PRAISE F

"The Letter," is a spellbind~~~~~~~~~~~~~~~~~~~~~~
a story of danger, failure, l~~~~~~~~~~~~~ound, forgiveness and
redemption. If you pick it up you won't be able to put it down.

–ELAINE WELLS

I planned to take several days to read "The Letter," however, once I
began, I was hooked. I could not put it down! Richard has written
a captivating novel exploring a wide range of human experiences
and emotions—sadness, anger, doubt, but also hope, love, compassion, and redemption. The characters are so real it is impossible
not to identify with them. I felt like I knew these people and had
shared their most intimate experiences. I'm a guy so I didn't expect
to get choked up, but as I read the last lines I couldn't help myself.
Needless to say, "The Letter" had a profound effect on me.

–FRANK C. DAVIS,
Melody Church, Pastor Emeritus
Mayor, City of Live Oak, Florida
Author, "Rasslin' With People,
The Eight People You Will Meet In
Life And Ministry!"

Wow. I loved "The Letter." I read it in just two settings and I liter-
ally had to keep reading until the end! I highly recommend it to
anyone who loves a great story packed with life changing truths.

–RAYMOND FRIZZELLE
Pastor and Author

"The Letter," is a 'you-can't-put-it-down' read. Adventurous
fiction, yes! Spiritually challenging, Yes! Crystal clear truth, YES!
Richard Exley once again captivates the reader with soul searching
drama — his best yet.

–JOHN MERRELL
Executive Director,
International Media Ministries (retired)
Founder and Director of Oral Learners Initiative

God-gifted master storyteller Richard Exley does not disappoint. I liked "The Alabaster Cross," but I truly loved "The Letter." It was a captivating read and I had trouble putting it down. I kept saying, "I'll read just one more chapter," but it turned into several. It invoked so many feelings—unresolved hurts, cripple emotions, danger, fears, romance and hope all crafted into one beautiful story.

–MELANIE KOCH
Author

"The Letter" by Richard Exley is a must read. It is a deftly sculptured story with the characters we came to know in "The Alabaster Cross." A letter creates anticipation. Will its words wound? Will its words soothe, comfort, reassure, and even heal, or will it leave more questions than answers? Read "The Letter," and discover its life changing truth for yourself.

–ORVILLE STEWART
Pastor

"The Letter" captured my emotions from the first page. I wept with those trapped in the excruciating web of deception. I held my breath, whether boating in the Amazon jungle or breathing the frosty air of the Rockies. The harsh realities of heart gaps left by an imperfect but loving father uncovered my own aches. Ultimately, I celebrated the welcome relief of long-awaited redemption. Like Bryan, I embraced the painstaking but profitable surrender to God's sovereignty. A must read for anyone who grapples with accepting the ways of God or navigating interpersonal relationships.

–REV. SANDY PHILLIPS,
Mom to three sons and Lead Pastor,
Oak River Church in Solon, Ohio

Although Richard Exley is my brother, I am not exaggerating when I say he has blessed the world with dozens of unique books covering a broad range of themes. I have read them all. One of his most popular books is *The Alabaster Cross,* an inspiring novel packed with poignant truths on life, relationships, new chances and so many other life principals. Now comes the much-requested sequel: *The Letter.* You do not want to miss this book; it will captivate you, provoke you and help you on your own life journey. Truly an inspiring read.

–DON EXLEY,
Church planter and career missionary to
Latin America

*The Letter...*I just read the last page and I still have tears in my eyes. What a beautiful story! So full of meaning, so touching. It's wonderful!

The message woven within the story was relatable, deeply touching, and ultimately encouraging. Love and forgiveness prevailed, over pain, hardship, even death. Prepare to take a journey that leads from the Amazon Basin to Colorado and back while entering into the hearts and minds of people who walk through the painful struggles of life, yet find healing and joy.

–ROBIN BOND

I couldn't wait for Richard Exley's sequel to "The Alabaster Cross," and I was not disappointed! Richard is a compelling writer and as I read "The Letter," I was riveted to every word. Every reader will find himself or herself in the story as the characters grapple with life issues and questions of faith. This is not a "one time" read for me. I will read it again and again. There are so many treasures yet to be discovered.

–MARILYNDA LYNCH

If you have been waiting, as I have, to hear the "rest of the story" from Richard Exley's gripping novel *The Alabaster Cross,* you will instantly be captured by *The Letter.*

Richard Exley, masterful storyteller, captivates you immediately by transporting you into Colorado's frigid January air. You see the fog created by the mailman's breath, you feel the cold slap you in the face, and the unforgettable scene is set. A letter arrives, and you are swept into a raw, compelling narrative.

Richard Exley writes a heartwarming and profound story, with real people who wrestle with passion and temptation, who fear being hurt. We relate to their struggles and root for them to win.

In short, *The Letter* will capture your emotions and your imagination and is definitely a "Must Read" book!

–Barbra Russell, MA, LPC
Counselor and Author of *Yes! I Said No!*

Nearly fifteen years ago, Richard Exley gave readers the gift of his first novel, *The Alabaster Cross.* As I finished reading the book, I knew in my spirit, there was a greater story to be told. Finally, the wait is over and the gift of his second novel is available. In *The Letter,* Richard continues to weave words that draw the reader into a continuing story that captivates and enthralls. As in his first book, Richard draws us into the story and the reader readily identifies with each character's joy and pain. You will feel you are a part of their struggles and triumphs. A powerful and poignant story!

–Dr Chuck Stecker
Founder, Executive Director
A Chosen Generation
Littleton, CO

RICHARD EXLEY

WORD & SPIRIT
PUBLISHING

DEDICATION

To Grandma Miller who introduced me to kerosene lamps and the art of storytelling.

Prologue

FORT COLLINS, COLORADO
1975

I have been writing for several hours, and my hand is cramping. Laying the cheap ballpoint pen aside, I massage my stiff fingers, noting with satisfaction the number of pages I have filled and torn from the yellow legal pad. Sometimes I think about getting a used typewriter and teaching myself to type, but I never seem to get around to it. There is an intimacy in putting a pen to paper that I can't imagine duplicating with a typewriter, an intimacy that is an integral part of the creative process for me.

Stretching, I realize the room has grown cold, and I note that the window above my makeshift writing desk is fringed with an intricate pattern of frost. In the distance, the snowcapped peaks of the Colorado Rockies jut into the brilliant blue of the winter sky. Belatedly I realize I have allowed the fire to burn down, so engrossed have I been in my writing. Moving to the stove, I open the door and poke at the coals. Opening the damper creates a draft, coaxing a small flame from the glowing embers, and I add some kindling before placing an armload of split pinion in the stove.

Having recently received a contract with a modest advance for my first novel, I am now beginning work on my second. Although my advance amounted to hardly more than grocery money, it will allow me to focus on my writing for the next four or five months without having to hustle odd jobs to keep body and soul together. I sometimes dream of having a bestselling novel, wondering what it would be like to be free from the financial pressure that has dogged my days for as long as I can remember. Even as a kid, I had to mow lawns and shovel snow to help my mother make ends meet. Living on the ragged edge of poverty was bad enough, but growing up without a father was what left me wounded in ways I still can't talk about.

I've made peace with my poverty; at least I think I have. Being divorced, I have only myself to think about, and my needs are few. Don't misunderstand me. I like to get paid for my writing, but what fulfills me is the work, not the pay. I'd be lying if I told you I wasn't looking forward to seeing my book in print, still I can't imagine that holding the first copy will be nearly as rewarding as the satisfaction I get from the writing itself. It's not easy, and I'm sometimes ready to pull my hair out, especially when I get bogged down and can't seem to figure a way out. Still, all things considered, this is who I am—a writer.

Glancing up, I see the rural mail carrier stopping at the end of my driveway. Even from this distance, I can see his warm breath fog the frigid January air as he lowers the window of his Jeep to deposit a fistful of mail in the sagging mailbox. I'm sure it's mostly junk; still, I reach for my parka and head for the door. The cold slaps me in the face, and my eyes smart. An arctic cold front has plunged temperatures to 17 degrees below, and the snow beneath my boots is nearly as hard as gravel.

Unconsciously I find myself comparing the bitter cold to the sweltering heat of the Amazon basin, and as I do, I am assailed with a host of bittersweet memories. It's been more than four years since Helen, Carolyn, and I launched our small boat and made our way down the Rio Moa toward Cruzeiro do Sul, on the first leg of our journey back to civilization; still the memories have the power to transfix me.

Determinedly I push them to the back of my mind as I open my dilapidated mailbox and retrieve my mail. A quick perusal of the contents confirms my suspicions. It's mostly junk, and I turn toward the house, eagerly anticipating the warmth of the stove. In the tiny mudroom, I stomp the snow off my boots and hang my parka on a wooden peg by the door. Tossing the mail on the counter, I stretch my hands toward the stove, savoring its warmth.

Out of the corner of my eye, I notice the edge of a tissue-thin, powder-blue, aerogram envelope. I don't know how I missed it when I glanced through the mail before tossing it on the counter, but I did. Now it draws me like a magnet. Could it be that Diana has written me after all this time? It's not likely, given the way we parted, but still, I hope.

I'm sure my optimism is ill founded. I haven't heard a word from her since I left the mission station, yet not a day passes that I do not think of her. I remember the way she looked the first time I saw her and how beautiful she was sitting in the swing beneath the towering samauma tree. Her eyes were the color of the Colorado sky, and her face was full of laughter, the afternoon sun highlighting her honey-colored hair. How gentle was her touch as she cared for me while I was recovering from malaria. The love we shared, brief as it was, still lives in my heart. Unconsciously I rub my chest where an all-too-familiar ache has taken up residence.

From my makeshift desk, I collect a sheaf of yellow pages and return to the warmth of the stove, determined to ignore the aerogram envelope and the memories it has invoked. Dutifully I scan the handwritten pages, noticing the cramped script. According to Diana, my handwriting matches my personality. She said I was hard to read. I don't like to think of myself as being closed, but I suppose she's right. It's not that I don't trust people. I just don't want to be hurt again.

With an effort, I turn my thoughts to my day's work, but the things I've written on the yellow pages are no match for the memories now playing on the screen of my mind. Diana is sitting in a wooden rocker with her injured leg propped on a makeshift footstool, a kerosene lamp on a wooden crate at her elbow. I am sitting on the floor beside her, and she is running her fingers through my hair. The only sound is the pinging of a gentle rain on the corrugated tin roof of the mission house. I am profoundly contented in a way I've never known. Pain, which has been so much a part of my life, is mostly gone, and what remains lurks unacknowledged on the edges of my mind. It will return, of that I am sure, but for now I push that thought from my mind and focus on the moment.

As always, that poignant memory morphs into darker ones from which I extract little pleasure, but no little pain. I've replayed the same scenes so often that they have cut deep grooves in my memory, like those on an extended-play album. My self-recriminations are without end. Did I do the right thing? Was I really thinking of Diana, or was I just being selfish? I try to imagine how things might have played out had I chosen differently, but I cannot picture a happy ending. Although I had made a semblance of peace with my past, at least as far as it concerned my relationship with my departed father, I was still a wounded soul with a long history of destroying those I loved. No matter how much it might pain me, I was determined to spare Diana that fate.

During those final days in the Amazon, we discussed every possible scenario, left no option unexplored. Late into the night, we planned and schemed and argued, but when all was said and done, we could not find a course of action suitable to both of us. Diana could not marry me and continue to serve as a missionary. Her denomination had a prohibition against ministers or missionaries marrying a divorced person. If she were to marry me, the Foreign Missions Department would rescind her appointment, and her denomination would defrock her. No matter how much we loved each other, I could never permit her to suffer such a loss or the inevitable public humiliation that would accompany it.

She offered to resign her appointment and seek reappointment with another missionary board with less stringent requirements regarding divorce and remarriage. It seemed like a workable solution at first blush, but the more we talked about it, the less feasible it became. Diana would have had to resign her appointment and leave the Amazon to return to the States to seek reappointment, without any guarantees. If she received an appointment with a new missionary board, she would have to spend months, maybe as long as two years, raising her support. No small task, given she would have few if any contacts within the new missionary organization. Even if she were successful, I could not imagine myself living as a missionary in the Amazon or any other Godforsaken place, no matter how much I loved her.

When I told her I would never consider living on the mission field under any circumstances, something seemed to die inside of her. Although I felt like a selfish jerk, I knew myself well enough to know that I didn't dare commit to something I could never live up to. I had already done that once, and I was still living with the consequences. Taking both of her hands in mine, I told her I loved her too much to lie to her or to myself. To do so, I explained, would be unspeakably cruel. I couldn't do that to her, not even to spare her this present pain.

For two or three days, she seemed to withdraw inside herself, and I set about making preparations for my trip downriver. She found me late one afternoon as Lako and I were putting the last of my things into his boat in preparation for leaving early the next morning. As she approached, Lako slipped away. I could tell she had been crying, but there was a stubborn determination in her eyes when she looked at me. She told me that since I had no intention of living on the mission field, she would give up her missionary work, marry me, and practice medicine in the United States.

I'm not sure how she expected me to react, but I surely disappointed her. Instead of taking her in my arms and crushing her to my chest, I turned and walked to the river's edge. Of course, her offer caused me no little conflict. I loved her, more than I ever imagined possible, and the thought of returning with her to the States made me dizzy with the possibilities. We could relocate in a small town high in the Rockies where she could practice medicine and I could follow my secret dreams of becoming a writer. It was what I had dreamed of; unfortunately, that's all it was—just a dream. I knew myself well enough to know my pride would never allow me to be a kept man, not even until I established myself as a published author. On another level, it made me feel like a jerk. She was willing to give up her calling, her life's dream, for me, and yet I wasn't even willing to swallow my pride and accept her offer. What could be more selfish than that?

Slipping behind me, she wrapped her arms around my waist and laid her cheek against my back between my shoulders. I loved her so much, and more than anything, I wanted to take her in my arms and cover her face with kisses, but I knew I didn't dare. If I allowed my resolve to waver even the least bit, I would be lost. Her willingness to sacrifice herself on the altar of our love was heartrending in its selflessness, but it would never work. It was a price neither of us could afford to pay. At least I was wise enough to know that. God had first claim on her life, and whether she realized it or not, turning her back on her calling would kill something vital inside of her. In time, she would come to resent me, to blame me for the loss of her life's purpose, and then her love for me would die. It was better, I reasoned, to suffer a clean break, painful though it might be, than to slowly destroy each other, as inevitably we must.

Removing her arms from around my waist, I turned toward the trail that led to the mission compound and the small house that had been my home these past weeks. I heard Diana sobbing, but I did not look back. She might have called my name, or it might have been a voice inside my head. I will never know, for I did not turn around to see.

There was only a hint of daylight touching the eastern sky the next morning when Lako and I made our way toward the river for the long journey back. I was torn up on the inside. The people I loved were here—Diana and Eurico—but I knew I couldn't stay. I refused to sacrifice their happiness in hopes of securing my own. No matter how much I wanted us to be together, I knew it would never work. As Lako turned the boat downriver, I choked back a sob and steeled myself for what lay ahead.

I hadn't allowed myself to relive those painful memories for several weeks, and with good reason. Each time I went there, I found myself battling depression, sometimes for days. What little joy the memories afforded me was far outweighed by the depression that followed. Deliberately I pushed the memories to the back of my mind and focused on the present. Outside the small window above my writing desk, the day was dying, winter's night coming with a rush. Placing the yellow sheets containing my day's writing on the makeshift desk, I turned toward the counter and picked up the tissue-thin, light-blue, aerogram envelope. The postage stamp was Brazilian, and with trembling hands, I carefully opened it, hoping against hope that Diana had finally written to me after all this time.

Chapter One

AMAZON BASIN
FAR WESTERN BRAZIL
1971

Helen stares through the airplane's small Plexiglas window with unseeing eyes at the uninhabited rain forest below. She is absolutely exhausted. Given the layovers in Miami and Rio, not to mention the delays in Manaus as a result of mechanical difficulties, she has been traveling nearly forty hours. In the seat beside her, Carolyn is sleeping, oblivious to the roar of the aircraft's engines and the turbulent flight, but Helen's troubling thoughts won't let her sleep. What began as an empty threat in an attempt to bring Rob to his senses has become a reality, and she can't help wondering if she has made a dreadful mistake.

Once more, she finds herself reliving the events that have brought her to this moment. First there was her mother's death, then Bryan's disappearance, and finally Rob's impatience when she continued to battle grief and depression weeks after her mother's funeral. He accused her of making a shrine out of her sorrow, and in short order, his impatience turned into indifference and then into a thinly veiled anger.

In the ensuing weeks, he began spending inordinate amounts of time at the church office. When he did come home, he was withdrawn, and his silent resentment tainted every interaction. After observing a number of flirtatious interactions between Rob and his secretary, she could only conclude they shared a dangerous and inappropriate attraction. When she confronted him, he laughed at her—she was imagining things, depression was making her paranoid. When she threatened to take her concerns to the church's official board, Rob just made light of her threats, telling her not to make a fool of herself. In desperation, she had booked this flight to Cruzeiro do Sul in Brazil's far western Amazon basin.

She had explained her decision to the congregation by telling them she was joining her brother, Bryan, in his attempt to learn what had happened to their missionary father. He had disappeared while on a mission of mercy into the Amazonian jungle more than twenty years earlier, and his unexplained disappearance haunted her still. There was an element of truth in her explanation, but in reality, she was desperately trying to bring Rob to his senses, to get him to realize their marriage was in serious trouble. Maybe, she had told herself, leaving him and their two boys to fare for themselves would help him realize how much they needed her.

With less than an hour before they were scheduled to touch down, she found herself remembering the morning of her departure. Parts of it she could only imagine, while other parts are so vivid, they nearly ripped her heart out.

In her mind's eye, she sees Rob unlocking the door to his office while winter darkness holds daylight hostage. Shedding his overcoat, he tosses it over the back of a nearby chair, before heading to the workroom to brew a pot of coffee. When it is ready, he fills a mug and returns to his desk, where he spends the next hour doing little more than shuffling papers. He was in no mood to work, but he couldn't bear to hang around the house while she finished packing. Every time she placed another piece of clothing in her suitcase, he felt as if she was mocking him. He kept hearing her voice inside his head—"I am a grown woman, an adult. You may ask me to reconsider my decision, you can even ask me to pray about it, but you cannot forbid me to go. I am not a child, and you are not my father!"

No matter how emphatically he had objected, she remained adamant. She was going to the Amazon whether he liked it or not. He tried to reason with her, but it was like talking to the wall. She refused to even discuss it with him.

He can't help thinking that she isn't the woman he married. When they married, she seemed the perfect pastor's wife—she was submissive, she served in ministry with him but never tried to usurp his authority, and she was more than happy to stay at home and raise their two boys. Something happened to her following her mother's death, or maybe it was Bryan's disappearance that triggered her strange behavior. In the weeks following those two events, she turned into a stranger, slowly sliding into depression. More often than not, he would come home in the evening to find her still in her housecoat, without makeup, her hair a mess. It was not unusual to find the breakfast dishes still on the table or stacked in the sink. Initially he had tried to comfort her, but try as he might, he could not reach her. Soon he lost patience, and his empathy morphed into resentment, then outright anger.

He grimaces as he recalls how things took a turn for the worse some weeks later, when Helen learned he had shared their marital struggles with Rita, his secretary. She had railed at him: "How could you confide in that woman? How dare you make her privy to the difficulties in our marriage? How would you feel if I confided in one of your board members? What if I told him that you were acting strange—working late, skipping dinners, not making love to me? What if I told him I suspected that you were involved with Rita?"

When he tried to brush her suspicions aside, suggesting an overactive imagination had made her jealous, she lit into him again. "Anyone can see that Rita has a thing for you, and you obviously enjoy it." Shaking her head wearily, she had continued in a tired voice: "I don't know if you're just too naïve to see what's happening, or if you simply enjoy playing with fire."

He's tired, maybe more tired than he has ever been, bone weary from the inside out. Placing his elbows on the desk, he buries his face in his hands and tries to pray, but the words get stuck in his throat. He wants to pray for strength and understanding, for help in becoming a better husband, but resentment renders him mute. He should pray for Helen—for her safety, for the healing of her wounded heart, for the restoration of their marriage—but he can't. Against his will, he finds himself wondering if it's already too late to restore their marriage, if things have already gone too far.

He is still nursing his melancholy thoughts when he hears someone in the outer office. Glancing at his wristwatch, he sees that it is barely seven o'clock. It's too early for Rita. Her workday doesn't begin until 8:30; still, he can't help hoping she has come in early. A moment later, the light in her office is turned on, and he hears her closet door open and then the clatter of coat hangers as she hangs up her coat. A couple of minutes later, she knocks on his office door. Opening it slightly, she asks, "May I come in?"

Without waiting for him to reply, she steps into his office and places a fresh cup of coffee on his desk. "What are you doing here so early?" he asks, noting the way her cashmere sweater complements her figure while accenting her blue eyes.

"I thought this might be a difficult morning, and I wanted to encourage you if I could."

"Thank you," he says, and she can't help noting how tired he looks. His eyes are bloodshot, with dark blotches beneath them.

Glancing at the cup of coffee steaming on the corner of his desk, and then back at him, she says, "It looks like it's going to take more than a fresh cup of coffee to perk you up."

"I'll be alright. I didn't sleep very well, and on top of everything else, I have a splitting headache. The muscles in my neck are all knotted up."

"Maybe I can fix that," she says as she positions herself behind him and begins to massage his neck and shoulders. As she does, he allows himself to relax, even though he realizes what they are doing is probably not a good idea. The pleasure he experiences as her fingers continue to work their magic is setting off alarm bells in his conscience, but he ignores them. He tells himself they are not doing anything wrong, but in his heart, he knows they are on dangerous ground. Never before have they been so familiar. Occasionally Rita has placed her hand on his arm while talking with him, or she has made it a point to brush his hand with hers while handing him a cup of coffee or some letters to be signed. If he is honest, he has to admit he has begun to look forward to those "chance" encounters. Nor is he completely innocent. On more than one

occasion, he has deliberately leaned over her shoulder to look at the church calendar while allowing his body to brush against hers. Although neither of them has said anything, they both realize that their friendship could turn into something more.

"I'm sorry, Pastor," she says, as she continues to massage his shoulders. "I may be speaking out of turn, but what Helen's doing is just plain selfish."

Not trusting himself to speak, lest he say something he might later regret, he mummers his assent.

"I don't understand how she can just leave you and the boys and go traipsing off to the Amazon. Surely she knows how demanding your ministry is. Not to mention how hard this must be on the boys."

Before she can say more, the lights in the office wing are turned on. Instantly she stops massaging Rob's shoulders and hastily moves to stand in front of his desk. Picking up some papers, he makes a show of giving her some instructions as Paul, his youth pastor, walks in.

"Good morning, Pastor," he says, while giving Rita a "what are you doing here?" look. Turning back to Rob, he continues, "I didn't expect to see you here. I thought you would be on your way to Denver."

"There were a couple of things I had to take care of before taking Helen to the airport, and Rita was kind enough to come in early and give me a hand." Glancing at his wristwatch, he says, "I better get going, or Helen will be in a panic." As if on cue, his private telephone rings. Ignoring it, he grabs his overcoat and heads for the door.

Arriving home, he sees that Helen has already moved her suitcases to the porch, where she is standing in the snow impatiently awaiting his arrival. "Where have you been?" she demands as soon as he gets out of the car. "Dallying with Rita, I suppose."

"What are you talking about? You know Rita's workday doesn't start until eight thirty."

He glares at her as she stomps the snow off her boots and goes inside to bid Robbie and Jake good-bye. They are standing together beside their grandmother when she enters the kitchen, their eyes large with apprehension. It pains her to see them looking so insecure, and for just a moment she considers calling the whole thing off. Instead, she gives them a tight smile as she kneels and opens her arms. After a moment's hesitation, they run to her.

Although the thought of leaving the boys nearly breaks her heart, she refuses to cry. They are already upset, and her tears would only make it worse. It pains her to realize that try as she might, she has not been able to completely shield them from what's happening between Rob and her. Now they cling to her, tears glistening in their eyes. "Why do you have to go?" Jake whines. From across the room, Rob's mother watches, her disapproval obvious.

Holding both boys in her arms, Helen squeezes them tightly, whispering her love in a voice only they can hear. After promising to pray for them every day, she tells them to obey their grandmother. Giving them a final hug, she brushes their foreheads with good-bye kisses before walking out the door, not daring to look back lest she break down.

The Letter

Rob has placed her luggage in the car, and he is impatiently tapping his fingers on the steering wheel when she gets in. Without a word, he puts their two-year-old Oldsmobile Cutlass in gear and guns the engine as they exit the driveway, causing the car to skid sideways on the snow-covered pavement.

It has been snowing since late yesterday afternoon, dumping more than eight inches of snow overnight, but by the time they reach the interstate, the snow has stopped. Unfortunately, the wind has picked up, blowing sheets of snow across the road, reducing visibility. Although the snowplows have been at work most of the night, the roads remain snow-packed, making driving hazardous. To further complicate things, they are running late. Rob's tardiness has aggravated Helen's already frayed nerves, and her thinly veiled anger lies between them like a ticking time bomb.

From time to time, she makes a show of looking at her watch while giving Rob a reproachful look. According to his calculations, they should make it to the airport in plenty of time; nonetheless, to appease her he accelerates. Suddenly they hit a sheet of ice, and the car spins out of control. For several seconds, it seems they will end up in the ditch, but Rob finally manages to get the Cutlass under control.

"What are you trying to do, kill us?" Helen demands, glaring at him.

Angrily Rob slams on the brakes, causing the car to skid sideways on the snow-packed highway before coming to a stop on the shoulder. An eighteen-wheeler, horn blaring, roars by, barely missing them. Jamming the transmission into park,

Rob opens the driver's door and gets out. "If you think you can do better," he fumes, "you can drive!"

Without a word, Helen slides across the seat and slams the door. Taking hold of the steering wheel, she shifts the transmission into drive. Rob tries to jerk the door open, but she has locked it. "Unlock this door," he screams while pounding on the window. "Let me in the car!"

Ignoring him, Helen checks the rearview mirror for oncoming traffic before pulling back onto the highway. Glancing in the mirror, she sees Rob waving his arms and running after her. She's tempted to drive off and leave him, but as her anger dissipates, she thinks better of it. A quarter of a mile down the road, she pulls onto the shoulder and stops.

When Rob finally reaches the car, he is gasping for breath. Since Helen is firmly ensconced behind the steering wheel, he makes his way to the passenger's side and gets in. As soon as he closes the door, she accelerates onto the highway. For several minutes, the only sound is Rob's ragged breathing and the whir of the tires on the snow-packed highway.

As angry as she is, Helen still cannot help wondering how things have come to this. Just a few months ago, she would have put their marriage up against anyone's; now she doesn't know if they're going to make it. Once they were best friends; now they're hardly civil to each other. Once they could talk about everything—the ministry, the boys, their dream vacation—anything. Some nights they would sit on the back porch, after putting the boys to bed, and talk for hours. Now they hardly talk at all. They exchange information necessary for running their household, but they never communicate. Rob seems to have lost all interest in making love to her, not that she minds, and it's been weeks since they've been intimate.

Against her will, she finds herself replaying a montage of moments involving Rob and Rita on the screen of her mind. At the time, each encounter seemed innocent enough, but in light of recent events, they have taken on an ominous tone. On more than one occasion, she dropped by the church unexpectedly only to find Rita and Rob alone in his office. It may have been perfectly legitimate—work-related—but she can't forget the guilty look on Rob's face or Rita's smugness.

A host of second thoughts assail her, and she can't help wondering if she is making a terrible mistake. Will her absence make Rob realize how empty his life is without her, or will he take advantage of the situation to spend more time with Rita? Be that as it may, it is too late to cancel her trip now. How would she explain her change of plans without appearing weak and indecisive? More importantly, if she backs down now, Rob will never take her concerns seriously.

Traffic picks up when they reach the outskirts of Denver, and she is forced to concentrate on her driving. Although she has been to Stapleton International Airport a number of times, she's not really familiar with the route. She is tempted to ask Rob to drive, but when she glances his way, his expression makes it obvious that he is expecting her to do just that.

Catching her eye, he asks, "Do you want me to drive?"

"I'm fine," she replies curtly.

Feigning a confidence she does not feel, she plows ahead, determined to do this on her own. Thankfully, there are a number of signs directing her to the airport, and she arrives with a few minutes to spare. Instead of turning into short-term parking as they had planned, she drives directly to the terminal, where she gets a skycap to help her with her luggage. After handing him her ticket, she turns toward Rob. Originally, he was going to bid her good-bye at the departure gate, but now there's no point. As angry as they both are, that would only prolong the agony. She gives him an awkward hug, which he barely acknowledges, then she turns and strides purposefully into the terminal. Although she hates to part this way, she cannot bring herself to apologize, nor can he. Pride locks them both in a stubborn silence, neither of them willing to make the first move toward reconciliation. She blinks back tears as she makes her way toward the departure gate. Inside her head, she hears the lyrics from a Neil Diamond song. Something to the effect that pride is the chief cause in the decline in the number of husbands and wives.

Helen is jerked back to the present when the aircraft touches down on the small airstrip that services this remote outpost in the far western Amazon basin. Beside her, Carolyn is yawning and rubbing sleep from her eyes as they taxi toward the nondescript building that serves as the terminal. Once the plane comes to a stop, they collect their carry-on bags and head to the exit at the front of the plane. As they descend the stairs, a wave of hot, moist air envelops them, and Helen feels perspiration soaking the back of her blouse. In an instant she is taken back to her childhood on the mission compound, with its sweltering heat and primitive living conditions.

While waiting for their baggage to arrive, she surveys the terminal with growing dismay. The small building looks like an ancient airplane hangar in desperate need of repair and a good cleaning. The magnitude of what she has done hits her anew when Carolyn asks, "What do we do now?"

"The first thing I'm going to do when we get to the hotel is take a bath," she says, feigning a confidence she does not feel. "After that we can sort things out. We'll have to find a boat and hire a guide to take us upriver to the mission compound, where I grew up. Hopefully, Bryan will be there."

In short order, their luggage is deposited on the concrete floor, and while Helen goes in search of a skycap to help them with their bags, a slovenly looking guy approaches, and without a word he takes their suitcases and heads for the exit. For a moment, Carolyn is too stunned to react, then she lunges after him. "That's our luggage," she hollers as he exits the building. Before she can reach him, he has hoisted their bags into the bed of a broken-down pickup and is standing beside it with the door open. He smiles, revealing a mouthful of tobacco-stained teeth, and motions for her to get in.

Glancing around, she realizes that Helen is nowhere to be found, and there isn't a police officer or a security guard in sight. Although her heart is hammering with fear, she is not about to let this jerk steal their luggage. Turning her back on him, she grabs a suitcase and drags it out of the pickup bed. While she is struggling with a second suitcase, Helen arrives and engages the driver in a conversation using mostly gestures. He speaks only a smattering of English, and she's forgotten what little Portuguese she knew as a child. Eventually he makes her understand that he is offering to drive them into town.

By now, Carolyn has wrestled their suitcases onto the side of the road, and she glares at Helen, who is smiling and nodding her head at the driver. Once more, he approaches Carolyn and attempts to reload the bags into the back of the pickup. She refuses to release her grip on the suitcases, and what ensues is a comical tug-of-war, and Helen breaks out laughing. "It's okay, Carolyn. He just wants to drive us into town."

"Absolutely not! There's no way I'm getting into that filthy truck with this guy. Look at him…"

"Be reasonable, Carolyn. It's a long walk into town, and our suitcases are heavy. Do you see any other options?" Turning to the driver, Helen motions for him to load the luggage. Once more, he reaches for the suitcases, but Carolyn glares at him, refusing to release her death grip on them. Finally, an airport employee walks over to see if he can sort things out. Although the language barrier makes it nearly impossible to communicate, he finally makes Carolyn understand that the driver is reputable.

Reluctantly she allows him to load their luggage. Climbing into the pickup, she can't help grimacing at the filth. The broken-down seat is grease-stained, and the floor is littered with trash. In an instant, she is carried back to her childhood. She grew up on the wrong side of the tracks, with an alcoholic father. Beat-up pickups and worn-out clunkers are old hat to her, but she had hoped never to see them again. Seeing her obvious dismay, Helen gives her an encouraging smile as she climbs in beside her. "It's going to be alright. Once you get a bath and some sleep, you'll feel better."

Chapter Two

For the better part of four days, Lako and I have been navigating the floodwaters of the Rio Moa while battling the elements: heavy rains interspersed with stifling heat, hordes of mosquitoes, and swarming sweat bees. The river is filled with all manner of debris—trash from the river margin, uprooted trees, and the bloated bodies of dead animals. A less-experienced boatman might have risked capsizing our small boat, but Lako manages the river's dangers with consummate skill. He has demonstrated his competence time and again these past few weeks, not only on the river, but also in several life-threatening situations. He has proven to be all Dr. Peterson said he was: the most knowledgeable guide on the river and a mateiro of unsurpassed skill.

Unfortunately, he is powerless against the black depression that now dogs my days. Learning what happened to my father after all these years has helped me make peace with my past, but I'm still subject to mood swings and bouts of anger. I was doing pretty well until I made the decision to leave Diana and Eurico and return to the States alone. Leaving them ripped my heart out, and I can't seem to regain my emotional equilibrium. I know I did the right thing—at least I think I did—but that doesn't make it easy. Much to my chagrin, I have discovered that doing the right thing doesn't necessarily feel good.

On top of everything else, I think I'm battling malaria again. I'm running a low-grade fever, my head is throbbing, and every joint in my body aches. It's not unexpected. Diana said I would probably experience reoccurring bouts of malaria from time to time. It's nothing like what I experienced the first time, but it is bad enough, and I cannot find a comfortable position in this small boat no matter how hard I try.

With a determined effort, I put my misery out of my mind and turn my attention toward the future. According to Lako, the Rio Moa should merge with the Rio Jurua shortly, meaning we should reach Cruzeiro do Sul sometime this afternoon. Hopefully I can secure passage on a barge going downriver without delay. Now that I've learned my father's fate, the thought of spending any more time in the far western Amazon basin is nearly more than I can bear. I'm sick of sleeping in hammocks under mosquito netting, and if I have to eat one more meal of rice and beans, I think I will puke. The thought of a Big Mac and fries is driving me nearly mad. As far as I'm concerned, I can't return to the States soon enough.

At long last I am ready to move forward with my life, but before I can do that, there are some things I must address. I'm deeply grieved by all the people I have hurt, especially my ex-wife, Carolyn, and my sister, Helen. When I return to the States, I will do what I can to make amends. There is no way I can undo the damage I have done, but at least I can acknowledge the fault was mine. I'm through blaming others for the mess I have made of my life and the pain I caused those who loved me. Helen may be able to forgive me, but I doubt if Carolyn can.

I must have dozed off, for when I awaken, Lako is maneuvering our small boat across the Rio Jurua's rain-swollen current toward Cruzeiro do Sul. I can't help noticing how different things look. When I headed upriver several weeks ago, the shantytown was located on dry ground, with a smelly accumulation of garbage and sewage beneath the elevated planks that formed a walkway leading from shanty to shanty. Now the river surrounds the shanties, which are perched on spindly stilts several feet tall, and the rain-swollen current has washed the garbage and sewage away. Closer to the river, there was a tawny beach cluttered with canoes of every size imaginable and heaps of bounty from the river and the forest—stacks of dried fish, bolas of raw rubber, mounds of palm fruits, and piles of rough-hewn timber. Among all that bounty, Indians and traders camped around driftwood fires, while children ran and played, oblivious to the adult world around them. Now all of that is gone, and the beach is underwater.

I can't help thinking that I've changed, too. I'm not the same man who shared Dr. Peterson's boat as we headed upriver toward the mission compound. When I boarded the *Flor de Maio* (the *Mayflower*), I was deeply troubled, a lost soul really. A lifetime of grief and anger had poisoned me, ruining all my relationships. It made me a terrible son to my departed mother. It estranged me from my sister, and it wrecked my marriage. I held my father responsible for the mess I had made of my life, and I blamed God for not answering a little boy's desperate prayers.

My parents were missionaries, raising my sister and me on an isolated mission compound in the far western Amazon basin. That should have afforded us lots of parental attention, but it didn't. Given our primitive living conditions, the work was never ending. My father labored long hours to carve the mission compound out of the jungle and to build a small house for our family. When he wasn't doing physical labor, he was busy studying, learning several different Indian dialects. He must have had a gift for languages, for he compiled extensive notes and vocabulary lists that are still used to teach new missionaries. In addition to all of that, he made regular treks into the jungle to preach the gospel to the Indians, often staying gone for two or three weeks at a time. His forays were not without risk. Danger lurked everywhere—an accident, a poisonous snakebite, a violent storm, a crippling illness, even a simple miscalculation, could result in death.

Like most children, I hungered for my father's attention, but I didn't know how to get it. When it wasn't forthcoming, I thought the fault was mine—maybe I had done something wrong, or perhaps I just wasn't good enough. Those feelings cast a dark shadow over my childhood, and they have tormented me my entire life. My father was a stern man. He was quick to discipline my sister and me, but he almost never hugged us. His lack of affection robbed me of my dignity, and it caused me to doubt my value as a person. Consequently, I ended up feeling worthless. His disappearance was just the final blow.

When he disappeared, I blamed myself. If I had been a better son, he would not have gone away; he would not have died and left me to grow up alone. The flaws in my reasoning are obvious now, but that's the way I felt as a boy, and I carry the scars with me to this day. After a time, my grief turned to anger and then to bitterness, and I came to hate him. I might hate him still if I had not discovered his journals. Without them, I might have never been able to forgive him, but through his writing, I became acquainted with another side of him. To my surprise, I discovered that although he was a stern man, he was not without love. The love he could never show, the things he could never say, were all there inside of him—he just couldn't express them. He was a flawed man to be sure, and an imperfect father; but as I am only now realizing, he was also a giant of a man—a missionary legend. At long last I have come to realize that the truth is never one-dimensional. It's a many-sided thing, and only when we embrace the whole of it can we find healing and peace.

I am not a whole man, not yet, but neither am I the angry man I used to be. I no longer blame my father, nor do I blame God. There's still much I don't understand—maybe I never will—but it seems to me that grief itself is not a fatal wound. It's the bitterness that kills, not the grief. Given time, our hearts will heal themselves. That's the way God made us; at least, that's how it seems to me.

My ruminating is cut short when the boat bumps against the river's edge. Moving as quickly as my aching body will allow, I climb out and drag the boat farther up the bank. Lako throws me a rope, and I secure it to a nearby tree. While I'm doing that, he begins unloading our gear. There's not much—a couple of hammocks, our mosquito nets, some rope, and a tarp. When I turn back to help him, he hands me my father's canvas satchel. It holds his Bible, carefully wrapped in oilcloth, and his final journal. To me they are more valuable than any earthly treasure. At last I stoop and pick up my small pack from the bottom of the boat. It weighs almost nothing, containing only my toothbrush and shaving gear, an extra pair of jeans, some underwear, three or four T-shirts, and my chambray shirt; still I am lightheaded when I shoulder my things and turn toward the inn located on the far side of the Praca do Triumfo (the Plaza of Triumph).

Hopefully I can get the same room I had before heading upriver. It's nothing to write home about, but it's as good as anything Cruzeiro do Sul has to offer, and the bathroom is just down the hall. I dump my gear near the front entrance and settle up with Lako. As he turns to go, I'm suddenly overcome with emotion. We are hardly close, but I do owe him my life. Had it not been for his knowledge of the rain forest, I might be buried in an unmarked grave deep in the jungle, just another victim of malaria. As I teetered near death, he brewed a concoction from the bark of the Cinchona tree and forced me to drink it, saving my life. Without his expertise, I would have never learned what happened to my father. At risk of his own life, he located the Amuacas, and he led me to Komi, who was with my father when he died.

He is hurrying down the street toward a small liquor store when I belatedly call his name. He turns toward me, his impatience obvious. I want to tell him how grateful I am, but I can't get the words out. For most of my life, anger has been the only emotion I allowed myself, and now I find I am tongue-tied. Once more I am my father's son, unable to express what I feel so deeply. I start toward him, but he waves me off. His addiction to *cachaca* (a cheap white wine) is fierce, and it is obvious it has taken hold of him.

After a shower I crash. Not even the street noise or the stifling afternoon heat or the too-small bed can keep me awake, and it is nearly dark before hunger arouses me. For a moment, I imagine I am back in Whittaker house, and in my mind, I can hear Euriko's irrepressible laughter. Diana is there, too, smiling softly as she calls my name. As I come fully awake, I realize I must have been dreaming. With an effort I push all memories of Diana and Euriko out of my mind. They promise pleasure, but experience has taught me they produce only pain. In time I might be able to enjoy them, but not now; the memories are too fresh, the pain still too raw.

After pulling on my only pair of clean jeans, I make my way to the small table in the corner. There is a pitcher of water, a washbasin, and a worn towel so thin I can nearly see through it. I splash the tepid water on my face, trying to scrub the last stubborn traces of sleep from my eyes. I finger-comb my dark hair before rummaging in my bag for a reasonably clean shirt. My fever has broken, and I am so hungry that even a plate of beans and rice is tempting.

When I step into the street, the sun is setting. In the distance, I can see the familiar redbrick cathedral located at the far end of the *Praca do Triunfo* (the Plaza of Triumph), and a short distance from there, I see the coffin maker's shop situated next to the *Ganso Azul* (the Blue Goose), one of Cruzeiro do Sul's principal bordellos. Turning the opposite direction, I make my way toward a small café located on the far side of the plaza. A slight breeze carries the smell of roasting meat to me, aggravating my already-ravenous hunger, and I quicken my step as I cross the plaza.

I pause at the door, scanning the noisy room in search of a table that might afford me a semblance of privacy. The small café is mostly filled with caboclos, making me something of a curiosity, as I am obviously a North American. Several patrons look my way as I move toward a small table located in a dark corner. They soon lose interest and resume their raucous banter. In short order, my food arrives, and I attack it, relishing the spicy flavor of roasted meat richly seasoned with onions and peppers. I am wiping my plate clean with a hunk of bread when the café suddenly grows quiet. Looking up, I see two women framed in the doorway. I recognize them instantly. The dark-eyed beauty is Carolyn, my ex-wife. Although I haven't seen her since our divorce, I would know her anywhere. The other lady is my older sister, Helen.

I have no idea what they are doing here, and I watch in a daze as they move toward the nearest empty table. Seeing Helen has generated a surge of all-too-familiar emotions, and I feel like a little boy again. When my mother was incapacitated by grief following my father's disappearance, Helen assumed the role of surrogate mother. She might have meant well, but I resented her efforts, and now that same resentment leaves a bitter taste in my mouth. I don't want her interfering in my life; never mind that I have mostly made a mess of it.

Even more confusing is Carolyn's presence. Our divorce was fairly acrimonious, and we have not spoken since it became final nearly two years ago. Since we had no children, there was no reason for us to stay in touch. Over time I came to realize the divorce was largely my fault. I was an angry man, incapable of giving or receiving love. Earlier today, I was determined to make amends to Carolyn for my insufferable behavior when I returned to the States. Not now. Her unexpected presence has awakened all the old hurts, and anger is like a knot in the pit of my stomach.

I'm tempted to storm across the room and confront them, but as the shock of seeing them begins to wear off, my anger slowly recedes, leaving my mind reeling. I keep asking myself what possible reason they could have for being here. The only thing I can conclude is that they are looking for me. But why?

While I'm wrestling with my thoughts, a waiter places two plates of steaming food on their table. I can't help noticing he can hardly take his eyes off of Carolyn. That's not surprising. With her thick auburn hair, coffee-colored eyes, and petite figure, she would attract attention in any crowd, but in this frontier outpost she is a rarity indeed. Helen is pretty enough herself, but she's no beauty—too many Whittaker genes.

They take their time eating, laughing and talking like old friends. I can't help thinking this is a side of Helen I have never seen. By nature, she is intense, not outgoing, and certainly not spontaneous. So, what has happened to turn her into this gregarious stranger?

I found it hard to believe when she wrote to tell me that she and Carolyn had become friends. While we were married, I don't think they even spoke to each other. Why would they? They have almost nothing in common. Helen is a believer. Carolyn is not. Helen is an "MK"—a missionary kid—while

Carolyn comes from a dysfunctional family with an alcoholic father. Helen is self-sufficient and fiercely independent, while Carolyn is needy. Yet here they are, at a frontier outpost in the far western Amazon basin, acting like forever friends. Go figure.

After they finish their meal, they linger over cups of *cafez-inbo*—Brazilian coffee made by boiling the grounds in brown sugar and water. It is so sweet and strong it makes my teeth ache when I drink it. Now their heads are close together, and it is obvious they are having a serious discussion. I wish I dared to move closer so I could eavesdrop on their conversation, but I cannot do so without risking being seen.

Thankfully, the table where I am seated is in a fairly dark corner, so I'm sure they haven't seen me. As far as Helen knows, I'm at the mission compound, or even deeper in the interior. If I lie low, I can probably avoid them altogether if that is what I decide to do. Still, my curiosity is working overtime, and I find myself trying to figure out what is going on. Why isn't Rob here? He and Helen never take separate vacations, although coming to this Godforsaken place could hardly be considered a vacation. Rob says shared experiences bond a couple, while unshared experiences separate them; so why isn't he here?

I still haven't figured anything out when they finally finish their *cafezombo* and exit the café. It is fully dark now, and I watch from the doorway as they walk across the plaza and enter the inn where I am staying. That complicates things. I will have to be doubly careful to make sure we do not bump into each other. If I decide to make my presence known, I want it to be on my terms and not by chance.

Chapter Three

Once I am back in my room, I realize my fever has returned, along with the joint pain and an exhaustion that makes it nearly impossible for me to put one foot in front of the other. Malaria is a beast, and these recurring bouts are hardly better. I shed my clothes beside the bed, hoping sleep will afford me a measure of relief. Unfortunately, sleep flees as I fight the too-small bed, my feverish sweat soaking the sheets making it impossible for me to find a position that is even remotely comfortable. As miserable as I am, it is not the fever or the pain that keep me awake, but my troubled soul. I thought I had made peace with my past, but as soon as I saw Helen and Carolyn, all the old resentments came flooding back. Much to my disappointment, I realize I have not fully rid myself of the anger that has defined me for so long.

In my misery, I cry out to the Lord. Little by little, my shame and helplessness is replaced by a life-giving memory. With my right hand, I grope for the alabaster cross that hangs from a leather thong around my neck. It was my father's. When he died, he left it to me, along with his final journal and his Bible. It took me more than twenty years, and a dangerous trek in the far western Amazon Basin, to recover them, but now they are mine. Lying in the dark, I can see his last words to me, written on the pages of his journal and now inscribed on my heart: *I leave you my alabaster cross, the earthly symbol of my eternal faith… I bequeath to you my Bible, for it is the Word of God. Hide it in your heart, and it will keep you wherever you go… Be a man of God, Bryan Whittaker, my precious son, be a man of God.*

That poignant memory fades, to be replaced by another. In my memory, the morning is gray, the air dead still and heavy with moisture. Near the river, the ground fog is so thick we can hardly see our boat. As Lako and I stow our gear, Komi stands watching, his arms folded, his weathered face a web of wrinkles. We are going downriver today, and I will probably never see him again. In my throat there is a lump the size of a man's fist, making it nearly impossible for me to speak. "Thank you, Komi," I finally blurt out, my voice breaking. "Thank you."

For a moment he says nothing, and I wonder if he understood me. Finally, he places his gnarled hand on my chest, and in his broken Portuguese he says, "You have great heart, Bryan Whittaker, much light."

That's what I cling to now, as I battle, not only the ravages of malaria's aftermath, but also the ache in my heart. It pains me to realize the hold the past still has on me. Yet, even as I come face-to-face with my shortcomings, I remind myself that I am not the man I used to be. The old Bryan would be feeding his anger rather than grieving over it.

After tossing and turning for the better part of an hour, I finally decide to get up. Even though I am physically exhausted, I can't sleep, so I pull on my jeans and make my way to the bathroom located at the end of hallway. Back in my room, I strike a match and light the kerosene lamp before reaching for my father's satchel. It still smells musty when I open it and retrieve his final journal. It is wrapped in oilcloth, which I remove. The pages are yellow with age, and in places the ink has faded. Carefully I leaf through the first few pages, straining to make out the faded words in the dim light. In a move reminiscent of my father, I pull the oil lamp close and begin to read.

All the entries are dated more than twenty years ago, and several of them were written before he left on his ill-fated mission of mercy. One in particular catches my interest, and I read it a second time.

I recently dreamed a prophetic dream in which the Lord dealt with my ego. In my dream there was only one character—me—only there were two of me. The first me was the real me. The other me was a musclebound monster. In my dream, we were standing on the edge of a cliff. The musclebound me was holding the real me high above his head as if he was going to hurl me to my death on the rocks below.

The real me attempted to reason with the other me—that musclebound maniac—but to no avail. "Why hurl me to my death," the real me pleaded, "when you could use your enormous strength and agility to pursue a career as a professional athlete?" He seemed not to hear me, and my death seemed imminent.

I awoke in a cold sweat. Instantly I knew that dream was a warning from God. The musclebound me was my ego, my ambition, the old man. So strong was he that I could not contend with him. He was immune to my most desperate pleas. God was my only hope, and there beside my bed I prayed that He would crucify that old man, and He did. God defeated him, but He did not destroy him. He broke his power, but he still lives. He is no longer the "strong man," holding me captive, but he is still to be feared. With determined deliberateness, I turn my back on him. By God's grace, I will starve this egomaniac. I will deny his unholy ambition, day by day, and thus reckon him dead!

As a believer, sin has no power over me except what I voluntarily give it. My "old self" is a broken man, pleading for my sympathy. "A crust of bread," he cries. "A helping hand for an old friend." So harmless, so pathetic, does he seem that I am tempted to share my life with him. When I do, however, I discover that he is almost immediately transformed into the "strong man" again. Experience has taught me that a single "yes" can undo a hundred "no's" and can put me under his tyranny once more. My only hope, then, is to deny him at every turn.

Placing my finger between the pages of my father's journal, I contemplate what I have read. Apparently, my father battled some "demons" of his own, overcoming them only with God's help. That gives me hope. His "demons" were ego and ambition, while mine is anger. If I understand what he has written, God breaks the stranglehold sin has on our will, but He does not destroy it. Once sin's power is broken, it is up to us to starve it into submission by resisting it at every turn. In my case, I must deliberately starve my anger by refusing to express it. I wish there were an easier way, a quicker way, but apparently there isn't.

I would like to read more, but my eyes are tired from straining to read in such low light. Finally, I blow out the lamp and make my way back to my cramped bed. It is late, I am still running a low-grade fever while fighting the aftereffects of my recent bout with malaria, and every joint aches. Still, I hope to get some sleep now that my heart is at rest. I may not be the man I want to be, but thank God I am not the man I used to be.

The sun is slanting through the small window, washing my cramped room in morning light when I awake. Glancing at my watch, I see it is nearly nine o'clock. Shortly after daybreak, I had been awakened by street noise—the blaring of a car horn, loud voices, and the roar of an unmuffled truck—but I must have fallen back to sleep. With an effort, I make my way to the window overlooking the plaza and gather my early morning musings, putting them into a semblance of order. After spending some time thinking and praying, I finally conclude that my best course of action is to meet with Helen and Carolyn. I'm still struggling with resentment at the thought that Helen followed me to the Amazon, but with God's help, I can deal with that. Who knows—maybe her being here has nothing to do with me? It's not likely, but who knows?

While I am still mulling these things over, I see Helen and Carolyn emerge from the inn and start across the plaza toward the café. They are greeted with wolf whistles, and for a minute they hesitate, not sure how to react. I'm not surprised they have attracted attention. In the far western Amazon Basin, attractive women are in short supply.

I can't help noticing they are dressed in similar fashion—colorful blouses, jeans, and hiking boots. On Helen, the outfit looks utilitarian, especially as she strides across the plaza with a determined, no-nonsense air. Carolyn, on the other hand, looks stunning, especially with the morning sun backlighting her auburn hair. Seeing her now, I am reminded of the way she looked in the meadow below Hahn's Peak in northwestern Colorado the afternoon I proposed to her. We had been hiking, and when we stopped in the shade beside a small creek, she took off her ball cap and shook out her thick hair. Her face was full of color, and her dark eyes sparkled. After taking an engagement ring, with an embarrassingly small diamond, from my pocket, I placed it on her finger. Being a man of few words, I simply said, "Carolyn, will you marry me?"

She burst into tears and flung herself into my arms. I could feel her heart pounding as I held her close. "Yes," she whispered softly. And then more fiercely, "Yes, Bryan, I will marry you."

We took our hiking boots off and rested our tired feet in the cold creek while discussing wedding plans. I had never given it much thought before, but one thing I knew: I wasn't getting married in a church. All of my memories of church were negative, and I wanted nothing to do with it. Like most girls, Carolyn wanted a church wedding, no matter how small, but I remained adamant. My pigheaded stubbornness nearly ruined a perfect afternoon, but we finally agreed on an outdoor wedding. "Look around," I told her. "You will never find a more beautiful cathedral than this."

Pushing that memory to the back of my mind, I breathe a quick prayer and head downstairs. By the time I reach the street, they are disappearing into the small café on the far side of the plaza. A host of turbulent emotions struggle in my chest as I slowly make my way across the square. A part of me is eager to tell Helen what I've learned about our father, but I can't help wondering if she will still try to mother me. Just the thought of it tempts me with anger.

When it comes to Carolyn, my emotions are all over the place. I'm ashamed of the way I treated her. When she needed me most, when she was dying for my love, I turned a cold shoulder, driving her into the arms of another. She was too needy to resist temptation but too full of love and goodness to live with her sin. I watched her die, day by day, hating herself for what she had done, but I never lifted a finger to help her; I never spoke a word to ease her guilt. Yet I'm angry, too! Seeing her again has been like picking a scab off an old wound, releasing all the pent-up hurt and bitterness. A part of me wants to make her pay for what she did, wants to make her suffer the way I suffered.

I'm still trying to sort through my feelings when I enter the café. Just inside the door, I pause to allow my eyes to adjust to the dimness. It is nearly deserted at this hour, and I have no trouble spotting Helen and Carolyn. Taking a deep breath, I head toward the table where they are struggling to communicate with the waiter, who doesn't speak English.

When he finally turns toward the kitchen to place their order, Carolyn sees me. She's obviously taken back by my sudden appearance, but she responds with surprising control. "Hello, Bryan," she says, giving me a tentative smile. "Long time, no see."

Helen turns, and at the sight of me she leaps to her feet, knocking over her chair. "Bryan," she gasps, embracing me in a fierce hug. For a moment I stand there awkwardly, not knowing exactly how to respond. The love I feel emanating from her washes over me like a healing balm, soothing my raw emotions. Finally, I give her a clumsy hug in return while trying to think of something to say.

"Let me take a look at you," she says, stepping back. After looking me over from head to toe, she asks, "Have you been sick?" Before I can respond, she continues, "You've lost weight. Quite a bit, I would say, from the looks of you."

She means well, or so I tell myself, but nonetheless, it feels like she's mothering me, and I don't like it. I'm tempted to react as I always have, but with an effort, I bite my tongue. Instead of making a sarcastic remark, I pull out a chair and take a seat across from her. "What in the world are you doing here?" I ask. "Is Rob with you?"

She hesitates before answering, as if trying to decide how best to explain. "Rob's at home. Someone has to look after the boys. Besides, he couldn't be gone from the church. This is a busy time, with Easter just around the corner."

The waiter returns and places a steaming plate of black beans and rice on the table before each of them. I order coffee and nod at Helen to continue. "It's kind of hard to explain," she says. "I guess I'm here for the same reason you are—to find out what happened to our father."

When I give her a skeptical look, she says, "I know this is out of character for me. I'm a creature of habit, as you well know. I never do anything spur of the moment. Rob says I never go anywhere without a thermometer, a hot water bottle, a gargle, a raincoat, an aspirin, and a parachute." She laughs nervously, and I can't help thinking there's more going on here than meets the eye, but I have no idea what it might be.

Although their food is getting cold, neither Helen nor Carolyn appears to have any interest in eating. Helen has shoved her plate aside, while Carolyn is nervously moving the beans and rice around on her plate. That she is extremely uncomfortable is obvious. Maybe I'm the cause, but I think there's more to it than that. It feels like they're keeping something from me.

"Enough about me," Helen says. "What are you doing here? I thought you would be at the mission compound or in the jungle."

The waiter has returned, and he now places a steaming mug of Brazilian coffee on the table before me. I take a sip, enjoying the special flavor of strong coffee brewed with brown sugar. Finally, I say, "Actually, I'm on my way home. Hopefully, I can book a cheap passage on a cargo barge going downriver to Manaus in the next couple of days. From there, I can fly to Rio and then to the States."

"Does that mean you've learned what happened to our father?" Helen asks. "Or have you given up?"

I give her the *Reader's Digest* version, telling her about Komi, who was with our father when he died. She wants more details, so I tell her he died after contacting yellow fever while treating the Amuaca Indians and that Komi buried him deep in the jungle. Finally, I tell her I have our father's satchel containing his Bible and his last journal. Her face is pale when I finish, and tears glisten in her eyes.

"I want to see his journal," she says in a voice choked with emotion. "And I want to see where he's buried."

Chapter 4

Carolyn excuses herself when we leave the café, and Helen and I head to my room. Knowing my sister is a neat freak, I hesitate at the door. My room is a mess—the bed is unmade, hammocks and mosquito nets are thrown in a corner, and my dirty clothes are strewn on the floor. Steeling myself for her disapproval, I open the door and allow her to enter before me. If she notices my mess, she doesn't say anything.

I direct her to the chair situated before the window overlooking the plaza before pulling my father's satchel from beneath the bed. The damp smell of mildew and old canvas is nearly overwhelming, and I can't help noticing the dark stains—probably my father's blood—on the canvas flap. Now my eyes are drawn to the leather patch that is stitched on the flap between the buckles. Although the leather is old and stained, there is no mistaking the initials carved into it—*H. W.*—Harold Whittaker.

Helen is staring in my direction, never taking her eyes off the satchel that once belonged to our father. When I place it in her hands, she is trembling, and her breathing is ragged. As I watch, she hugs the satchel to her chest, and silent tears leave wet tracks down her cheeks. It is such a private moment I feel like I should look away, but I can't tear my eyes away from her face. It is like looking into her soul, and maybe for the first time in my life, I feel like I truly know my sister. To my chagrin, I belatedly realize that her grief was as great as my own. I can't help wondering why I am just now realizing how much she has suffered.

"What's in here, Bryan?" she asks, fumbling with the buckles.

"Not much in terms of earthly goods. When Komi gave it to me, there were a couple of fishhooks, a spool of fishing line, a pocketknife, and a stub of a pencil. The only truly valuable items were our father's Bible and his final journal, and they are only valuable to us."

Taking my father's pocketknife from the pocket of my jeans, I hand it to her. "I thought you might like your boys to have this."

As she turns it over in her hand, her face lights up with a memory. "I can't tell you how many times I saw our father use this very knife to sharpen my pencil or to dig a splinter out of my finger." After another moment, she asks, "Are you sure you don't want to keep it for yourself?"

"I'm sure. Besides, he left me his alabaster cross." Reaching inside my shirt, I pull it out. Taking it off, I hand it to her. "In his journal you will find a final letter to each of us—to you, to me and to Mom. I haven't read what he wrote to you or Mom, but in my letter, he left his cross to me. His words are indelibly inscribed on my memory: 'Bryan, I leave you my alabaster cross, the earthly symbol of my eternal faith. Wear it all the days of your life as a symbol of your covenant with the Lord.'"

My voice is thick with feeling, causing Helen to give me a long look before she hands the cross back to me. After studying it for a moment, I bring it to my lips before placing the sweat-stained leather string over my head and tucking the cross inside my shirt.

"Something has happened to you, hasn't it?" she probes. "You're different."

When I nod, she continues, "Can you tell me about it?"

"Someday, maybe. Right now, I think you should look at our father's journal, especially the letter he wrote to you."

I watch as she takes the journal from his satchel and removes the oilcloth in which it is wrapped. She carefully refolds the oilcloth and lays it aside before opening the journal. When she does, a wave of emotions plays across her face. In an instant I am right there with her, reliving the moment when I opened it for the first time. The pages were yellow with age, and in several places the ink had faded or ran together; nonetheless, I felt closer to him than I ever did when he was alive. While he lived, he was always so distant, so private, but there, on the pages of his journal, he bared his soul. Knowing how emotional that was for me, I offer to leave so she can have some privacy.

"Please stay," she says. "I don't want to be alone."

As she begins to read, I move quietly around the room, stuffing my dirty clothes back into my bag and making my bed. When the room is reasonably straight, I stretch out on the bed and contemplate my future. Although I was never a very good student, I am seriously considering enrolling in college when I get back home. Maybe I will study photography with an eye toward photojournalism, or perhaps I will take some creative writing courses. The possibility of being a writer excites me. Like my father, I am mostly tongue-tied, but put a pen in my hand and all the inarticulate yearnings of my soul seem to find their voice. Who knows, maybe I will fail. Still, I'm not going to allow the fear of failure to keep me from trying.

I must have drifted off to sleep, only to awaken a short time later. Helen is weeping softly, and I want to comfort her, but I don't know what to do. I've never been good at that sort of thing. I'm tempted to pretend I'm still asleep, but if I refuse to comfort her, I will never forgive myself. All my life I've been turning a blind eye to the sufferings of others, a deaf ear to their silent cries for a shoulder to lean on. Not now. Not this time.

Making my way across the room, I kneel in front of her and clumsily take her in my arms. When I do, her soft weeping erupts into harsh sobs. It feels awkward, but I force myself to hold her while she sobs into my shoulder. After a time, her tears seem to exhaust themselves, and she reaches for her purse in search of a tissue.

"I'm sorry, Bryan. I don't usually make such a spectacle of myself." When I don't say anything, she continues, "I haven't been myself since Mother died. Rob's grown tired of my moodiness. He says I'm making a shrine out of my sorrows. Who knows, maybe I am."

Of course, I don't know what to say, so I just sit there. Taking a deep breath, she continues, "This is a difficult time for Rob and me. We seem to have lost our way. I don't know if we're going to make it."

Her disclosure stuns me, but I try not to let it show. In my mind, Rob and Helen have always been the perfect couple. I know I should say something, but once again, I'm at a loss for words. Seeing Helen like this—nervously shredding a tissue, her eyes red and puffy from crying—has left me more than a little confused.

When it becomes apparent I'm going to remain silent, she continues, speaking so softly I have to strain to hear. "In *Dante's Inferno,* the writer takes a walk and suddenly finds himself disoriented, and so begins his journey into the various levels of hell with these words: 'In the middle of the journey of our life I found myself in a dark wood.'"

Her reference to *Dante's Inferno* is wasted on me, but I'm having no difficulty understanding her despair. "That best describes what is happening to me," she laments. "In the middle of my own journey, I suddenly found myself in a dark wood, and I don't know if I can find my way out."

Her hopelessness is tearing my heart out. I've been there, and I know how helpless it makes you feel. She's obviously embarrassed, but now that she's started to bare her soul she is determined to continue. "It feels like I'm just going through the motions, sleepwalking instead of living. I've become a terrible mother to my children, and God knows I haven't been a good wife to Rob."

Putting my hand on her arm to comfort her, I interject, "Helen, you may feel like a terrible mother, but I'm sure you're not. Even sleepwalking, you're a better mother than most women I know."

Giving me a tired smile, she says, "Thanks, Bryan. That's kind of you to say, but you haven't heard the worst yet. I think Rob may be involved with another woman."

"That's absurd," I blurt out before I can stop myself. I don't mean to make light of her concerns, but I can't imagine Rob doing something like that. He's a pastor, for heaven's sake!

"I know it sounds preposterous," she concludes, "but I don't know how else to explain his actions. He's been avoiding me, working late—or so he claims. He has no interest in making love to me, and we haven't been intimate in weeks, maybe months."

I'm still trying to wrap my mind around that when she adds, "I think he's involved with his secretary. She's divorced. Her name is Rita. I have no idea if they're sleeping together, but if they're not, it's only a matter of time. Anyone can see that she's infatuated with him."

When it becomes apparent I have no advice to give or even words of comfort, Helen manages to compose herself. Finally, she takes a deep breath before suggesting that I invite Carolyn to join us so we can talk about what needs to be done in preparation for going upriver to the mission station.

Chapter 5

STERLING, COLORADO
1971

Darkness comes early on the high plains of Northeastern Colorado in late winter, and it is fully dark when Rob makes his way toward his car. Earlier it was sleeting, before an arctic cold front dropped the temperatures into the single digits, and the windows on his Oldsmobile Cutlass are covered with a sheet of ice. After starting the car and turning on the defroster, he uses the scraper to clear the windshield. It is slow going, and he can't help thinking that he should have taken the Board's suggestion and built a small garage, or at least a carport, to shelter his automobile. They wanted to include it in the plans when they built the new facilities, but he vetoed it, fearing some of the congregation might think it too extravagant.

Having finally scraped the windows clean, he climbs wearily into the car. For two or three minutes, he stares into the darkness while soaking up the warmth of the heater. The last thing he wants to do is go home. With Helen gone, things aren't the same. His mother is doing the best she can, but her strict discipline makes Helen's stern parenting style seem almost permissive. Mealtimes used to be fun. Following dinner, they had often lingered around the table laughing and talking. First Robbie and then Jake would tell a bad joke or share some amusing antic, causing all of them to erupt in laughter. Now meals are a tense affair punctuated by his mother's stern rebukes: *"Eat with your mouth closed." "Use your napkin." "Don't wipe your hands on your jeans."* And of course, *"Clean your plate. There are starving children all over the world, and you're wasting food."* He tried reasoning with her, but she was intractable. Now he and the boys rush through meals with hardly a word, only too eager to leave the table.

Honesty makes him acknowledge that even before Helen left for the far western Amazon Basin, things were difficult. They tried to keep their disagreements from the boys, but a tense atmosphere soon infected the family. Painfully polite, but terse exchanges replaced the comfortable camaraderie he and Helen once enjoyed. Occasionally their tempers flared in the boys' presence, causing them to cringe in fear. Soon Robbie and Jake crept through the house as silent as ghosts, their rambunctious exuberance a thing of the past.

He sighs wearily before finally turning on the headlights. The parking lot is slick, causing the Cutlass to fishtail slightly as he eases onto the street. He tries to concentrate on his driving but soon finds his mind wandering. With Helen in the Amazon, his thoughts frequently turn to Rita. He's being foolish and he knows it, but he tells himself there's no harm in just thinking about her. Of course, he knows better, but he chooses to indulge his fantasies anyway. Never mind that he has counseled countless others to carefully guard their thought lives.

Without consciously deciding to do so, he finds himself driving by her house. The kitchen light is on, and he catches a glimpse of her as she prepares dinner. For just a moment, he's tempted to drop in for a cup of coffee, but with a stern resolve he dismisses that ill-conceived thought. As much as he hates to admit it, he knows he's playing with fire. Helen was right—Rita is attracted to him—and he enjoys it!

As he turns the corner toward home, he reflects on the situation in which he now finds himself. Never in his wildest imaginings would he have thought himself capable of being attracted to another woman. He's a minister, for heaven's sake, a married man and the father of two boys. So how did this happen? With painful clarity, he reflects on the fact that once a boundary between a man and a woman is crossed, it is almost impossible to reestablish it. Over the past several months, the boundaries in his relationship with Rita have been breached in a myriad of small ways, but none more critical than the morning when she gave him a massage. He knew they were moving onto dangerous ground, but tension had knotted his neck and shoulders and he had a splitting headache. Relief seemed cheap at any price. The pleasure he experienced as her fingers worked their magic set off alarm bells in his conscience, but he ignored them.

That was a defining moment—and a critical factor in what is happening now. In that moment, nothing more was communicated than this: *Our friendship could turn into something else.* He could have closed the door and carefully restricted their relationship, but he didn't. And because he didn't— because he did nothing at all—he left the door open, and that moment took on a life of its own. Even though he is not yet willing to admit it, he is plunging headlong toward disaster.

He is still wrestling with his thoughts when he turns into the driveway and hits the garage door opener. Once inside the garage, he turns off the ignition, but he remains in the car. Replaying his memories of Rita has left a bitter taste in his mouth. He is sick with shame and lives in fear that someone will discover their relationship. He loves God, he knows what they're doing is wrong, but he can't bring himself to break it off. The best he can do is tell himself that he will never allow their relationship to become anything more than an emotional attachment. He vows he will never allow it to become physical; he couldn't live with himself if he did.

Once more he indulges in rationalization, telling himself that it's not his fault he's attracted to Rita. Not entirely, anyway. If Helen hadn't run off to the Amazon, none of this would be happening. Never mind that he and Rita were "sparking" long before Helen headed to Brazil. Thinking of Helen, he experiences conflicting emotions. He's angry with her, yet he misses her too. That is, he misses the efficient way she cared for the boys and managed their home. She seemed to do it so effortlessly that he hardly noticed. The house was cleaned, the laundry done, the meals prepared, and the boys taxied to and fro as if by magic. He never lifted a finger.

His mother is doing the best she can, but it's not working very well. She's almost seventy years old, and she seems overwhelmed. The boys miss their mother, and they mope around the house. Meals are tense affairs where he feels caught in the middle. The boys don't like the way his mother cooks, and they often refuse to eat, which creates a scene. His mother expects him to discipline the boys, to make them eat everything on their plates and to show her more respect. Yet he often feels she is overbearing and insensitive to how difficult this is for them.

Rita has offered to help, but that hardly seems a good idea. His mother is very territorial and would undoubtedly resent her. Not to mention the fact that Rita's presence would confuse the boys. Besides, his mother is discerning by nature, and he fears she would immediately sense something awry in their relationship.

He is still mulling over his situation when the door leading into the garage from the utility room is opened, throwing a shaft of light into the car. "There you are," his mother says. "I thought I heard the garage door open. What in the world are you doing sitting in the dark?" Before he can answer, she continues, "We've been waiting dinner on you, and the food's getting cold."

Although Rob retreated to his bedroom as soon as he got the boys in bed, it was after two o'clock before he finally fell into an exhausted sleep, only to be tormented by guilt-ridden dreams in which he was charged with adultery. In his dreams he stood shamefaced before a presbytery board of his peers. After hearing his lurid confession, they defrocked him and dismissed him from his church. He awoke sick with shame, his heart pounding. The dreams were prophetic, a warning from God; of that he was sure.

As much as he dreads it, he knows he has to speak with Rita—the sooner the better. They must get their relationship back on a purely professional footing. Although they have never done anything even remotely physical—discounting the massage, of course—the attraction between them is undeniable, and it must be dealt with immediately, albeit with utmost care.

Driving to the church office, he tried out several approaches in his mind, searching for just the right tone. He wanted to make sure she knew how much he cared for her, and he wanted to be especially careful not to hurt her. An unfaithful husband and a bitter divorce had wounded her in ways that still weren't completely healed. The last thing he wanted was to reopen those old wounds. Why, he wondered, had he ever let things get to this point? Helen had tried to warn him, but he had brushed her concerns aside, suggesting that she was imagining things. Now, no matter how carefully he handles his conversation with Rita, she is likely to be hurt.

Although he intended to talk with her as soon as she came into the office, he kept finding reasons to put it off, and it was late afternoon before he finally decided to bite the bullet. Taking a deep breath, he punched the intercom button. "Rita, I realize it is late, but I really need to speak with you before you go."

"Give me just a minute," she replied before dropping her car keys back into her purse. Stepping into the ladies' room, she quickly checked her makeup before applying a little lipstick. Giving her hair a final pat, she headed for his office.

In spite of himself, Rob couldn't help noticing how attractive she was. She had put in an eight-hour day, and yet she looked like she had just stepped out of a fashion magazine. She had a knack for coordinating her outfits in a way that few women could, and inadvertently he caught himself comparing her stylish appearance with Helen's more pedestrian look. For a fleeting moment, he was tempted to disregard his plans to speak with her and simply enjoy the moment, but he steeled his resolve.

"Should I make fresh coffee?" she asked, giving him a warm smile.

"That won't be necessary," he replied, as he moved to shut the office door.

Although he was attempting to appear relaxed, she couldn't help noticing how tense he was. Placing her hand on his arm, she asked, "What is it? Have I done something wrong?"

Without a word, he directs her to the leather couch in front of the picture window that overlooked a snow-covered field. Once she is seated, he situates himself on the adjoining love seat and studies the floor between his feet. Finally, he clears his throat. "Rita," he says, choosing his words carefully, "you are a very special person, and I truly enjoy working with you. You have an innate understanding of the ministry—its unique pressures and demands—and that makes you easy to talk to. Although I probably shouldn't admit it, I often find myself sharing things with you that I'm not comfortable sharing with anyone else, not even Helen. I can't help thinking that you would make some pastor a wonderful wife and helpmate in the ministry."

Something about Rob's manner and careful choice of words makes her uneasy, and when he pauses, she interjects, "I'm not sure what you're trying to say, but you're making me uncomfortable. I feel like the 'other shoe' is about to drop."

"I'm sorry. I don't mean to make you feel that way. What I'm trying to say is that you're a very attractive woman and I enjoy your company, probably more than I should. That's a dangerous thing for a man in my position."

He pauses, giving her a chance to respond. When she doesn't say anything, he continues, stumbling over his words. "If I'm not mistaken, I think you may have feelings for me, as well."

Placing her hand on his arm, she smiles in a mischievous kind of way. "Rob, you're so cute when you're embarrassed. Of course, I'm attracted to you. What woman wouldn't be? But I know you're married, and that's that. End of story."

"Do you realize how dangerous this is?" he asks. "If we ever allowed our feelings to get out of hand, it would be disastrous. Divorce for a man in my position is out of the question, and even a hint of a scandal could ruin my ministry."

"Surely you don't think I would ever do anything to hurt you or your ministry?" she asks, aghast at the thought.

"Of course not. Not knowingly anyway, but emotions often have a will of their own."

"So where do we go from here?" she asks. "Assuming I still have a job."

"Of course, you still have a job. I couldn't do without you." In a lighter tone, he continues, "If I didn't have you, who would keep track of my calendar, pick up my laundry from the cleaners, and run my errands, not to mention bring me coffee?"

"Don't forget the massages."

"As much as I enjoy your massages, we will have to forego them in the future. Any form of physical contact is strictly off-limits. It's simply too dangerous."

Following that conversation, they made a concerted effort to get their relationship back on a professional footing. She made it a point to strictly adhere to the official office hours, never arriving early and always leaving right on time, even if Rob was working late. They were painfully polite with each other, never saying anything that could in any way be misconstrued. But she couldn't control her thoughts. Several times a day, she caught herself thinking, "He's attracted to me…" And she couldn't help wondering if his admonition to be careful wasn't, in a backhanded sort of way, a suggestion that their relationship might become something more.

For his part, Rob sorely missed the "innocent" flirting and playful exchanges that had been so much a part of their friendship. In fact, the more he restrained himself, the more obsessed he became. Of course, he convinced himself that he would never allow things to get out of hand, refusing to even consider the possibility that he might be capable of being unfaithful to Helen. Although he realized that reestablishing the boundaries were mandatory, another part of him wished he had never had that conversation with Rita.

From time to time, he asked her to bring him a fresh cup of coffee in hopes that they might inadvertently touch hands when she handed it to him. To his disappointment, she was always careful to place it on the coaster on the corner of his desk. Once or twice he complained of a tension headache, hoping she would offer to give him a massage, but she pretended not to hear, or she offered to get him a couple of aspirin. Several times he came in early, secretly hoping that she might do the same, but she never did. When she continued to ignore his none-too-subtle hints, he decided to take matters into his own hands, although he would have never admitted as much, not even to himself. He deliberately put off preparing the materials for the monthly board until the last minute so he would have an excuse to ask her to work late.

On the surface, his request seemed innocent enough, but Rita suspected it signaled a return to the way things used to be. Once the boardroom was ready and the packets of materials had been laid out for each board member, she returned to the office area and called Rob on the intercom. "Is there anything else you need before I go?"

"If you have a minute, please step into my office."

When she opened his office door, he was standing before the picture widow staring into the darkness. For several seconds, maybe even as long as a minute, she remained just inside the door, waiting for him to acknowledge her presence. Finally, she cleared her throat discreetly. Taking a deep breath, he turned and said, "Sorry. I didn't hear you come in. Please close the door."

As she walked across the room toward him, he couldn't help noticing the soft rustling of her skirt and the subtle fragrance of her perfume. For a moment they stood side by side without speaking. In the distance, they could see the traffic moving on the street, the red taillights of the passing cars reflecting off the snow. Stepping behind her, he slipped his arms around her waist, drawing her close, and she nestled into his arms. Finally, she asked, "Are you sure we should be doing this?"

"I'm sure we shouldn't be doing this," he murmured into her hair. "Nothing good can come of it."

Turning so she could face him, she took a deep breath before speaking. "If nothing good can come of this, then why are you tempting me?"

"I can't seem to help myself," he replied, not even attempting to hide his misery. "I know what we are doing is wrong, and I hate myself for being so weak. It doesn't matter if I love you or not—I can never divorce Helen. It would destroy my ministry. Besides, I couldn't do that to my boys or to the church."

"I understand, I really do," she replied. "What I can't understand is why God would allow us to fall in love, just to make us miserable." She paused before asking, "Can loving each other be wrong if we're careful to make sure no one gets hurt?"

"That's the problem. In situations like this, someone always gets hurt, usually the children or the betrayed spouse. Still, even knowing the risks we're taking, I'm not willing to give you up."

The clock on the office wall chimes, and Rob gives her a final squeeze before releasing her. "You'd better go. It's almost time for the board meeting. It wouldn't look good if one of the board members showed up early and you were still here."

"I know," she murmurs, resignation coloring her words.

Back in her office, she locks her desk, puts her coat on, picks up her purse, and heads for the parking lot. On the short drive home, she finds herself replaying what just happened. Of course, she feels guilty—Rob is a married man, a father, and a pastor—but she tries to rationalize it away. She would never do anything to deliberately hurt him, or Helen, for that matter. It's just that her heart goes out to him. He's such a good man, and Helen doesn't seem to love him, as she should. Alone in the car, she whispers into the darkness, "All I want to do is give him the love he deserves."

Chapter 6

AMAZON BASIN
FAR WESTERN BRAZIL
1971

The three of us—Helen, Carolyn, and myself—are meeting in my cramped hotel room to discuss their plans. Although they've been in Cruzeiro do Sul for nearly three weeks, they have not made any progress in their attempt to hire someone to take them upriver. That should have made it easier for me to convince them to return to the States, but that wasn't the case. Helen is adamant about going to the mission compound, and she refuses to listen to reason. Frustrated, I move to the window and stare across the plaza, making a determined effort to keep my temper in check. When Helen gets something in her mind, she can be really stubborn. The curse of our Whittaker genes, I suppose.

Once I have my anger in hand, I rejoin my sister and Carolyn at the small table in the corner of my room. Carolyn remains silent, content to let Helen and I work this out between ourselves. Speaking as calmly as I can, I try once more to explain the dangers of going upriver, especially during the rainy season, when the rivers are flooded and filled with debris.

"Bryan," Helen says, speaking patiently as if to a dull child, "you are not going to talk me out of this. I didn't come this far just to turn around and go home. I want to see the mission compound where we grew up, and more importantly, I want to see where our father is buried."

Against my better judgment, I acquiesce, worn down by her obstinate determination. "The first thing we will have to do is find a boat," I say, as I return to the window and try to think where we might find something suitable for the trip upriver. Thinking out loud, I muse, "I was fortunate enough to connect with Dr. Peterson shortly after I arrived. He had chartered a fairly large boat for a six-month expedition to conduct ecological studies in the far western Amazon River Valley. His itinerary coincided with my own, enabling me to hitch a ride. I left him when we reached the mission station, which is located about ten days' journey up the Rio Moa. He continued upriver and is not scheduled to return for another three, maybe four weeks."

"That's not a problem," Helen interjects. "Carolyn and I won't need a boat that big anyway. All we need is something small, just large enough to get the two of us to the mission compound."

Wearily I reply, "Remember, you're going into the interior, which means you will have to take all of your supplies with you. When I set out with Dr. Peterson, every available inch of the *Flor de Maio* was covered with provisions and equipment."

"Oh, I hadn't considered that," Helen reflects. "So, what do you think we will need, say, for four or five weeks?"

"More than you might imagine, but we can figure that out once we locate a boat and a guide."

"What about the *mateiro* who served as your guide?" Carolyn asks, injecting herself into the conversation. "Would his boat be big enough to take us and our supplies upriver?"

"That may be your best bet, but I have to warn you— Lako can be a challenge."

"In what way?"

"He's a drunk. When I met him, he was passed out in the alley behind the Blue Goose, his head resting in a puddle of his own vomit. I was ready to dismiss him out of hand, but Dr. Peterson assured me he was the finest guide on the river. He said, 'Keep him sober, and you won't find a more capable guide. There aren't more than a handful of people in all of Amazonia who have his skills.'"

"So, how did you keep him sober?" Helen asks impatiently.

"Once we were headed upriver, I had Eurico go through his things and throw out every bottle of *cachaça* he could find."

"Who's Eurico?" Carolyn asks.

"He's a nine-year-old street urchin—what the locals call a *Peixote*. His parents died of malaria when he was only six years old, leaving him an orphan. When I met him, he had been living on the streets for three years. He subsisted by selling chewing gum, shining shoes, and begging."

"That's so sad," Helen interjects, thinking of her own two boys.

"I know. Yet he's the most optimistic person I've ever met. He has an infectious grin and an indomitable spirit. He's a born hustler and wise beyond his years. He introduced me to Dr. Peterson and found Lako for me."

Smiling, Carolyn asks, "When can we meet him?"

"That will have to wait until you get to the mission station. He's living with one of the missionaries now, a medical doctor from Minnesota. Her name is Diana Rhoades."

Without intending to, I have allowed special warmth to color my words, and Carolyn has picked up on it. Undoubtedly, she is comparing my feelings for Eurico and Diana to the coldness with which I often treated her. Glancing at her, I see a tear slip down her cheek, and I am reminded that when she needed me most, I withdrew inside myself, leaving her to face life alone. No matter how hard she tried to reach me, I refused to respond. Little wonder she divorced me.

"If he's a drunk," Helen asks, refocusing me on the task at hand, "how did he become such a renowned guide?"

"He wasn't always a drunk," I reply. "According to Dr. Peterson, he turned to drink following the deaths of his wife and three children."

"How did they die?"

"Malaria. They fell prey to the most recent epidemic to strike Cruzeiro do Sul. That was three or four years ago. The same epidemic that made Eurico an orphan."

"It makes me sad to think how cruel life can be," Carolyn muses.

"Be that as it may," Helen says, taking charge once again. "He sounds like our best bet, so where can we find him? I would like to get things underway as soon as possible."

"That could be a problem. After I settled up with him, he headed straight for the liquor store. By now he's probably sleeping off a drunk somewhere, but only God knows where."

Helen presses me. "Surely you can find him?"

"Maybe. I suppose I could hit the bars and liquor stores and see if anyone has seen him. He's well known to the locals, both as a guide and a drunk. Of course, finding him is one thing—sobering him up and convincing him to take you ladies upriver is an altogether different matter."

"Of course, he will agree to take us," Helen says dismissively. "Why wouldn't he?"

I've had just about all I can take of her "know it all" ways, and it's all I can do to keep my temper in check. Biting back my angry words, I reply, "First of all, he's just completed a grueling twelve weeks in the interior. Secondly, it's dangerous. Our lives were at risk—and not just from the jungle. We had a harrowing escape after being captured by the Amuacas. Thirdly, he might not like being saddled with two women who know absolutely nothing about roughing it in the interior."

For an instant, anger flashes in her eyes, but it is quickly replaced by concern. "I had no idea you were captured by Indians. What in the world happened?"

I give her the *Reader's Digest* version, leaving out the most harrowing details, concluding with our escape. "An old woman who remembered our father helped us escape. The medicine he brought saved her life, and she felt indebted to him. According to Lako, our father told her that I would come one day. Apparently, I look enough like our father that she recognized me."

"Bryan, that's absolutely amazing! I mean, what are the chances of that happening, especially after more than twenty years?" When I nod in agreement, she continues, "It had to be the Lord's doing. There's no other explanation."

It might well have been the Lord's doing, but Carolyn has gone ghostly pale, and I can tell that the thought of being captured by the Amuacas is terrifying her—and rightly so. Although it is the twentieth century, they have had little or no contact with the outside world and live a Stone Age existence. They are fierce warriors and have been known to kill outsiders on contact. Little wonder, considering every contact with the white man has been disastrous. The rubber barons enslaved them, and the white man's diseases decimated their population.

Helen is fascinated by my account and seems oblivious to Carolyn's angst. "Don't leave us hanging," she says. "How did you escape?"

"When it was fully dark, the Indians built a large fire in the common area in front of the longhouse and began dancing around it. It was weird. Firelight flickered off their painted faces, giving them a ghoulish appearance. Suddenly the shaman emerged from the darkness, shaking his rattles and chanting. Slowly he moved from dancer to dancer, placing a gourd containing hallucinogenic drugs of some kind to their lips. The dancers were soon stoned. Several fell into a stupor where they were, while others wandered off into the darkness and passed out. According to Lako, they experience visions and/ or visitations from the spirit world while in their drug-induced stupors. Only the shaman can interpret them, and his interpretations would determine whether we lived or died.

"When most of the tribe was stoned, the old woman crept through the darkness to where we were. She quickly cut the vines binding our hands and feet and led us away from the village. We followed her up a nearly invisible trail, which she said would take us into a valley that the Amuacas considered haunted. Her brother lived there as an outcast, and she said if we could make it to that valley, he would give us sanctuary. The steep trail was grueling, even for Lako. For me, it was nearly impossible. I had injured my knee weeks earlier, and it was still giving me trouble. Every time I took a step, it felt like someone was driving an icepick into it. Somehow, I managed to keep going, the thought of being recaptured by the Amuacas forcing me to push through my pain, and by daylight we were descending into the haunted valley.

"Here's where events take their most usual turn. The old woman's brother—his name is Komi—turned out to be the Indian who came to the mission compound seeking our father's help on that fateful day so long ago. When our father fell prey to the plague that had decimated the Amuaca village, Komi cared for him, and when our father died, he buried him."

I return to the window once more and stare out, not seeing the Plaza, but an image burned into my memory. I see the place where my father is buried beneath a towering samauma tree deep in the rain forest. Carved in its base is a crude cross. Unconsciously I finger the alabaster cross hanging from a leather cord around my neck.

"What is it?" Helen asks as she comes to join me at the window.

"I was just thinking of our father," I say, my voice thick with emotion. "He was a complex man, impossible for a seven-year-old boy to understand. He was a private person, a solitary man, and I mistook his silence for rejection. Growing up, I couldn't help doubting his love, but through his journals I have come to understand how wrong I was. He truly loved me, and you also."

She places her hand on my arm to comfort me, and I immediately regret my emotional display. Like my father, I am a solitary man, and I wear my stoicism like a suit of armor, afraid to let anyone see the frightened little boy who lives inside this grown man's body. Abruptly I turn from the window and stride across the room. At the door, I glance back and mumble, "I better see if I can find Lako."

Chapter 7

Locating Lako and sobering him up took some doing. After forcing him to take a cold shower and drink nearly a gallon of black coffee, he was in a surly mood. He glared at me while clenching and unclenching his fists in an attempt to keep his hands from trembling, as I explained that my sister wanted to hire him to take her and a friend upriver to the mission compound.

"Absolutely not!" he snarled while cursing under his breath. Helen had authorized me to offer him twice the amount he had charged me if necessary, but to no avail. When I continued to press him he lunged to his feet, shoved me out of his way, and staggered out the door.

Helen was furious but undeterred. She was sure there had to be other reputable guides. "If you can't locate one, I will do it myself," she said, thrusting out her chin stubbornly. I reminded her that she had been searching for a guide for more than three weeks and she still had no idea where to find one, not to mention the fact that she could barely order breakfast in Portuguese. Carolyn laughed. "He's got a point, Helen."

Exasperated, she walked to the window and stared down at the street. For a minute or two, her shoulders slumped, and

I thought she was finally coming to grips with reality. Surely she could see how impossible the situation was. I glanced at Carolyn, who must have been thinking the same thing, for she seemed relieved. I could tell she was ready to get on the next flight back to the States.

I should have known better. Helen is as stubborn as our father. When she turned from the window, her jaw was set, and her eyes blazed. "You could do it, Bryan. You could be our guide."

I started to protest, but she plunged ahead. "How hard can it be? All you have to do is follow the river upstream until we get to the mission compound. Please, Bryan. You know how much this means to me."

Once more I try to reason with her. I remind her that when we leave Cruzeiro do Sul, the last traces of civilization will disappear. We will be completely on our own, and the deeper we venture into the interior, the more unforgiving it becomes. Danger lurks everywhere. It wears many faces. An accident, a snakebite, a violent storm, a crippling illness, even a simple miscalculation can result in death.

Carolyn needs no convincing, but Helen seems deaf to my most determined efforts. Finally, I tell her about Diana's near-fatal plunge down the mountain and the injuries I suffered in my ill-fated attempt to rescue her. I describe the miserable night we spent on the mountain while Eurico went for help. Without embellishment, I describe killing the jaguar that attacked me, and how close I came to death. Sparing no punches, I tell them of the violent storm that practically destroyed the mission compound and Eurico's nearly fatal bout with meningitis.

Nothing I say moves her, and once more I'm reminded that she is our father's daughter. Like him, she is goal oriented, and once she sets her mind on a task, nothing can deter her—neither danger nor logic. With or without me, she is going upriver. I want to remind her that she has two sons who need her, and that while her determination is admirable, to ignore the risks is downright foolish. I want to, but I don't. When I see the naked desire in her eyes, my heart hurts. It mirrors my own need to reconnect with my father, and in spite of my determination to dissuade her, I find myself wanting to help her.

With an effort, I play the devil's advocate one last time and address the logistics. "Even if I am willing to take you to the mission compound, we will still need a boat. There's no guarantee I can find one, and if I do, it could be expensive."

"How much money are we talking about?" She asks.

"I'm not sure, but probably twelve to fifteen hundred dollars, just for the boat. Then we will have to buy supplies and gear. We will need gasoline for the boat, hammocks, mosquito nets, tarps, cooking utensils, and foodstuff. That will run another four or five hundred."

Helen grimaces and chews her lip. I don't want her to be disappointed, but I can't help hoping the cost is prohibitive. Going upriver with an experienced guide is dangerous, but going without one is sheer madness. I have no doubt that I can find the mission compound if all goes well, but let an emergency arise and I will be hard pressed to deal with it. I'm not the tenderfoot I was when I arrived three months ago, but I'm certainly no *mateiro*.

After considerable thought, she says, "Let's do it. It's a lot of money, but I would never forgive myself if I turned back now."

For the next three days, I make the rounds talking to everyone I know in a futile attempt to find a reputable guide and/or a boat someone is willing to sell. As a last resort, I go in search of Lako. Of course, he is drunk, and when he sees me approaching, he glares at me and spits on the ground. "Don't you ever give up?" he growls. When I don't bother to answer, he stares at me defiantly. "The answer is still no. I won't take your sister to the mission compound. Not now. Not ever!"

Taking a wad of Brazilian *reals* from my pocket, I count out the equivalent of one thousand dollars. Lako continues to shake his head, but I can see the hunger in his eyes. He cannot help calculating how much *cachaca* (cheap white wine) that wad of *reals* will buy. Finally, I say, "I want to buy your boat."

He licks his lips, and I can tell that he is sorely tempted. His addiction to *cachaca* is fierce, and according to my calculations, he's probably already drunk up all the money I paid him. He cannot tear his eyes off the wad of *reals* I have shoved across the table toward him, and I can tell it is all he can do not to reach for them. With trembling hands, he pours the last of the *cachaca* into a cracked cup and gulps it down, before putting his hands beneath the table between his knees.

With deliberate slowness, I add a couple hundred more dollars' worth of *reals* to the stack on the table. "If you won't take my sister upriver, then sell me your boat and I will take her myself." When he still hesitates, I continue, "When we return in six or eight weeks, I will sell your boat back to you if you like."

We seal the deal with a handshake. I suppose I should feel satisfied, but any sense of accomplishment is tainted with a strong dose of guilt. I cannot help thinking that I am helping Lako destroy himself. Without his boat, he will never be able to make a living as a *mateiro*. With painful clarity I see his future. He will spend his days sweeping out saloons before drinking himself into an early grave. Maybe that was his destiny regardless of anything I did or did not do, but I cannot help feeling I am contributing to his demise.

As I make my way back to the inn where Helen and Carolyn await my return, I find myself considering what lies ahead. As apprehensive as I am about challenging the rain-swollen currents of the *Rio Jurua* and the *Rio Moa*, which are filled with all manner of debris—trash from the river margin, uprooted trees, and the bloated bodies of dead animals—it is nothing compared to the angst I feel at the thought of facing Diana. I don't know what I fear most, her complete rejection or the renewal of our ill-fated romance with its inevitable gut-wrenching parting.

Chapter 8

STERLING, COLORADO
1971

It's after nine thirty as Rob replaces the board agenda, the minutes, and the monthly financial report in a file folder before putting it in his briefcase. The monthly meeting of the official board has adjourned, and he tries to hide his impatience, as several of the board members appear to be in no hurry to depart. Normally, he would enjoy their fellowship, but tonight he has other plans. Rita is preparing a late dinner, and he is eager to join her.

In his saner moments, he realizes that his rendezvous with her is inappropriate, even foolish, but he has convinced himself they aren't doing anything wrong—just two friends sharing a meal. Nonetheless his conscience nags him with troubling questions: *If you are not doing anything wrong, then why are you keeping it a secret? How would Helen feel if she knew what you are doing?* Scriptures memorized years ago return to convict him: "Abstain from all appearance of evil." And "Do not lust in your heart after her beauty or let her captivate you with her eyes.... A man who commits adultery has no sense; whoever does so destroys himself."

In his heart of hearts, Rob knows he is playing with fire, but he has convinced himself he can handle it. He tells himself he would never be unfaithful to his wife, never mind that his feelings for Rita are a betrayal of his marriage vows: *To forsake all others and cleave only to his wife as long as they both shall live.*

He's well aware that when good people commit adultery, it is seldom a sudden thing. Slowly, one small step at a time, they allow themselves to be drawn in. With each succeeding step, they tell themselves they will go this far but no farther. Unfortunately, their good intentions are just that—good intentions, nothing more. Although he can't admit it to himself, he is blindly following in their footsteps.

As pastor, he has helped several men negotiate infidelity's treacherous waters. Again and again, he has counseled them never to underestimate their capacity for sin. He has warned them that no matter how good their intentions, they are no match for their wayward emotions. Now he turns a deaf ear to his own counsel. He is different. He is unique. He can handle it. Or so he tells himself.

The last of the board members have finally gone, and Rob is preparing to lock up when Dave Underwood returns. "Pastor, may I have a word with you?"

Glancing at his watch, Rob replies, "Actually it's pretty late, and I should get home to the boys. If what's on your mind isn't too pressing, maybe we could meet for breakfast in the morning."

"If you don't mind, I think it would be better if we talked tonight. What I have to discuss with you is best handled in private."

Something in Dave's demeanor makes Rob uncomfortable, but he does his best not to show it. Placing his keys and his briefcase on the conference table, he takes a seat and motions for Dave to join him. "I hope this won't take too long," he says. "It's been a long day and I'm tired."

Dave chews his lip and studies his hands, and Rob can't help thinking how out of character this is. Dave is normally fun loving and outgoing, not uptight at all, so what's going on? Finally, Dave takes a deep breath and forces himself to look Rob in the eye. "I don't really know how to say this, so I'm just going to dive in. Over the past three or four weeks, I've dreamed the same dream at least two, maybe three times. In my dream, you and Rita are together, like on a date. You are both dressed up, and you're in a fancy restaurant. Not here in Sterling, but someplace else, maybe Denver or Colorado Springs. When you leave the restaurant, you get in a cab and it takes you to a swanky hotel. In my dream, I see you check in and pick up a room key before getting on the elevator together. That's when I wake up."

Shame washes over Rob, and he feels his heart beating slow and heavy in his chest. In an instant, he remembers his own dream, and he cannot help but feel that God is trying to warn him; nonetheless, he does his best to appear puzzled but unconcerned. Finally, he asks, "Do you have any idea why you would dream something like that?"

"Not really," Dave replies. "I'm ashamed to admit it, but at first I thought God was showing me that you and Rita were having an affair. But then I realized you would never do anything like that."

When Rob doesn't say anything, he continues, "After praying about it, I decided it might be a warning from the

Lord. With Helen gone to the Amazon, it would be just like the devil to try to trip you up. That's why I'm telling you. So you can be extra careful."

"Have you discussed this with anyone else?" Rob asks. "Your wife maybe, or another board member?"

"Of course not."

"Good. You were wise to come to me. The enemy would like nothing better than to use your dream to start a rumor suggesting that Rita and I are having an affair."

Puzzled, Dave asked, "Are you saying my dream was inspired by the devil?"

"Absolutely not, but if the wrong people got hold of it, it could be devastating."

"So, what does it mean?" Dave asks, more than a little confused. "Did I just eat too much pizza, or is this dream from the Lord?"

"Only you can know for sure. For instance, when I awake after receiving a dream from the Lord, I'm absolutely convinced it was from Him. I don't know how to explain it except to say that I know that I know that I know!"

Nodding his head, Dave says, "That's exactly how I felt, especially after I dreamed the same dream a second and third time. I knew it was from the Lord. I just wish I knew what it means."

Rob chews his bottom lip as if in deep thought before replying. "One school of dream interpretation teaches that all of our dreams are about ourselves, regardless of who is in our dreams. If that was the case, then this dream would have nothing to do with Rita or myself. It would be all about you."

Shaking his head, Dave says, "Who came up with that crazy idea? It doesn't make any sense to me."

"Maybe I can help you understand," Rob suggests. "The psychologist who introduced me to this school of dream interpretation used a personal experience to illustrate what he was talking about. He told us that he dreamed the same basic dream over and over again. In his dream, his wife was emotionally involved with another man. The other man was always a famous person. Sometimes he was a powerful politician or a professional athlete or a Hollywood celebrity. In his dream, he would try to reason with his wife, telling her that she was destroying their marriage by her involvement with these other men. She brushed his concerns aside saying they were just friends, nothing more.

"Each time he dreamed that dream, he would awake feeling frustrated and angry with his wife, although in real life she had never given him any reason to distrust her. Early one morning he awakened after dreaming that dream yet again. Slipping out of bed in the predawn darkness, he tugged on his robe and made his way downstairs to his study. Silently he prayed, 'God, why do I keep dreaming this same dream over and over again?'

"In his heart, he heard God say, 'That dream is not about your wife. It is about you and Me, and you're breaking My heart.' In an instant, he realized that although he was a nominal Christian, he was reserving a part of his heart for other things. He went on to tell us that he surrendered his life fully and unconditionally to the Lord that morning and that he never dreamed that dream again."

Frowning, Dave asks, "Are you suggesting God is trying to tell me I'm not completely committed to Him?"

Putting his hand on Dave's arm to reassure him, Rob says, "I'm not suggesting anything like that. I'm simply saying that our dreams, even the ones that come from God, often come to us in parables. Therefore, we need to be very careful how we interpret them and with whom we share them."

After Dave leaves, Rob shuts off the lights and locks up the building. He is still somewhat troubled by Dave's dream, and he can't help feeling it was a warning from the Lord. With a determined effort, he convinces himself it has nothing to do with him and Rita. They might be attracted to each other, but they have no plans of allowing their feelings to get out of hand. Yet on another level, he can't help thinking how thankful he is that it was Dave who received that dream and not someone else. Dave trusts him, and it will take more than a dream to cause him to question his pastor's integrity.

Chapter 9

Driving out of the church parking lot following his conversation with Pastor Rob, Dave is deeply troubled. As much as he wants to believe Rob's explanation, he can't escape a growing conviction that something isn't right. His dream was too vivid, too clear. He isn't a person given to dreams—in fact, he can't remember ever having a prophetic dream before. He isn't ready to conclude that Rob and Rita are having an affair, but he is absolutely convinced the Lord is trying to tell him something.

On the drive home, he recalls several troubling incidents involving Rob and Rita. Once he had dropped by the church office after hours only to discover they were both "working late," although the rest of the staff had left for the day. They were sitting on the leather couch and adjoining love seat in Rob's office. Their coffee cups were nearly empty so they must have been there for a while. There was an open calendar on the end table and what looked like two or three letters that may have needed the pastor's signature. He couldn't hear what they were saying, but it was obvious they were having a serious conversation. At one point, Rita seemed to be consoling Rob. She reached over and placed her hand on his arm while leaning close to speak to him. To be sure, the office door was open and there was the table between the couch and the love seat, but they seemed to share an inappropriate familiarity.

Another time he spotted them flirting in the supermarket parking lot—or so it appeared to him. The driver's side window on Rita's automobile was open, and Rob was leaning down talking to her. She was laughing, and his face was animated and full of emotion. As he turned to go, she reached up and touched his cheek before mouthing a sultry good-bye.

Rob had watched Rita drive away before turning toward his own car. When he did, he found himself face-to-face with Dave, who was pushing a full shopping cart toward his pickup. Before he could stop himself, Dave had blurted out, "What was that all about?"

For a moment, Rob had seemed flustered, but then he had brushed Dave's concern aside with a wave of his hand. "How goes it, Dave?" he asked with feigned enthusiasm. Noting the cart full of groceries, he continued, "How did Lisa get you to do the shopping?"

Dave started to tell him that Lisa was sick, but Rob wasn't listening. "Dave," he said, with a shake of his head, "you're a better man than me. Helen's always trying to get me to do the grocery shopping for her, or at least help her get the groceries, but so far I've managed to avoid it."

When Dave reached his pickup, he had begun unloading the sacks of groceries while Rob continued his nervous chatter. After putting the last bag of groceries into the truck, he had bid Rob good-bye with a sick feeling in his heart. Try as he might, he could not get the image of Rita touching Rob's cheek while mouthing a sultry good-bye out of his mind. He wanted to believe the best, but he couldn't help feeling that something was amiss.

As he replayed those two incidents, and several others, in his mind, he was deeply troubled, especially in light of his dreams. Although he has steadfastly refrained from discussing his concerns with anyone, lest he unfairly taint Pastor Rob's character, he now feels he has no choice but to confide in someone.

When he arrives home the children are in bed, and Lisa is ensconced on the couch with a book. Slipping a bookmark between the pages, she stands to give him a hug. Noting his somber expression, she asks, "What is it? Did something happen at the board meeting?"

"No. Nothing like that, but I do need to discuss something with you."

Taking her hand, he directs her toward the kitchen. "Maybe you could make some coffee. This may take a while."

Although Lisa wishes he would just tell her what's troubling him, she knows better than to push. Words do not come easy for him, and experience has taught her that if she tries to push him, he will just clam up. He will talk, but only in his own time.

Without a word, she turns toward the counter and begins preparing a pot of coffee. While it is brewing, she cuts two pieces of homemade apple pie and places them on dessert plates before setting them on the kitchen table. When the coffee is ready, she fills two mugs, adding three spoonfuls of sugar and a heavy dose of cream to hers.

After joining Dave at the kitchen table, she says, "Okay. What is it?"

Before replying, he takes a bite of apple pie and chews slowly. Finally, he asks, "Is there anything about Rob's relationship with Rita that bothers you?"

"You mean other than the fact that Rita idolizes him?"

"What do you mean?"

"Oh, come on, Dave. Anyone can see she has a thing for him. If I were Helen, I sure wouldn't have gone traipsing off to the Amazon with that woman around."

"Do you think Rob's aware of Rita's feelings?"

"Of course, he is! She's so transparent. I think he enjoys it. I mean, what man doesn't enjoy the attention of an attractive woman?"

"Do you think you're the only one who has noticed this?"

"Are you kidding me? You guys may be blind to this sort of thing, but virtually every woman in the church knows that Rita has a crush on Pastor Rob."

After taking a sip of her coffee, Lisa says, "Enough with the questions. Tell me what's bothering you."

For the next several minutes, he tells her what he's observed, concluding with his dreams and his conversation with Pastor Rob. When he finishes, silent tears stain her cheeks. "I was afraid something like this might happen. When it comes to light, it's going to kill Helen and the boys, not to mention what it will do to the church."

Reaching across the table, Dave takes her hand. "I know things look bad, but let's not jump to conclusions. I'm not ready to conclude Rob is having an affair. Maybe the Lord is just warning us so we can pray a hedge of protection around him. Or perhaps the Lord wants us to intervene, to save Rob from himself, before he does something really stupid."

The living room clock chimes on the half hour, and Rob gets to his feet while Lisa collects their coffee mugs and dessert plates. She rinses them before placing them in the dishwasher as he heads toward the bathroom to brush his teeth. He's already in bed when she finishes in the kitchen, but he's not asleep. Although he's exhausted, he can't turn off his troubled thoughts, and he suspects it's going to be a sleepless night.

He's still awake sometime later when a car turns into the driveway, its headlights casting deformed shadows on the bedroom wall. Glancing at the luminous face of the bedside alarm clock, he sees that it's after midnight. *Who can that be at this hour of the night?* he wonders, as the headlights are turned off. He's pulling on his jeans when the doorbell rings. Stuffing his feet into his slippers, he heads for the front door.

Chapter 10

When Dave turns on the porch light, he is amazed to see Paul Blair, the youth pastor, standing on the steps. They are friends, but hardly the kind who just drop in unannounced, especially at this late hour. Nonetheless, he opens the door and invites him in.

"I'm sorry to barge in on you like this," Paul apologizes, "but I really need to talk to you."

Waving his apology off, Dave says, "Think nothing of it. Would you like a cup of coffee?"

"Why not?" Paul says, as he follows Dave into the kitchen. "I'll probably be up all night anyway."

He takes a seat at the kitchen table while Dave moves to the sink to rinse out the coffeemaker. While he's preparing a pot of coffee, he studies Paul out of the corner of his eye, noting how troubled he appears. Although he has never considered himself a particularly perceptive person, even he can tell something is bothering him.

The coffee is just finishing brewing when Lisa enters the kitchen. She quickly fills two mugs before joining the men at the table. Turning to Paul, she asks, "Cream or sugar?" For a moment he doesn't seem to hear her. Belatedly he mumbles, "No, thank you. Black is fine."

For a time, Paul simply stares at the steam rising from his coffee without speaking. Finally, he says, "Maybe I'm making something out of nothing. I'll let you be the judge of that."

He takes a sip of his coffee before continuing, "I had to make an unscheduled hospital call this evening. One of the McGregor twins had an emergency appendectomy."

Before Lisa can ask, he adds, "He's fine. Anyway, it was late when I left the hospital. I go right past Rita's house on my way home, and Pastor Rob's car was parked in her driveway. I probably wouldn't have given it a second thought, except it was nearly eleven and Helen is in Brazil."

"What are you suggesting?" Dave asks.

"I don't know," Paul replies, obviously uncomfortable. "Maybe nothing, but it just didn't seem right. I can't think of any reason for Pastor Rob to be at Rita's house at that time of night."

"Why tell us?"

"I trust you, Dave. You're Pastor Rob's best friend. I guess I was hoping you could talk to him before he does something stupid, if it's not already too late."

"Dave," Lisa interjects, "maybe you should tell Paul about your dreams."

After thinking about it for a moment, Dave relates his prophetic dream. "I've dreamt that same dream three times in the last month."

"That's heavy, brother," Paul says. "Real heavy."

Turning to Paul, Lisa says, "Maybe I'm speaking out of turn, but I would like to ask you a couple of questions if I may?"

"Of course."

"May I be perfectly candid?"

"Certainly."

"What do you think about Rob and Rita's relationship? Are they too familiar with each other?"

"What do you mean?"

"Let me ask it another way. Have you ever seen them flirting or interacting in a way that made you uncomfortable?"

In an instant, Paul has a flashback to the morning Helen was leaving on her trip to the Amazon. It was barely seven o'clock, but Rob and Rita were already at the office. He couldn't be certain that anything inappropriate was going on—that is, he didn't really see anything—but he heard a lot of scurrying around when he opened the door to Rob's office. And he remembers how uncomfortable he felt.

"Yes," he concedes reluctantly, "there have been times when I observed them acting in ways I thought were inappropriate."

"And?" Lisa presses.

"Let's just leave it at that. I'm not comfortable sharing any details."

The living room clock chimes one, and Paul pushes back from the table. "I really should be going." At the door, he hesitates. Turning to Dave, he says, "I know it's late, but I was wondering if you would consider driving into town with me so you can verify that Rob's car is parked in Rita's driveway?"

"Do you really think that's necessary? Besides Rob has probably left by now."

"Granted," Paul concedes, "but in situations like this, it's important to have more than one witness. Hopefully, I'm overreacting, but if something inappropriate is going on, we need to make sure we have documented everything."

Reluctantly Dave dons his coat and hat before following Paul out into the frigid night. They drive in silence, each of them absorbed in his own troubling thoughts, and it is well past 1 a.m. when they drive slowly past Rita's house. The living room light is on, and Pastor Rob's car is still parked in her driveway. Paul circles the block before parking down the street where they have a clear view of the house. The drapes are closed, making it impossible for them to see into the house, but from time to time they see silhouettes moving about.

Reaching into the back seat, Paul snags his camera bag and drags it to the front. "What are you doing?" Dave asks, as Paul takes his 35 mm Minolta out of the bag.

"Two witnesses are good," Paul replies, "but visual evidence is even better."

"Isn't it too dark to get a picture?"

"I'm using high-speed black-and-white film with a wide-open aperture so we'll be alright." Dave has no idea what Paul's talking about, but since Paul's a camera buff he'll take his word for it.

Dave watches from the car as Paul slips down the street to stand in the shadows in front of Rita's house. He quickly shoots two or three frames and then moves to relocate. When he does, the front door opens unexpectedly, throwing a shaft of light across the driveway. For an instant, he is fully exposed before he ducks behind a thick shrub. Belatedly, the light is shut off, and Rob steps onto the porch, clearly visible in the glow of a nearby streetlight. Rita follows him outside, and they embrace before Rob descends the steps and turns toward his car.

The shrub where Paul is hiding is hardly more than an arm's length from Rob's car, and he is sure Rob will see him. His mind is racing, but he cannot come up with any kind of a reasonable explanation to explain why he is there. Desperately he tries to shrink within himself, hoping against hope to make himself invisible. Finally, Rita waves good-bye to Rob and shuts the door. Without even a glance in Paul's direction, Rob starts his car and eases out of the driveway. He drives slowly down the block and turns the corner before turning on his headlights.

Paul is trembling as the aftermath of the adrenaline rush leaves him shaken. Once more he studies the house to make sure the drapes are fully closed before easing out from behind the shrub and hurrying down the street toward his car. Jerking the door open, he collapses on the seat.

"Wow!" he manages to say, gasping for breath. "I thought I was a goner. If Rob had turned his headlights on, he would have spotted me for sure!"

After catching his breath, he puts his Minolta in the camera bag and turns to Dave. "So, what do you make of that?"

"It certainly looks bad. If it was anyone but Pastor Rob, I would say they were having an affair, but Rob's not that kind of man. He's a pastor, for heaven's sake, a man of God."

"I'm sorry to disillusion you, Dave, but pastors are human, too."

"Maybe so, but it's hard to think of Pastor Rob that way. He has a beautiful family. I'm sure he and Helen have the normal struggles we all have, but I can't imagine Rob risking his family for a fling with Rita. It just doesn't make sense."

"Maybe you're right," Paul concedes. "Maybe there is a reasonable explanation, but for the life of me, I can't imagine what it might be."

When it becomes apparent that Dave isn't going to say any more, Paul starts the car and eases down the street. He makes a right turn onto Highway 6 heading west toward Atwood. At this late hour, the highway is deserted; nonetheless, he drives well below the speed limit as he tries to make some sense of the evening's events. Finally, he says, "At some point we will have to get the entire board involved. Of course, we will have to contact the district office, as well. Normally we would call our presbyter first, but since Rob's the presbyter, that's not an option."

"What happens when the district gets involved?"

"I'm not sure exactly how it works, but I know the district presbytery will conduct some kind of investigation. At some point, probably early on, they will talk to Rob. Of course, we will have to tell them what we know."

The seriousness of the situation weighs heavily upon both of them, and they drive without speaking until Paul turns into the driveway leading to the farmhouse where Dave and Lisa live. It's bitterly cold, and a gust of wind rocks the car, but they hardly notice. Finally, Dave says, "Maybe we should talk with Rob before we do anything else. Isn't that what Jesus tells us to do? Something to the effect that if a brother sins, you should go to him privately before you make a big deal about it."

"I suppose you're right," Paul concedes, "but I hate the thought of confronting Pastor. When he gets angry, he can be pretty intimidating."

"Intimidating or not, I don't think we have a choice," Dave replies, reaching for the door handle. "I'll set up a meeting with Pastor Rob. Once it's arranged, I'll let you know."

Chapter 11

AMAZON BASIN
FAR WESTERN BRAZIL
1971

To my surprise, the journey upriver has gone remarkably well in spite of the rain-swollen rivers with their abundance of debris. That's not to say it has been easy, for it hasn't been. Day after day we have battled the elements: heavy rains interspersed with stifling heat, hoards of mosquitoes, and swarming sweat bees. Neither Helen nor Carolyn has complained, although they are obviously miserable. The worst are the sweat bees. Desperate for the salt in our perspiration and saliva, they scramble over our faces, crawling into our mouths, our nostrils, and our ears. They are stingless, but their sharp mandibles pinch, tempting us to swat at them continually. Before I could warn Helen and Carolyn, they had crushed several of them, setting off a suicidal frenzy by the fallen bees' enraged sisters. Belatedly I told them to ignore the little buggers, that they would leave once they were satiated—but kill one of them, and the rest would go crazy.

I am not nearly as proficient as Lako; still, I manage to erect a serviceable camp each night. Even though they are exhausted from the long days on the river, both Helen and Carolyn pitch in. Carolyn gathers firewood while Helen helps me stretch a tarp between four trees, making an effective shelter from the rain. Beneath it we hang our hammocks and arrange our mosquito nets. Once that is done, I build a fire and prepare a simple meal—usually fried plantains, a slab of bacon, and some beans. One evening I caught a large catfish, and we cooked it on a green spit over glowing coals. We ate it with our fingers, pulling the succulent flesh off the bones and popping it into our months.

Each night follows a familiar pattern. If it is not raining, Carolyn and I sit around the fire, drinking coffee, black and sweet with brown sugar, but seldom conversing. Helen usually retreats to her hammock with one of our father's journals. Reading is difficult given the faded ink and the dim light emanating from the lantern hanging from a nearby branch; nonetheless she is engrossed. The things she is learning about our father fascinate her. His writings reveal a different side of him, a kinder, gentler side.

"Bryan," she calls from her hammock, "listen to this entry dated November 7, 1939."

Getting up from the fire, I go and stand beside her hammock as she reads aloud. In the glow of the lantern, I can see that her eyes glisten with tears and her face is full of feeling.

Tomorrow is the big day. Our containers have already been shipped to Miami, and in the morning we will get on a train that will take us from Denver, Colorado, to Miami, Florida, where we will board a ship bound for Rio de Janeiro. From Rio we will travel to the frontier outpost of Cruzeiro do Sul, where we hope to hire a boat and a guide to take us deeper into the interior of the far western Amazon Basin. To my knowledge, no other missionary has ever gone there. We plan to establish a mission's outpost to use as a base for our forays into the jungle. Our vision is to preach the gospel to unreached Indians who have had little or no contact with the outside world. My parents are supportive of our missionary call, but Velma's parents think I am out of my mind. They simply cannot conceive of how a loving father could take his wife and young child to such a "Godforsaken place" (to use their words).

I love Velma and little Helen as much as any man could love his wife and daughter, but as the apostle Paul wrote, "...None of these things move me, neither count I my life dear unto myself, so that I might finish my course with joy, and the ministry, which I have received of the Lord Jesus..." (Acts 20:24).

Where we are going is dangerous, and we may well die there. That being the case, I considered shipping our things in caskets. In the early years of the twentieth century, many of the missionaries going to Africa did exactly that. Given conditions on that Dark Continent, they knew they would most likely die and be buried there—still, they did not hesitate to go. They were not only determined to live for Christ, but also ready to die for Him if need be.

In the end, I decided against the caskets. Velma's parents were already nearly beside themselves, and I didn't want to do anything that might push them over the edge. Nonetheless, I cannot help admiring those early missionaries to Africa— both their practicality and their commitment.

It is late and we have an early call in the morning, so I should probably blow out the lamp and get to bed.

Lord, I ask You to protect Velma and little Helen even as I offer my life to You. I don't want to die, but if my death will advance the cause of Christ, then let me be a willing sacrifice. In Your holy name I pray, amen.

For a moment, we are both quiet as we contemplate our father's journal entry, but even more, his closing prayer. Finally, Helen asks, "What do you think of that? Sounds almost like he had a premonition of things to come, doesn't it?"

"Maybe," I muse. "I don't know if he had a premonition of his death or not, but it sure sounds like he was willing to die for Christ. I used to think his attitude was selfish and uncaring, but I don't feel that way anymore. After reading his journals, I know how much he loved us."

"I know. I got goose bumps when I read, '*I love Velma and little Helen as much as any man could love his wife and daughter.*'"

I linger a few minutes longer before returning to the fire, when I realize Helen has fallen asleep with our father's journal open on her chest. Using the tail of my shirt as a potholder, I reach for the coffeepot nestled in the coals and splash scalding hot coffee into my tin cup. Squatting on my heels, I blow on my coffee to cool it before taking a sip.

Across from me, Carolyn pokes a stick in the fire, sending a shower of sparks flying into the night. Without consciously intending to, I find myself studying her. She's unusually attractive, beautiful really, with her expressive eyes, thick auburn hair, and shapely figure. Even now, after several days on the river, she is still stunning. It's easy to see why I fell in love with her. Unfortunately, her good looks blinded me to the irreconcilable differences that doomed our marriage from the start. I was a pragmatist. She was a hopeless romantic. I was stoic. She was sentimental. I hadn't shed a tear in years. She cried over everything—weddings, movies, poems, even little puppies. We were both wounded souls, but we dealt with our wounds differently. Her wounds made her needy; mine made me angry. She was clingy, while I was emotionally distant. She tried too hard, while I hardly tried at all.

Staring into the fire, with the sound of the river in the background and nightbirds calling, I find myself replaying the words that portended the end of our marriage. We had only been married a short time, but already there were deep fissures in our marriage. I told her she was smothering me, that I couldn't breathe, that I needed some space. For what seemed a long time, she didn't say anything, and when she finally spoke, her voice was so sad I knew her heart was breaking. "If you're asking me to love you less," she said, "I can't do that." When I didn't say anything, she continued, her voice cracking. "It's kind of sad, isn't it? You want me to love you less, and I want you to love me more."

That, in a nutshell, was our problem, and it doomed our marriage.

The melancholy mood I have kept at bay by sheer determination since leaving Cruzeiro do Sul now washes over me. Nothing pains me more than remembering the way I have mistreated Carolyn. Unfortunately, she isn't the only person I have wounded. It seems I have damaged or destroyed nearly every relationship I've ever had. I know God has forgiven me—at least I want to believe that He has—but that doesn't change the past.

More than anything, I want to apologize to Carolyn, but I don't know where to start. After all this time, what can I possibly say that will make any difference? No matter how sincere, my apology cannot undo the damage I have done. I don't expect Carolyn to forgive me for the heartless ways I treated her. That would be asking too much, but at least I would like her to know that she was not to blame. The fault was all mine.

She stares into the darkness, deep in thought, while I study her more closely—not her physical appearance, but the person she has become. There may still be traces of the needy, insecure person she was when we married, but I haven't seen even a hint of it thus far. When I watch her interacting with Helen, or coping with the discomforts we face every day on the river, or simply sharing camp chores, I see a person who is comfortable in her own skin, a person who is at peace with herself.

Helen says Carolyn's still in love with me and deeply regrets our divorce. I find that hard to believe after the way I treated her. In any case, she has done nothing to indicate she feels that way. Initially I expected her to be distant, even hostile toward me, considering how acrimonious our divorce was, but that's not been the case. Instead she treats me like a casual friend or a distant cousin. She's cordial, but that's all.

"Do you think we will reach the mission compound tomorrow?" she asks, interrupting my ruminations.

"I think so, but I can't be sure. With the river this high, all the landmarks look different. Besides, this is only my second trip upriver. I'm not sure I would recognize any landmarks in any case."

She continues to poke at the fire, causing the sparks to dance in the darkness. Finally, she says, "Tell me about Diana and Eurico."

I take a sip of my coffee and try to organize my thoughts before responding. "Like I told you before, Eurico is an orphan. His parents and siblings died when he was only six years old, and he has been on his own ever since. He's a born hustler, and he was able to keep body and soul together by shining shoes and begging, not to mention doing just about any kind of odd job he could find.

"I must have looked like an easy mark, because he set out to hustle me. That turned out to be a good thing—maybe one of the best things that has ever happened to me. He introduced me to Dr. Peterson and convinced me to hire Lako as my guide. In the process, he wormed his way into my heart."

Just thinking about the little guy causes my mood to lift, and I find myself smiling as I anticipate our coming reunion. "You're going to love him. I know you will. He has the most infectious smile and an irrepressible optimism."

"What about Diana?" Carolyn asks with a contrived casualness. "Tell me about her."

Her question tempts me to revisit memories better left undisturbed. With a determined effort, I sidestep them and describe Diana in the most benign terms possible. "She's our age, or just slightly older, with a heart of gold. As a medical doctor, she could be earning a handsome salary in the States, but instead she chooses to serve as a medical missionary in this Godforsaken place."

"What about her family?" Carolyn presses. "Is she married? Does she have children?"

"According to Eleanor—that's Gordon Arnold's wife—her mother died of breast cancer when she was still in medical school. Her father's a surgeon practicing in Minneapolis."

When I pause to refill my tin cup with the last dregs from the nearly empty coffeepot, Carolyn says, "And…"

My delaying tactics do not fool her, and I grin sheepishly before continuing, "Diana's single and has never been married, which means she has no children. She's really attached to Eurico. In fact, I suspect she would like to adopt him, but I don't know if that's possible."

"Is she pretty?"

Her question gives me pause, and in my mind's eye, I see Diana as she was the first time I laid eyes on her. She was examining a feverish Indian baby in the tiny clinic at the mission compound. Her blond hair was pulled back, but a few strands had worked loose and she had to keep brushing them out of her eyes. Her movements were economical, and she was totally engrossed in her work—still, nothing could disguise her natural grace.

She seemed unaware of my presence, but I couldn't take my eyes off of her. She was wearing a white lab coat over blue jeans and some kind of pullover shirt. The lab coat was loose-fitting, but it could not hide the pleasing contours of her body.

"Well," Carolyn presses, "is she pretty?"

"She's attractive," I say, being careful to make sure my voice gives nothing away. "Her hair is naturally blond, at least I think it is, and her eyes are blue. What makes her attractive, however, is her inner strength. She knows who she is, and she has a strong independent streak."

When I pause, Carolyn gets to her feet and tosses the last of her coffee into the fire before saying, "Obviously she's not needy like me..."

I watch her walk through the dark toward her hammock with an ache in my heart. Without intending to, I have drawn an unfavorable comparison between her and Diana, at least in her mind. I certainly didn't intend to, and it pains me to realize that beneath Carolyn's poised self-assurance, there remains a trace of the insecure little girl she was when we married. I cannot help thinking that no one goes through life unscathed. We're all wounded—just in different ways.

Chapter 12

When the boat is fully loaded, I start the outboard motor and let it warm up before motioning for Helen to shove us off. Although our boat is small, it is overloaded, and it is all she can do to push it off the sandbar. With a lunge, she shoves it into the river and hoists herself into the boat before giving me a thumbs-up. It's the rainy season, and the current is strong. If I hadn't started the engine before shoving off, we would be drifting downstream with little or no control. Now I turn the boat into the teeth of the current and accelerate, heading upriver.

After days of overcast skies and incessant rain, the sun has finally broken through. It is streaming in broad beams through the towering trees, and across the river the rain forest is draped in swirls of early morning mist. Two scarlet macaws are splashes of red against the green canopy, and I cannot help but marvel at the wild beauty of this place.

Although all three of us are ready for our trip upriver to end, only Helen is truly eager to reach the mission compound. It's been more than twenty years since our father disappeared while on a mission of mercy into the jungle, forcing our mother to return to the States with Helen and me in tow.

Only God knows what secret dreams Helen harbored in her heart all those years while secretly hoping to return one day to the place of her childhood. As each day brings us closer to our destination, she becomes more animated. It's like she has a homing instinct drawing her back.

This morning she was a bundle of energy, breaking camp with unbridled enthusiasm, taking the hammocks and mosquito nets down and storing them in the boat while humming to herself. This is a side of my sister I have never seen. She's always been diligent in everything she did, but not necessarily joyous. Like our parents, she kept a tight rein on her emotions, but here in the wilds of the far western Amazon Basin, she is morphing into a different person.

I wish I could share her enthusiasm, but my memories of the last days I spent at the mission compound are bittersweet at best. All the good things I remember—the friendship I shared with Gordon, the meals Eleanor prepared, reading my father's journal by the light of a kerosene lamp at the rough-hewn table in Whittaker House, sitting in the swing under the towering *samauma* tree drinking sweet tea with Diana, and Eurico's miraculous recovery from meningitis—are overshadowed by the pain of our parting. There's no way I can go through anything like that again.

In contrast to Helen's unabashed enthusiasm, Carolyn slouches against a bundle of provisions and stares straight ahead with unseeing eyes. Once or twice Helen tries to engage her, but she gives up when Carolyn refuses to respond. I watch it all from the rear of our small boat, one hand resting on the throttle of the outboard motor. I can't be sure, but I believe last night's conversation about Diana has triggered her old insecurities. This is the Carolyn I had lived with, and while I can't read her mind, I recognize the signs. Her eyes are bleary from lack of sleep, and I suspect she spent a good part of the night comparing herself to Diana although she has not even met her. In her mind, Diana is everything she's not—strong, independent, and self-reliant. As much as Carolyn would like to be that kind of woman, she is sure that she is not and will never be.

When we were married, her insecurities made her needy, causing her to seek validation from others in ways no self-respecting person would. It was painful to see, and embarrassing, and my heart hurt for her. This is the part of Carolyn that had caused me to pull away. I couldn't cope with it. Her neediness was too great, and it threatened to consume me. I just wish she could see herself the way others see her—not needy, but competent and capable.

The sun is low in the sky, and the day is nearly done when we round one final bend in the Rio Moa and watch as the mission compound emerges from the deepening shadows. Helen is nearly giddy with excitement while I am filled with mixed emotions. As much as I look forward to reuniting with Euriko, I am filled with apprehension at the thought of seeing Diana, considering the way we parted. Of course, I'm not sure how Gordon and Eleanor will feel about seeing me, either.

As I ease through the debris near the shore, seeking for a place to beach the boat, I catch sight of a small figure out of the corner of my eye. It is Eurico! I would recognize him anywhere. As I watch, he discards his fishing pole and runs toward us, as I ease the boat against the muddy bank. "Bryan!" he shouts, his voice barely audible above the sound of the river. "I knew you would come back. I knew it! I told Diana you would, but she didn't believe me."

He runs into my arms, and I scoop him up and crush him to my chest in a bear hug. Off to one side, Helen and Carolyn are taking it all in, and belatedly I introduce them. Eurico hardly gives Helen a glance, but Carolyn captivates him, and for the first time since I've known him, he is speechless.

"Let's go see Diana," he says, tugging at my hand impatiently.

I make excuses, that being the last thing I want to do. "It's nearly dark," I say, "and we need to get the boat unloaded. Why don't you see if you can find Gordon and let him know we're here? In the meantime, we will get our things moved up to Whittaker House if it's still available."

Helen is all eyes as we lug our provisions up the path toward the mission compound. For her, it is like stepping back in time. She is experiencing it all as she did when she was an eleven-year-old girl—the towering trees shutting out the sky, the sound of the river, the calling of the nightbirds. When we finally step into the clearing and catch sight of Whittaker House, she gasps. The house that loomed so large in her memory is not large at all. If the truth be told, it is hardly more than a cabin, albeit a well-built cabin.

We dump our supplies on the front porch and step inside. The construction is simple. The roof is made of corrugated tin nailed directly to rafters made from rough-cut lumber.

The walls are covered with wood planks of various widths that have been neither painted nor stained, giving the house a lingering aroma of raw wood even after all these years. Stained planks of random widths make up the flooring. They are pulling apart in places, and I can only conclude that our father must have put them down before they were completely seasoned.

Carolyn stands just inside the door as Helen moves about the small rooms, her face lightening up from time to time as a familiar object reminds her of a childhood memory. Pulling out a chair at the rough-hewn table our father built, she sits down. Turning toward me, she says, "I can almost hear Father saying grace or reading to us from the Bible, with the kerosene lamp pulled close to illuminate the pages."

I nod, not trusting myself to speak as my throat is thick with feelings generated by my own memories. Finally, I say, "One night I slipped out of bed and tiptoed to the doorway that opened into the kitchen. As you may recall, there was no door in those days, only a flimsy curtain, and I pulled it back just enough to let me peek out. Father was reading the Bible, his lips moving as he mouthed each word. Mother had loosened her hair, allowing it to fall around her shoulders. She was slowly brushing it, and I remember marveling at the way it caught the light from the lamp. After a time, Father got up and reached for her hand. I watched as Mother allowed him to lead her to their bedroom. I cannot ever remember seeing our father's face so full of feeling or our mother's more beautiful. I was too young to realize what was happening, but even then, I knew it was special."

We hear footsteps on the porch, and before Carolyn can open the door, Eurico bursts in and runs to stand beside me, while glancing shyly at her. I stand three inches over six feet, but Gordon Arnold towers over me, and now his huge frame fills the small room. I reach to shake his hand, but he envelops me in a hug. Getting up from the table, Helen extends her hand to Eleanor, who has stepped up beside him. "I'm Helen Thompson," she says, "Bryan's sister, and this is my friend Carolyn."

For a moment no one says anything, and an awkward silence fills the room. Turning to Carolyn, Eurico asks, "Did Bryan tell you about the crocodile that nearly overturned our boat?"

"No, he didn't," Carolyn replies with a smile, "but I think I would rather hear it from you anyway."

Everyone laughs, and the tension is broken. Before Eurico can launch into his tale, I tousle his hair and say, "Let us sort things out with the Arnolds before you regale Carolyn with your wild tales."

He is sorely disappointed, but he brightens when Carolyn winks at him and mouths, "Later."

In short order, Eleanor has decided that Helen and I will sleep in Whittaker House. If Eurico is willing to give up his room for a few nights, Carolyn can stay with Diana—if it's agreeable with Diana, of course. Turning to Gordon, she says, "There's a big pot of vegetable soup simmering on the stove. Why don't you fetch it while I introduce Helen and Carolyn to Diana."

Without waiting for a response, she starts toward Diana's small clinic, motioning for us to follow. Helen and Carolyn descend the porch steps, and start down the path after her, but I remain on the porch. They've only gone a short distance when Eleanor stops, and turns toward me. "Bryan, aren't you coming?"

"I'll help Gordon with the soup," I reply, as I turn to follow him, thankful for an excuse to delay seeing Diana.

Chapter 13

Diana is straightening up her small clinic when Eurico bursts in, followed by Eleanor and her entourage. "Bryan's here," he shouts, nearly bursting with excitement. A sudden rush of emotion flushes her face, and she quickly turns away, lest Eleanor and the newcomers see how Eurico's announcement has ignited her emotions. Giving them a tentative smile while trying to control her wildly vacillating emotions, she says, "I'll be right with you."

To buy time, she rearranges some medical supplies even as she tries to make some sense of Bryan's return. She's hoped and dreamed of this moment, but never in her wildest imaginings did she think it would really happen, not given the way they parted. She can't help wondering if he has finally realized he can't live without her. Maybe he is ready to take her up on her offer to give up her missionary appointment and return to the States with him.

For a moment, she lets herself imagine what life would be like with him. They could move to a small town high in the Rockies where she could work with an older doctor who is nearing retirement, or perhaps she could go into private practice for herself. Things might be tight financially for a while, but neither she nor Bryan are materialistic, so that wouldn't be a problem.

Maybe they could buy a small house or a cabin on some acreage and fix it up. Bryan is handy with tools, and she has a knack for decorating, so it would be fun. In her mind's eye she sees their bedroom, with a large window overlooking a meadow with a mountain stream flowing through it. In the distance, she can envision snowcapped peaks jutting into the brilliant blue of the Colorado sky. A queen-sized bed with a handmade comforter nearly fills the small bedroom, and she imagines the love they will share nestled together beneath the covers on cold winter nights.

The small living room will have an oval-shaped braided rug, a leather couch, a couple of chairs, and an ancient wood-burning stove for heat. In one corner Bryan will have a small antique desk that he's spent hours refinishing until it gleams with a dark luster. He will spend his days at that desk writing his first novel on a salvaged typewriter. When she comes home at the end of a long day at the clinic, they will sit in front of the fire with only a kerosene lamp for light. She will sip her coffee and listen, enthralled, as Bryan reads what he's written that day. From time to time, she will make a suggestion regarding character development or a twist in the plot. Occasionally he welcomes her input, but more often than not, he says, "I don't tell you how to treat your patients, so don't tell me how to craft my novel." He softens his words with a smile, but she gets the message.

Sometimes they will reminisce about their time in the Amazon Basin. She will remember how he looked the first time she saw him standing in the doorway to her small clinic with a battered Nikon camera hanging on a leather strap draped over his shoulder. Although he looked a little worse for the wear after spending weeks on the river, she still thought he was one of the best-looking guys she had ever seen. The contrast between him and the diminutive Dr. Peterson was startling.

They will remember her near-fatal plunge down the rain-slick mountainside and his desperate attempt to reach her. They spent the night huddled together on an outcropping of rocks waiting to be rescued. Her leg was broken, and she was in shock. All night he held her close, using his body warmth to ward off hypothermia. During the weeks of recovery, they fell in love while spending hours together.

On long summer evenings, they will sit on the small front porch drinking sweet tea while Eurico fishes in the creek. When he returns with a stringer of brightly speckled brook trout, Bryan will build a small fire in the fire pit and fry them in a cast-iron skillet. On summer weekends, she will pack a picnic lunch, and the three of them will take long hikes exploring the wilderness areas high in the Rockies.

All of this she imagines in a flash, and now her heart is beating fast as she tries to control her emotions. She can't allow herself to get her hopes up. Another disappointment would kill her. Nonetheless, she can't imagine any other reason Bryan would return to the mission compound. After rearranging some final items, she wipes her sweaty palms on her lab coat, takes a deep breath to calm herself, and turns toward Eleanor and the women who have come with her.

Although the tall woman smiles warmly, there is a no-nonsense air about her. Diana can't help thinking that she seems vaguely familiar, but for the life of her, she can't place her. Perhaps she's a pastor's wife from one of her supporting churches. Maybe she met her during itineration. While she is still trying to place her, the woman introduces herself. "I'm Helen Thompson, Bryan's sister."

Her words hit Diana like a punch in the stomach. Suddenly it all makes sense. Helen's the reason Bryan has returned to the mission station—it's not because he can't live without her. Now she feels foolish, like an immature schoolgirl with a crush on a guy who doesn't know she exists. How could she do this to herself? Didn't Bryan make his feelings plain enough when he left?

As if from a great distance, she hears Helen speaking, but she's having trouble connecting the words. "This is my friend Carolyn," Helen says, gesturing toward a shapely woman with a beautiful complexion and dark luminous eyes. In an instant, Diana has a flashback. It is the wee hours of the morning, and she is dozing in a rocking chair in the bedroom at Whittaker House. Bryan is battling malaria and nearly delirious with fever. As he thrashes about in his feverish sleep, she hears him calling for Carolyn. As if adding insult to injury, she realizes this dark-eyed beauty must be Bryan's ex-wife. What is she doing here? How could Bryan do this to her?

With a Herculean effort, she maintains her composure. She has no idea what, if anything, they know about her ill-fated relationship with Bryan, but she is determined to give nothing away. As if from a great distance, she hears Eleanor speaking.

"I've sent Gordon and Bryan to get a pot of vegetable soup I've had simmering all afternoon. I thought we could all eat at your house. I hope you don't mind."

Despite how warmly Gordon greeted me, it is readily apparent that my unexpected appearance has unsettled him. As we make our way toward the cottage, he shares with his wife Eleanor, he pauses and turns toward me as if to speak, and then he seems to think better of it and resumes walking. I'm sure he's wondering what I'm doing here—and with good reason. When Lako and I headed downriver toward Cruzeiro do Sul, on the first leg of my journey back to civilization, I never expected to set foot on the mission compound again. In fact, I was determined to leave the far western Amazon Basin and never return, and I told Gordon as much.

Stepping out from under the towering trees, we cross a small clearing, as the last of the afternoon light succumbs to the encroaching night. I follow Gordon up the steps, but rather than going inside their small house, he makes his way to a rough-hewn rocker sitting near the middle of the porch. As I watch, he strikes a match and touches it to the wick of the kerosene lamp on the small table beside his rocker. I study his face as he sits there in the shadows, concern etched in his features. After a moment, I walk to the far end of the porch and stare into the darkness. For several minutes, the only sound is the rustling of the wind in the trees and the creaking of Gordon's rocker.

Finally, he clears his throat and says, "Before we rejoin the ladies, there's something we need to talk about." When I turn toward him, he motions for me to have a seat in the rocker situated beside him. Instead, I slouch on the porch rail and force myself to look him in the eye. I think I know what he's going to say, and I don't blame him. He's probably going to tell me that as much as he likes me, it would have been better if I hadn't come back. He might even suggest I leave at first light.

"Before I say my piece," he says, "why don't you tell me what you're doing here."

His words are soft-spoken and his tone is kindly, but I get the message loud and clear. I'm not welcome, and I'd better have a good reason for being here. Although I'm tempted with anger, as I've always been when dealing with authority figures, I swallow my pride and make every effort not to be defensive.

"Let me begin by saying I don't blame you for being upset, especially given the way Diana and I parted." Then I proceed to tell him about my unexpected encounter with Helen and Carolyn in Cruzeiro do Sul. After giving him the relevant details, I spread my hands in a gesture of helplessness and ask, "What else could I do? I couldn't let them attempt the trip upriver alone."

"I suppose not," he says.

After a moment, he continues, "Bryan, in many ways you are like a son to me, but your presence here is disruptive, especially to Diana. The way you left nearly killed her. She's still not over it. Maybe she never will be."

His words are like sharp knives opening old wounds, and for a moment I relive our painful parting. Diana offered to give up her missionary appointment and return with me to the States. As tempting as that was, I loved her too much to allow her to sacrifice herself for me. Besides, I knew it would never work. In time she would have come to resent me for forcing her to give up her calling. Unfortunately, there was no way I could make her understand, and as I walked away, I knew I had once again wounded her, albeit in an unforgivable way.

With an effort, I push that unwelcome memory aside and turn my attention to Gordon. I want him to know that it was kindness, not cruelty, that made me do what I did. Unfortunately, I've never been good with words, so I just sit there in the darkness staring at my hands for the longest time. Finally, I manage to say, "I never meant to hurt her," my words coming out in a strangled whisper.

"I don't suppose you did," he continues, "but it doesn't really matter. The truth is, you wounded her in ways that may have damaged her permanently. It's like she's sleepwalking, just going through the motions. If it wasn't for Eurico, I don't know what she might have done. Hurt herself, maybe. That little guy's been her salvation."

He pauses, and in the stillness, I hear the soft sound of the river. Getting to my feet, I walk to the end of the porch and stare into the darkness, shame and regret eating a hole in my heart. I don't blame Gordon for feeling the way he does, nor do I think he means me any harm. Still, his disapproval wounds me in ways that take me back to my childhood, and now it's my father's voice I hear inside my head. Well do I remember his harsh words and the damaging effect they had on my fragile psyche. Many a time I slinked away like a whipped pup from one of his tongue lashings, to seek a hiding place where I tried in vain to heal my wounded soul. He never came looking for me. Not once.

From a distance, I hear Gordon, his soft-spoken words making his feelings crystal clear. "I don't know what your intentions are, but I'm asking you to stay away from Diana. You've sorely wounded her twice, and if I can help it, I won't allow you to hurt her again."

Without a word, I leave the porch and search for the path in the darkness. Although it is nearly pitch-black, I manage to find my way back to Whittaker House, where I retrieve a flashlight before heading for the river. As I descend the porch steps, I hear the murmur of voices from Diana's cottage, but the words are indistinguishable. The voices and the lamplight spilling from the window promise companionship, but I know better. Eurico would surely welcome me, but my presence would only cause Diana pain, and that's the last thing I want to do.

Chapter 14

STERLING, COLORADO
1971

It is nearly 6 p.m., and Rita has gone for the day, when Dave and Paul knock on the door to Pastor Rob's office. Although they have prayed earnestly regarding this meeting, neither of them feels very hopeful. It highly unlikely that anything truly positive can come of it. More likely, it will simply further strain their relationship with Rob, maybe even damage it beyond repair. If he is guilty of adultery, it will likely portend the termination of his ministry, at least to the church in Sterling.

Without bothering to get up from behind his desk, Rob calls a curt, "Come in."

When they enter, he motions them to the two chairs immediately in front of his desk while continuing to examine a file folder full of papers. "So," he asks abruptly, setting the papers aside, "what's so important that I have to stay after hours to meet with you?"

Dave's nerves are already raw, and Rob's condescending tone and obvious impatience grate on him. He cannot help feeling that Rob has played him for a fool, brushing aside his concerns and dismissing his prophetic dreams. Sensing his growing frustration, Paul places his hand on Dave's arm to calm him, but to no avail. Ignoring Paul, he demands, "What were you doing at Rita's house at one o'clock in the morning?"

Stunned, Rob counters, "What are you talking about?"

Without a word, Paul slides a photograph across the desk. When Rob picks it up, he is shocked to see it is a photo of his car parked in Rita's driveway. The license plate on his car is clearly visible, as are the numbers on Rita's house.

Stalling for time, he studies the photograph while searching for a plausible way to explain why he was at Rita's house at that time of night. Finally, he asks, "Where did you get this?"

Reaching across the desk, Paul retrieves the photograph and replaces it in the inside pocket of his sports coat. "I took that picture on Tuesday night. Actually, it was early Wednesday morning. Dave was with me."

"I can't believe this," Rob says, disbelief coloring his words. "I can't believe you guys were actually spying on me."

"We weren't spying," Paul counters, "but that's hardly the point. What we want to know is, what were you doing at Rita's house at one a.m.?'"

"And what I want to know," Rob demands, barely able to control his anger, "is what you think gives you the right to interrogate me?"

When Paul doesn't reply, he continues, "How long have we known each other? A little more than five years? In all that time, have I ever given you any reason to question my integrity?"

"No sir, you haven't," Paul says, refusing to be intimidated. "Not until recently. Not until this business with Rita."

Turning to Dave, Rob asks, "What about you, Dave? I thought we were friends. I've always had your back, and I thought you had mine. And now you pull something like this. Why are you out to get me?"

"Don't be ridiculous, Rob," Dave protests. "If we were out to get you, we wouldn't be here. We would have taken that photograph straight to the board and then to the district superintendent."

"Pastor," Paul says in a conciliatory tone, "we're not here to accuse you, but to give you a chance to put our concerns to rest. We would like nothing more than to put this whole thing behind us."

Rob is angry, but he's scared, too. He knows only too well what the district superintendent would think if he got hold of that incriminating photograph. And then there's Helen. If she saw it she would go ballistic! Thank God she's in the Amazon. How could he have been so careless—stupid, really? He must have been out of his mind to park his car in Rita's driveway. What was he thinking, for heaven's sake?

With an effort, he reins in his emotions before speaking. "I can't overstate how deeply grieved I am by your actions. Relationships are built on trust, and I'm not sure I will ever be able to trust either of you again. At least not the way I've trusted you in the past."

Pausing, he looks hard at Dave and then at Paul to make sure they know how grievously they have wounded him—a wound from which their relationship may never recover.

Even though he knows Pastor Rob's actions are highly suspicious, Dave can't help feeling in the wrong somehow. To his chagrin, he belatedly realizes that Rob is a master manipulator. This is a side of his personality he's never seen.

"Is there an explanation for my presence at Rita's house in the wee hours of the morning?" Rob asks rhetorically. "Of course, there is, but if you trusted me, you wouldn't require one. If you trusted me the way I've always trusted you, we wouldn't be having this conversation. As far as I'm concerned, I don't owe you an explanation. My integrity speaks for itself, but to make sure we can put this thing to bed, I'll tell you why I was at her house.

He pauses, considering his words before continuing. "As you may recall, Rita has a sixteen-year-old son. He is living with his father and stepmother out of state. On the night in question, Rita got a telephone call from her ex informing her that Chad had been in a serious auto accident. Although he was in the hospital, his injuries were not life-threatening. Unfortunately, he had been drinking, and the girl who was with him was killed.

"Rita was beside herself when she called me. She blamed herself for Chad's drinking. She was sure it was her fault. The divorce was especially hard on him, and he blamed her. She couldn't help thinking that if she had forgiven her husband's repeated infidelities, they would still be married, and Chad wouldn't be in trouble. The longer she talked, the more hysterical she became, and when I couldn't calm her, I was concerned she might harm herself. That's why I went to her house. Of course, if Helen had been here, she would have gone with me, but as you know, she's in Brazil with her brother."

Dave remains skeptical, but Paul has a sheepish look on his face and stammers out an apology. "I'm sorry, Pastor. I don't know what I was thinking." Taking the photograph out of the inside pocket of his sports coat, he makes a show of ripping it into tiny pieces before dumping them on Rob's desk. Finally, he asks, "Do you want me to resign?"

"That's a good question," Rob muses. "Let me think about it for a few days, and I'll get back to you."

After making a final attempt to apologize, Paul excuses himself, but Dave remains seated. "Pastor," he says, "I want to believe you, I really do, but I'm still deeply troubled. I can't put my finger on it, but something just doesn't feel right. There are too many coincidences."

The incoming call light blinks on Rob's phone, and simultaneously they hear the phone on Rita's desk ringing. It's after hours, so Rob lets it go to the answering machine. As few seconds later, his private line rings, and he says, "I better take this. It could be my mother or one of the boys."

Dave gets up and walks across the room to the picture window and stares into the darkness, deep in thought. He and Rob have been close friends for a number of years, but he's never seen him act this way. His emotions seem to be all over the place. Even the way he is talking on the phone is strange, furtive somehow, not at all the way a man would, talk to his boys, certainly not the way he would talk to his mother. He doesn't want to believe it, but he can't help thinking that Rob is talking to Rita.

"Sorry about that," Rob says as he hangs up the telephone.

"No problem," Dave replies. "So, how are the boys? No problems at home, I hope?"

For a moment, Rob seems confused, as if Dave's question makes no sense. "No. No, of course not. They're fine."

Returning to the desk, Dave remains standing while he studies his friend. Finally, he asks, "May we have a word of prayer before I go?"

"I don't think so," Rob replies.

Without a word, Dave exits the office. After he is gone, Rob castigates himself once again for parking his car in Rita's driveway. In the future, he will have to be more careful. Next time he will park a few blocks away and walk. Still, he can't help thinking that coming up with that story about Chad was a stroke of genius. Hopefully, Dave and Paul will keep it confidential. If they were to approach Rita, his whole explanation could fall apart. Maybe he should give her a heads-up—but on second thought, probably not. There's no reason to worry her, and besides, he doesn't want her thinking he would throw Chad under the bus to save his own skin.

On another level, he is more than a little uncomfortable. He's always prided himself on being a man of integrity, and it troubles him to realize how easily he has lied. Something his district superintendent said recently now comes to mind: "It's easy for a man to lie when he's living a lie." Is that what he's doing—living a lie? With an effort, he dismisses that troubling thought as he brushes the scraps of the incriminating photograph into the wastebasket.

Chapter 15

Lisa is sitting in the Blue Bird Café, nervously toying with her second cup of coffee while waiting for Rita to join her. Lunch was Dave's idea. She was hesitant at first, but he persuaded her. He said that if Rita's son had actually been in a serious automobile accident, she would need all the emotional support she could get. On the other hand, if Pastor Rob had fabricated the whole thing, they needed to know. Reluctantly she had agreed, but she is still uncomfortable.

Glancing at her wristwatch impatiently, she sees that Rita is almost fifteen minutes late. Punctuality is a high priority in the Underwood family, and she finds herself muttering one of Dave's truisms under her breath: "Early is on time. On time is late, and late is unacceptable."

She lets her gaze wander to the parking lot, where the sun is shining brightly, and a Chinook wind is attacking the snow with a vengeance. It's a welcome reprieve from the bitter cold, but she fears it won't last. March on the high plains of northeastern Colorado is known for its spring blizzards. She still remembers the blizzard of 1959, when the snowdrifts reached the eaves of the houses. As a teenager, she enjoyed the adventure—being out of school for several days and leaping off the roof into snowdrifts higher than a tall man's head—but as an adult, it has lost all appeal. She's ready for spring!

As she continues to stare out the window, she watches an eighteen-wheeler with a load of cattle pull onto Highway 6 as Rita turns into the parking lot. She noses her 1965 Mustang into a parking space between a muddy pickup and a shiny new Pontiac Grand Prix. Grabbing her purse, Rita heads for the entrance of the café, being careful not to brush against the dirty pickup.

Although she's nearing forty, no one would know it. She's still a striking woman. Today she's wearing bellbottom jeans, a peasant blouse, a fringed jacket, and boots—hardly her normal church attire—and Lisa almost doesn't recognize her.

She pauses in the doorway to scan the dining room before spotting Lisa in a back booth. As she heads her way, Lisa cannot help noticing the admiring glances that follow her. It's not hard to imagine why Pastor Rob would be attracted to her, and for a moment the bitter taste of resentment nearly chokes her. How dare this woman tempt their pastor and destroy his family? How dare she threaten the unity of their congregation?

"Sorry I'm late," Rita says as she slides into the booth across from Lisa and takes the menu the waitress hands her. "A glass of water with lemon please, and a cup of decaf coffee."

The waitress returns, and they order—a cheeseburger and fries for Lisa and a Monte Cristo sandwich for Rita with a small side salad. When their food arrives, Lisa cannot help noticing how slowly Rita eats. More than two-thirds of her Monte Cristo sandwich remains when Lisa devours the last bite of her cheeseburger.

The waitress refills Lisa's coffee cup and takes her empty plate away. After swallowing a bite of her Monte Cristo sandwich, Rita wipes her mouth with her napkin and says, "My curiosity is nearly killing me. What was it you wanted to discuss with me?"

Lisa hesitates a moment before speaking, trying to think of the best way to begin. Finally, she simply says, "Dave and I heard about Chad's accident and we want you to know how sorry we are." She pauses before continuing, "If finances are an issue, Dave and I would like to help. Perhaps we could buy you a plane ticket so you can fly out to be with him."

"What are you talking about?" Rita stammers, confused. "Chad hasn't been in an accident... You must be mistaken."

She is fairly certain Lisa is misinformed; nonetheless, a knot of fear swells in the pit of her stomach. If something were to happen to Chad, it would destroy her. It's been bad enough being estranged from him, living hundreds of miles apart, but she comforts herself with the hope of one day being reconciled. She has told herself repeatedly that as he gets older, he will realize that the slant his father has put on the divorce is only partly true. Yes, she filed for divorce, but only after Brad had a series of affairs.

Yet, even as she tries to convince herself there is no cause for concern, a dark thought takes shape in her mind. If Chad had been in an accident, keeping it from her is exactly the kind of thing Brad might do. He has made it clear he would like nothing more than to further alienate her from her son. What better way than to let Chad believe she doesn't care? She doesn't want to believe Brad would do such an evil thing, but given his history of sadistic behavior, she wouldn't put it past him.

With trembling hands, she pushes her half-empty plate to one side and leans across the table toward Lisa. Although she is trying desperately to control her emotions, she is freaking out. The mere thought of something happening to Chad, no matter how remote the possibility, is simply unbearable. Finally, in a voice shaky with fear, she manages to say, "I'm fairly certain you must be mistaken. If Chad's been in an accident, I would surely know about it."

"I'm sure you would," Lisa replies, as she reaches across the table to squeeze her hand. "Dave must have misunderstood Pastor Rob."

For a moment, Rita just stares at her in confusion. If Brad had contacted him, Rob surely would have gotten in touch with her. Finally, she manages to ask, "Are you sure this came from Pastor Rob?"

When Lisa simply nods, Rita picks up her purse and hurriedly exits the café. Lisa's heart hurts as she watches her go. From Rita's reaction, she can only conclude that Rob was being disingenuous. That being the case, they've got a mess on their hands. When the congregation discovers what's going on, it will tear the church apart—not to mention what it will do to Helen.

Finally, she places a handful of coins on the table and picks up the check. At the cash register, she pays for lunch and exits the café, battling both grief and anger. Like a broken record, the same question keeps playing over and over in her mind: *How could Pastor Rob have allowed himself to become entangled in such a sordid mess?*

RICHARD EXLEY

Rita is deeply hurt and furious as she guns her Mustang out of the parking lot. When it comes to her only son, she is a momma bear! No one had better say anything about him, or they will answer to her—and that includes Pastor Rob Thompson. Why in the world would he tell Dave Underwood that Chad had been in an auto accident if it wasn't true? It makes no sense. Yet, if Chad was in an accident, why didn't Rob get in touch with her? Vacillating between fear and anger, she struggles to make some sense of the situation.

She is still furious ten minutes later when she parks her Mustang beside Rob's Oldsmobile Cutlass and makes her way up the sidewalk toward the private entrance to his office. Using the key he gave her, she lets herself in. He is not at his desk, although it's covered with books and commentaries. His Bible is open beside his typewriter, and it appears he is working on his sermon for tomorrow's service. Glancing at his open Bible, she is surprised to see the text he has chosen. It is the story of David's adulterous affair with Bathsheba, and he has underlined the prophet's words with a red marker: *"Then Nathan said to David, "You are the man!"*

A moment later, Rob emerges from the workroom carrying a steaming cup of freshly brewed coffee. Although he is nearing forty, he's aging well, with just a touch of gray in his dark hair, which she thinks makes him look distinguished. He's just under six feet tall, with a runner's lean build and sharp features. He's not really handsome in a conventional way, but there's something about him that demands attention. Today she hardly notices.

Giving her a warm smile, he says, "What a pleasant surprise."

As delighted as he is to see her, he can't help feeling uneasy. Without consciously intending to, he finds himself glancing out the window to make sure they are alone. The parking lot is empty except for his Cutlass and her Mustang, which are parked behind the church, making them impossible to be seen from the street. Still, try as he might, he can't help thinking that Paul might show up unexpectedly, or one of the board members. If that were to happen, he doesn't have any idea how he would explain Rita's presence.

Belatedly he realizes that something is troubling her. "Are you okay?" he asks.

"Has Chad been in an auto accident?" she demands, barely able to control her emotions.

"Not that I'm aware of," he replies, trying to appear genuinely puzzled. "If there was an emergency, surely Brad would call you, wouldn't he?"

Now that she is reasonably sure Chad has not been in an accident, her anxiety is morphing into full-blown anger. Through clenched teeth she asks, "Did you tell Dave Underwood that Chad had been drinking and that he'd had an accident?"

"What are you talking about?" Rob demands, feigning surprise.

"Don't lie to me!" Rita hisses, glaring at him.

Without responding, Rob walks across the room and stares out the window, deeply troubled. He's ashamed of the man he's become—a liar and an unfaithful husband—never mind that he and Rita have never been sexually intimate. He's afraid, too. It seems his whole life is coming apart—his ministry and his marriage. The ancient words of the wise man keep going over and over in his mind: *"He that covereth his sins shall not prosper…"*

Rita has followed him across the room, and now she demands, "Did you tell Dave Underwood that Chad had been drinking when he crashed his car?"

"Yes," he says, forcing himself to turn around and face her, "but I can explain."

She's stunned and confused. Her mind is reeling. Blind with anger, she slaps him and pounds his chest with her fists. As her anger slowly exhausts itself, he tries to hold her, but she shoves him away. "Don't touch me!" she hisses. "How could you do this to me? How could you lie about my son? What were you thinking?"

"I'm truly sorry, Rita, but I had to tell Dave something. He and Pastor Paul saw my car in your driveway at one a.m. and demanded an explanation. Paul even had a photograph that was pretty incriminating—the license plate on my car and the numbers on your house were clearly visible. They threatened to take it to the district superintendent unless I could explain what I was doing at your house. I was desperate, and on the spur of the moment, that story about Chad was all I could come up with."

Wearily Rob returns to his desk, where he collapses in his executive chair as a migraine headache takes shape behind his eyes. His vision blurs, then narrows, as his peripheral vision becomes dark. For a few seconds, he sees flashing lights and then the pain starts. He fumbles in his desk drawer before finally finding a bottle of Excedrin. He shakes two tablets into his hand and swallows them dry.

Rita takes a seat in one of the side chairs in front of his desk. She's still angry—how dare he malign her son to protect himself!—but now she's beginning to realize the seriousness of their situation. He looks frightened, and that concerns her. He's usually in control, a step ahead of every situation, but now he seems at a loss, and it appears things are spinning out of control. Even though his marriage and ministry are at risk, she can't help thinking of herself. What will he do now? Will he end their relationship? If he does, how will she cope?

Hesitantly she asks, "What about us? What happens now?"

When he doesn't answer immediately, she continues, "Are you sorry you fell in love with me?" She fears his answer, but she has to know.

He chews his bottom lip as he considers his response, the migraine making it difficult for him to think. Finally, he says, "I'm deeply grieved to discover I'm not the man I thought I was—a man of God and a faithful husband. I'm sorry for betraying Helen and for the pain this will cause her. I'm sorry for putting the church in the middle of this mess. If it comes out, a lot of people are going to get hurt. Most of all, I'm sorry for transgressing God's holy law and for discrediting the ministry."

It feels as if her heart has stopped, and she can barely breathe. It seems her worst fears are about to be realized. She's never allowed herself any illusions regarding their relationship. From the beginning, she knew it would never be more than this—stolen moments, intense longings, and unfulfilled desires. Still, the thought of losing what little they've shared is heartbreaking.

After a painful pause, he continues, "I'm sorry about a lot of things, and I wish none of this was happening, but as crazy as it may be, I'm not sorry for falling in love with you."

"What's the worst thing that can happen?" she asks, ready to face the worst now that she's assured of his love. "Walk me through it so I can prepare myself."

"Worst-case scenario: Paul and Dave take that photo and their suspicions to the district superintendent. Then the district Officials will conduct their own investigation. To start with, they will probably want to talk with both of us, separately, of course. So we will have to get our stories straight."

"Can they force us to talk with them?"

"They can't force you to talk to them," he replies, "but if I refuse, they will probably defrock me."

"So, what do we tell them?"

"As little as possible. Admit to nothing other than being careless and unthinking in our work habits. Never, under any circumstances, admit that our relationship is anything other than professional. We are not attracted to each other. We are not emotionally involved, and we are definitely not having an affair. Deny! Deny! Deny!"

"Will that work?"

"It's not likely to alleviate their suspicions, but without a confession from either of us, there's not much they can do."

"Does it make any difference that we haven't actually committed adultery?"

"Probably not. Even if we haven't been physically intimate, we are involved in an inappropriate relationship. Besides, who will believe us, given that incriminating photo?"

"I thought you said Paul ripped it up."

"He did, but I'm sure he has the negative or another copy."

"What are we going to do?"

"Nothing for the moment. Who knows—maybe they will drop the whole thing. It's not likely, but they might."

Deeply shamed, Rob gets up from behind his desk and begins pacing, his thoughts in turmoil. How could he have been so foolish? Helen tried to warn him, but he wouldn't listen. Now he cannot get the words of his sermon text out of his mind—*"You are the man!"*

Was this how David felt when the prophet confronted him? Probably. Did he wish a thousand times that he could go back and relive those fateful moments? Undoubtedly. Would he have done anything differently? Who knows?

When Rob pauses in front of the picture window, Rita walks up behind him and slips her arms around his waist. Laying her cheek against his back she whispers, "I'm sorry, Rob, so sorry. I never intended for any of this to happen."

Now he hears himself repeating a poem he plans to use in tomorrow's sermon:

"Oh, the price we pay, for just one riotous day. Eternities of regret and grief, and sorrow without relief."

Chapter 16

Dave and Lisa were not in church the following Sunday, a sure sign that something was terribly wrong, and Rob noted their absence with no little concern. They never missed a service, and he couldn't help thinking he was to blame. By now, Dave had to know his explanation for being at Rita's that fateful night was pure fabrication. Fabrication nothing! To Dave's black and white way of thinking, it was an outright lie. It grieved him to think that his actions had wounded Dave's faith and damaged their friendship, but he didn't know what he could do about it. Apologize perhaps, or try to explain that his relationship with Rita was purely platonic, but he could hardly expect Dave to believe him. Unconsciously, he found himself reciting under his breath a line his mother used to quote when she suspected he was being less than truthful: *"Oh, what a tangled web we weave when at first we set out to deceive."*

As the service progressed, he found himself increasingly distracted. He kept replaying last night's dream over and over in his mind. In his dream, he was entering the pulpit and announcing his text. As he did so, the congregation gasped and began whispering to one another and pointing at him. Belatedly he realized that although his suit coat and tie were impeccable, from the waist down he was totally nude—shamefully exposed.

With an effort, he pushes that dream—and the shame it has spawned—out of his mind. Determinedly he turns his attention to the service, only to be blindsided again. Now he is plagued with the thought that Dave may have discussed his suspicions with any number of congregants. From time to time, he catches himself surveying the congregation in an attempt to scrutinize each worshiper, carefully searching their faces for any sign that their attitude toward him has changed. Finally, he concludes that if Dave has shared anything with anyone, it isn't readily apparent from their demeanors; nonetheless, he still feels vulnerable.

The choir finishes its final number, and he hesitates a moment before stepping into the pulpit. As he is announcing the text, Dave and Lisa slip in and take a seat in the rear of the sanctuary, causing him to momentarily panic. His heart pounds, and his breath comes in ragged gasps. Dave's tardy entrance has thrown him off stride, and he can't help feeling it was designed to do just that. Without intending to, he finds himself wondering whether Dave has the incriminating photo with him, wondering whether he intends to confront him right here in front of the entire congregation?

Taking a deep breath, he forces those troubling thoughts from his mind and reads his text, stumbling over several of the words: *"And Nathan said to David, Thou art the man... Now therefore the sword shall never depart from thine house; because thou hast despised me, and hast taken the wife of Uriah the Hittite to be thy wife."*

As his eyes sweep over the congregation, he castigates himself for choosing this passage and for the sermon he has prepared. In retrospect, it seems almost an admission of guilt. It's not, of course, but he sees Dave give Lisa a knowing look—or so it appears to him. Paul also seems unnerved, and Rob suspects the same thought has occurred to him. Out of the corner of his eye, he sees Rita shift uncomfortably in her seat, while twisting a decorative handkerchief. Her distress is obvious, and he can't help wondering if she fears he is about to make a public confession.

So heavy is the condemnation pressing down upon him that for a moment he is tempted to do just that: to set aside his sermon notes and come clean with the congregation. *Surely,* he tells himself, *they will believe me if I explain that my only sin was allowing myself to become emotionally involved with Rita, nothing more. But what if they don't believe me? What if they conclude my confession is self-serving, simply an attempt to defuse the situation? What if they decide that incriminating photo is proof enough of adultery?* Reluctantly, he concludes the risk is too great. He has too much to lose. He's just going to have to press on and let things play out.

Turning to his sermon notes, he begins in a shaky voice, "What we have here is a spiritual tragedy. David, known as a man after God's own heart, has betrayed himself and his God. It would be easy to conclude that he was an evil man, a hypocrite, pretending to be a godly man, but I don't believe that's the case. David did an evil thing, to be sure. He had Uriah the Hittite killed, and he took Uriah's wife to be his own wife"—here Rob hesitates, stumbling over his words—"but that did not make him an evil man. Good people do bad things, but they are not necessarily bad people, albeit they suffer terribly. For a while, they may maintain a spiritual façade, and they may even fool their friends and family, but at the core of their being, they are dead! Where once there burned a holy fire, now there are only ashes."

Dave glances at Lisa, and when he catches her eye, he whispers, "Is he describing David, or is he referring to himself?"

She simply shrugs her shoulders and turns her attention back to the sermon as Pastor Rob continues, "There are moments of sinful pleasure, to be sure—the excitement of the hunt, the thrill of the conquest—but the end is death. Death to the adulterer's relationship with God. Death to the adulterer's marriage, for even if he manages to keep the facts of his adultery secret, his very secrecy will rob his marriage of its intimacy. Death to the adulterer's self-respect, for he has betrayed his own values. Even if no one else ever finds out, he knows. He knows he is not the faithful husband and godly father he appears to be. He knows he is not the spiritual leader nor the man of integrity his friends think he is." He pauses for effect and then continues in a sober tone. "It's a terrible thing to know that you are not the man your family and friends think you are."

When Lisa glances at Dave, she is surprised to see that silent sobs are shaking his shoulders while tears stain his weathered cheeks. She can't help thinking that he never cries. Never! Leaning close, she whispers, "What is it, Dave? Why are you weeping?"

A fresh wave of grief sweeps over him, and he buries his face in his hands in an attempt to muffle his sobs—but it is no use. Several nearby worshipers turn to see what the commotion is about. Finally, Dave slips out of the pew, then stumbles into the foyer and down the steps toward the car. After a moment, Lisa follows. Getting into the car, she slides across the seat and puts her arm around him. When she does, he buries his face against her shoulder. At last his weeping subsides, and he manages to say, "Rob's not talking about King David. He's describing himself, and it's breaking my heart."

Immediately following the close of the service, Rob slips out the side door of the sanctuary and heads for his office. If the congregation finds his sudden disappearance unusual, so be it. He is simply in no mood for small talk. As crazy as it might seem, the only person he wants to talk to is Rita. Never mind that their inappropriate relationship is the source of all his troubles.

Once inside his office, he locks the door and leaves the lights off. Sitting behind his desk with his face in his hands, he castigates himself. How could he have been so foolish? Why didn't he listen to Helen? She tried to warn him. If he'd had an ounce of common sense, he would have avoided Rita like the plague. Unfortunately, common sense proved to be no match for temptation. If he is honest with himself, he has to admit that even now, as shamed and miserable as he is, he is not willing to give Rita up.

It makes no sense. He is risking everything that is important to him—his marriage and family, his ministry, his reputation, even his livelihood—and for what? An illicit relationship that's going nowhere! As much as he cares for Rita and enjoys the excitement of their relationship, he cannot imagine divorcing Helen or giving up his ministry. So, why is he unwilling to terminate their relationship? He can only conclude that sexual temptation has rendered him temporarily insane.

His ruminating is cut short when someone knocks loudly on his office door. For an instant, he imagines it might be Rita, but then he realizes that given the circumstances, she would never risk it. Besides, she wouldn't knock. She has a key to his office door. So, who can it be? Maybe a concerned board member or a disgruntled parishioner, not anyone he wants to see.

When he continues to ignore the knocking, it becomes louder and more insistent. "Robert Thompson, I know you're in there. Open this door right now. I want to speak with you!"

He can hardly believe his ears. What is his mother doing here? She should be at home preparing lunch for the boys.

For a moment, he considers slipping out through his private entrance and heading for the parking lot, but then decides against it. Reluctantly he makes his way toward his office door, concluding that since he will have to face his mother sooner or later, he might as well get it over with. When she gets like this, there's no avoiding her. Never mind he is an adult with children of his own.

As soon as he opens the door, she strides into the room with a grim determination. "What in the world are you doing sitting here in the dark?" she demands. Without giving him a chance to reply, she switches on the overhead lights and opens the blinds, flooding the room with bright sunlight.

Turning back to Rob, who has retreated behind his desk, she continues, "I think it's time we talked. I don't know what's gone amiss between you and Helen, but I suspect it has something to do with your secretary, and I intend to get to the bottom of it."

Pretending to ignore her, he shuffles some papers, but all the while his mind is racing. It's obvious his mother senses something is awry, but he has no idea how much she knows or suspects. She is spiritually perceptive, and he's never been able to fool her—still, he has no intention of admitting anything. Instead he gives her a puzzled look before asking, "What in the world are you talking about?"

Unfazed, she replies, "I'm talking about you and Helen. Anyone can see that something has changed in your relationship. It's not like Helen to go traipsing off to the Amazon Basin without you. Even the boys sense something is wrong. They're not themselves."

Choosing his words carefully, he tells her, "Helen hasn't been herself since her mother died. She's been depressed, and it's put a strain on our relationship. It's affected the boys, too, as you've noticed." Spreading his hands in a helpless gesture, he concludes, "I tried to talk her out of going to the Amazon, but she was insistent. There was nothing I could do."

She considers his words for a moment, then asks, "How did her depression affect you?"

"What do you mean?"

"You've changed, Rob. You used to be a family-first kind of husband and father, but not anymore. Since I've been here, you've worked late a lot of nights. It feels like you don't want to come home. The boys say you never have time to play with them anymore."

She's right, but he's not about to admit it. Instead he explains, "The church has grown, and things are a lot busier now, not to mention the added responsibilities of being a presbyter. You've been around ministry your entire life, Mother. You know a pastor's work is never done."

"I do know a pastor's work is never done," she concedes, "but I also know that a busy pastor with a depressed wife is an easy target for the enemy."

"What are you implying?" he asks, trying not to sound defensive.

Her brows furrow in concentration, and she chews her bottom lip, as if trying to make up her mind. Finally she says, "As hard as it may be for you to believe, your father and I went through a difficult time in our marriage when we were just a little older than you are now. The church wasn't growing, and he was receiving a lot of criticism. To make ends meet, I took a job as a receptionist in an attorney's office, so I wasn't as attentive to your father as I should have been. He was dealing with a lot of disappointment and self-doubt, making him easy prey for the enemy. Anyway, one of the ladies working at the church began spending a lot of time with him. Without intending to, he became infatuated with her. Thankfully, before anything could happen, I confronted him. At first, he became defensive and accused me of having an overactive imagination. Things might have turned out badly if your father hadn't been sensitive to the Holy Spirit. Thankfully, when the Lord began dealing with his heart, he repented. He confessed his feelings to me, and together we put some safeguards in place to protect him from further temptation.

"I see you exhibiting many of the same behaviors that alerted me to the dangers your father was facing—he was becoming increasingly indifferent to me, he was creating 'legitimate' projects at the church so he could spend time with her, and he was willing to share his struggles with her, especially the struggles we were having in our marriage. There's more, but I think you get my point."

His mother's words are like darts piercing his soul, but he is not about to admit that to her. Instead he counters, "Mom, you're reading more into my situation than it merits. Granted, things are a little strained between Helen and me, but I'm not infatuated with another woman. I don't mean to sound disrespectful, but I think you're projecting my father's shortcomings onto me."

His words sorely wound her, and that grieves him, but he hardens his heart lest he acknowledge the truth of her observations. Without another word, she gets to her feet and walks to the door. With her hand on the door handle, she pauses and turns toward him. In a voice he has to strain to hear, she says, "'He that covereth his sins shall not prosper: but whoso confesseth and forsaketh them shall have mercy.'"

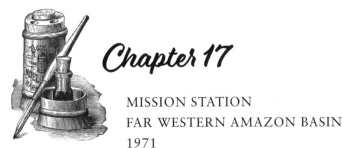

Chapter 17

MISSION STATION
FAR WESTERN AMAZON BASIN
1971

G uided by the flashlight's narrow beam, I make my way down the muddy path toward the river where our boat is tied up. Troubled though I am by Gordon's words and the situation with Diana, I'm still careful to keep a sharp eye out for the deadly pit vipers that inhabit this part of the Amazon Basin. According to Lako, they hunt at night, identifying their prey through the heat-detecting sensors embedded around their lips. Fortunately, I encounter no snakes, and when the trail opens on a high sandbar overlooking the river, I pause to survey its wide expanse. Although the temperature is moderate, the air is heavy with moisture, and humidity has pasted my shirt to my back. Hordes of insects buzz around my head, preparing for a feast.

Being careful where I step, I collect an armload of fallen branches and arrange them in preparation for building a fire. The wood is damp, but that suits my purpose as I want a smoky fire to ward off mosquitoes. Working quickly, I arrange the fallen branches and place several handfuls of dry grass and twigs to serve as tinder. I strike a match, being careful to shield it from the breeze that has sprung up. Touching it to the grass, I watch it ignite. In a few seconds, it has spread to the twigs, and soon I have a small but smoky fire. The smoke irritates my eyes, but dealing with it is better than battling the insects.

It's the rainy season, and to the west the sky over the Serra Divisor is boiling with thunderheads. Nearer, the night is electric with lightning, the air smelling of fresh ozone. Downdrafts, cold and heavy with moisture, trouble the towering treetops, and I'm reminded of the violent storm that nearly killed Eurico. The wind tore a large branch off a tree, hurling it like a spear. It struck him in the head, ripping a large gash in his scalp and giving him a concussion.

Squatting on my heels, I stare into the fire as the storm continues to build. I can't help thinking that if Gordon is not exaggerating, I've wounded Diana in ways I can't even begin to comprehend. My intentions may have been noble, but when I walked away from her, I ripped her heart out.

Given my complicated relationship with Diana, I can't imagine how I allowed Helen to convince me to bring her upriver. Guilt, I guess, considering how I had treated her most of my life, or maybe I was harboring an unacknowledged desire to see Diana one last time. Whatever the reason, it was a mistake. I can see that clearly now. Nothing good can come of this. Not for Diana and not for me. As Gordon said, my presence here is disruptive.

I'm tempted to haul our stuff back down to the river and reload the boat for an early departure in the morning, but Helen would never agree to that. This is her only chance to revisit the place where we grew up, and she's determined to make the most of it. Besides, she's not the problem; I am.

Another possibility is taking shape in my mind, but the mere thought of it fills me with dread.

The fire has burned down, so I add two or three dead branches and hunker down as the first huge raindrops dimple the surface of the rain-swollen river. A jagged flash of lightning illuminates the riverbank, and for a moment I think I see a huge crocodile and my blood runs cold. Frantically I search the area near the fire, trying to locate my flashlight. Without it I am blind. Even now that huge croc could be creeping closer, but without my flashlight I have no way of knowing.

Realizing the fire is my only protection should that huge reptile decide to attack, I move to place it between us. When I do, I step on something that causes me to turn my ankle, and I nearly fall. To my relief, I discover I have stepped on my misplaced flashlight. Squatting down, I dig it out of the mud, and with trembling hands I switch it on, directing its powerful beam toward the crocodile. To my relief, I discover that what I thought was a huge croc is just a log the river has cast up on the bank.

With a crash of thunder, the storm erupts, loosing a deluge of rain that drenches me in an instant. Hurriedly I kick the fire apart and watch for a moment to make sure the downpour has extinguished every spark. When all that remains is blackened embers floating in a puddle of muddy water, I make my way up the rain-slick path toward Whittaker House.

By the time I reach the clearing that harbors both the small house my father built and Diana's cottage, I am soaked to the bone. Whittaker House is dark, so I assume Helen is still enjoying Diana's hospitality. Through the heavy downpour,

I can just make out the lamplight spilling from the windows of her cottage, but the storm has obliterated the murmur of voices. I can't help noting the contrast between the two cottages. Hers is full of light and laughter, while Whittaker House is dark and empty, an apt reflection of the way I feel. The ones I love—Diana and Eurico—are in her cottage, but I dare not go there.

A wave of loneliness engulfs me as I mount the steps and stomp the mud off my boots before opening the door. The storm is roaring in my ears as I feel my way to the kitchen table, where I strike a match and light the kerosene lamp. I strip off my wet clothes and towel myself dry. Once I've found a clean pair of jeans and a T-shirt, I return to the kitchen. I use a match to light a burner on the kerosene cookstove and put some coffee on to boil. Rummaging through our provisions, I find a hunk of bread, some cheese, and some smoked fish, which I wash down with coffee, scalding hot and black.

The intensity of the storm is increasing, and the pounding of the rain sounds like handfuls of gravel hitting the tin roof. In the distance, I hear what sounds like trees breaking and crashing, and I am thankful for the shelter of Whittaker House. I cannot help but marvel at its durability. Having withstood violent storms like this for more than thirty years, it is irrefutable proof of my father's carpentry skills. Thinking about it now, I can only marvel at his resourcefulness. There were no lumberyards in the jungle, so he had to cut the trees and mill the boards himself before he could even start building. It was backbreaking work, but I never heard him complain. The end product was not fancy, but it is durable and weatherproof.

As I finish my meager meal, the storm seems to be easing a little, and I'm tempted to get a second cup of coffee and sit on the porch. Instead I rinse my dishes and place them on a towel on the counter before heading to bed. I leave the lamp burning for Helen, but I turn it down low. Just outside my bedroom door I pause, letting the pungent order from the kerosene lamp take me back to the childhood I spent in this very house.

I'm exhausted, but my mind is too troubled to sleep. I toss and turn, trying to get comfortable while wrestling with my thoughts. I can't stay here; Gordon has made that plain enough. Yet neither can I expect Helen to give up her plans to accommodate me. That wouldn't be fair to her. She's put a lot of time and money into this trip, and she's every bit as emotionally vested in this endeavor, as I was when I set out to discover what happened to our father. I consider and discard any number of ideas as unworkable. Always my mind returns to the possibility that first occurred to me earlier this evening while I was at the river. As I consider it now, the mere thought of it fills me with dread.

I'm still searching for a less risky solution when I hear Helen slip in the front door. She tiptoes to my bedroom door and opens it a crack. Now that the storm has passed, moonlight is streaming through the window beside my bed. I'm sure Helen can see me in the faint light, so I force myself to breathe deep and regular, pretending to sleep.

"Bryan," she whispers, "are you awake?"

When I don't respond, she closes the door softly and returns to the kitchen. Whittaker House is small, and through the thin walls I hear her strike a match and I assume she is lighting the kerosene cookstove. The pump handle squeaks as she fills the teakettle before putting it on the stove to heat. She is talking softly to herself as she rummages through our provisions in search of tea. Finally, I hear her pull out a chair, and in my mind's eye, I see her sitting at the table sipping her tea, deep in thought. I can only imagine what she is thinking.

Chapter 18

I'm sitting on the porch of Whittaker House, enjoying my second cup of coffee, when Helen joins me. "Some storm last night," I say. When she nods in acknowledgment, I continue, "I expected to see more damage, some trees down maybe, but it's just broken branches and smaller debris scattered about."

Looking around, she says, "I don't remember this place being so beautiful. As a child, I guess I never really paid much attention."

She takes a sip of tea before setting her cup on the porch rail and descending the steps. As I watch, she makes her way through the wet grass to a host of colorful flowers. Most of them are unfamiliar to me, but I do recognize some orchids. Their colorful petals are decorated with sparkling beads of water from last night's storm, and the blending of light and color is truly amazing.

"Are these orchids?" she asks, bending down to pick one. When I acknowledge as much, she picks several more in various colors and carries them to the porch. Handing them to me, she heads into the house. Over her shoulder she says, "I'll be right back." A couple of minutes later, she returns with a mason jar half full of water. Taking the orchids from me, she carefully arranges them in the jar before setting them on a wooden crate situated between our chairs. Although I am not much into decorative ambience, I have to admit the orchids add a nice touch.

"Do you remember how Mother loved flowers?" she asks. Without giving me a chance to reply, she continues, "We used to go on walks looking for the perfect flower. Sometimes you came with us, but you were always wandering off on your own. Flowers never held much interest for you."

I grin at her in acknowledgment before taking a sip of my coffee. "I guess flowers just aren't my thing."

"Mother knew the names of practically all the flowers, or so it seemed to me. Still, the thing I remember most are the bouquets she made for the table. It was her way of brightening things up, although if I remember correctly, our father wasn't all that impressed."

When I simply nod, she turns her attention to the small bouquet of orchids sitting on the wooden crate between us. "Who knows? She may have used this very jar, or one like it, for a vase."

The orchids, or more particularly the mason jar, have resurrected an old memory, and not a pleasant one. *Mother and Helen are arranging a bouquet of wildflowers for the table when Father walks in. Mother senses his mood and turns away, but Helen, being a child, does not. "Look, Daddy," she exclaims excitedly, thrusting the mason jar of flowers toward him. "Aren't they pretty?"*

Ignoring her, Father addresses our mother. "Velma, how many times have I told you not to waste your time picking flowers? Your time could be better spent weeding the garden or canning vegetables."

Taking the bouquet of wildflowers from Helen, he walks to the porch rail and dumps them out. Mother is angry, I can tell, but she doesn't say anything. Instead, she goes to the stove to finish preparing supper. Helen puts plates and glasses on the table while fighting back tears, but Father acts as if nothing is amiss.

Memories like that dominated my childhood and helped shape the damaged man I became. I'm sure there were good memories, too, but they were overshadowed by the hurt my father inflicted, intentionally or otherwise. He was not physically abusive, but his sternness and lack of affection wounded me in ways that haunt me still. Thank God we found his journals, or I might have gone to my grave without ever knowing that he loved Helen and me.

Noticing my coffee cup is empty, Helen takes it from me and goes into the house to refill it. When she returns, I tell her, "You don't have to do that. I can get my own coffee."

"It's no trouble," she says. "With three guys in our family, I'm used to serving. I'm always getting one of them something." For just a moment, there is a hint of something in her eyes—homesickness for her boys or concern for Rob and their marriage—and then it is gone. I would like to ask her about it, but before I can, she takes a seat on the porch rail facing me. "So, what happened to you last night?" she asks. "I thought you were having dinner with us."

It's the question I've been dreading, and I take a sip of my coffee before responding. "It's complicated," I say, before giving her the *Reader's Digest* version of my failed relationship with Diana. My throat is tight, and my eyes are damp as I describe our final parting. When I finish, we sit for a minute or two without speaking. Finally, she says, "May I ask you a question?"

Reluctantly I agree, and she looks at me intensely before asking, "If you truly love Diana, why did you walk away?"

Why, indeed?

Once more I try to explain my reasons, being careful to emphasize how it wouldn't be fair to Diana if I let her sacrifice her missionary calling for me. Helen just shakes her head before replying, "That sounds noble, Bryan, but I'm not buying it. I think you're just afraid of being hurt again. Besides, you have no right to decide what's best for Diana."

Her words hit a nerve, and before I can stop myself, I blurt out, "And you have no right to tell me how to live my life!"

Anger has made my words harsh, and I lunge to my feet and storm off the porch. As I stride across the clearing toward the path that leads to the river, I hear Helen calling my name. "Bryan," she says, "please don't go."

The old Bryan would have ignored her, but already I'm regretting my angry outburst. At the edge of the clearing, I stop. For several seconds, maybe as long as a minute, I stand there, trying to calm myself. Finally, I return to the porch, breathing a prayer under my breath, "Lord Jesus, help me."

Nothing is harder for me than apologizing; still, I take a deep breath and force myself to tell Helen I'm sorry for my angry outburst. She is stunned, and well she might be, for I've never apologized to her before. "Maybe you're right," I say. "Maybe I was afraid of being hurt. Not that it really matters now. Whatever my reasons, I know I never meant to hurt her."

When Helen doesn't say anything, I continue in a voice that is hardly more than a whisper, shame tainting every word. "Apparently, I've hurt Diana in ways I can't even comprehend, at least that's what Gordon told me. According to him, she is barely functioning—"Hanging on to her sanity by her fingernails," were his exact words. He's convinced I'm putting Diana at risk just by being here, and he wants me to leave immediately. I'm not sure how he feels about you and Carolyn."

"Well, that explains what I was sensing at dinner last night."

When I raise my eyebrows questioningly, she continues. "It felt like there was an elephant in the room, but no one would talk about it. A couple of times I asked Gordon where you were, but he never really gave me an answer. Eleanor tried to put everyone at ease, but Diana seemed to be sleepwalking, just going through the motions."

"Funny you should say that. That's exactly how Gordon described her. He said she might have actually hurt herself if it hadn't been for Eurico."

"So, what are we going to do?"

"I'm not sure. I don't see how I can stay here, given Gordon's feelings. Besides, being near Diana is ripping my heart out."

"Have you considered talking to her? If you truly love each other, maybe you can work things out."

"That will never happen," I say. "She will never trust me again."

"Why wouldn't she? Lovers quarrel and make up all the time. Very few couples make it to the altar without a crisis or two."

"That's true enough, I suppose, but most couples do not have our history. Some sins are past forgiving—or so it seems to me."

We sit in silence for several minutes, each of us immersed in our own thoughts. Finally, Helen speaks. "Bryan, I don't mean to pry, but it feels like there's something you're not telling me."

She's hit the nail on the head, but how can I tell her about the unspeakable thing I did when Eurico was desperately fighting for his life? The mere memory of it leaves freezer burns on my soul. I drop my eyes and study the porch floor between my muddy boots. Without looking at her, I say, "There are some things I can't talk about, at least not yet. Maybe never.

"Helen," I ask, changing the subject, "do you still want to see where our father is buried?"

"Of course, but I thought you said it was too dangerous."

"It is dangerous, but I can't stay here. I can't risk hurting Diana more than I already have."

When she hesitates, I say, "I'm not even sure I can find where he's buried, but I'm willing to give it a shot if you are."

When she still hesitates, I add, "If something happens to me, it's no big deal, but you have a lot more to consider. You have two boys who need their mother. I don't have to tell you what growing up without a parent is like. And then there's Rob."

Finally, she says, "Let me sleep on it and see how I feel in the morning."

Chapter 19

Although it is still dark, Helen has been awake for hours, having spent the better part of the night wrestling with her decision. She has a painful yearning to see the place where her father is buried, but at what cost? Bryan has been brutally frank concerning the risks involved in the trek upriver. Danger and even death may await them. Does she have the right to put her life at risk when her boys need their mother? Yet this may well be her only chance to kneel at her father's grave and finally close this chapter of her life. Consciously or unconsciously, she's been waiting all her life for this moment, and if she walks away now, she may regret it for the rest of her life.

Having made her decision, she slips out of bed and puts on her shirt and jeans before tiptoeing to the kitchen, where she lights the kerosene lamp. At the sink, she uses the pump to fill the teapot before putting it on the stove to heat. Although she would prefer a china teacup, she settles for a heavy mug. When the water reaches a boil, she fills the mug and allows the tea to steep. Pulling the kerosene lamp close, she picks up a pen and puts it to paper.

If anything should happen to her, she wants to leave something for her two sons. A letter telling them how much she loves them is hardly a substitute for a living and breathing mother, but she knows the value of the written word. Her father's journals have been a gift from God, especially the letter he wrote to her just before he died. As she thinks about it now, her throat grows tight, and she mouths the words of Hebrews 11:4: *"...and by it he being dead yet speaketh."*

When she finishes the letters to her sons, she carefully folds them and puts each letter in a separate envelope, on which she has written each boy's name. Once she seals them, she hugs them to her heart and whispers a prayer only a mother can pray. She will leave the letters with Carolyn, to give to Rob for Robbie and Jake if she doesn't make it back.

Finally, she picks up her pen once more and writes:

Dear Rob:

It is not yet daylight, and I am sitting at the table my father built when I was just a child. A host of memories flood my mind—simple meals eaten together as a family, schoolwork done under my mother's watchful eye, the sound of my father's voice reading Scripture during family devotions, and Bryan's impatience. He was always squirming, and Father was constantly correcting him. As a child, he could never sit still.

Of course, the defining memory is of the last night we spent together before Father disappeared. The table was covered with supplies—rice, beans, coffee, smoked meat, bandages, medicine, and other medical supplies.

Mother was helping him pack by checking things off a long list as he stowed them away. On more than one occasion, this careful attention to detail meant the difference between life and death. In the jungles of the Amazon Basin, a person seldom gets a second chance.

When Father finished packing, he put on his spectacles and reached for his Bible. Without being asked, we all ceased what we were doing and gave him our attention. Our family devotions followed a prepared reading schedule, and that night's passage was Isaiah 43:1–3.

"But now thus saith the Lord that created thee, O Jacob, and he that formed thee, O Israel, Fear not: for I have redeemed thee, I have called thee by thy name; thou art mine. When thou passest through the waters, I will be with thee; and through the rivers, they shall not overflow thee: when thou walkest through the fire, thou shalt not be burned; neither shall the flame kindle upon thee. For I am the Lord thy God, the Holy One of Israel, thy Saviour."

These many years later, I still remember tears glistening in my mother's eyes when Father finished reading. If I try, I can still hear his voice as he took her hand and said, "The Lord has spoken to us through His Word. No matter what dangers I may face, He will see me safely through."

Only, God did not see him safely through, and that has been a nagging concern for me all these years. I can't help wondering if God can truly be trusted. I probably shouldn't feel that way, but it is what it is.

Why do I rehash all of this? Because tomorrow or the next day, Bryan and I are going upriver to visit my father's grave. Bryan has been there only once, and he is not sure he can locate it again, but we have to try. It is the rainy season, and the rivers are swollen and powerful, making travel especially dangerous. In addition, there is the ever-present threat of accident or illness, not to mention the hostility of the Amuacas.

I don't mean to sound melodramatic, but danger lurks everywhere in the Amazonian rain forest, and I may not make it back. The thought of losing my life without making things right with you is more than I can bear, hence this letter.

I'm terribly sorry for the way I left you at the airport. I was angry, and my pride wouldn't allow me to reach out to you. With the perspective of time and distance, I can see that I have been a perfect "bitch" for weeks, maybe months. Concealing my friendship with Carolyn and deliberately allowing you to be tormented by my unexplained long-distance phone calls was just plain evil. Please forgive me.

In my hurt and anger, I may have overreacted to Rita. I still believe she has designs on you, but I should have trusted you more. You are a man of God and a wonderful husband and father. Falling in love with you and marrying you was the best thing that ever happened to me. I love you more now than I ever have, and I look forward to spending the rest of our lives together.

> *With all my love,*
> *Helen*

Dawn is coloring the east windows with soft light when Helen finishes her letter to Rob. After folding it carefully, she places it in an envelope and seals it. She collects all three letters, walks out on the porch, and stretches, trying to relieve her cramped muscles. Her heart hurts as she considers her marriage, and she prays desperately that the wounds she and Rob have inflicted on each other can be healed without leaving permanent scars.

It is full daylight when she finishes praying, and on an impulse she decides to join Carolyn and Diana for a cup of tea before telling Bryan she has decided to take him up on his offer to visit their father's grave. Diana is alone on the porch when she arrives. Her Bible is open in her lap, and a cup of tea is steaming on the crate beside her.

"Would you care for a cup of tea?" she asks, giving Helen a tentative smile.

"Please," Helen replies, as she lowers herself into the adjoining rocker.

While Diana is preparing a second cup of tea, Helen replays the conversation she had with Bryan in her mind. It seems obvious to her that he is desperately in love with Diana, but for some reason he thinks he has burned his bridges. She can't help wondering what he could have possibly done that love cannot heal.

"Here's your tea," Diana says as she places a teacup on the crate between their rockers.

For several minutes, they rock in silence, giving Helen a chance to study Diana out of the corner of her eye. She's beautiful, and it is easy to see why Bryan would be attracted to her. Unfortunately, she seems deeply grieved, and her smile never reaches her eyes. On an impulse, Helen asks, "So, what happened with you and Bryan?"

When Diana takes a sip of tea before replying, Helen adds, "He's still in love with you, you know."

"I hardly think so," Diana counters. "When we parted a few weeks ago, he made his feelings pretty clear."

"Don't be too sure. Bryan's not easy to understand. He often pushes people away when he really wants to hold them close."

"What do you mean?"

"Love scares him. He's afraid of being hurt again. Without really understanding what he is doing or why, he shoves people away."

"Have you discussed this with Bryan?"

"Just briefly."

"What did he tell you?" Diana asks.

"Not much, really. Just that he wasn't willing to let you sacrifice your missionary calling for him. He said that wouldn't be fair to you."

Unbidden tears slide silently down Diana's cheeks as she relives their painful parting. The rejection she felt that evening, as Bryan removed her arms from around his waist and walked away without a backward glance, is still painfully raw. Getting up, she walks to the end of the porch and stares in the distance toward the river.

After a couple of minutes, Helen goes to stand beside her. "I told him he didn't have the right to make that decision for you."

Diana smiles ruefully. "I'm sure he appreciated that."

"Hardly."

Taking a deep breath, she says, "Loving Bryan isn't easy. He keeps breaking my heart."

Helen nods empathetically, and Diana continues, "I don't understand him. He says he loves me, but when I offer to resign my missionary appointment and return to the States with him, he turns me down cold. No explanation. Nothing."

"Could you really do that, give up your calling?"

"For Bryan, I think so."

"My father used to say that if a person was truly called, there was no turning back."

"I've thought a lot about that," Diana says, "don't think I haven't. Here's my conclusion. Medicine is my calling. That's how I serve God. I wouldn't be giving up my calling if I resigned my missionary appointment to practice medicine in the States. I would simply be changing assignments, like a pastor going to a different church."

Choosing her words carefully, Helen says, "Bryan's afraid that in time you would come to regret your decision. Perhaps you would even blame him. If that were to happen, it would poison your love, and he can't bear the thought."

"Did he tell you that?"

"Not in so many words, but yes."

Throwing up her hands in a gesture of exasperation, Diana says, "That's what makes Bryan so difficult. He's so closed. You can't talk anything through with him."

"If there's any chance for you and Bryan," Helen ventures, "you will have to make the first move. Bryan's convinced he's hurt you in ways that are past forgiving and that you want nothing more to do with him. To complicate things, Gordon has asked him to stay away from you."

"That infuriates me!" Diana fumes. "Gordon means well, but he has no business interfering in my private life."

"He's just trying to protect you. He doesn't want to see you get hurt again."

Neither Helen nor Diana hears Carolyn approach, and they are startled when she asks, "Who's trying to protect whom?"

Without responding, Diana excuses herself and goes inside. After an awkward moment, Helen extracts three envelopes from her shirt pocket and hands them to Carolyn. "Bryan and I are going upriver tomorrow in search of our father's gravesite. He's made it clear we may be risking our lives, so I thought I would write to my three guys just in case something happens and I don't make it back."

Puzzled, Carolyn says, "Are you sure you want to do that? I mean, have you considered the consequences for your boys if anything were to happen to you?"

When Helen doesn't respond, Carolyn continues, "What made Bryan change his mind? I thought he said it was too dangerous."

"Who knows? Maybe he finally realized how important it is to me. Besides, it's probably not all that dangerous anyhow."

"Then, why did you write these letters?"

"As a precaution, that's all. Now, promise me you'll keep them safe until I get back. And if per chance something unforeseen happens to me, I want you to give them to Rob."

"Of course," Carolyn says, "but I still think you're making a mistake."

Chapter 20

The coffee is boiling, and I am frying bacon in a cast-iron skillet when Helen returns to Whittaker House. "Where have you been?" I ask, just to make conversation.

"I was having a cup of tea with Carolyn and Diana," she replies as she unwraps a loaf of Eleanor's home-baked bread and cuts several slices for toasting in the skillet.

At the mention of Diana, my heart aches. I sometimes wish I had never allowed myself to fall in love with her, considering how much pain it has caused both of us. At other times, I'm simply thankful for the love we shared, and I know I would gladly do it again, even knowing how painful our parting was.

Using a long-handled fork, I remove the bacon from the skillet and place it on two plates. Helen pours the hot bacon grease into a tin can, leaving just enough in the bottom of the skillet to toast the bread. While she is doing that, I pour two mugs of coffee, black and sweet, just the way the Brazilians like it.

When the toast is ready, Helen joins me at the table. I'm hungry, and without thinking, I wrap a piece of toast around a slice of bacon and take a bite without returning thanks. Helen clears her throat, and I realize what I have done. "Sorry," I say. "Would you like to ask the blessing, or do you want me to do it?"

"Please give thanks," she says, bowing her head.

When I finish, Helen has a pensive look on her face. "Listening to you pray," she muses, "is almost like listening to our father. You sound so much like him, or maybe it's just being here—in this house, at this table, where we spent so much time as children." Her voice trails off, and she takes a sip of coffee before taking a bite of bacon and bread.

"Well," I say, "have you given any more thought to going upriver to see our father's grave?"

"I thought about it nearly all night," she replies. "I hardly slept a wink."

"And…"

"I've decided to do it."

"Are you sure? It could be dangerous."

Before she can respond, Eurico bursts in. After giving me a hug, he picks up a thick slice of bread and wraps it around several pieces of bacon. Although he is small for his age, slight really, he has a voracious appetite. I'm used to it, but Helen watches in amazement as he devours the bacon and bread in short order and reaches for the last piece of toast.

Once we have finished eating and cleaned up the kitchen, I get a pencil and prepare to make a list of the things we will need. I use one of Lako's old lists as a guide and then add to it. He always planned to supplement our supplies by hunting and fishing, but I'm not comfortable with that. I'm not a *mateiro*, and it would be an unnecessary risk to count on supplementing our foodstuff with fish and wild game.

When Eurico realizes what I am doing, he gets excited. "I want to go," he says. "Take me with you."

I don't want to disappoint him, but there is no way I'm taking him with us. It's simply too dangerous. If something were to happen to him, it would kill Diana.

"Please," he begs. "Pretty please."

I reach over and tousle his hair affectionately. "We'll have to let Diana make that decision."

Before I can say another word, he darts out the door and heads for the clinic at a dead run. Shaking my head, I turn to Helen and say, "I don't envy Diana having to tell him no. He's got his heart set on going with us."

Carolyn sticks her head in the door and calls, "May I come in?"

Without waiting for a reply, she walks to the kitchen table, which is now covered with supplies. I'm putting things into packs as Helen marks them off my list. "Let me give you a hand," Carolyn says, reaching for a twenty-five-pound bag of black beans.

"Thanks," I say, taking the beans from her, "but no thanks. Let me pack our supplies. There's a method to my madness."

We are just finishing up when Eurico returns. He is downcast, and Carolyn asks, "What's up, little guy? You look like you've lost your last friend."

"Diana says I can't go with Bryan," he mumbles. "She says it's too dangerous."

Carolyn tries to comfort him, but he brushes her aside. "Diana should know I can handle myself in dangerous situations." Turning to Bryan, he says, "Tell them, Bryan. Tell them what I did when you and Diana fell down the mountain."

Grinning at Eurico, I say, "You were the hero that day. If it hadn't been for you, Diana and I might have died."

"Are you serious?" Helen asks.

When I nod, she says, "Let's hear it—the whole story."

I pour the last of the coffee into my mug before recounting our harrowing adventure. "We were returning from a medical emergency in a Kachinawanian village a half day's hike from here when Diana slipped on the muddy trail and plunged down the mountain. She probably would have fallen to her death if she hadn't hit a tangle of vines and underbrush. As it was, she suffered cuts and bruises, a severe concussion, and a badly broken leg.

"The instant I saw her cartwheeling down the mountain, I leaped after her. The mountain was steep, and I lost my footing and plummeted head over heels, ending in a tangle of brush overlooking a sheer drop-off of more than one hundred feet. I wasn't injured nearly as badly as she was, but I was in no shape to get either of us back up the mountain."

"Tell them what I did," Eurico says excitedly. "Tell them what I did."

I take a swallow of coffee before continuing. "First, Eurico carefully worked his way down the mountain, bringing my rifle and Diana's backpack, which contained a water bottle, a few aspirin, and some smoked fish. Although he didn't want to leave us, considering how seriously we were injured, I convinced him to go for help. He hiked back to the mission compound alone and returned twenty-four hours later, bringing Lako and the Arnolds with him.

"Lako proved to be every bit as competent as Dr. Peterson said he was. In short order, he set Diana's broken leg and rigged a splint for it. Then he and Gordon improvised a lift to bring her up the mountain. She was in pretty bad shape—dehydrated and in excruciating pain. Once they got her back on the trail, they placed her on a stretcher and immediately set out for the mission station. There was no way I could keep up with them given my injured knee, but they had no choice but to go on. Diana was their first priority, and she was in no condition to spend another night in the jungle.

"Eurico refused to leave me, and we soon fell behind. By this time, my injured knee was swollen nearly twice its normal size, and the pain was excruciating. Every time I took a step, it felt like someone was jabbing an ice pick in it. I fell several times, and I might have died there, but Eurico would not let me quit. It was long after dark when we finally reached Whittaker House, where I collapsed on the porch, unable to drag myself inside."

When I finish, Eurico is wearing a huge grin and flexing his muscles while enjoying the admiration of Helen and Carolyn.

"So," Carolyn asks, "is that why Diana walks with a slight limp?"

"Exactly. The fact that she walks as well as she does is pretty amazing considering Lako set her leg without the aid of an X-ray."

From a distance we hear Diana calling for Eurico. He's reluctant to leave us, but I give him a gentle nudge to start him on his way. When he is gone, Carolyn says, "What a remarkable young man."

Suddenly Gordon's burly frame fills the doorway. "How about a cup of coffee?" he says as he steps into the small kitchen/living room combination.

"We're fresh out," I say, "but it will only take a minute to brew a pot." He looks around for a place to sit, but with all the stuff we've packed for the trip upriver, he can't find an empty chair. "It's pretty cluttered in here," I say. "Why don't you and Helen go out on the porch, and I'll bring the coffee when it's ready."

As they head for the porch, I turn toward the coffee grinder, but Carolyn waves me off. "Let me do this," she says.

After moving a couple of packs, I straddle a chair and watch Carolyn move about the kitchen. Without intending to, I find myself recalling how much I used to enjoy watching her putter around in the kitchen in the early days of our marriage. Once I slipped up behind her and wrapped my arms around her slim waist. Burying my face in her thick auburn hair, I whispered, "Even in the kitchen, you fill me with bedroom thoughts." She laughed and said, "Hold that thought till later. Right now, I need to finish dinner."

Placing a scoop of coffee beans in the hand grinder, she studies it for a minute trying to decide exactly how it works. Unable to figure it out, she glances my way. "I guess I'm going to need your help after all. If you'll grind the beans, I'll clean the coffeepot."

By the time I've finished grinding the coffee beans, she's washed the coffeepot and filled it with water from the hand pump at the sink. Handing it to me, she watches as I dump six scoops of ground coffee, along with a healthy dose of brown sugar, into the water. She hands me a match, and I light the kerosene stove. Soon the rich aroma of brewing coffee fills the room.

While waiting for the coffee to finish, Carolyn and I sit across the table from each other and struggle to make small talk. Given our painful past, we are not completely comfortable with each other, and neither of us seems to know how to bridge the gap. I would like to tell her how sorry I am for all the hurt I caused her while we were married, but I don't know where to start. I want her to know that she was not to blame, that the responsibility was all mine. In my heart of hearts, I know I never set out to hurt her, but in my brokenness, I couldn't seem to help myself. I wish I could explain that to her, but I can't help thinking any attempt to do so would only seem self-serving, as if I were making excuses. Besides, "I'm sorry" seems so trite in light of the hurtful things I did. Anyway, what good would an apology do at this late date? It could never undo the hurtful things I've done. In fact, apologizing might simply open old wounds, doing more damage than good.

Finally, the coffee is ready, and Carolyn fills two mugs with hot coffee, black and sweet, and heads toward the front porch. I linger a moment more before filling two more mugs. I can't help thinking I have squandered another opportunity to right the wrongs I have done to Carolyn. Pushing that thought to the back of my mind, I follow her out to the porch, where I hand a mug of steaming hot coffee to Gordon and keep one for myself.

Gordon and Helen are deep in conversation and hardly bother to acknowledge our presence, which is fine by me. I am only too happy to let them talk. Carolyn finds a chair and joins them at the far end of the porch. I make myself comfortable on the porch steps and sip my coffee while staring at Diana's cottage.

I can't help thinking that Gordon is a good man, but he can be overbearing at times, and I am still smarting from his remarks regarding Diana and me. The last thing I want to do is cause Diana more pain, but I cannot help resenting him for interfering in our lives, no matter how good his intentions. He has made it clear that I am not welcome here and that the sooner I return to Cruzeiro do Sul, the better.

I'm still pondering these things when Gordon downs the last of his coffee and hands his empty mug to Helen. Getting to his feet, he says, "Well, I best be going." Turning to me, he continues in a hopeful tone, "I couldn't help noticing your packs. Have you decided to return to Cruzeiro do Sul?"

"Don't you wish," I say, taking a perverse pleasure when I see a momentary flicker of disappointment cloud his features.

Ever the peacemaker, Helen hastens to add, "Bryan and I are going upriver in the morning in search of our father's grave."

Visibly concerned, he turns to me. "Bryan, do you think that's wise? A trek upriver is a risky venture anytime, but during the rainy season, it's doubly dangerous." When I don't respond, he presses me, "Are you sure you know what you're getting yourself into?"

He's right, of course, but I brush his concerns aside. With a feigned confidence, I assure him I have things well under control. He's unconvinced, and seeing he's making no headway with me, he turns to Helen. "I realize how desperately you want to see where your father is buried, but I beg you to reconsider. In my estimation, your chances of finding your father's grave and returning safely are no better than fifty/fifty at best."

Although I have already detailed the dangers to Helen, Gordon's concern seems to affect her in a way my warnings did not. I watch as she chews the corner of her bottom lip—a habit she's had since childhood and a sure sign she's stressed. Pressing his advantage, Gordon urges her to think of her children. "You know how hard it was to grow up without your father. Surely you don't want your boys to grow up without their mother."

When Helen continues to vacillate, he tries another tack. "I realize Bryan's capable, but he's no *mateiro*. A venture like this would be dangerous with the most experienced *mateiro* to guide you, but without a skilled guide, it is sheer foolishness! If anything goes wrong, Bryan will be hard pressed to rectify the situation."

"That's enough, Gordon," I say, anger giving my words a hard edge. Although I agree with his assessment, I resent him rubbing my nose in it.

Finally, he sighs in exasperation before descending the porch steps. He has taken no more than two or three steps down the path before he stops and turns back toward us. "What you are proposing to do is more dangerous than you can imagine. I implore you to reconsider. I would hate for anything to happen to either of you." When neither of us responds, he turns and walks toward the small house he shares with his wife, Eleanor.

Chapter 21

Later that afternoon, Gordon returns and hands Helen an envelope with her name on it. "This came for you. It was in that bundle of mail Bryan brought from Cruzeiro do Sul. I didn't get a chance to go through it until a little while ago." With that he turns and heads toward Diana's clinic to deliver her mail.

Once he has gone, Helen opens the envelope and extracts the letter. As she reads it, her face turns deathly pale, and her breathing becomes shallow and erratic. Carolyn starts toward her, but she motions her away. With an effort, she composes herself before carefully refolding the letter and placing it in the envelope. A tear leaks from the corner of her eye, and she quickly brushes it away before stepping off the porch. I watch as she strides determinedly down the path toward the river. My heart tells me I should go after her, but I hesitate. Whatever is bothering her is probably none of my business—or so I tell myself. Besides, I never know what to say in situations like this.

Yet I cannot help remembering how many times I walked away when the last thing in the world I wanted was to be alone. How my heart yearned for someone to care enough to come after me. No one ever did except Carolyn, and I shoved her away. How different my life might have been had I responded differently. Instead of pain, there might have been hope. Instead of loneliness, there might have been love. Regret woos me, and for a moment I am tempted to wallow in self-pity, but with an effort I resist it. What's done is done, and no amount of regret can change it.

Out of the corner of my eye, I see Carolyn watching me. Her face is full of sadness—a sadness I put there—and I would give almost anything if I could undo the hurtful things I've done. She has every right to despise me, but what I see in her eyes is not disgust, but compassion, maybe even love. Although how she could love me after the way I've hurt her is more than I can imagine.

Crossing the small porch, she tentatively places her hand on my arm. The warmth of her touch resurrects memories better left buried, and I am tempted to walk away. Instead, I will myself not to overreact as I continue staring at the spot where Helen disappeared as she fled down the path toward the river. "Go to her, Bryan," Carolyn urges me. "She needs you."

I hesitate a moment more, torn between the man I used to be and the man I am becoming. The man I used to be would ignore Helen's pain as well as Carolyn's gentle prompting, but I will no longer allow myself to do that. Although I am my father's son—his genes being deeply imbedded in my psyche—I yearn to be different. The father I knew as a child was a stern man, unable to show affection except on rare occasions. As a result, I grew up bent, and like him, I have difficulty expressing my deepest feelings. It's easier to just walk away. Even now, I am tempted to leave Helen to fend for herself, but I won't. No matter how difficult it is, I am determined to be there for her.

Taking a deep breath, I step off the porch and start down the path in search of her. As I near the river, I see her huddled on a sandbar. Her knees are drawn up, with her arms clasped tightly around them, and she is crying harshly. Seeing her like that is ripping my heart out. I can only imagine what tragic news that letter may have contained. Maybe something terrible has happened to one of the boys. Maybe Rob has been in a fatal auto accident. Maybe...

Not knowing how to comfort her, I simply sit down beside her and put my arm around her shoulders. When I do, she collapses against me, seeming to take comfort from my presence. After a time, her harsh crying subsides into soft sobs and finally ceases.

Without a word, she hands me the envelope, wrinkled and tear stained. When I hesitate, she motions for me to open it. Dreading what the letter might contain, I slowly extract it from the envelope and unfold it. The single sentence seems to leap off the page at me, and in an instant, I appreciate Helen's distress. *"A word to the wise: When the cat's away, the mice will play."* It was signed, *"A Concerned Friend."*

Although the message is deliberately ambiguous, its meaning is plain enough. If the "concerned friend" is not exaggerating or being disingenuous, it appears Helen's suspicions regarding Rob and Rita were well justified. I don't want to believe Rob is capable of this kind of betrayal, but it seems obvious something is amiss. I'm stunned. How could he do something like this to Helen or to the boys? Handing the letter back to her, I ask, "What are you going to do?"

Without answering, she gets to her feet, walks to the river's edge, and stares across its wide expanse. After a few minutes, she rejoins me on the sandbar, and we sit in silence with our backs against a large driftwood log. I want to say something to comfort her, but words fail me. Anything I can think of seems trite. After a time, her grief morphs into anger, which gives way to a grim determination. Finally, she says, "I want to go home immediately. I'm not going to let that evil woman steal my husband and destroy our family."

Chapter 22

When we return to Whittaker House, Carolyn is already packing our supplies and equipment. With a perception I am only now learning to appreciate, she has correctly discerned our situation and is making preparations for an early departure downriver. She pauses when we walk in and glances a question in Helen's direction. Helen seems not to notice, and without a word, she continues toward the small room at the back of the house that serves as her sleeping quarters. Although she has closed the curtain that serves as a door, we can hear her muttering angrily as she slams her personal gear into her backpack.

I would like to tell Carolyn what is going on, but I don't feel it's my place. If Helen wants to confide in her, she will have to do it herself. "Things have changed at home," I say as I survey the packs Carolyn has readied for transporting to the boat. "Helen wants to head back as quickly as possible. We will leave for Cruzeiro do Sul at first light."

While Carolyn continues packing our gear, I begin moving it down to the river. It is nearly dark when I place the last of our things in the boat and secure it for the night. Hordes of insects swarm around my head, and I am tempted to return to Whittaker House to escape them, but I decide against it. I need some time alone to sort through my feelings. It turns out nothing is as it seemed. I always saw Rob and Helen as the perfect couple, and now I find out their marriage is in trouble. As implausible as it seems, Rob may be involved with his secretary. I could never have imagined that, not in a thousand years.

Then there's Carolyn. Given the way I treated her as our marriage was ending, I assumed she hated me, and with good reason. Much to my surprise, I discover she has become a believer, and on top of that, she and Helen have become best friends. To make things even more confusing, Helen claims that Carolyn is still in love with me. That's hardly likely, but I have to admit that while Carolyn has gone out of her way to appear nonchalant toward me, I have sensed a growing attraction. To be perfectly honest, being around her has been more than a little disconcerting. Although our marriage was a shipwreck, I find I still have feelings for her. Not love necessarily, but compassion, maybe even pity. Of course, I would never allow myself to become involved with her, and I am sure she feels the same way about me. Still, the emotions she's stirred in me are confusing, especially considering my feelings for Diana.

While trying to make sense of all of this, I have been gathering driftwood in preparation for building a fire, in hopes the smoke will discourage the ravenous insects that are nearly driving me mad. Moving quickly, I arrange the driftwood before placing a handful of dry grass and some small twigs beneath it. I strike a match, being careful to shield it from the wind, and ignite the grass. In almost no time, I have a small but smoky fire. I squat close to it and endure the smoke, hoping it will disperse the insects.

It is fully dark now, and the forest is alive with a cacophony of night sounds—the bark of a spiny tree rat, the call of an owl, hoatzins hissing and huffing in a grove of mungubas, and a dozen caimans croaking on the other side of the meander. Familiar sounds I remember from my childhood, and comforting.

Suddenly the night is rent by the bloodcurdling scream of a panther. In an instant, I am carried back to the night Diana and I spent on the side of a steep, rain-soaked mountain. We were both injured—she with a concussion and a broken leg. I had severely injured my knee while plunging down the mountain in an ill-fated attempt to rescue her. Sometime in the middle of the night, a sense of danger had jerked me awake, and I reached for my rifle. Staring into the darkness, I spotted a pair of yellow eyes glowing in the night. I barely had time to raise my rifle before that big cat launched himself at me. I don't remember firing, but I saw the muzzle flash an instant before he crashed into me. When he bowled me over, I thought I was a goner, but by some miracle I had killed him with my first shot. He was already dead when he hit me.

The panther screams again, somewhat nearer this time, jerking me back to the present, and I find myself wishing for my rifle. Unfortunately, it's back at the house. I ended up leaving it there when I had too much to carry on my final trip to the boat. Reminding myself that it is usually only old or crippled panthers that attack humans helps ease my mind;

nonetheless, I hastily add more fuel to the fire and position myself so the river is at my back and the fire is between the jungle and me.

I listen intently, but all I hear is the buzzing of insects and the sound of the river. In the distance, I hear the screech of a nightjar—what the natives call a *Rasga mortalb*. Well do I remember the first time I heard it. Lako and I were sitting around our campfire deep in the jungle when I heard what sounded like someone tearing a piece of cloth. Startled, I blurted out, "What was that?" Giving me a strange look, Lako said, "That's the bird of death. Soon someone is going to die."

Of course, I dismissed his words as primitive superstition, but now they return to haunt me. Given the dangers we will face on the flood-swollen Ria Moa on our return trip to Cruzeiro do Sul, I can't help thinking that death is a very real possibility. I don't mean to be melodramatic, but the danger is real and can't be ignored.

With our departure just hours away, I find my thoughts turning toward Diana and what a confusing hodgepodge they are. I am nearly sick with wanting to see her, and yet I cannot imagine what possible good could come of it. I cannot think of a single thing we haven't already said, and when I remember our last parting, the pain is nearly more than I can bear. I don't think either of us could go through that again.

Reason tells me that no matter how much we love each other, our situation is impossible. Yet I am tempted to think there must be some possibility we have overlooked, some solution we haven't considered. My heart tells me love will find a way—although I cannot imagine what it might be—and I am almost willing to risk whatever pain and disappointment rejection might bring on the off chance that we could build a life together. A saner part of me reminds me that I am not the only one at risk here, and I cannot bear the thought that I might break Diana's heart yet again.

Like a damaged record, my mind replays Gordon's rebuke over and over again: *"I don't suppose you meant to hurt her, but it doesn't really matter. The truth is, you wounded her in ways that may have damaged her permanently. It's like she's sleepwalking, just going through the motions. If it wasn't for Eurico, I don't know what she might have done. Hurt herself maybe. That little guy's been her salvation."*

With an effort, I put his words out of my mind and poke at the dying coals with a long stick, sending a shower of sparks upward. Belatedly I add more driftwood to the fire. When it is blazing brightly, I arrange my lengthy body into a more comfortable position on the damp riverbank and try to imagine what might have been if I had chosen differently.

Had I been willing to join Diana on the mission field, we might have adopted Eurico and built a life of our own. Although I cannot imagine myself as a missionary per se, I am handy, and my skills would have proved useful, especially in a primitive place like the far western Amazon Basin. Freed from the mundane tasks of survival, Diana could have devoted herself to caring for her patients.

Try as I might, I can't make myself believe it would have ever worked out. No matter how much I love her, I can't imagine spending my life in a Godforsaken place like this.

Nor could I allow her to give up her missionary calling to practice medicine in the States. In time, she would have come to resent me, and the love we shared would have died a slow and bitter death, tainting whatever good memories we shared. As hideously painful as our parting was, it is better this way. Better a clean break than a slow death—or so I tell myself.

Chapter 23

It is still dark, and a thick layer of low-hanging clouds is threatening rain as Carolyn and I climb into our small boat. Helen holds it steady as Carolyn makes a nest for herself among the supplies. I make my way to the stern, where I check the connection on the gas line. Satisfied, I tug on the pull cord again and again. To my disgust, the outboard engine refuses to start. I pump the bulb on the gas line and fiddle with the choke before jerking on the pull cord yet again. This time the engine sputters and coughs, spewing an oily cloud of exhaust before finally settling into a steady rhythm. I nod at Helen, and she shoves us off before stepping into the boat.

This is the third day we have spent on the river since leaving the mission compound. The weather has been miserable, with a steady drizzle drenching us from morning till night, and it looks like we are in for more of the same today. As I turn the boat down river, I can't help comparing the miserable weather to the melancholy mood that has settled upon us. It started with Helen, and like a contagious infection, it spread to Carolyn, and now it has infected me. The rain may chill our bodies, but this dark mood chills our souls and drains our spirit.

It is so unlike the excitement and sense of adventure that characterized our earlier trip upriver. Helen had been nearly giddy with excitement, and her enthusiasm infused us all. After more than twenty years, she was returning to the place where she grew up. She passed the endless hours in the boat by regaling us with long-forgotten memories from her childhood on the banks of the Rio Moa, deep in the far western Amazon Basin. Her memories, unlike mine, were filled with light and laughter, and I couldn't help wondering if we grew up in the same family. More likely, the difference was perspective—she chose to remember positive experiences while I did the opposite. As a result, she has always been an optimistic person, unlike me.

Unfortunately, our mother's death and her troubled marriage have combined to knock the wind out of her. The anonymous letter she received a few days ago was simply the last straw. No matter how hard she tries, she can't stop replaying it over and over in her mind: *"A word to the wise: When the cat's away, the mice will play."* Now she vacillates between abject despair and seething anger.

Carolyn has attempted to cheer her up, but to no avail. I haven't fared any better. Several times I pointed out things I thought might capture her attention—a primitive homestead with a canoe pulled up on the riverbank, a huge anaconda swimming in the murky water in the flooded rain forest, a blue morpho butterfly. Although she showed little or no interest, I still regaled her with information I had learned from Dr. Peterson. I told her that the blue morpho is among the largest butterflies in the world, with wings spanning from five to eight inches. I pointed out that their vivid, iridescent blue coloring was a result of the microscopic scales on the backs of their wings, which reflect light. Normally, sighting such an exotic species would have excited her, and she would have asked a hundred questions. Now she simply grunts while scanning the Rio Moa with unseeing eyes, her thoughts a million miles away.

We spend the rest of the afternoon in silence, huddled under our ponchos as the rain continues to fall, and it is nearly dark as I scan the riverbank for a suitable campsite. I have been so preoccupied with concern for Helen that I haven't paid much attention to the weather. Belatedly, I realize a storm is brewing, and overhead the sky is boiling with dark and ominous clouds. The wind is roaring, whipping the rain-swollen Rio Moa into a mass of whitecaps, and our small boat is taking a terrible beating. Lightning streaks across the sky, and thunder explodes overhead. Suddenly the sky erupts in a full-fledged deluge, and the driving rain nearly blinds me. Our ponchos offer some protection, but not much, and the rain stings like pellets. I fight to keep our boat from capsizing while desperately searching for a place to beach it.

Lightning momentarily illuminates the darkness, and I catch a glimpse of Helen and Carolyn desperately clinging to the boat to keep from being pitched overboard. I tear my eyes away from them just in time to see a huge tree crashing toward us. The surging current has undercut its root ball, and the sixty- and seventy-mile-per-hour wind has uprooted it. I have only an instant to react, and I desperately attempt to turn the boat, but the current is too strong. It catches the boat broadside and flips it over just as the huge tree crashes down on us, driving our capsized boat deep under the surface of the river.

The force of the massive tree takes me deep underwater, and I desperately search the murky depths for Carolyn and Helen until my lungs are about to burst. Frantically I lunge for the surface, where I take greedy gulps of air before plunging back down into the blackness. Helen is a strong swimmer, and she may be able to save herself, but I have no idea whether Carolyn can swim or not. Desperately I search the dark water, but I can't see a thing. There's no sign of either of them.

My lungs are on fire, my muscles are cramping, and I am beyond exhaustion, but I refuse to give up. Each time I fight my way back to the surface, I scream their names as loudly as I can, until my throat is raw, but it is no use. The rush of the river and the roaring of the wind drown out my cries. Taking a huge gulp of air, I plunge beneath the surface one final time, where I search frantically in the darkness for any sign of them.

Having exhausted all hope of saving either of them, I attempt to swim to shore, but I don't have the strength. The current is strong, and it carries me downstream as the storm continues to roar. I can hear trees crashing in the jungle as the wind-driven rain hammers the river. An occasional streak of lightning momentarily illuminates the darkness, and I strain to scan the river for some sign of Helen or Carolyn, but it is no use. The rain blinds me. I don't want to believe it, but I fear they have drowned, and with that knowledge a black despair threatens to overwhelm me. I am beyond exhausted, both physically and emotionally, and I am tempted to give up, to allow myself to succumb to the paralyzing cold and numbness, to just let my battered body sink into the depths of this dark river.

But I don't. Each time the surging river attempts to suck me into its depths, my will exerts itself. Instead of giving up and yielding to the oblivion of death, I find myself choking and gagging as I fight to keep my head above the surface of the river so I can suck in another gulp of life-sustaining oxygen. This vile river may take my life, but not without a fight. No matter how exhausted I am, or how heavy and waterlogged my clothes become, I will never give up. My only hope now is to try to stay afloat until the river makes a sharp turn carrying me close to the bank. When it does, I may be able to grasp a low-hanging branch and pull myself onto solid ground.

I don't know how long I fight to stay afloat—forever, it seems—and when I began to cramp, I fear the end is near. The pain is excruciating, knotting my muscles, making it nearly impossible for me to keep my head above the surface of the river. As the current is sucking me down, for what I fear may be the last time, I fling myself upward, thrashing about with a superhuman effort. Suddenly a jagged flash of lightning illuminates the night, and I see a huge log rolling in the current. Desperately I hurl myself at it, realizing it is my only hope. Somehow, I manage to make it to the log. It is slick, and no matter how hard I try, I can't get a grip. I claw at it, digging my fingernails into the wet bark. For an instant, it seems I have a grip, and I fight to hang on even as I feel myself slipping. I try to wrap my arm around it, but I am paralyzed with cramps and I can't lift my arm high enough to get it around the log. I scream in frustration and pain as the log slips away, breaking and tearing my fingernails. At the last instant, my jacket snags on a broken limb that is jutting out of the log, and I find myself being dragged down the river.

Knowing my jacket could rip loose at any moment, I desperately fight to get a grip on the branch. It is about the size of a man's wrist and jagged on the end where my jacket is caught. Somehow, I manage to wrap my torn fingers around it, but it is slick, and I know I will never be able to maintain my grip if my jacket tears loose. Somehow, I have to hook my arm over that branch—it is the only way I can be sure of hanging on. Gritting my teeth, I fight to lift my arm, then scream in pain when cramps knot my muscles. For an instant, I lose my grip, and only my jacket keeps me from being swept away.

My muscles are knotted with cramps, and my torn fingers are stiff with cold, still I manage to get a grip on the branch once again. Realizing I will never be able to lift my arm high enough to get it over the branch until the cramps exhaust themselves, I tighten my grip and pray. After a while, the cramps begin to ease a little, and I decide to give it another try. Gritting my teeth against the pain, I force my elbow up and over the branch and pull my battered body against the log.

I must have passed out, for when I come to, the storm has spent itself, and a full moon makes the night nearly as bright as day. The storm-swollen Rio Moa is as powerful as ever, but a sharp bend in the river has created an eddy that is now pushing the log into the bank. Carefully I work my jacket loose from where it is snagged and shove off the log toward the shore. Near the bank, I manage to take hold of some low-hanging branches and pull myself out of the river, where I collapse on the muddy ground.

I am wet, cold, and totally exhausted. My entire body is covered with gooseflesh, my teeth are chattering, and I'm shivering uncontrollably. I force myself to my feet and stumble into the jungle in search of some kind of shelter. Given my wet clothes and exposed position, hypothermia is a real danger. Thankfully, it has stopped raining; nonetheless, the ground is soaked, and finding any kind of shelter that is somewhat dry may be impossible.

The terrain near the river is flat and tangled with undergrowth. Without a machete, the going is tough. Although the moon is full, almost no light penetrates the dense foliage overhead, and I can hardly see my hand in front of my face. Nonetheless, I forge ahead, knowing to do otherwise is to die.

Finally, I stumble upon a downed tree with an enormous root ball taller than my head. Some earlier storm must have taken it down, for the roots overhead are interwoven with a thick layer of leafy vines, and the ground beneath them is nearly dry and covered with a heavy layer of leaves. It looks inviting, but I hesitate. Without a light, I can't be sure it is uninhabited, and it seems a likely place for a snake. I am shivering uncontrollably, and after a moment I throw caution to the wind and crawl in, burrowing deep into the dry leaves in an attempt to warm myself.

Chapter 24

At the first hint of daylight, I force myself to crawl out of the root ball where I spent the night. My clothes are wet, and I am cold, but nothing like last night. Immediately my thoughts turn to Carolyn and my sister. Reason tells me they have drowned, but I refuse to accept it. I have survived and one or both of them may have escaped the river, as well. It's not likely, but I cling to that slim possibility like a drowning man clings to a life preserver. Even now, they may be huddled on the riverbank, waiting for me to find them.

With that thought in mind, I retrace my steps toward the river. The undergrowth is dense, and without a machete to hack my way through it, the going is rough. I scramble over rocks and crawl under branches. Thorns tear at my clothes. Occasionally I stick my hand into a nettle and get stung, but I keep going. Finally, I stand on the bank above the eddy and scan both sides of the river for any sign of Helen or Carolyn. There is nothing—not a scrap of clothing or a bit of debris from the boat, or a tendril of smoke. Desperately I scream their names until my throat is raw, but there is no response.

Although I am exhausted from my ordeal in the river, I force myself to spend the entire day searching the riverbank and the encroaching jungle for any sign of them. It is early evening when I finally give up and seek a sheltered place to spend the night. The sun has warmed my body and dried my clothes somewhat, but now it is starting to rain again, and I must find shelter, or I will suffer another miserable night, wet and cold.

It is nearly dark when I stumble onto a shallow cave cut into the side of a small hill. The opening was obscured by a tangle of vines, and I almost miss it. It is barely deep enough for me to crawl into, but it will protect me from the rain.

My stomach is growling with hunger as I try to make myself comfortable inside my cramped shelter. All I've had to eat since our boat capsized was some partially spoiled fruit that I was able to pick up off the ground along with some wild berries. It was tasty enough, but it did little to satisfy my hunger. If I am going to survive, I will have to do better than that.

I may have escaped the river, but I'm not out of the woods yet. I have nothing—no food, no equipment, no compass, and no way to start a fire—just the clothes on my back. My best chance of being rescued is to stay close to the river. There's not a lot of boat traffic this time of the year, but it's my only hope. No one will find me if I wander around in the jungle.

Lying in the darkness, I berate myself for my stupidity. According to Lako, the first rule of survival is to have an emergency pack. Well do I remember his careful instructions: "If you have an accident," he said, "your emergency pack is the only thing between you and death. It should have a first aid kit, a cigarette lighter and/or matches, a small supply of rice, beans, smoked fish, drinking water, mosquito nets, ponchos, a machete, and a flashlight. Pack it with balsa wood chips to make it buoyant. It must be waterproof or have a waterproof rubber liner. If you are in a boat, it should be fastened to you with a cord or a strap at all times."

We had a well-stocked emergency pack, but I didn't bother to attach it to myself or to one of the others, and now I am suffering the consequences. Without any way to make a fire, I am cold and hungry, and without mosquito nets, I am being eaten alive.

Lying in the darkness, I'm blindsided by a wave of grief when I think of Helen and Carolyn. I can't help blaming myself. I never should have agreed to take them to the mission compound in the first place. Helen's threat to buy a boat and go upriver on her own was a hollow one, and I knew it. If that had been possible, she would have already done it, rather than wasting time hanging around Cruzeiro do Sul until I showed up. So, why did I give in to her against my better judgment? I wish I knew—guilt, maybe, for never being there for her when she needed me. Whatever the reason, it was the worst decision of my life. As a result, Helen and Carolyn are most likely dead, and I will have to live with that if I survive.

I've never been one to weep, but now great sobs rack my body, and I bend double with grief. I can't help thinking what this is going to do to Helen's boys. The accidental death of a parent can be a crippling blow to a child, sometimes scarring him for life. It may even cause him to lose his faith. I should know. That's what happened to me.

And now it's happening again. My newfound faith is shaken. Once more, I feel God has betrayed me. How could He fail to protect Helen when He knows how much her boys need their mother—and if someone had to die, why not me? Surely, I deserved death more than she did, and more than Carolyn for certain. Through clenched teeth, I groan, "Would to God I had died in their stead."

I don't know how I'm going to face Rob. How will I explain to him that I let Helen drown? He will blame me. But he's not innocent, either, and that thought makes me mad. If he hadn't been fooling around with his secretary, Helen never would have come to the Amazon. Now I turn my anger on him and his pigheaded behavior. Around and around my emotions go, a deadly cocktail of grief and anger.

Whatever progress I have made toward becoming a whole man is now at risk. All my old resentments are boiling up again. The only difference is that this time I blame myself rather than my father. Of course, I hold God ultimately responsible, for He has all the power. He could have prevented this tragedy, but He did nothing. At least that's how it seems to me.

Chapter 25

When I crawl out of my shallow cave, I note with thankfulness that the sky is clear above the towering *samauma* trees. A day without rain would be a blessing, allowing my tattered clothes to fully dry. A more serious concern is my feet. My hiking boots are soaked, and walking in them all day yesterday has rubbed my feet raw. I would like to take them off and check my feet, but I decide against it. I have no medicine, so what's the point? Besides, if I remove my boots, I may not be able to get them on again.

Gritting my teeth against the pain, I start walking. The trail I follow is overgrown, and it looks like it hasn't been used in years. After about twenty minutes, I push through a tangle of vines and step into a small clearing. Across the way, I see a log situated in direct sunlight, and I limp toward it. Easing myself to the ground, I sit with my back against it with my legs stretched out before me. The sun is bright, and I luxuriate in its warmth. Later today, I may curse the heat, but right now I gladly soak it up.

A hundred feet overhead, the treetops are alive with a troop of red howler monkeys, the air thick with their musk—a mix of body odor, urine, and feces. The smell is enough to gag me, but it is their screaming that grates on my nerves and makes my head ache. Dr. Peterson likened it to the sound of a demonic wind screaming through the rigging of a ship. He said it was their way of staking out their territory. I'm tempted to move on to escape them, but the sun is warm, and I have no energy; besides, there's no guarantee they won't follow me.

I haven't eaten anything other than a handful of berries and some half-rotten fruit in nearly forty-eight hours, and I am faint with hunger. What I wouldn't give for a sirloin steak and a baked potato with butter and sour cream. Right now, I would even settle for some of Komi's roast monkey, two or three live tree grubs, plump and wiggly, and a swig of Lako's premasticated manioc drink. Since thinking about food simply aggregates my hunger, I push all thoughts of eating out of my mind and try to concentrate on the situation at hand.

When I do, a fresh wave of grief hits me. Once more, I castigate myself. Helen and Carolyn have most likely drowned, and it's my fault. Had I been more observant, I would have seen the storm building and sought shelter before it hit. Had I been a more experienced boatman, I wouldn't have overreacted and capsized our boat. Had I been more vigilant, I surely could have saved one or both of them. Had I been... The list of my failures and shortcomings goes on and on. The more I think about it, the more debilitated I become.

I am nearly paralyzed with regret, and I might have spent the entire day wallowing in self-pity had I not recalled something my father wrote in one of his journal entries. I don't know what brought it to mind—the Holy Spirit, maybe—but once I thought of it, I couldn't get it out of my mind. I can't recall his exact words, but the essence is clear in my mind: *"If only" are the two saddest words in the human vocabulary. They focus on the past, and the past can't be changed. Try replacing "if only" with "next time." "Next time" focuses on the future, and with God's help I will do better. I will learn from my failures, but they will not define me. My past will not determine my destiny!*

Reaching inside my shirt, I finger the alabaster cross my father bequeathed to me. I can almost hear him say, "Be a man of God, Bryan Whittaker, be a man of God." I'm not sure I know how to be a man of God, but I know it won't happen if I sit here feeling sorry for myself. I may never become the man of God my father envisioned, but it won't be because I didn't try.

With renewed determination, I push my self-incriminating thoughts aside and turn my attention to my situation. If I'm going to survive, I will need all my wits about me. The nearest help is at the mission compound, at least a three-day journey upriver by boat, maybe longer given the flooded river's strong current. Without a boat, the only way is a trek through the jungle. That's probably a six or seven-day ordeal, and there's not even a hint of civilization between here and there. My other option is going downriver toward Cruzeiro do Sul. It is farther, but there are a number of primitive homesteads scattered along the river in that direction. My best hope is to try to make it to one of them.

Having finally made a decision, I push myself to my feet and turn toward the river, hunger gnawing at my belly. High overhead, the monkeys are screeching and feasting on fruit impossible for me to reach. The ground is littered with their discards, and I search among them for something salvageable. Here and there, I spot a piece of half-eaten fruit, and I quickly devour it, trying not to think about what I'm doing.

I can't help thinking that I could probably eliminate two or three days' travel if I cut through the jungle, as opposed to following the river's meanderings. It's tempting, but a saner part of me knows it's foolish. Without a compass, I could easily wander around in circles. Besides, I'm hoping to be rescued by a passing boat, or to stumble onto a homestead, which makes following the river the logical thing to do.

I retrace my steps from yesterday, and by mid-afternoon I find myself back at the river. For several minutes, I scan the riverbank, searching once more for some sign of Helen or Carolyn. I know it's a long shot, but I can't help myself. Against all reason, I refuse to give up hope. Somehow, some way, they may have survived. Of course, I see nothing, not even a hint that would indicate they are alive, and my heart is heavy when I finally head downriver.

If this was the dry season, I could walk on a sandy beach at the river's edge, but now it's underwater. In fact, the flood-waters of the Rio Moa cover a wide expanse of the river margin, and I am forced to fight my way through a tangle of underbrush as I follow its meanderings.

Without a cleared trail, walking is not easy, and I run into dead ends—impassable bushes, an impenetrable thicket of bamboo, and a tangle of uprooted trees. When I do, I have no choice but to retrace my steps and try to find a way around these barriers. All of this is exhausting and makes for slow going, not to mention it is time consuming. To complicate things, I must constantly be on the lookout. Danger is everywhere. The river margin is a favorite haunt for wild boars, crocodiles, anacondas, and various poisonous snakes.

If Lako were here, he would know what to do, and I rack my brain for any tidbits of knowledge I might have gleaned from him. Unfortunately, when we were together, I was so consumed with my own issues that I didn't pay him much mind. Now all I can remember is a disgusting concoction he made from boiled and mashed manioc roots. To prepare it, he put huge wads of the mashed roots into his mouth to collect his saliva, then he spit it back into the mixing bowl to start the digestive process. The object was to create a food source that provided quick energy. It tasted terrible, but it worked!

As I hike through the tangled underbrush near the river margin, I rack my brain trying to recall what he said about the manioc plant. If I remember correctly, it's indigenous to the Amazon Basin—a bush of some kind. He might have even pointed it out to me. That being the case, I may be able to find some growing wild. Of course, I have no way of making a fire, so if I am lucky enough to come across some of the bushes, I will have to eat the roots raw.

I haven't made a lot of progress, but knowing how quickly darkness comes in the Amazon, I begin searching for a place to spend the night. I'm having trouble finding anything suitable, and it is almost dark when I encounter a tangle of downed trees blocking my way. My initial reaction is frustration. There is no way I can safely climb over them. I can't risk it. If I fell and broke an ankle or a leg, I would be done for. Weary as I am, I prepare to force my way through the dense undergrowth in an attempt to work my way around the downed trees. When I do, I realize that what I've been considering an insurmountable obstacle may actually be the shelter I've been seeking.

Lying down on my belly, I attempt to worm my way under the outer rim of the fallen trees. It's no use. There's simply not enough room. I start digging, using my hands in an attempt to create enough space for me to slip through. Although the ground is not particularly hard, it is intertwined with all manner of roots. Given my injured fingers, digging is excruciatingly painful, and I'm making little progress. I need something to dig with, a sharp rock or a stout stick.

The ground is littered with broken branches, and I soon find a stout one that has a jagged point on one end. Wielding it like a pick, I attack the ground with renewed vigor. In short order, I have enlarged the space beneath the fallen tree's huge trunk just enough for me to slip under it.

There's just a hint of daylight left, and I work quickly to enlarge my den. By breaking off a number of dead branches from overhead, I create enough space to allow me to sit up. Then I turn my attention to the ground. To my surprise, it is surprisingly dry—just a little damp. After removing some debris to make my "bed" more comfortable, I scatter leaves that I hope will protect me from the dampness. If it rains during the night, I will probably get wet, but the tangled mass overhead should give me some protection.

Tomorrow I will have to search for food. Hopefully, I can find some edible berries or some fruit that is within reach. Manioc roots may be my best bet; unfortunately, I am not sure what a manioc bush looks like. I'm still contemplating other possible sources of food when an exhausted sleep overtakes me.

Sometime later, I awake to the sound of snorting and grunting. The moon is bright, but it sheds little light on the floor of the rain forest, and I can see almost nothing. No matter. My ears tell me everything I need to know. A wild boar has caught my scent and is aggressively attacking the tangle of fallen trees in an attempt to get to me. I sense more than see an ugly snout with sharp tusks rutting around in the space I enlarged in order to belly-crawl under the tangle of fallen trees. His strength is enormous, and dirt flies in all directions as he thrusts his head from side to side. He is wild with bloodlust, and his vicious grunts and foul breath make me sick with fear.

My first instinct is to retreat, and I press my back against a tangle of branches as far as possible from the opening where he is digging. In less than a minute, he has enlarged it enough to thrust his ugly head into my cramped space. Sensing victory, he renews his efforts, flinging tangled roots and dirt in all directions. If I don't do something and do it quickly, he will work his way under the huge tree's fallen truck. When he does, his ugly tusks and sharp teeth will make short work of me.

My heart is racing as I fumble in the dark for the stout branch I used as a digging tool. It's not much of a weapon, but it's all I have. Grasping my digging stick as tightly as I can with both hands, I stab at the huge boar's tiny eyes with all my might, the force of my thrust vibrating in my arms and shoulders. The boar jerks his head back, roaring with pain and rage, and I hear him crashing through the underbrush as he runs off.

My legs are trembling, and I feel weak in the aftermath of the adrenaline rush. After a few minutes, my heart rate returns to normal, but I don't relax my vigilance. I don't think he will return tonight, but I'm not taking any chances.

Chapter 26

DENVER, COLORADO
1971

Rob studies himself in the full-length mirror. The dark blue, three-piece suit is conservative without being too severe, the shirt and tie carefully coordinated, the shoes stylish. There is absolutely no hint of timidity, no suggestion of guilty uncertainty, not even a shadow of fear, yet on the inside he feels like a man preparing for his last meal. Fragments of misapplied Scripture haunt him: *"....He was numbered with the transgressors....He was despised and rejected of men....he was brought as a lamb to the slaughter...."*

Putting those thoughts out of his mind, he picks up his briefcase and leaves the hotel room. The drive to District Headquarters is accomplished mechanically, and all too soon he finds himself easing his two-year-old Cutlass into a cramped parking space. Glancing at his watch, he realizes he is almost fifteen minutes early, so he decides to remain in the car rather than endure the humiliation of facing his peers a moment before it is absolutely necessary. Unfortunately, the frigid temperatures soon force him to change his mind, and he carefully makes his way across the icy parking lot toward the District Office.

As he waits in the outer office, the members of the presbytery board begin arriving, and his apprehension increases as he watches them file into the conference room. They are his colleagues—or at least they were. He has served on the presbytery board with them, and yet today they will sit in judgment on him.

Occasional bursts of laughter punctuate the indistinguishable drone of conversation that filters out of the conference room, aggravating his anxiety as the minutes drag by. With an effort, he forces himself to appear at ease, but on the inside the acid of regret eats at him. Extracting a roll of antacids from his coat pocket, he breaks off five or six and hastily chews them, seeking some relief. It is futile, for his painful discomfort is much deeper than indigestion.

A scene from Shakespeare's *Macbeth* fills his mind, and he watches in tormented fascination as Lady Macbeth, unable to sleep, walks back and forth in the lonely watches of the morning. As she paces, she rubs her hands and moans unhappily, "Out damned spot! Out I say! Here's the smell of blood still! All the perfumes of Arabia will not sweeten this little hand."

Then he sees himself—haggard, driven by despair, full of regret, knowing full well the die is cast, that it is probably too late to save his ministry. He can't help thinking this is how Esau must have felt: "For ye know how that afterward, when he would have inherited the blessing, he was rejected: for he found no place of repentance, though he sought it carefully with tears."

The protracted delay is a two-edged sword, postponing the inevitable confrontation, yet every minute feeds fresh fuel into his already overactive imagination. His stomach is on fire, forcing him to devour the remaining antacids. Nervousness tempts him to pace, but his pride refuses him this release. Picking up a church periodical, he thumbs through it, seeking something to read, but the words blur so he puts it down and yields to the tempting torment of hindsight.

For an awful minute, he hates Rita, he hates the January morning when she massaged his stiff neck, he hates the late-night dinner they shared at her house, and he hates the desperate love that binds them together. Most of all, he hates himself—hates his weakness, hates his need for her, and hates his inability to break it off. He feels trapped, and he hates that feeling too.

"Rob Thompson."

At the sound of his name, he looks up and sees Mike DuPree, one of the presbyters. "If you would come with me, please? We're ready to see you now."

Entering the conference room, he is a striking figure, the picture of confidence and composure, but on the inside, he is full of shame and self-loathing. George Chambers, the district superintendent, directs him to a chair at the end of the table with a wave of his hand and says, "I believe you know these gentlemen."

When Rob nods, he continues, "I'm sure all of us are aware of the purpose for this meeting. Still, allow me to begin by outlining the events that have brought us together. Approximately a week ago, I met with Paul Blair, Pastor Thompson's youth pastor, and Dave Underwood, one of the board members at the church. They asked to meet with me concerning Pastor Thompson's relationship with Rita Wallace, his secretary. Before contacting the District Office, they met with Pastor Thompson in an attempt to resolve their concerns. Unfortunately, nothing was resolved, and they felt they had no choice but to contact me. They also gave me a photograph of Pastor Thompson's car parked in Rita Wallace's driveway. There was a date and time stamped on the negative—February 24, 1:27 a.m. These are serious concerns, which, if proven, may require disciplinary action by this body."

Turning to Rob, he asks, "Would you like to respond?"

Very deliberately, Rob looks around the table, taking time to look each man in the eye, forcing them to either meet his gaze or look away. Finally he speaks, quoting King David, "For it was not an enemy that reproached me; then I could have borne it: neither was it he that hated me that did magnify himself against me; then I would have hid myself from him: But it was thou, a man mine equal, my guide, and mine acquaintance. We took sweet counsel together, and walked unto the house of God in company... Yea, mine own familiar friend, in whom I trusted, who did eat of my bread, hath lifted up his heel against me."

He pauses, letting his words sink in. "I thought you were my friends. I thought you knew me. I thought you knew the kind of man I am. Do you really believe I could betray my wife and humiliate my sons? Do you truly believe I would jeopardize my ministry and risk my family's financial security for a fling with my secretary? Do you really think I care so little about my relationship with the Lord? What kind of a man do you think I am?"

Reaching into his briefcase, he removes a fist-sized rock and places it in the center of the table. Slowly he looks around the table, pausing to look each man in the eye once more. "Let him who is without sin cast the first stone."

After a moment of stunned silence, the superintendent addresses him sternly. "Pastor Thompson, let me remind you that the presbyters are not on trial here. This meeting is about your actions and the charges that have been brought against you. Are we clear on that?"

For a moment, Rob stares at him before finally saying, "Yes, you've made yourself perfectly clear."

Picking up a yellow legal pad, the superintendent studies it for a moment before directing a series of questions at Rob. "What is your relationship with Rita Wallace?"

"She's my secretary."

"What were you doing at her house on the night of February twenty-third?"

"We were having dinner."

"At midnight?"

"Not by design. We had a lengthy board meeting. Then Dave Underwood asked to speak with me, so it was late when I finally got away from the church."

"Approximately what time was that?"

"At least ten thirty, maybe later."

"Do you think it appropriate to have a private dinner with your secretary in her home, especially at that time of night?"

"In retrospect, I would concede it was inadvisable. In fact, I considered canceling dinner when I realized how late it was, but I decided against it. Rita had gone to a lot of trouble, and I didn't feel right disappointing her."

"Has she ever prepared dinner for you and your wife?"

"No."

"Doesn't that seem strange to you?"

"What do you mean?"

"She's never prepared dinner for you and Helen, but once your wife is out of town, she makes a special meal just for you."

"When you put it that way, I suppose it does seem odd, but let me explain. On board meeting nights, I don't go home until after the meeting, which can be pretty late sometimes. Rita knows my mother puts the boys to bed early and then retires herself, so she offered to make dinner. At the time, I didn't give it a second thought. As far as I was concerned, she was just being kind."

"What time did you arrive at her home?"

"Maybe ten-forty-five."

"How long does it take to eat a leisurely dinner? Thirty minutes? Forty-five minutes? An hour at most?"

"Probably."

"For now, let's assume you spent one hour over dinner. You said you arrived at approximately ten-forty-five." When Rod nods an acknowledgment, he continues, "One hour for dinner makes it eleven-forty-five. Pray tell us why you were still there after one o'clock in the morning?"

"We were talking. I guess time got away from us."

"Just talking?"

Without giving Rob a chance to respond, he asks, "Did you tell Dave and Paul that Rita's son was in a serious auto accident?"

"I did."

"Did you also tell them that Rita was so upset that you thought she might hurt herself?"

"I did."

"Neither of those statements was true, were they?"

"No."

"Why did you lie?"

Shrugging his shoulders, Rob says, "What can I say? It was stupid. I panicked."

While the superintendent takes a minute to look through his notes, Rob studies the men seated around the conference table. What he sees is not encouraging. Although none of them appear to take any pleasure in the proceedings, they do seem skeptical. He can't blame them. If the roles were reversed, he would be skeptical too. Although there's no proof of adultery, things do look bad.

Clearing his throat, the superintendent asks, "How does Helen feel about your relationship with Rita?"

In an instant, Rob flashes back to a Sunday night in late October. *Helen has slipped out of bed and is huddled on the living room couch when he finds her. The diffused light from a streetlamp halfway down the block glistens on her tear-damp cheeks. Reaching for a tissue, he moves to dry her tears. When he touches her, she turns away, as if his touch is repulsive.*

"How could you?" she hisses. "How could you?"

Lunging to her feet, she towers over him. Anger makes her face hot and her eyes flash. "How could you confide in that woman? How dare you make her privy to the difficulties in our marriage?"

Interrupting, he demands, "What are you talking about?"

"I'm talking about you and Rita. It's obvious she has a thing for you, and anyone can see you enjoy it. That scene in the driveway yesterday was so transparent. I've been up most of the night, and I've given this a lot of thought. Rita has to go. If you don't replace her, I will go to the church board."

The superintendent speaks again: "Please answer the question. How does Helen feel about your relationship with Rita?"

"She's fine with it," Rob manages, hoping he sounds convincing. "In fact, Helen and Rita are friends."

"Is there anything about your relationship with Rita that you would consider inappropriate?"

"What do you mean?"

"Are you attracted to her or she to you?"

"I like her, if that's what you mean. She's a loyal employee and a hard worker. I would be hard pressed to find a better secretary."

"Both Dave and Paul feel there's more to it than that. They each described instances when it appeared you and Rita were overly familiar. They also noted that you and Rita have a habit of working late after everyone else has gone for the day."

The questions and accusations continue for another hour, but in the end the presbytery board is forced to conclude there is no evidence to prove he is guilty of anything other than poor judgment. They give him a written reprimand and strongly recommend that he replace Rita. They also ask to meet with both him and Helen as soon as she returns from the Amazon.

He is exhausted when the meeting is finally over and more than a little relieved. As grueling as it was, it could have been far worse. Two things, however, trouble him—their recommendation that he replace Rita and their request to meet with him and Helen. He has no intention of complying with either request. Of course, he will be more circumspect in the future, but he is not about to terminate Rita.

Chapter 27

Rob makes a quick stop in the men's room before exiting the District Headquarters. He is tired, more tired than he's ever been. Not just physically tired, but bone weary from the inside out. His head is pounding, and he considers getting a hotel room rather than making the two-hour drive to Sterling, but in the end, he decides against it. By the time he reaches the interstate, the snow is really coming down and the wind is picking up. If it continues at this rate, his two-hour drive could easily turn into a three- or four-hour ordeal.

He tries to concentrate on his driving but finds himself thinking about Rita. As insane as it is, given what he's just been through, he needs her, longs for her touch, for the comfort of her love. It makes no sense. He should be making plans to end their relationship, not planning their next clandestine rendezvous. He should be thanking God that he escaped today's ordeal with nothing more than a reprimand and vowing never to allow himself to become involved in an inappropriate relationship again. Instead, he's resentful. Instead of taking responsibility for his actions, he's angry with Dave and Paul. He can't help feeling this is entirely their fault.

Helen crowds into his thoughts, and in spite of himself, he feels guilty. She's his wife and the mother of his children. She deserves better than this. Although he has not made love to Rita, nor does he intend to, he has given her a part of his heart, a part that should belong only to Helen. He tries to deny it, but in his heart of hearts, he knows better. He's guilty of emotional adultery, and no amount of rationalization will change that. He vowed to forsake all others and love only Helen, but he has betrayed her, and he has betrayed the Lord. These thoughts weigh heavy upon him as he drives through the snow-covered night, but he cannot bring himself to even think of ending his relationship with Rita.

Somewhere between Fort Morgan and Sterling, the full weight of his situation comes crashing down. For the first time, he realizes that he is trapped without a way out. Whatever he does now, people he cares about are going to get hurt and hurt badly. He couldn't break up with Rita even if he wanted to. She's not a vindictive person, but he has no way of knowing what she might do. Well it has been said, "Hell hath no fury like a woman scorned."

Yet, he cannot continue the status quo, either. Already their relationship is taking on a life of its own; becoming more and more physical, and he knows it's only a matter of time before they will become sexually intimate. Although he still vows it will never happen, he knows he is only kidding himself. And once they cross that line, there will be no going back.

He can only imagine how Helen will react when she returns from the Amazon and learns that the district presbytery has reprimanded him for his relationship with Rita. He doesn't think she will leave him, but she will insist that Rita has to go. If she refuses to leave quietly, everything could blow up. He could find himself facing the district presbytery again, with Rita testifying against him. He could be defrocked and dismissed from his church. Helen might even divorce him.

It is nearly eleven o'clock when he finally rolls into town. He's dead tired and would like nothing more than to go directly home and fall into bed, but Rita is expecting him. Tired as he is, he's tempted to throw caution to the wind and just park in her driveway, but he knows that's not wise. Instead he leaves his car a couple of blocks away and walks back to her house. Thankfully, it is late, and most of the houses are dark. There's little chance anyone will see him, still he feels vulnerable, like a thousand pair of eyes are watching him.

As soon as he rings the doorbell, Rita opens the door, and he quickly steps inside. The drapes are closed, and the lights are low. There's a small fire in the fireplace, a carafe of coffee on the coffee table, and Rod McKuen's "The Sea" is playing on the stereo. Taking his coat, she directs him to the couch. After hanging it in the coat closet, she comes to sit beside him.

Although she is desperate to know what happened at the meeting, she doesn't ask. Instead she takes his hand in both of hers and studies his face. He looks dead tired, but beyond that, his face gives nothing away. Finally, he takes a deep breath and begins. "It went pretty much the way I thought it would. Without any real proof of wrongdoing, there wasn't much they could do other than reprimand me."

Relieved, she asks, "Does that mean you're still our pastor?"

"Yes, at least for the time being."

"What do you mean?"

"The district officials aren't likely to do anything else, but Dave and Paul could stir up trouble if they have a mind to. A word here or there to the right people is all it would take."

"Are you okay?" she asks, sensing his mood. "Was it terrible?"

"It wasn't fun, I can tell you that. I lost a lot of respect in the eyes of the men who serve on the presbytery board. I'm not sure they will ever think of me the same way again. To tell you the truth, I feel like damaged goods."

Running her hand over his chest, she says in a sultry voice, "You don't feel damaged to me."

When his only response is a tired smile, she realizes the day's ordeal has taken more out of him than she expected. "Is there something you're not telling me?"

"I don't think I can do this," he says, his voice breaking. "I don't think I can do this."

He seems so sad she thinks her heart will break, but she's also frightened. She can't help feeling this may be the end of their relationship, or at least the beginning of the end. "What do you mean?" she probes. "You're scaring me."

"I'm all torn up on the inside."

He's sobbing, and now she's really scared. She's never seen him like this, and she doesn't know what to do.

"It feels as if God has forsaken me. I try to pray, but I don't feel anything."

Now great, ragged sobs tear at his throat, and he slides off the couch, falling facedown on the floor. "God," he sobs, "don't cast me away. Whatever You do, please don't cast me away. Don't take Your Holy Spirit from me, or I will surely die."

He weeps and prays but finds no relief, for always between him and God is Rita and his unwillingness to give her up. Yet even his feelings for her are ambivalent, a love/hate kind of thing. He hates her. He hates his need for her. He hates his guilt and his sin, yet the thought of life without her is unbearable. Even as he hates her, he desperately needs her.

After a long while, his grief seems to exhaust itself. He stops sobbing but remains seated on the floor, his back against the couch, his head bowed. Rita sits on the floor beside him, and he puts his arm around her shoulders and pulls her close.

Too late, he realizes he is no longer the master of his destiny. Sin is. He wants things to be the way they once were before sin led him astray, but there's no going back, no undoing the things he has done. Like Esau, he finds no place of repentance, though he seeks it with tears and strong cries.

Chapter 28

AMAZON BASIN
FAR WESTERN BRAZIL
1971

For thirteen days, I fight my way through the tangled river margin, subsisting on whatever fruit and berries I can find. My clothes are in tatters; my face and arms are scratched and bruised; and I am covered with insect bites. My feet are painfully raw and swollen. I am weak from hunger and nearing the end of my strength when I stumble upon a trail that is not completely overgrown. It leads to a small clearing, where I see what appears to be a homesteader's open-walled hut. It has a thatched roof and sits on a platform of split *buriti* with a few posts from which to hang hammocks for sleeping.

When I catch sight of it, my heart leaps, and for the first time in several days, I believe I may get out of this alive. I'm sure the homesteaders will be more than happy to help me when they learn I can pay. Pioneers have a harsh life, and cash money is in short supply. What I need is food and a boat, or a canoe, to take me downriver to Cruzeiro do Sul.

I shout a greeting in my halting Portuguese, but I get no response. Cautiously I step into the clearing, noticing for the first time that there is absolutely no sign of life anywhere. No barking dog, no smoke from a cooking fire, no children playing, nothing. To my dismay, I realize the homestead is deserted. Whoever lived here at one time is now gone.

My disappointment is acute, and I'm tempted to despair. Weak as I am, I don't think I have the strength to go on. Desperately I search the area, convinced there must be something here that I can use to help save myself—a misplaced tool, a hidden cache of food, or something. All I find are flat, rusty tin cans, discarded cardboard boxes, and a circle of rocks around a burned-out cooking fire. No food, no tools, nothing that I can use.

It is starting to rain again, so I crawl into the homesteader's abandoned hut, thankful for the thatched roof and the platform of split *buriti*. For the first time in days, I have a roof over my head, and although the platform is hard, it is dry and level. It is still early in the day, but as exhausted as I am, I fall into a troubled sleep, and in my dreams, I relive the nightmare that has befallen me.

I awake in a panic, fear and desperation causing my heart to race. Slowly the nightmare fades, but the despair it has birthed remains. For the hundredth time, I relive the tragic night in my mind. I experience it all again—the violent storm, the turbulent river, the moment our boat capsized, and my frantic attempts to rescue Helen and Carolyn. I know I did everything in my power to save them, but my failure haunts me still. Guilt weighs heavy upon me, and I fear it is something I will have to live with for the rest of my life. Survivor's guilt, someone called it.

My entire body is aching with hunger, so I force myself to search the area in hopes of finding some fruit or berries. Some distance from the hut, I find an area that looks like it was once a garden plot. It's pretty well overgrown with bushes. On an impulse, I uproot one and study the roots. They look vaguely familiar, kind of like the manioc roots Lako boiled and mashed to make his bitter-tasting concoction. If they are, I am in luck. Of course, I have no way to make a fire so I will have to eat them raw, but as hungry as I am, that won't be a problem.

On my way back to the homesteader's hut, I surprise a wild chicken, which takes off running and flapping its wings. I run after it, but as weak as I am, I have no chance of catching it. Reluctantly I give up the chase and return to the area where I kicked it up. As I am bending down to pick up my bundle of roots, I spot a nest containing four eggs. I immediately crack one of the eggs and suck the protein-rich contents from the shell. Under different circumstances, I might be repulsed by the thought of eating a raw egg, but now I quickly devour a second one. The last two I save for tomorrow.

It is nearly dark when I return to the hut, and I quickly pick through the discarded debris in search of a flattened tin can that I can use for a scraper. When I find a suitable one, I sit on the floor and scrape the rough peeling off what I believe to be a manioc root. It looks something like a sweet potato. It's tough and vaguely sweet, but nonetheless it dulls my hunger.

Sometime later that night, I awake with a violent headache, my stomach is cramping, and I feel nauseous. I am so weak I can barely crawl to the edge of the raised platform, where I vomit violently but feel no better. All I can figure is that the raw eggs must have made me sick. All night long, I battle shortness of breath and dizziness, my stomach continues to cramp, and I have the dry heaves. When morning comes, I finally fall into a restless sleep.

All day long, I sleep fitfully, and when I awake sometime in the late afternoon, I feel totally wrung out. My heart is racing, and it feels like I'm having a panic attack. Deliberately I take several deep breaths and try to calm myself. I'm badly dehydrated, but now I'm afraid to drink from the nearby spring, fearing it might be contaminated. Or maybe the raw eggs made me sick.

Finally, my raging thirst overcomes my fear, and I venture into the night. I make my way to the spring, where I lie on my belly and thrust my face into the cool water. I drink a couple of swallows, then pause. When my stomach doesn't react, I drink some more but not too quickly. As I drink, I notice my heart rate seems to be slowing down a little. I probably spend thirty or forty-five minutes at the spring, drinking small amounts, then pausing, before my thirst is quenched. Finally, I return to the homesteader's deserted hut.

I'm hungry, but the thought of eating a raw egg makes me queasy, so I decide to try a little more manioc root. I feel around in the dark until I locate the flattened tin can I used for a scraper. The peeling is tough, but I manage to scrape most of it off. I sit on the raised platform with my feet dangling off as I chew the barely edible root. It's a clear night, and overhead the stars are brilliant. I locate the Southern Cross and to its left Alpha and Beta Centauri, then Scorpio. My father showed them to me when I was just a little boy, and I've never forgotten. Out of nowhere I catch myself wondering if I will ever have a son. If I do, I vow to teach him all the things my father never had a chance to teach me.

By the time I've finished eating most of the root, I'm feeling strange. I'm short of breath, and I feel a headache coming on. I try to stand, but I'm so dizzy I stagger like a drunk. My stomach knots in pain, doubling me over as a wave of nausea hits me, and I vomit violently. I hang my head over the edge of the raised platform and heave again and again until I think I am going vomit my insides out. It's a replay of last night, only worse, and all night long I battle shortness of breath and dizziness, my stomach continues to cramp, and I have the dry heaves yet again. I've never been this sick, not even with malaria, and sometime in the wee hours of the morning, I pray to die.

Another day and night pass while I battle delirium and hallucinations. My stomach is knotted with cramps, and in my madness, I'm convinced a huge anaconda has entwined itself around me and is attempting to crush me. I accidently throw myself off the raised platform as I thrash about wildly in a desperate attempt to free myself. It's no use. No matter how hard I try, I cannot escape, and the crushing pain in my stomach is squeezing the life out of me. I must have passed out, for some time later I come to wet and cold. It is raining again, and somehow, I manage to pull myself back onto the split *buriti* platform.

I cannot tell the difference between hallucination and reality, and it goes on hour after hour. Now a vicious wild boar, with curving tusks as sharp as razors, is attacking me, and I lash out with my feet, kicking and screaming. Then I'm in a johnboat, when a red-eyed crocodile, with a head almost a meter long, attacks the boat. I'm scrambling for my pistol when she slams the side of the boat, her powerful tail driving us sideways before capsizing our boat. Then I am in the river, and she has my legs in her jaws and is dragging me beneath the dark water.

Finally, on the morning of the third day, I awake in my right mind. It takes several minutes for me to reorient myself. Little by little, I recall what has happened and where I am, and when I do, a sense of helplessness nearly overwhelms me. With a determination that can only be the product of my Whittaker genes, I force myself to sit up. I will not quit. I may die here in this Godforsaken place, but it won't be because I gave up.

My thirst is raging, and weak as I am, I stumble to the spring. Without a cup of any kind, I am forced to lap up water like a dog. When my thirst is quenched, I realize I am covered in dried vomit, and the stench is disgusting. It takes what little strength I have to peel off my tattered clothes. Below the spring is a pool for collecting water, and I ease my abused body into it. The water is cool, and I'm shivering; nonetheless, I take my time. Without soap it is not easy to get clean, but after some determined scrubbing, most of the filth is gone.

Thankfully, the sun is high in the sky and the day is warm when I crawl out of the pool, and my body dries quickly. I collect my filthy clothes, nearly gagging at the stench of vomit, and return to the pool where I bathed. Since I have no soap, I decide to let my clothes soak while I sit in the sun and enjoy its warmth. I am weak from hunger, but I haven't seen any fruit or berries nearby. There are several more manioc bushes nearby, or at least what I thought were manioc bushes, but I will starve before I eat another manioc root. I'm convinced they're what is poisoning me.

Once I have rested, I return to the pool and scrub my filthy clothes until they're reasonably clean. After spreading them over some bushes to dry, I return to the open-walled hut, where I see the two wild chicken eggs I had saved from my first day here. My whole body aches with hunger, but I'm afraid to eat them. What if that's what is making me so desperately ill? I don't think they are, but I can't take that risk. I don't think I could survive another episode like the last one. It would kill me.

When my clothes are dry, I get dressed and return to the abandoned hut once more. When I do, I can't help noting how little strength I have. Just that small effort has worn me completely out. Two weeks with almost nothing to eat plus food poisoning have just about done me in. My only hope of survival is to continue following the river toward Cruzeiro do Sol, but I don't know if I have the strength to fight my way through the tangled river margin. Still, I don't really have a choice. If I stay here, I will die.

As weak as I am, death doesn't seem like such a bad option. Of course, I would never do anything to deliberately end my life, but it is tempting to just sit here in the sun until the end comes. If everything I have been taught about heaven since I was a child is true, then death would be a welcome relief. No more pain or suffering. No more disappointments or broken relationships.

Fragments of sermons I heard as teenage boy, then promptly forgot, now play in my mind, and I mull them over with an interest I've never had before. I can't help wondering if I will really be reunited with my parents in heaven. Will Helen be there, and Carolyn?

Thinking of being reunited with my father brings his last words to mind. He recorded them in his journal, in a letter he left for me, and I have inscribed them on my heart. *"Death is not far away now, and I could welcome it with open arms, knowing that to be absent from the body is to be home with Christ, were it not for you. I hate the thought of leaving you to grow up without a father."* He also left me his alabaster cross, and now I extract it from inside my shirt, where it hangs from a leather string about my neck. It was a symbol of his faith and his covenant with the Lord.

As I study it, turning it over in my hand, I sense his nearness in the same way I sensed his presence when I knelt at his grave at the base of that towering samauma tree in the far western Amazon Basin. Kneeling there, I poured out all the hurt and anger I had held against him since he disappeared while on a mission of mercy when I was just seven years old. Forgiving my father gave me a new lease on life, and now that my own death is near, the sense of his presence gives me the grace to finally forgive myself for the mess I've made of my life.

My throat is tight as I begin making a mental list of my sins. Of course, at the top of the list is the bitterness that has defined my life. It poisoned all my relationships and destroyed any chance of happiness I might have had. The enormity of the hurt I have inflicted on others and myself is almost beyond telling. Were it not for the grace of our Lord, I would despair.

Haltingly I pray, "Lord, if I wasn't convinced You have already forgiven me, I could never forgive myself. But because I am forgiven, I can forgive myself."

For several minutes, I bask in His presence as His love floods my soul; tears of gratefulness sliding silently down my cheeks. Finally, I take a deep breath and begin, "With Your help, Lord Jesus, I forgive myself for hating my father. I forgive myself for abandoning my mother when she needed me. I forgive myself for resenting my sister and for pushing her away when she tried to get close. I forgive myself for hardening my heart against Carolyn and for the cruel ways I pushed her toward divorce. I forgive myself for walking out and leaving Diane to face Eurico's death alone. I forgive myself for rejecting her love and for hurting her in ways from which she may never recover. And now the big one: I forgive myself for not being able to save Helen and Carolyn from drowning."

When I finally finish, I am sobbing, not with grief but with gratefulness. I am totally wrung out, but on the inside, I am free. No longer do I feel a need to punish myself, or to sabotage every relationship, or to undermine any success I might have. Weak as I am, I may not survive, but if I do, I vow to be a true man of God. A man my father would be proud of.

# Chapter 29

Morning is just a hint on the horizon when I pick up my stout walking stick and leave the homesteader's hut, heading for the river margin. An undulating layer of mist is suspended over the trail about eye level, herded by the heat of my body into little eddies that taper into the forest. Although the temperature is moderate, the humidity has pasted my ragged shirt to my back. In this moment, I loathe the Amazon Basin. I hate the heat and humidity, along with the disease-carrying insects and parasites that flourish here. I hate the isolation and the primitive living conditions. Most of all, I hate the harsh environment that has taken those I love from me.

Thrusting those troubling thoughts from my mind, I turn my attention to the task at hand. There's no trail through the river margin, so I use my walking stick to force my way through the undergrowth. I can't see the river, but I can hear it a few meters away. The lazy, meandering body of water we navigated on my first trip upriver to the mission compound is gone. The rainy season, with the help of several severe storms, has turned it into a swollen torrent, strong and sullen.

Three hours later, the sun has burned the low-lying mist away, and when the Rio Moa makes a sharp bend, I find myself on a point of land jutting into the river. From that vantage point, I have a clear view upstream. In the distance I see what appears to be a good-sized boat approaching, and my heart leaps, but I'm afraid to get my hopes up, lest my eyes are playing tricks on me.

As I continue to stare upriver, the boat begins to take shape as it draws nearer. It is still some distance away, but I can tell it is a broad-bellied houseboat. As it comes closer, I see it is painted a bright blue with *Flor de Maio* (Mayflower) in large white letters on its hull. Although I recognize the boat, it is nearly more than I can comprehend. I have prayed to be rescued, but never in my wildest dreams did I think Dr. Peterson would be the one to rescue me.

I stand as far out on the point of land as I can and wave my arms wildly in a desperate attempt to get the boat's attention. The current is strong, and it is pushing the boat away from the point on which I am standing. I'm not sure if anyone has seen me, and I am sick with disappointment when it looks like they are going to pass me by. My hope surges when the boat makes a slow turn and works its way across the current to the eddy on the far side of the point on which I am standing.

I watch in amazement as the captain eases the broad-bellied boat up against the bank. Two deckhands leap ashore and quickly secure it. In my excitement I try to run toward the boat, but I stumble and take a hard fall. Before I can get up, the deckhands are there, lifting me to my feet. I recognize both of them from my earlier trip upriver, but neither of them seems to recognize me. As we near the boat, I can hardly believe my eyes. Dr. Peterson is standing in the bow, and Helen is beside him. At the sight of her, my heart leaps with joy. I never expected to see her again, but she has miraculously survived. Now I franticly scan the deck in search of Carolyn, but to my dismay, she is nowhere to be found.

The deckhands help me aboard, and in an instant Helen is there, laughing and crying as she throws herself into my arms. "Bryan," she says, disbelief coloring her words, "we thought you were dead."

I clutch her tightly to my chest and try to speak, but I can't. My emotions are all over the place. She's crying, and I'm crying. We're mumbling incoherently, not making any sense. We cling to each other, unable to let go while our tears flow—tears of joy and tears of sorrow.

Finally, I break free and scan the deck once more. I recognize the captain—sometime in the past his nose was broken and now it sits a little crooked on his face. Dr. Peterson is standing beside him, looking as animated as I remember. There are several others, but nowhere do I see Carolyn. Turning back to Helen, I ask, "Where is she? Where is Carolyn?"

Whatever joy Helen experienced when she discovered I was alive is replaced by a primeval grief. She doesn't need to say anything. Her grief-stricken face tells me everything I need to know. Carolyn is dead. I shouldn't be shocked. I've known all along that her chances of survival were slim to none, but when I saw Helen alive, I dared to hope. Now I'm crushed. It's like experiencing her death all over again. It feels like my heart is being ripped out, and I fall to my knees sobbing. In an instant Helen is kneeling beside me, wrapping her arms around me, mingling her tears with mine.

I have no idea how long we cling to each other in our grief, but after a while I feel the vibration of the engines as the captain eases the *Flor de Mayo* away from the bank and turns her downriver. When I can finally bring myself to lift my head and look about, the foredeck is deserted. Apparently, the captain, as well as Dr. Peterson and his team, had the courtesy to allow Helen and me to grieve alone.

We move into a small patch of shade, where we sit with our backs braced against a bag of rice. We both have a hundred questions, but neither of us feels like talking. Carolyn's death has rendered us mute, and we sit together, locked in sorrowful silence. My tears are endless, as are hers.

Sometime later, a deckhand brings each of us a plate of black beans and rice. It is my first real meal in more than two weeks, and although I am sick with grief, I devour it. Helen picks at hers before pushing it aside. Finally, I steel myself and ask her about the night of the big storm.

Before responding, she takes a moment to gather her courage. When at last she speaks, her voice is soft and filled with pain. "When that huge tree fell on us, capsizing our boat, I thought we were all going to die."

When I nod in agreement, she continues, "I was driven deep underwater, but I've always been a strong swimmer, and I fought my way to the surface, where I grabbed on to the branches of that same tree."

"What about Carolyn?" I ask. "Did you see her?"

"Only for an instant," she says, grimacing. "There was a flash of lightning, and I saw her struggling in the current before it swept her away."

She's weeping now, guilty tears, bitter tears. I try to console her, but she is locked somewhere inside herself, and I cannot reach her.

Finally, she forces herself to look at me, her face full of anguish. "Maybe I could have saved her, but I didn't even try. All I could think about was my boys."

I take her in my arms, and she buries her face against my chest. "You couldn't have saved her," I say, remembering my own desperate attempts that fateful night. "You did the right thing, Helen. Your boys need you."

I would like to know how she escaped the river and the particulars of her rescue, but now is not the time to press her for details. It will probably take four or five days to reach Cruzeiro do Sul, and we will have plenty of time to talk.

Chapter 30

My emotions are all over the place. One minute I am nearly giddy with excitement at the prospect of returning to the States. The next minute I am mute with grief as I consider Carolyn's death. Although we were divorced, I cared about her, especially now, since making peace with my past. Her death means I will never have the opportunity to undo the damage I did to her, and that grieves me deeply. I hurt for Helen as well. She has lost a dear friend, and she blames herself for not saving her. It doesn't make sense—there was no way she could have saved Carolyn; in fact, she would have probably drowned herself if she had tried—still self-blame is seldom logical, and my words of comfort fall on deaf ears.

I am regaining my strength more quickly than I expected. This is just the second day since my rescue, but already I am feeling like a new man. It is amazing what a little rest and plenty of rice and black beans will do. Ever the scientist, Dr. Peterson has questioned me at length. He wants to know how I survived—where I slept at night and what I ate. He was particularly fascinated when I told him I got food poisoning after eating raw manioc roots, or at least what I surmised were manioc roots. After I described my symptoms, he simply shook his head. "That wasn't food poisoning. You were suffering from acute cyanide poisoning, and you're very fortunate to be alive."

Then he launched into a scientific lecture. Had the topic been anything else, my eyes would have glazed over, but this time he had my attention. "The manioc root is widely known as 'cassava,' except in the far western Amazon Basin. South America grew and consumed cassava hundreds of years before Christopher Columbus first voyaged here. It is a hardy crop that is resistant to drought and does not require much fertilizer. It's a rich source of carbohydrates, and it provides more calories per acre than other cereals. Today it is a primary component in the diet of millions of people around the world."

Growing impatient, I interrupt him. "Dr. Peterson, I don't mean to be rude, but could you focus on the part about cyanide poisoning?"

He doesn't like to be interrupted, and I can tell he is miffed; nonetheless, he yields to my prompting. "There are two types of cassava: bitter and sweet. Bitter cassava contains high levels of two compounds capable of releasing toxic hydrogen cyanide. Sweet cassava contains the same compounds, but in significantly lower quantities. Given your symptoms, I suspect you got hold of some bitter cassava. The only reason it didn't kill you is because you ate such small amounts."

"If it's so poisonous, how can millions of people subsist on it?"

"Proper preparation is the key. Eating raw or even improperly prepared cassava can kill you. In the case of sweet cassava, simple boiling does the trick. Removing the toxins from bitter cassava is considerably more complicated."

Having delivered his lecture, Dr. Peterson goes in search of the captain. When he has gone, Helen comes to join me. For several minutes we sit in silence, each of us locked in our own thoughts. We are both grieving, Carolyn's death impacting us in profound ways. I can't help thinking that I will never get to tell her how grieved I am for the ways I treated her when we were married. She loved me passionately with a fierce determination, but I pushed her away. She was a wounded soul with a fragile self-image, and my rejection pushed her over the edge. I would give almost anything if I could go back and relive those tragic days. How differently I would treat her. Maybe my love could not heal her, but at least I would try my best to protect her from this cruel world.

Determinedly I push my self-incriminating grief into a private place, to be dealt with at some future date, and turn my attention to Helen. When I do, I cannot help noticing how terribly sad she looks. I would like to say something to encourage her, but her pain is too deep for words. Instead, I slip my arm around her shoulders and pull her close. She is weeping now, silently, her face buried against my chest. It feels awkward, but good, too, and I can't help thinking that the Lord is changing me. I am no longer an angry, bitter man. I still struggle with a lifetime of conditioning, but with God's help I am learning to reach out to others.

After a time, she dries her tears, squares her shoulders, and says, "I need to talk about it."

When I nod, she begins, "Some of this you already know, but I need to start at the beginning, so bear with me. When that huge tree fell on us, I thought we were all going to die. I was driven deep underwater, but I fought my way to the surface. The current was pushing me downstream, but I was able to grab hold of a branch on that tree before it swept me away.

"Once we capsized, I never saw you again. Of course, I hardly expected to. It was pitch-black, and the rain was blinding. There was a flash of lightning, and for an instant, I caught sight of Carolyn before the current swept her away.

"Apparently some of the tree's root ball was still connected to the bank, because instead of carrying the tree downstream, the current pushed it into the riverbank, where it got hung up. Although I was dazed, I knew it was just a matter of time before the current would sweep it away and me with it. Using the branches, I pulled myself out of the water and scrambled up the riverbank. Hardly had I reached the safety of the river margin before the current ripped the tree loose and swept it away.

"I spent a miserable night, wet, cold, and grief-stricken. When morning came, I searched the riverbank but saw no sign of either Carolyn or you. I thought both of you had drowned."

When she pauses, I interject a question. "So, how did you survive without any food or survival gear?"

"God must have been looking out for me, because I found our emergency pack floating among some debris in an eddy some distance downriver. I got a long branch and tried to snag it, but I couldn't reach it. Having no other choice, I stripped off my clothes and eased into the water. It was creepy swimming among all that debris, but I knew I had to have that pack. My survival depended on it."

She continues, but I am hardly listening. Instead, I am considering what she said about God looking out for her. A part of me wants to believe God was doing just that, but I sense my old cynicism rearing its ugly head. I mean, if God was really looking out for us, why did we capsize in the first place? And if God was looking out for Carolyn, I can't help thinking He didn't do a very good job. These are the kind of thoughts that had plagued me as a child following my father's disappearance, turning me into a cynical soul and ruining all my relationships. Now such thoughts make me feel guilty, but I can't pretend they're not real. I'm not angry with God, just confused, and maybe disappointed.

Turning my attention back to Helen, I listen as she tells me that once she had the emergency pack, she felt she was going to survive. "I had to," she says. "My boys need me.

"Like you, I had a choice. I could head downriver toward Cruzeiro do Sul, or I could go upriver toward the mission compound. The mission compound was closer, so I set out in that direction. It was harder going than I expected."

"You can say that again," I say with a grimace, as I survey my ragged clothes and abused body. I can't help thinking that my sister is one tough woman. Not many people, man or woman, could do what she did.

"We were on the river three days before we capsized," she says. "Given the strength of the current, I knew we had traveled a considerable distance, so I figured it would take me ten or twelve days to make it back to the mission compound."

When I nod in agreement, she continues, "I don't know how you made it without a machete."

I just shrug my shoulders and motion for her to go on. "The rain was the worst, and after the first two or three days, I wondered if I would ever be dry again. Finding a reasonably dry place to spend the night was nearly impossible. I ended up sleeping in the most unlikely places. Thankfully, I had a tarp to use as a ground sheet and a mosquito net to keep the bugs out."

I tell her about the wild boar that tried to attack me, and she tells me about her encounter with a crocodile. "For once, it wasn't raining, so I was sleeping in the open near the fire. Before crawling inside my mosquito net for the night, I placed several large limbs on the fire. Sometime later, I awakened with a start—God must have poked me, I guess. Across the fire I saw a huge crocodile creeping toward me. For a moment, I was paralyzed with fear, then I leaped out from under the mosquito net and grabbed the largest limb out of the fire. With a roar, the crocodile charged at me, its huge jaws gaping wide open. With all my might, I thrust the burning end of that long branch down his throat."

As amazing as her account is, I can't help focusing on one comment: *"I awakened with a start—God must have poked me, I guess."*

When she finishes her story, I ask, "Do you really believe God woke you?"

"Of course," she replies without a moment's hesitation.

I want to believe, I really do. I want to believe that God is looking out for us, but there are too many instances when it seems no one was watching over us. Sure, it would be easy to say that Helen and I were spared because God was looking after us, but what about Carolyn? Why wasn't He looking out for her? Why did He let her drown?

Helen seems to have talked herself out, and we sit in silence for some time. It is raining again, not hard, but steady. Thankfully, we are sheltered under an overhang, so we're staying dry. The day is fading, and I feel the throbbing of the engine change tempo as the captain slows the boat to search for a place to camp for the night.

Chapter 31

Suddenly I'm jerked awake, and for a moment I'm disoriented, unable to remember anything other than the terrifying scream still echoing inside my head. Turning my head slightly, I see the stubborn embers of last night's cooking fire glowing in the darkness. Nearby, someone is snoring, and a short distance away; I hear the sound of the river. Slowly it comes back to me. This is the third night following my rescue, and in the light of the moon, I can make out the silhouette of the *Flor de Mayo* snugged up against the riverbank.

Fragments of my troubling dream return, as real as the night around me. In my dream, Carolyn is sorely injured and unable to save herself. "Bryan," she screams, "please help me." Although it was just a dream, I cannot help feeling it was more than that. Maybe the Lord is trying to tell me that Carolyn is still alive and that it is up to us to find her. I have to admit, that hardly makes sense. At this late date, it's not likely she's alive, and if she is, I wouldn't know where to find her. I would have to be crazy to share my thoughts with Dr. Peterson or the captain. They would think I had lost my mind, and rightly so.

Tired as I am, sleep won't come, so I lie in my hammock and try to remember the details of my dream. It's no use. No matter how hard I try, all I can remember is Carolyn's terrifying scream and the sense that she was seriously injured and in desperate need of my help. Eventually I fall asleep, only to dream the same dream a second time. Carolyn is calling my name, and I am blindly slashing my way through the tangled underbrush of the river margin in a desperate attempt to locate her. Just when I am about to find her, I'm suddenly jerked awake, my heart pounding, Carolyn's scream ringing in my ears.

I pull the mosquito net back and ease myself out of my hammock, trying not to make a sound lest I awaken the others. Squatting beside the fire, I stir up the coals and add a handful of small branches before putting the coffeepot on to boil. When the coffee is ready, I fill a tin mug and take a sip, savoring the sweetness of the brown sugar flavoring the coffee. With cup in hand, I make my way to the river's edge and study the sky as the first hint of daylight bleaches the darkness above the towering trees across the river.

My thoughts are troubling, and I worry over them like a dog with a bone. I know it's foolish to think Carolyn might still be alive, but I can't rid myself of that thought. I tell myself that even if she didn't drown in the river, there's no way she could survive in the jungle without a machete and provisions. I almost convince myself, but not quite. Against all logic, I can't help thinking, *But what if she is alive? What if my dreams are her way of communicating with me, her way of calling for help?*

Behind me, the camp is stirring, and Helen comes to join me on the riverbank. We stand side by side as the sun inches its way up the sky. The river margin is filled with tendrils of fog, reminding me of Spanish moss hanging from the branches of live oak trees. The sun's first rays are laying bright bars of gold across the river while it turns the wisps of fog into fleeting shadows of light. The morning is so beautiful that I'm nearly tempted to fall in love with the Amazon, but then I remember that beneath its serene beauty, there crouches a malevolent beast.

I take a final sip of my coffee before throwing the dregs into the river and turning toward camp. When I do, Helen places her hand on my arm. "What is it, Bryan? What's troubling you?"

I'm tempted to brush her concerns aside as I have done for most of my life, but something stops me. Instead I ask, "Do you think there's any chance Carolyn might still be alive?"

My question takes her by surprise, and she studies me before replying. "No. I don't think so. As much as I would like to believe she survived somehow, I don't think it's possible."

Without replying, I head up the path, and she hurries to join me. Just before we reach camp, I stop and turn toward her. "Do you think it is possible for people we care about to communicate with us through our dreams?"

She hesitates before responding, choosing her words carefully lest she offend me. "I'm not sure about people being able to communicate with us in dreams, but I know God does."

Intrigued, I press her. "Tell me more."

"The Bible is filled with numerous examples," she explains. "The first one that comes to mind is when an angel of the Lord appeared to Joseph in a dream. He told him to take the baby Jesus and flee to Egypt because King Herod was going to try to kill the child."

When I nod but don't say anything, she asks, "Why this sudden interest in dreams?"

Quickly I tell her about my dreams of Carolyn. I conclude by saying that I think she is still alive and I believe the Lord wants us to save her. Helen knows God sometimes moves in supernatural ways, yet I sense her hesitancy. She wants to believe, but having come to grips with Carolyn's death, she is finding it difficult to think she might still be alive. I can't help thinking that if I can't convince her, I will never be able to convince Dr. Peterson or the captain.

Finally, she says, "I can't say I'm convinced your dreams are from the Lord, but they could be. If you truly believe we should search for Carolyn, I will support you."

I didn't realize how much I needed her encouragement until that moment. Taking a deep breath, I say, "Thank you. You have no idea how much that means to me."

She gives me a tentative smile. "I'm sure you realize it's not going to be easy to convince the others."

When we reach camp, the crew is busy breaking camp in preparation for our departure. I approach the captain and ask if I may speak to him and Dr. Peterson about a private matter. He suggests we return to *Flor de Mayo,* where Dr. Peterson and Helen join us.

Once onboard, the captain leads us to the poop deck, where he makes himself comfortable on an upturned five-gallon bucket and proceeds to fill his pipe. When he gets it going, he turns his attention to me. In a kindly voice he asks, "Well, young man, what's this about?"

Now that we're all together, I'm hesitant to begin. Last night the dream was so real I was absolutely convinced Carolyn was alive. Now I'm not sure. In the light of day, I can't help doubting myself. Maybe I'm just trying to make up for the way I treated her when we were married. Or maybe this is my way of coping with survivor's guilt. I don't want to believe that, but...

Clearing my throat, I begin, "I have reason to believe that Carolyn may still be alive. I would like to return upriver so we can search for her."

Before I can say more, Dr. Peterson interrupts, "I don't mean to be insensitive, but what you're suggesting is simply not possible. The fact that you and Helen survived is truly remarkable, but to suggest Carolyn is still alive after all this time just doesn't make sense. She almost certainly drowned, but if she did manage to escape the river somehow, she could never have survived this long in the jungle."

Allowing his voice to take on a more sympathetic tone, he continues, "I realize it's hard to lose a friend, but denying reality isn't going to make it any easier."

Taking a puff on his pipe, the captain turns to Dr. Peterson. In a reasonable voice, he says, "Carolyn is most likely dead, I'll grant you that, but let's hear what Bryan has to say." Turning to me he says, "Bryan, two days ago you seemed ready to believe Carolyn was dead." When I nod, he continues, "So, what made you change your mind?"

Instead of trying to explain, I ask, "Do you believe it is possible for those we love to communicate with us in special ways, like in dreams?"

Immediately Dr. Peterson shakes his head, skepticism clearly visible in his expression, but the captain seems thoughtful, so I press my point. "Twice last night, Carolyn came to me in a dream. It was as real as anything I've ever experienced. In my dream, she was alive, but seriously injured. She was calling my name and pleading for help."

That's too much for Dr. Peterson. He is a scientist, and he's skeptical of anything that cannot be proven empirically. Turning to the captain, he says, "I think we've heard enough. Let's be on our way."

As he turns to go, the captain lays a huge, work-calloused hand on his arm. "I know this sounds far-fetched, but let's hear Bryan out before we write him off."

Jerking his arm free of the captain's hand, Dr. Peterson glares at him. "What's to hear? The girl drowned, and it's going to take more than a couple of dreams to change that."

A rush of anger threatens to consume me, and I'm ready to tear his head off. Sensing my anger, Helen puts a calming hand on my forearm. In the past I would have shoved her hand away and turned my anger on her, but now I restrain myself.

Turning to Dr. Peterson, she says, "I know it's been a long expedition and that you're eager to reach Cruzeiro do Sul, but we're talking about a young woman's life. Granted, it's not likely she's alive, but what if she is? Would you really turn your back on her?"

"Absolutely not! If I thought there were any chance she was alive, I would search the jungle until we found her, no matter how long it took. What I'm not willing to do is waste three or four days conducting an utterly hopeless search."

Ever the negotiator, Helen says, "What difference will three or four more days make? If there's even the remotest chance Carolyn's alive, we have to search for her. That's the only humane thing to do."

Dr. Peterson snorts in disgust. "This is ridiculous," he storms. "I chartered this boat, and I'm ready to continue downriver. If Bryan wants to stay here and search for the woman, I say give him whatever he needs and let's be on our way."

With that, he turns on his heel and starts toward the rear of the boat. When he realizes the captain hasn't moved, he turns and glares at him. "What are you waiting for? This is my charter, and I'm ready to go."

It's all I can do not to throw him in the river, but I restrain myself, and it's a good thing, too. His temper tantrum and the disrespectful way he addressed the captain has worked in our favor. Although the captain maintains a measure of dignity, it is obvious that he is angry through and through. "It may be your charter," he says through clenched teeth, "but the *Flor de Mayo* is my boat, and I'm still the captain. On my boat, my word is law!"

Without another word, he takes the wheel and orders the crew to cast off. He carefully backs the boat into the current and deliberately turns upstream. Dr. Peterson starts to protest, but he thinks better of it when the captain glares at him, daring him to speak.

Chapter 32

Although I'm thankful the captain has made the decision to go upriver in search of Carolyn, I am apprehensive as well. My dreams seemed real enough when I dreamed them, but now I can't help thinking they might have been just that—dreams. I mean, what do I know about interpreting dreams? Maybe they were nothing more than the product of my overactive imagination. Who knows? I may be making a fool of myself by insisting we search for Carolyn, but I can't bring myself to back down. Chances are, we will never find her, but if I don't search for her, I will never be able to live with myself. If there is even the slightest chance she's alive, we have to do everything in our power to save her.

As we plow upriver against the current, I consider every possibility and try to imagine every scenario. Although Helen and I were rescued at different locations, days apart, we both stayed near the river, where the crew on the *Flor de Mayo* spotted us. Apparently, Carolyn didn't do that; maybe she was injured and couldn't make it to the river, or perhaps the crew failed to see her. Either way, we're going to have to search the jungle, and that's no easy task. Given the nearly constant rain, the tangled undergrowth, the hordes of insects and all manner of poisonous snakes, searching for her will be a risky endeavor. Well it has been said that in the jungle, death wears many faces.

When the captain asked me what I had in mind, I suggested we begin our search just downriver from where our boat capsized and on the opposite side of the river from where Helen and I were rescued. I explained to him that we had already searched the south side of the river while trying to work our way back to civilization. To my way of thinking, if Carolyn is alive, she must be on the north bank or somewhere in the jungle adjoining the Rio Moa.

Going upriver against the rain-swollen current is slow going, and although we keep a sharp lookout, we spot nothing to suggest Carolyn might still be alive. The mood on the *Flor de Mayo* is tense. The boat's crew, as well as the expedition team, was eager to return to civilization, and the delay did not set well with them. To a man, they are convinced the search is ill conceived and a total waste of time. Only the captain's stern resolve keeps them in line.

Once we reach the area where the storm capsized our boat, we form two-person search teams and wade into the jungle. Of course, Dr. Peterson and several of his team refuse to take part. It is killing work, hacking our way through the tangled underbrush of the river margin, while hordes of sweat bees drive us nearly mad. The heat and humidity combine to suck the life out of us. Whatever strength I thought I had regained soon evaporates, leaving me limp with exhaustion; nonetheless, I slog on. What choice do I have? If Carolyn is still alive, we have to find her.

Although I maintain a brave front, I'm sorely tempted to give up and call the search off. I can't help thinking that if my dreams were truly from God, He would have surely guided us to Carolyn instead of letting us stumble around like the blind leading the blind. What kind of God would make this so difficult? And what about Carolyn? Doesn't He care about her? I struggle to keep a tight rein on my irreverent thoughts lest I allow my doubts to turn into bitter cynicism. I've gone that way before, and it leads to a dark place, a place to which I never want to return.

Day by day, the crew is becoming more resentful, and each evening Helen and I eat alone unless the captain joins us. Although neither of us speaks of it, we can't help noticing the disparaging glances they cast our way. If I'm reading the mood correctly, we are going to have to call this search off before long or we will have a munity on our hands. I can't really blame them. Searching the jungle adjoining the river is brutally hard work, and with little hope of finding Carolyn, they are ready to call it quits.

In some ways, this is worse than being lost in the jungle. No matter how exhausted I became, I knew I had to keep going. It was my only chance of survival. Now I battle indecision. A hundred times a day, I am tempted to give up and call the search off. And a hundred times a day, I resist the temptation. No matter how much resentment comes my way, no matter how foolish I may look, I owe it to Carolyn to keep searching.

Just as I am finishing my second cup of *cafezinbo*, two crewmen stagger into camp carrying an improvised stretcher. In an instant I am on my feet, and Helen is right behind me.

Taking one end of the stretcher, I help the exhausted men place it near the fire. Although we try to be gentle, Carolyn groans in pain as we set it on the ground. Behind me Helen gasps, and in the flickering firelight I see that Carolyn has an ugly gash in the side of her head and insects have ravaged her face and arms.

Someone has brought a first aid kit, and Helen is gently bathing her wounds. I can't help noticing that Carolyn's leg is bent at an awkward angle, and when I try to straighten it, she screams in pain before passing out. I'm no doctor, but I can tell that her breathing is shallow and irregular. She appears to be dehydrated, and even in this faint light, I see she is nothing more than skin and bones.

Thankfully the *Flor de Mayo's* first aid kit is well stocked, and I select a World War II–type morphine pack and inject Carolyn. Almost immediately her pain begins to ease, and I examine her leg more carefully. It is broken about midway between her knee and her hip. It is critical that we set it as best we can and put a splint on to immobilize it.

I motion for Helen to hold her shoulders, and I position myself at her feet. Using my right hand, I begin exerting pressure on the broken femur while pulling her heel toward me with my left hand. Although Carolyn is heavily sedated, she still groans in pain as I work to set her broken leg. When I feel the ends of the bone slide into alignment, I quickly wrap it in a crude splint. I am sweating profusely, and my hands are shaking when I finish.

Someone hands me a cup of coffee, and Helen pats me on the shoulder. "Good job, Bryan."

The captain is questioning the two crewmen who found her, so I move closer and listen in. "It was nearly dark, and we were crossing a small clearing on our way back to the boat when I noticed several vultures circling overhead."

The speaker is old beyond his years, with tobacco-stained teeth and a long scar running nearly from his ear to the corner of his mouth, but there is kindness in his eyes. "We headed that way on the off-chance it might be the woman—or at least her body."

Someone hands him a plate of black beans and rice, and he pauses to stuff his mouth before continuing. "She was lying in a crumpled heap at the base of a towering tree. She most likely fell while attempting to climb the tree. Probably trying to reach the fruit that was hanging about ten meters overhead."

He takes another huge bite of rice and beans before resuming his account. "At first we thought she was dead, but she turned out to be alive, but barely."

I listen for several minutes more but learn almost nothing else, so I return to where Helen is keeping vigil at Carolyn's side. One by one, the others drift off to seek their hammocks, thankful the search is finally over. Soon the camp grows silent except for the calling of the nightbirds, the murmur of the river, and the snoring of exhausted men.

Now that Carolyn has been found, the adrenaline that kept Helen and me going has drained away, leaving both of us wiped out, especially Helen. At my insistence, she leaves Carolyn's side and retreats to her hammock, after telling me to wake her in a couple of hours. Once she has gone, I take Carolyn's limp hand in my own. Her nails are broken, her skin raw in places, not at all like the carefully manicured hand I remember from our days together. Thankfully, the morphine has eased her pain, but her sleep is restless, and from time to time she moans softly. Once I thought I heard her call my name, but I may have just imagined it.

The fire has burned down to a few stubborn coals, so I poke at them until I coax a small flame, then I add three or four pieces of wood. In the firelight, I study her profile. Seeing her this way makes my heart hurt. She was always picture-perfect, every hair in place, her makeup flawless. Now her auburn hair is a tangled mess, her face bruised and covered with insect bites. I want to touch her cheek, just to let her know that I am here, but I don't, lest I wake her.

By maintaining the strictest discipline, I have negotiated the two years since our divorce with only an occasional memory of the love we once shared. I dare not go there, for while the memories promise comfort, they bring only pain. Tonight, however, I am powerless against the past, and a host of bittersweet memories wash over me. I close my eyes tightly, and a poignant memory comes into focus.

It is our wedding day, and I am standing in a high mountain meadow just below Hahn's Peak north of Steamboat Springs, Colorado. Carolyn is walking across the meadow to join me, a bouquet of wildflowers native to the Rocky Mountains in her hand, and sunlight shimmering off her auburn hair. Her face is full of love, and the way she looks at me makes my heart ache with desire.

Like always, a second memory now superimposes itself on the first. *We are honeymooning in a rustic cabin high in the*

Rockies when I awaken in the dead of night to find Carolyn weeping silently in bed beside me. She tries to convince me it is just tears of joy, but when I press her, she admits she is sad because none of her family was present to share her special day. That was my doing. I had insisted on a small wedding with just a few friends and no family. It wasn't the first time I hurt her, nor would it be the last. It seemed I had a special talent for causing her pain, a talent that would eventually destroy our marriage.

This bittersweet reminiscing goes on for most of the night as I maintain my vigil at Carolyn's side. While the memories give me fleeting moments of intense joy, reminding me why I fell head over heels in love with her, in the end I am nearly overwhelmed with a sense of loss, with the sense that I have ruined something rare and special. Sitting alone in the darkness, I am tempted to believe that in time we might be able to rebuild the love we once shared. In my saner moments, I realize it is nothing more than a pipe dream.

Carolyn groans, calling me back to the present. Gently I lift her head and help her drink a few swallows of water. When I do, I notice her lips are cracked and dry. Rummaging in the first aid kit, I find some lip balm and carefully apply it. To my surprise, I realize that caring for her has awakened feelings I thought were dead and gone, or maybe I had just repressed them.

Just before daylight, she regains consciousness. She is confused initially, but little by little she becomes aware of her surroundings. Slowly she realizes that she is no longer alone in the jungle, injured and helpless. Nearby she sees a fire, and not far away someone is snoring. I watch as she turns her head and catches sight of me. When she does, she gasps, "I thought you were dead."

"No such luck," I reply, trying to make light of it.

Her eyes are huge in disbelief, and she keeps saying my name over and over. Kneeling beside her, I gently take her ravaged hand in mine. When I do, she hugs it to her chest. "Oh, Bryan, I thought you were dead, and I didn't know how I was going to live without you."

Exhausted, she closes her eyes as sleep reclaims her, while I replay her words over and over in my mind. Maybe Helen was right. Maybe she does still love me, although I can't imagine how she could. Taking a tight rein on my emotions, I tell myself not to make too much of her words. Given the harrowing experience she has endured, she most likely won't even remember what she said when she fully recovers.

Nonetheless, I continue to kneel beside her, enjoying the way she grips my hand even in sleep. As strange as it may seem, in this moment I feel closer to her than I ever did when we were married. During our marriage, her neediness threatened to swallow me whole, and I pushed her away lest her love consume me. Now it feels good to be needed, maybe even loved.

My legs are cramping, and I need to change positions, but when I try to slowly extract my hand, she squeezes it tight. "Don't leave me, Bryan. Please don't leave me."

Chapter 33

STERLING, COLORADO
1971

It is late Friday afternoon when Rita hands Rob a cablegram in a sealed envelope before taking a seat in one of the side chairs in front of his desk. He studies the envelope for a moment before opening it. After quickly scanning the cablegram, he reads it a second time more slowly. Without a word, he hands it to her.

Dearest Rob: Coming home. Arrive Tuesday 6:38 pm. Flight number 3827. Life-changing trip. Many dangers. Carolyn seriously injured. Please forgive me. You are my life. Love Always. Helen.

Rita's hand is shaking when she finishes reading, and she quickly places the cablegram on Rob's desk before hiding her hands in her lap. She tries to smile, but her heart is breaking. Helen is returning home to take her rightful place as Rob's wife. She supposes it was inevitable, but she has refused to think about it. Given a little more time, she is convinced she could win Rob's heart. But time is running out, and she feels her dreams slipping through her fingers.

She should be happy for Rob and Helen, but try as she might, she can't feel anything except panic. How many times did she tell herself not to fall in love with Rob? How many times did she tell herself nothing good could come of it? She knew it would end this way, that in the end he would choose his wife and his ministry over her.

"Are you okay?" she hears him ask, as if from a great distance. He is kneeling over her, offering her a drink of water, and belatedly she realizes that she must have fainted. The same thing happened when she learned Brad was divorcing her. This is worse, she thinks. As painful as the divorce was, it was also a relief. She remembers telling a friend that it was like the merciful death of a loved one after a long illness. Of course, you grieve, but you're relieved as well. At least she was. Her love was a long time dying, but when the divorce was final, she was ready to move on with her life. Today there's no relief in sight. As she contemplates the end of her relationship with Rob, there's just grief, unspeakable, gut-wrenching grief.

He helps her to her feet and walks her across the room to the leather couch. Outside the picture window, evening has fallen, and in the distance, he hears the sound of traffic in the street. Slipping his arm around her shoulders, he pulls her close. She wills herself not to respond, but she is powerless to resist. Nestling into his embrace, she buries her face against his chest. Although she is determined not to cry, bitter tears stain her cheeks as he kisses her hair and tells her everything is going to be all right. She wants to believe him, but she knows better. No matter how much he says he loves her, she will never be anything but a plaything to him. Already she senses a subtle shift in his feelings. It's too vague to be described but too real to be denied. He may be whispering his love to her as she snuggles in his arms, but she's not fooled.

Even now, he's distancing himself from her as he turns his heart toward Helen.

As she continues to weep, he grows impatient. "Rita, get hold of yourself. You knew Helen wasn't going to stay in the Amazon forever."

"This changes everything," she sobs. "Everything. I will never get to see you."

"Of course, you will," he consoles her. "We will just have to be more careful."

Yet even as he tries to reassure her, he is feeling relieved. With Helen back in the picture, he can begin to extricate himself from his relationship with Rita, carefully, of course, so as not to offend her. He cares deeply for her, maybe even loves her, but he is smart enough to know their relationship isn't going anywhere. Sure, he has talked about divorcing Helen, and they have dreamed about a life together, but that's all it was, just talk. The trick will be to break it off without inciting her wrath.

Rita does not think of herself as a homewrecker, nor does she have any desire to hurt Helen or the boys, but she is not going to give Rob up without a fight. She never intended for it to come to this. In the beginning, it was just a game, some innocent flirting, but it soon took on a life of its own. Now her feelings for Rob are all-consuming, and the thought of losing him is more than she can bear. She might be able to share him with Helen, but she's not giving him up, not if she can help it. In the deepest part of her being, a tiny seed germinates and begins to poison her soul. At this moment, it is not yet a thought, barely even a feeling, but it takes root and begins to grow.

~~~

Rob is at the gate, awaiting Helen's flight nearly thirty minutes before it is scheduled to arrive. He paces the corridor, too nervous to be seated. His emotions are all over the place. As eager as he is to see her, he can't escape the sense of dread that holds him captive. Sooner or later he will have to tell her about the rumors that are circulating regarding his relationship with Rita. Better, he reasons, for her to hear it from him than to be blindsided by gossip. Of course, he will also have to inform her about his meeting with the district presbytery.

Extracting the folded cablegram from the inside pocket of his sport coat, he rereads it for what seems the hundredth time, focusing in particular on Helen's declaration of love: *"Please forgive me. You are my life. Love Always. Helen."*

With a poignant rush of emotion, he recalls when she was truly his life and he hers. They were newlyweds and in Bible college, both working part-time jobs and as poor as church mice. A hot date was an ice cream cone dipped in chocolate from the drive-in. Still, they somehow managed to scrape enough money together to buy a used stereo from the second-hand store. Many a night they sat on the living room floor in their tiny apartment listening to Bobby Goldsboro sing his signature hit, "Honey."

Their first congregation was small and the demands of ministry manageable, so they had lots of time for each other. In the summer, they picnicked under towering cottonwood trees along the Arkansas River. In the winter, they ice-skated on frozen ponds swept clean of snow by bitterly cold winds. Afterward they snuggled by a bonfire, roasting hot dogs and drinking hot chocolate.

Once, they hiked to a secluded canyon, where they baked tinfoil-wrapped potatoes in hot coals and broiled two-inch-thick T-bone steaks over the open flames. As the sun slid beneath the rim of the towering canyon wall, they lay side by side on their sleeping bags and watched the stars decorate the night sky. Later they made love, both their bodies and their souls merging. When they married, they had been true innocents; consequently, the love they shared was pure and uninhibited, free of shame, and untainted by past experiences.

"So," he muses, "where did we go wrong?"

Before he can formulate an answer, Helen's flight arrives, ten minutes early, and he joins the rush of people moving toward the arrival gate. As family and friends greet the deplaning passengers, his anxiety intensifies. Helen is nowhere to be seen, and he can't help wondering if she missed her flight, or, God forbid, changed her mind about coming home. He is about to give up and look for a pay phone when he sees Bryan pushing a wheelchair down the jet bridge.

His first thought is that Helen has injured herself, and then he sees her walking just behind Bryan. Belatedly he realizes the injured woman must be Carolyn. If she hadn't been with Bryan and Helen, he would never have recognized her. Her face is badly bruised, and there's a large bandage on the side of her head. A plaster cast encases her leg from her hip to her toes.

A moment later, Helen sees Rob. Instantly she steps around Bryan and hurries toward him. Just before she reaches the end of the jet bridge, she pauses, suddenly unsure of herself. The memory of their angry parting is indelibly imprinted on her heart, and now it returns with a rush. She can't help thinking he might still be holding a grudge. Then he smiles, revealing the boyish grin that stole her heart so many years ago, and opens his arms. With a cry of joy, she hurls herself at him, and when he crushes her to his chest, she feels safe for the first time in months. Gone are the hurt feelings, the angry words, and the punishing silence.

Now she is weeping, with relief and joy, her tears giving vent to all the pent-up emotions that have weighed heavy upon her these past months. Her heart is so full it's about to burst. There are so many things she wants to say, so many things she wants to tell him, but she doesn't know where to start. Placing her mouth close to his ear, she whispers, "Rob Thompson, I love you." And then again, with more intensity, "Rob Thompson, I love you so much."

At the baggage claim, they collect her luggage and bid Bryan and Carolyn good-bye. Carolyn's roommate has come to drive her home, and Bryan is going to crash at a friend's house. When they are alone in the car, Rob kisses her long and tenderly, then he asks if she would like to have dinner before they make the two-hour drive home.

"That would be wonderful," she says, "especially if we can go someplace special."

"What do you have in mind?"

"I would love to go to the Four-Forty Club, if you think we can afford it."

"Tonight, we can afford anything." Giving her a hug before starting the car, he adds, "When we're together, I feel rich!"

The hostess seats them at a secluded table near the fireplace and hands them each a menu. Although she's starving, Helen can hardly look at the menu for staring at Rob. A lock of hair has fallen across his forehead, and when she reaches across the table to brush it back, she realizes he has silver highlights in his dark hair. Is that something new, she wonders, or has she simply been too self-absorbed to notice? Studying his face in the candlelight, she sees something else she has never seen before—a delicate web of wrinkles at the corner of his eyes— what her mother used to call crow's feet. It appears the last few months have been as hard on him as they've been on her. She feels a flutter of anxiety when she realizes how close they came to losing each other.

Once they place their orders, she reaches inside her purse, extracts a stained and wrinkled envelope, and hands it to him. Before opening it, he looks at her questioningly. "What's this?"

"Just something I wrote to you when I thought I might die in the Amazon. Just read it. It's pretty self-explanatory."

Extracting the small pocketknife that he always carries from his pants pocket, he slits the envelope and removes the letter. He quickly reads it, then goes back and rereads the final paragraphs a second time.

I don't mean to sound melodramatic, but danger lurks everywhere in the Amazonian rain forest and I may not make it back. The thought of losing my life without making things right with you is more than I can bear, hence this letter.

I'm terribly sorry for the way I left you at the airport. I was angry and my pride wouldn't allow me to reach out to you. With the perspective of time and distance, I can see that I have been a perfect "bitch" for weeks, maybe months. Concealing my friendship with Carolyn and deliberately allowing you to be tormented by my unexplained long-distance phone calls was just plain evil. Please forgive me.

In my hurt and anger, I may have overreacted to Rita. I still believe she has designs on you, but I should have trusted you more. You are a man of God and a wonderful husband and father. Falling in love and marrying you was the best thing that ever happened to me. I love you more now than I ever have, and I look forward to spending the rest of our lives together.

> *With all my love,*
> *Helen*

When he finishes reading, his chest is tight and his throat hurts. "Thank you," he finally manages to say. Carefully he refolds the letter and replaces it in the stained envelope. When he starts to hand it back to her, she says, "Keep it. It's yours."

Chapter 34

Rob had every intention of making a full confession to Helen, but she was so happy and their reunion was so perfect that he couldn't bring himself to spoil it. Instead, he took a few days off and drove Helen and the boys to a condo at Breckenridge. He was an accomplished skier, and he spent the mornings on the challenging blue and black runs, while the boys took lessons on the bunny slope. Helen was still recovering from her ordeal in the Amazon, and she was only too happy to lose herself in a good book while ensconced on the love seat in front of the fireplace. The four of them spent the afternoons playing table games or taking leisurely drives through the snow-covered mountains.

After putting the boys to bed each evening, Rob and Helen talked late into the night, careful to avoid any mention of the things that had nearly destroyed their marriage. Instead they focused on renewing their relationship. Together they dreamed about their future. Some nights they braved the frigid cold to soak in the hot tub located on the balcony just outside their bedroom. Later they made love that was both tender and passionate. It was a nearly perfect time, marred only by Rob's guilty conscience, which he tried to ignore. If Helen sensed it, she pretended not to notice.

On their final night in the condo, she put the boys to bed before joining Rob in the living room. He was deep in thought and hardly acknowledged her presence when she placed a steaming mug of hot chocolate on the end table beside him. She has brought her father's journal, intending to share some portions with Rob, but sensing his mood, she now sets it aside. For some reason, he seems to have no interest in talking about her experiences in the Amazon. Each time she brings it up, he deftly turns the conversation to other things. Although his disinterest has hurt her feelings, she has been careful not to react. Swallowing her disappointment once again, she places her hand on his arm and asks, "Is something troubling you?" When he doesn't respond, she presses, "What is it?"

In an instant, Rob realizes there will probably never be a better time to tell her about Rita and the mess with the district presbytery board, but try as he might, he can't bring himself to do it. The very idea renders him mute. He can't bear the thought of watching the love in her eyes turn to disappointment and then anger. He knows it will be much worse if she hears it from someone else; nonetheless, he decides to put it off till later.

Taking a sip of his steaming hot chocolate, he gives her a tentative smile. "I guess I'm feeling kind of depressed at the thought of leaving in the morning." Shrugging his shoulders, he adds, "I wish we could stay longer, but duty calls."

"What do you have there?" he asks, belatedly noticing her father's journal on the coffee table.

For just an instant, she wishes she hadn't brought it. If he treats it with the same disinterest that he has shown at any mention of her experiences in the Amazon, she doesn't know what she will do. Picking it up, she carefully removes the oilcloth before replying, "This is my father's final journal. Komi, the Indian who was with my father when he died, gave it to Bryan."

Unbidden tears are glistening in her eyes, and she hugs the journal to her chest before continuing. "There's nothing, absolutely nothing, my father could have left us that I would treasure more. Through his writing, he has given me a glimpse of his heart. For the first time in my life, I feel like I know him. Really know him."

Taking a tissue from her pocket, she dabs at her tear-damp eyes before opening the journal. The pages are brittle with age, and in places the ink is so faded it is almost impossible to read. Carefully she turns the pages until she comes to the entry she is seeking. Risking a glance at Rob, who is watching her intently, she clears her throat and begins to read.

Dearest Helen:

After days and days of rain, the sun is finally shining, warming my tired bones. Nonetheless, I fear my death is near. I am not afraid of dying for I take comfort in the words of Jesus: "I am the resurrection, and the life: he that believeth in me, though he were dead, yet shall he live." When I take my final breath here, I will take my first breath of eternal life!

Still, if I am totally honest, I have to admit that I hate the thought of dying, not because I fear death, but because I hate the thought of leaving my family. I hate the thought of not being there for you as you grow into the woman God has called you to be. I hate the thought that I won't be there to walk you down the aisle on your wedding day. I hate the thought that I won't be there to dedicate your babies to the Lord, and I hate the thought that I won't have a chance to tell you how special you are and how much I love you.

It shames me to remember how little affection I showed you as you were growing up. Thinking about it now, I recall the hunger in your eyes when you looked at me. My heart hurt with love for you, but I didn't know how to express it. I left that up to your mother, but I now realize you needed a father's love also. If I could do it again, I would hug you every day and tell you how much I love you. I would kneel beside your bed and pray with you every night and kiss you on the forehead before blowing out the lamp.

I take comfort because I know how strong you are. In many ways, you are stronger than Bryan, maybe even stronger than your mother. In the days ahead, you will have to be strong for both of them. That's a heavy load for a girl your age, but I have no doubt that you will manage. Your faith is strong. It always has been.

I would like to think Bryan might follow in my steps and become a missionary, but in my heart, I know God has other plans for him. As my death draws near, I have an ever-growing conviction that my missionary mantle will be passed on to you. And I am convinced that your ministry will far exceed my own and through you my ministry will live on.

You are truly a daughter any father would be proud of, and I am so thankful the Lord allowed me to be your father. I love you more than I could ever say, and I always will.

> *With all my love always,*
> *Father*
> *January 1949*

When she finishes reading her father's letter, she can't look at Rob lest she see disapproval in his eyes. For what seems a long time, they sit in silence, the only sound being the crackle of the fire and the creaking of the condo as the temperature outside plunges into the single digits. Finally, Rob clears his throat and says, "That's quite a letter." Although his words are complimentary, there's something in his voice that makes Helen feel uncertain.

Determinedly she pushes her concerns aside and bares her heart. "That letter, and all I've been through these past weeks in the Amazon, has given me a new perspective on my life."

Before she can say more, he interrupts, "What do you mean, a new perspective?"

Although there's more than a hint of challenge in his tone, she decides to ignore it. Choosing her words carefully, she replies, "I've never thought of myself as a particularly strong person, but my father's words have encouraged me to look deeper. In doing so, I've discovered a strength I never knew I had.

"Maybe you have to be pushed to your limits before you really discover how strong you are. For instance, I could have never imagined myself capable of surviving alone in the jungle for more than a week, but I did. If I hadn't discovered a strength I never knew I had, I would have died. Either I would have drowned, or I would have perished in the jungle."

"Your survival probably had more to do with God's protection than any special strength you might have," Rob says dismissively.

"I'll grant you that! But if I hadn't been strong, I might have given up and died before Dr. Peterson's expedition found me."

His words have wounded her. Instead of rejoicing with her, he seems to be belittling the things the Lord has been affirming in her heart. A sob catches in her throat, but she pushes it down, determined not to let him see her cry. Moving to the fireplace, she pokes at the fire before adding a couple of logs. When the fire is blazing, she moves to the window and stares out at the night, trying to figure out how things could have gone so wrong.

Once she has regained her composure, she turns to face him. "Why are you doing this? Why are you belittling me and discrediting everything I experienced in the Amazon?"

Her heart's cry is plain enough, but Rob cannot bring himself to relent. Instead of taking her in his arms and comforting her, he continues to challenge her. "I know your father's letter means a lot to you, but I would counsel you not to make too much out of it. No doubt he wanted to believe you would carry on his missionary work, but only God can call a person to the mission field."

"Of course, you're right," she replies, too hurt to argue.

For reasons he can't explain, not even to himself, Rob feels threatened by her self-confidence and newly discovered spiritual identity. Something inside of him wants to belittle her, wants to demean her father's words. He hates what he's doing, but he can't seem to help himself. Now he says, "I hope you're not going to tell me you feel called to the mission field."

She should just let it go, but she can't. Instead she tries to make him understand. "Maybe. I'm not sure. All I know is that when I was at the mission station, it felt like I belonged there."

Disgusted, Rob says, "So, I guess you expect me to resign the pastorate and follow you to the mission field."

"No, Rob," she says wearily, "that's not what I expect you to do. I'm your wife, a pastor's wife, and I will serve where you serve. You've always had a heart for missions, and I couldn't help but wonder if perhaps you had a missionary call on your life. That's all."

"Well, let me make one thing perfectly clear. I'm called to be a pastor, and I will always be a pastor. I have a heart for missions, but I will never be a missionary!"

His eyes are blazing with anger, and Helen's heart is breaking. Glaring at her, he says, "I'm going for a walk. I need some air." Without another word, he puts on his ski jacket and storms out the door.

She is stunned. Just minutes ago, they had been enjoying hot chocolate and intimate conversation, and now Rob is on the warpath. Trying to make some sense of the situation, she replays their conversation over in her mind. Try as she might, all she can come up with is that Rob is threatened by the woman she has become. If she knows her heart, that's the last thing she wants to do, but how can she make him understand that all she wants to do is serve with him?

Although she's exhausted, she's too agitated to go to bed. Instead, she carries their cups into the kitchen, where she rinses them before placing them in the dishwasher. After straightening the living room, she curls up on the love seat and stares at the dying embers in the fireplace. She can't help wondering if this is what their life is going to be like—times of intense closeness suddenly torn apart for no good reason.

Against her will, she finds herself reliving the dreadful days leading up to her decision to go to the Amazon. With painful clarity, she remembers their heated arguments, the punishing silence, her depression, and his late nights at the church. Although she tries to ignore it, she can't help cringing at the memory of the familiarity she witnessed between Rob and Rita. She can only pray that all of that is behind them.

Chapter 35

Rob watches Rita drive away before turning and walking up the sidewalk toward the front of the house. Hitching a ride home with her wasn't a good idea, but Helen left immediately after the service ended, leaving him stranded at the church. She's never done that before, and he fears the worst. Maybe one of the boys became ill, or perhaps Helen did. It's not likely, but why else would she rush off the way she did?

As soon as he opens the door, he knows something is amiss. Helen is not in the kitchen preparing Sunday dinner, and the boys are nowhere to be found. He hangs his overcoat in the hall closet and calls, "Anybody home?" as he makes his way from room to room. Finally, he sees Helen sitting on the back deck staring into the distance. "What in the world is she doing out there?" he mutters to himself.

He shivers as he steps onto the deck. Even though the sun is shining brightly, a brisk wind off the snow-covered Rockies makes it uncomfortably chilly. Helen seems oblivious to the chill. He calls her name, but she simply continues to stare into the distance. Finally, he sits down in the chair beside her and touches her arm. When he does, he notices that she is clutching a crumpled sheet of paper.

"What's that?" he asks.

Without a word she hands it to him, her hand trembling with pent-up anger and an unspeakable grief. As he takes it from her, she suddenly turns on him. "How could you do this to me?" she demands, spitting the words at him. "How could you do this to our boys?"

He's shocked by the force of her words, but before replying, he smoothes the crumpled sheet of paper and quickly scans it.

Dear Helen:

Thankfully, you are home. I only hope you are not too late. While you were away, he has been playing. Has he told you about the incriminating photo and the investigation by the district? Probably not. Ask him, you need to know.

A Concerned Friend

He feels like he's been sucker-punched, and his head is spinning. In retrospect, he realizes he should have told Helen what was going on the minute she stepped off the plane. He knew something like this was a possibility, but he could never find the right time to tell her. Or maybe he could never find the courage to tell her. If he had come clean with her, she would have been hurt, and terribly angry, but at least she would have heard it from him and not from an anonymous "friend." Now, no matter what he says, she will view it with suspicion. She will wonder if he is telling her the whole truth or if he is holding something back.

Finally, he manages to ask, "Where did you get this?"

"I found it in my Bible. I have no idea how it got there."

When he doesn't respond, she asks, "Are you going to tell me what this is about, or should I just wait for another letter?"

Taking a deep breath, he lays out the bare facts as quickly as he can—his late-night dinner with Rita, the incriminating photo, and his hearing before the district officials. When he finishes, her face is deathly pale, and a single tear slides down her cheek.

A dark cloud obscures the sun, and a gust of wind chills them. Reaching for her hand, he says, "It's cold out here. Let's continue this inside."

Pulling her hand away, she asks, "Do you love her?"

He hesitates before answering, and that's all the answer she needs. She hardly hears him as he goes on to explain that he has feelings for Rita, but he doesn't know if he's in love with her. He hastens to add that he has no intentions of ever leaving Helen or the boys.

"Have you made love to her?"

"Absolutely not!"

She continues to question him, her voice sounding strangled. "Have you kissed her? Have you touched her?"

"Helen, stop," he pleads. "You don't want to do this. It will serve no good purpose."

"Just tell me the truth."

The Letter

"You couldn't bear the truth."

"Have you kissed her?"

"Yes, if you must know, I have kissed her. I kissed her because she was there for me when you weren't, because she took the time to understand me when you were so self-absorbed that you hardly noticed whether I was around or not. You made a shrine out of your grief. You cared more about the dead than you did about the living—our boys or me. It pains me to say this, but Rita cares about me in ways you never have."

Helen's heart is breaking. The man who vowed before God to forsake all others, to love and cherish only her all the days of his life, has betrayed her. He claims he hasn't made love to Rita, but she doesn't know whether to believe him. What difference does it make? Whether or not he has made love to her doesn't really change anything. He has given Rita a part of his heart that belonged only to her, and that's adultery, even if they haven't had sexual intercourse.

Wave after wave of grief washes over her, and she wishes she had died in the Amazon. She wishes she had drowned when their boat capsized. She wishes she had perished in the jungle. Death would have been better than this. She's sobbing now, quietly. With each sob, it feels like a piece of her heart is being ripped out.

She can't help wondering what happened to the man she fell in love with. What happened to the man she married? He was a good and decent man, a man of integrity, a man who loved God. This man—her unfaithful husband—is a stranger. She doesn't know him. Or maybe she never knew him. Maybe their entire marriage was just make-believe; maybe it was all an elaborate charade. Maybe Rita isn't even the first woman he has been involved with.

A hundred incidents, seemingly innocuous at the time, now seem ominous when seen in this new light. She remembers a church picnic where they were playing keep-away, and he and Rita were wrestling over the ball. At the time, it seemed like innocent fun, but in retrospect it seems sexual, almost lurid. How could she have been so trusting, so naïve?

As crazy as it sounds, she feels ashamed. How will she ever face her friends? What will they think of her when they find out her marriage wasn't all it appeared to be? Maybe they already knew, or at least suspected, that Rob wasn't the perfect pastor and faithful husband she thought he was. At least one person did—the anonymous writer who signed her letters "A Concerned Friend."

Every special memory she has of their thirteen-year marriage is now suspect. She can't help wondering if Rob was leading a double life even when it seemed their marriage was solid. Did the board meetings really last that late? Were those late-night phone calls truly pastoral emergencies, or just a ruse to get out of the house? When they were intimate, was he really making love to her, or was he fantasizing about someone else? When he stormed out of the condo in Breckenridge, was he just going for a walk, or did he find a pay phone and call Rita? Reason tells her she's overreacting, that her entire marriage was not a sham, but her overwrought emotions are immune to reason.

The Letter

The wind has picked up, and the temperature has plunged, as so often happens in the early spring on the high plains of northeastern Colorado. Helen is chilled to the bone, and her teeth are chattering. Against her better judgment, she allows Rob to put his sports coat around her shoulders and lead her into the house. Once inside, she stumbles to the bedroom, where she throws herself facedown on the bed. He sits on the bed beside her and softly rubs her back until she finally stops shaking.

When she is able to compose herself, she says, "I won't share you."

"What do you mean?"

"In time I may be able to forgive you, but Rita will have to go."

Chapter 36

FORT COLLINS, COLORADO
1975

Almost four years have passed since I returned from the Amazon. While there, I discovered I had a budding talent for photography, and when I returned to the States, I considered enrolling in Colorado State University to pursue a degree in photojournalism. After thinking about it, I realized that while I have a good eye, there's no art in my photography, nothing to set it apart. I soon discovered that while my aptitude for photography was limited, I had a gift for writing. Put a pen in my hand and the words just seem to flow out of me. While still enrolled at CSU, I published three short stories based on my experiences in the Amazon. Those stories caught the attention of a small publishing house. When they offered me a contract, I began work on my first novel.

Rob and Helen attempted to reconcile, and for a time it seemed they might make a go of it. I saw Helen from time to time, and although she put on a brave front, I could sense something was not right. I encouraged her to confide in me, but she never did. Too many Whittaker genes, I guess. A couple of times I drove to Sterling on the weekend. Although Rob and Helen were painfully polite toward each other, even I could see things were strained. Rob was gone a lot. "Working," Helen said, but I couldn't help but wonder. I wanted to ask her if the "thing" with his secretary was resolved, but I didn't. Even the boys were different. Gone was their rowdy exuberance and ready laughter. Now they crept through the house like ghosts, lest they shatter the fragile façade their parents tried to maintain. By the time the weekend was over, I was only too eager to return to my garage apartment with its comforting solitude.

Through a series of painful revelations, Helen was able to verify that the anonymous letters from a "concerned friend" were sent by Rita herself in an attempt to break up Rob and Helen's marriage. At Helen's insistence, Rob finally replaced her, but it was messy. Nearly half the congregation felt Rita had been unjustly fired and demanded a vote of confidence. It was close, but a slim majority of the congregation voted to retain Rob as their pastor. The fallout was brutal. Charges and countercharges were exchanged, and nearly forty percent of the congregation left the church. Needless to say, all of this took a terrible toll on Rob and Helen's relationship. He blamed her for insisting that Rita had to go, and she blamed him for involving himself in an inappropriate relationship.

Who knows how things might have worked out if it hadn't been for Rob's accident. When he attended a men's retreat with a group of guys from the church, several of them carpooled, but he chose to drive to drive his own car. He left the retreat in the wee hours of the morning following the opening service. Why he left and where he was headed remains a mystery. Some have suggested that he was going to meet Rita at a mountain hideaway, but that's only speculation. According to the Colorado Highway Patrol, he died in a one-car accident, late Saturday night, on Highway 50 west of Canon City. Later I learned that a heavy rain had caused a rockslide in the narrow canyon, blocking the highway. Apparently, Rob lost control of his car trying to avoid the huge rocks and plunged into the Arkansas River.

Helen grieved terribly, and for a time she blamed herself. Watching her grieve was like reliving my own childhood, and I feared for her boys. I knew only too well how crippling it could be for a child to loss a father, so I made sure to spend as much time as possible with them. We went camping at Chambers Lake, located in the mountains above Fort Collins. For a week, we hiked and fished. At night we sat around the campfire and talked. Little by little the boys shared their anger, their fears, and their grief.

In time, Helen regained her equilibrium, although she continued to grieve, not only Rob's death but also all its ramifications. Her whole identity changed. She was no longer the wife of a pastor. For the first time in years, she had to work outside the home. Now she was a widow with two young children to support. I encouraged her to remarry. She was still young, barely forty, and her boys needed a father. She dated a few times, but nothing ever came of it. When I pressed her, she told me she was thinking of applying for a missionary appointment. I wasn't really surprised. The far western Amazon Basin and its indigenous people called to her. Like our father, she wanted to take the gospel to those who had never heard it.

The Rocky Mountain District eventually approved her missionary application, and she is currently itinerating to raise monthly support. She plans to settle in the Peruvian Amazon and minister to the indigenous people groups who inhabit the jungle and live in relative isolation from the rest of the world. To tell you the truth, I think she's crazy, but I have never seen her look more alive.

When we returned from the Amazon nearly four years ago, Carolyn was recovering from her ordeal in the jungle. I had set her broken leg as best I could, given the primitive conditions in which we had found ourselves. Nonetheless, the orthopedic surgeon had to rebreak her femur and surgically insert a rod and some screws. Her rehab was slow, but when she recovered, she was as good as new. Her experience in the Amazon was traumatic, to say the least, and she still doesn't like to talk about it, but I believe it changed her in positive ways. Having survived a near-drowning, nearly two weeks alone in the jungle without food or equipment, and a broken leg has made her self-reliant. Occasionally I see glimpses of the insecure person she used to be, but for the most part, I'm amazed at her self-confidence.

It wasn't easy, but I followed through on my vow to apologize to her and take responsibility for the way I had treated her during the last weeks of our marriage. As our marriage was falling apart, she had clung to me, loving me with a fierceness that threatened to suffocate me. As a result, I pushed her away. My rejection exacerbated her insecurities and drove her into the arms of another. When I learned of her adultery, I was sorely wounded and vowed never to forgive her. She wept and begged for my forgiveness, but I turned my back on her. I never missed a chance to shame her. In fact, I took pleasure in it. In the end, she shouldered the blame for all that was wrong in our marriage, and I let her, even though I could see it was killing her.

I told her I didn't expect her to forgive me, but at least I wanted her to know that the failure of our marriage wasn't entirely her fault. In fact, most of the fault was mine. I told her about my father wound and how it had crippled me emotionally. I told her that when we married, I was incapable of loving anyone. It was a harrowing conversation for both of us, and there were a lot of tears. In the end she forgave me, although I can't imagine how she did it.

To my surprise, I discovered I enjoyed her company, and we began doing things together. Not dating, just hanging out. Sometimes we picnicked in the park or took long drives to see the fall colors when the aspens turned. In time, we became good friends, something we never achieved while we were married. She told me about nursing school, and we discussed the novel I was writing. I might have fallen in love with her all over again—but for my feelings for Diana.

When I left the mission station four years ago, my heart was breaking, but I was sure I would get over Diana in time. Painful as our parting was, I was convinced it was the right decision. I simply could not allow her to sacrifice her missionary call for me. No matter how much we loved each other, I was convinced it would never work. I still think I made the right decision, but I was wrong about getting over her. Not a day goes by but that I think of her, and anytime I date, which isn't often, she's the standard by which I judge all others. So far no one has measured up, not even close.

The Letter

I know it's not likely, but I cling to a secret hope that one day Diana will contact me. There's no reason to think she will, but still I cling to that hope. And given another chance at love, you can be sure I would never walk away. No matter what the risks, I would gladly take them. If these last four years have taught me anything, it's that the joy of loving Diana and being loved by her far outweigh any hurt we might suffer. I know that now, but I fear it is too late. Still, I hope.

Chapter 37

I've been writing for several hours, and my hand is cramping. Laying the cheap ballpoint pen aside, I massage my stiff fingers, noting with satisfaction the number of pages I have filled and torn from the yellow legal pad. Belatedly, I realize that the room has grown cold, and I notice the window above my makeshift writing desk is fringed with an intricate pattern of frost. In the distance, the snowcapped peaks of the Colorado Rockies jut into the brilliant blue of the winter sky.

Moving to the stove, I poke at the coals and open the damper, creating a draft that coaxes a small flame from the glowing embers. I quickly add some kindling before placing an armload of split pinion in the stove. In almost no time, the fire is blazing, and I stand there a moment more, enjoying the warmth.

Glancing up, I see the rural mail carrier stopping at the end of my driveway. Even from this distance, I can see his warm breath fog the frigid January air as he lowers the window of his Jeep to deposit a fist full of mail in the sagging mailbox. I'm sure it's mostly junk, but still, I reach for my parka and head for the door. The cold slaps me in the face, and my eyes smart. An arctic cold front has plunged temperatures to minus-17 degrees, and the snow beneath my boots is nearly as hard as gravel. Unconsciously I find myself comparing the bitter cold to the sweltering heat of the Amazon Basin, and when I do, a host of bittersweet memories assail me. It's been more than four years since Helen, Carolyn, and I launched our small boat and made our way down the Rio Moa toward Cruzeiro do Sul, on the first leg of our journey back to civilization; still, the memories have the power to transfix me.

Determinedly I push them to the back of my mind as I open my dilapidated mailbox and retrieve my mail. A quick perusal of the contents confirms my suspicions. It's mostly junk, and I turn toward the house, eagerly anticipating the warmth of the stove. In the tiny mudroom, I stomp the snow off my boots and hang my parka on a wooden peg by the door. Tossing the mail on the counter, I stretch my hands toward the stove, savoring the heat.

Out of the corner of my eye, I notice the edge of a tissue-thin, powder-blue aerogram envelope. I don't know how I missed it when I glanced through the mail before tossing it on the counter, but I did. Now it draws me like a magnet. Could it be that Diana has written me after all this time? It's not likely, given the way we parted, but still, I hope.

I'm sure my optimism is ill founded. I haven't heard a word from her since I left the mission station, yet not a day passes but what I think of her. I remember the way she looked the first time I saw her and how beautiful she was sitting in the swing beneath the towering samauma tree. Her eyes were deep blue, reminding me of the Colorado sky in winter, her face, with its high cheekbones, was full of feeling and the afternoon sun was highlighting her golden hair. How gentle was her touch as she cared for me while I was recovering from malaria. The love we shared, brief as it was, still lives in my heart. Unconsciously, I rub my chest where an all-too-familiar ache has taken up residence.

Pushing those memories to the back of my mind, I collect a sheaf of yellow pages from my makeshift desk and return to the warmth of the stove, determined to ignore the aerogram envelope and the memories it has invoked. Dutifully I scan the handwritten pages, noticing the cramped script. According to Diana, my handwriting matches my personality. She said I was hard to read. I don't like to think of myself as being closed, but I suppose she's right. It's not that I don't trust people. I just don't want to be hurt again.

Outside the small window above my writing desk, the day is dying, winter's night coming on with a rush. With an effort, I turn my thoughts to my day's work, but the things I've written on the yellow pages are no match for the magnetism of that aerogram envelope lying on the counter. Placing the yellow sheets containing my day's writing on the makeshift desk, I turn toward the counter and pick up the aerogram envelope. The postage stamp is Brazilian, and with trembling hands I carefully open it, hoping against hope that Diana has finally written to me after all this time.

Dear Bryan:

Please forgive me for presuming on your kindness. Were it not for Eurico, I would not trouble you, but I have nowhere else to turn. I have discovered a rather large lump in my breast. It may be nothing to be concerned about—a cyst or a benign tumor—but there is no way to be sure without returning to the States and having it checked out.

Eurico and I are flying to the States in late March or early April. I will be checking into the University of Colorado Hospital in Aurora. Worst-case scenario: The tumor is malignant. In that case, I will have a mastectomy followed by radiation therapy and perhaps chemotherapy.

Here's my dilemma. I have no one to take care of Eurico. I would leave him here with Gordon and Eleanor, but they are going home on furlough and he can't stay by himself. I have no family, or I would leave him with them. As you may recall, my mother passed away several years ago after a lengthy battle with breast cancer. About eighteen months ago, my father suffered a massive heart attack and died suddenly.

I feel awkward asking for your help, but I don't know what else to do. You may be married with a family of your own by now, and if you can't do this, I will understand.

Sincerely,
Diana Rhodes

Her letter knocks the wind out of me, and I stumble to my makeshift desk and collapse in my chair. I replay her words over and over in my mind—*Worst-case scenario: The tumor is malignant. In that case, I will have a mastectomy followed by radiation therapy and perhaps chemotherapy.* I'm in shock. My heart refuses to believe it. This can't be happening to Diana. She's too young, too vivacious, too full of life!

Sometime later, I realize the cabin has grown cold and outside a full moon has risen; it is nearly as bright as day. The moonlight reflecting off the snow seeps in through the windows, casting deformed shadows on the far wall. I should rekindle the fire and turn on the lights, but Diana's news has left me disoriented. Ordinary tasks now seem impossible. Finally, I put an armload of wood in the stove and stir up the fire, but I leave the lights off. The semidarkness matches my mood, and I realize I haven't grieved like this since my father disappeared while on a mission of mercy in the far western Amazon rain forest nearly twenty-five years ago.

Of course, I will take care of Eurico. I've missed that little guy more than I can say. The thought of his infectious smile and enthusiasm for life is the only thing that makes Diana's news bearable. I survey my tiny cabin, and for a moment I'm embarrassed. Where will he sleep? There's only one bedroom. Where will we put his things? Then I remember that everything he owns will probably fit in a duffel bag with room left over. And if anything, the mission house is even more primitive than my cabin.

I'm scared. Mind-numbing scared. I can't imagine a world without Diana. Although we haven't spoken since our painful parting four years ago, I always took comfort in the knowledge that she was there. If anything happens to her, I will never forgive myself for walking away. If only I had accepted her offer to return to the States with me and practice medicine here. Worst-case scenario, we would have had four good years together. Now the only time we may have could be fraught with sickness and death. How could I have been so stupid? What was I afraid of, for heaven's sake?

If Diana gives me another chance, I won't throw it away, I can promise you that. Of course, she may have no interest in rekindling our relationship, and I couldn't blame her, considering the pain I have caused her. Still, I hope. According to Helen, there's no obstacle love can't overcome, and I love Diana, so maybe, just maybe, we can make it work this time.

Chapter 38

MISSION STATION
FAR WESTERN AMAZON BASIN
1975

Looking up from the little Indian girl she is examining, Diana sees Gordon ambling toward the clinic. He has a fist full of mail, and she hopes she has a letter from Bryan. It's been more than two months, actually almost three, since she posted her letter to him. It normally takes four to six weeks for a letter to reach the States and an equal amount of time to receive a reply—that is, if anyone is coming upriver from Cruzeiro do Sul. Otherwise, the mail might be delayed until Gordon picks it up when he journeys downriver for supplies.

Lifting the little girl off the examining table, she gives her a hug before handing her mother a small packet of antibiotics. They are just leaving when Gordon walks in, his huge frame filling the small room. Waving an envelope at her, he says, "I think this is what you've been looking for. Let's hope it's good news."

Taking it from him, she glances at the address, instantly recognizing Bryan's cramped handwriting. Picking up a nearby scalpel, she carefully cuts the seals and unfolds the tissue-thin paper. Her hands are trembling, and she turns her back as she begins to read, lest Gordon sees how nervous she is.

The Letter

Diana:

I cannot tell you how grieved I am to learn you have a lump in your breast. I'm glad you're coming to the States to have it checked out. Given your family history, this must be especially hard for you. Please don't jump to any conclusions. As you pointed out in your letter, it may just be a large cyst or a benign tumor. If it turns out to be something more serious, the University of Colorado Hospital is the place to be. It is a top-flight cancer treatment hospital specializing in the latest treatment protocols.

Of course, I will take care of Eurico while you're recovering. I've missed that little guy terribly. I live in a small cabin just west of Fort Collins, in the foothills, about eighty miles from Aurora. He will love it. The thought of seeing him gives me the strength to deal with your situation. I'm sure it will turn out to be nothing serious; still, I won't rest easy until all of this is behind you.

I don't know if Carolyn has been writing to you or not, so forgive me if this is old news. You inspired her to go into nursing, and she enrolled in nursing school upon her return to the States. She graduated last December and now works at the University of Colorado Hospital in the oncology department. She has a two-bedroom apartment a few blocks from the hospital and insists you stay with her, that is, if you haven't made other arrangements.

When you get to Cruzeiro do Sul, send me a cable with your flight information, and I will meet your flight. I wish the circumstances were different; still, I am eager to see you and honored that you thought of me in regard to Eurico.

Be careful on the river, it can be treacherous this time of the year. Hopefully, you are going downriver with Gordon and Eleanor. He is an experienced boatman, and you will be in good hands. Safe travels.

Your friend forever,
Bryan

P.S. I am holding you in my prayers.

When she turns to Gordon, tears are glistening in her eyes. Softly he asks, "Are those tears of joy, or has Bryan disappointed you again?"

In an instant, she is defensive. Gordon may mean well, but he has no right to imply Bryan can't be trusted. She wants to defend him, and she's tempted to give Gordon a piece of her mind, but she thinks better of it. Instead, she thrusts the letter at him, saying, "Here, read it for yourself."

While Gordon scans the letter, she walks to window and stares down the path that leads to the river. Granted, Bryan has hurt her in the past, but not deliberately, and not out of cruelty. One time she may have thought that was the case, but now she believes his actions were motivated by his concern for her. His thinking may have been misguided, but she believes his heart was right.

It's been more than four years, but in her mind, she can see the day of his departure clearly. It was just after daylight, and a ground fog gave the mission station and the surrounding rain forest an ethereal appearance. Bryan moved in and out of the fog as he made his way toward the river and away from her. She was tempted to run after him, but her pride wouldn't let her. Instead she just stared at him through tear-blurred eyes as he walked out of her life; all the while, her heart was breaking.

Did she make a mistake? Probably. Well she remembers Helen's counsel, having replayed it over in her mind at least several hundred times. *"If there's any chance for you and Bryan, you will have to make the first move. He's convinced he's hurt you in ways that are past forgiving."* Is she ready to make the first move? Maybe, but only if he still has feelings for her.

She can't help wondering if he's married or in a serious relationship. Surely not or he would have mentioned it in his letter, wouldn't he? Unconsciously she rubs her breast, hating and fearing the lump that now dictates her life. If it's malignant, that will squelch all possibilities of renewing her relationship with Bryan. She couldn't put him through what she endured as her mother battled cancer. Months of radiation treatments followed her radical mastectomy, then chemotherapy when the cancer spread, and the side effects were hideous. The pain was unbearable, she was nauseous all the time, she lost all of her hair and was so weak she could hardly walk across the room. When she finally died, she was nothing but skin and bones. If her own tumor is malignant, that's likely what she's facing, and she shudders at the thought. It's simply too hideous to imagine.

She can't help thinking that no man in his right mind would choose to marry a deathly ill woman mutilated by a radical mastectomy. Certainly not Bryan, she thinks, remembering how he abandoned her when he thought Eurico was dying.

Gordon calls her name, and she turns from the window. "Nice letter," he says, handing it to her. "Be careful. Guard your heart. I don't want to see you get hurt again."

Before she can reply, he continues, "It will probably take Eleanor and me four or five days to get things finished up here. That means we could probably head downriver by Wednesday. Will that work for you?"

"No problem. Eurico and I will be ready."

Once he leaves the clinic, she brews a cup of tea and takes it to the porch, where she settles on the swing. Opening Bryan's letter, she rereads it, slowly this time, searching for nuances of meaning in his carefully crafted words. His concern is obvious enough, and she tries to decide if he is just being compassionate or whether he still has feelings for her.

The Bryan she remembers was a man of few words and not given to flattery. If he said something, he meant it. Holding his letter close to her heart, she allows herself to believe he still cares for her. Maybe he even loves her.

A gust of wind, cold and heavy with moisture, troubles the towering treetops, and over the Serra Divisor a storm is brewing. Nearer, the evening is electric with lightning, the air smelling of fresh ozone. Throwing the dregs of her tea off the porch, she locks the small clinic and hurries toward her cottage just ahead of the first drops of rain.

Once inside, she lights the kerosene lamp and prepares to start supper for Eurico and herself. Then she remembers that he is spending the night with the Arnolds. They are the closest thing he will ever have to grandparents, and they dote on him. She can't help smiling as she pictures him playing checkers with Gordon. He is fiercely competitive and studies the board intensely before making a move. Maybe Gordon allows him to win, she doesn't know, but Eurico relishes his triumph while Gordon pretends to pout. Eleanor rewards him with a huge piece of chocolate cake and even allows Gordon a small slice as a consolation prize.

With the evening stretching before her, she wanders through her small cottage with its simple furnishings. Braided rag rugs add color to the dark planks that make up the floor. Empty fruit crates set on end serve as end tables, and kerosene lamps provide the only light. The gentle pinging of the rain on the corrugated tin roof reminds her of the evenings she and Bryan spent together while her broken leg was mending.

Making herself comfortable on the couch, she relaxes, allowing her mind to revisit the past. A collage of memories now plays through her mind like slides projected on a screen. In the first, it is night, and the room's only light comes from the full moon that spills its soft glow through the small window beside her bed. Bryan is napping in the chair beside her, and she turns her head so she can study his profile. He has a strong face with chiseled features and deep-set eyes. He needs a haircut, his unruly locks falling over his forehead and curling over his collar. She would like to touch his face, but she doesn't want to wake him.

He must have sensed something because he opened his eyes and smiled at her. When he did, she reached over and brushed his hair back before allowing her fingers to rest on his cheek. In a husky voice, she asks, "Have I ever told you what a good-looking man you are?"

"I don't think so," he replies with a grin, "but I'm all ears if you would like to tell me now."

Giving him a playful punch, she says, "The first time I saw you, I thought you were the best-looking man I had ever seen."

"You're kidding me."

"No. I'm serious."

"You could have fooled me. You hardly looked my way. It seemed like you only had eyes for Dr. Peterson, and later, over dinner at the Arnolds, you virtually ignored me."

"Dr. Peterson is an old friend. I could hardly ignore him."

"So, are you going to tell me how good-looking I am or not?"

"I don't think so. You might get the big head."

They both laugh, and then she asks, "Are you ever going to kiss me?"

Leaning over, he brushes her forehead with a kiss.

"That's not a kiss."

Taking his face in her hands, she kisses him on the mouth. In an instant, he responds. Kneeling beside her bed, he takes her in his arms and kisses her passionately. Why they finally break, she is flushed but manages to say, "Now, that's a kiss!"

That memory dissolves to be replaced by another, and now she relives the night they spent together on the steep mountainside following her accident. Although they were not far from the equator, they were wet and chilled to the bone. One of the phenomena of the rain forest is the incredible evaporation of moisture from the wet jungle floor that continues after the sun has set, sucking heat out of the muggy air. Given their wet clothes and exposed position, they were in danger of hypothermia.

She remembers waking sometime in the night shivering violently. Bryan wrapped his arms around her and spooned his body against hers in a desperate attempt to share his meager body warmth with her. It helped some, but his closeness is what she remembers now, how their bodies fit together as if they had been made for each other. "Please, Lord Jesus," she whispers. "Please give us another chance at love."

She must have dozed off, for she awakens with a crick in her neck. In the tiny bedroom, she undresses and blows out the kerosene lamp. Once in bed, she unconsciously messages her breast, hoping against hope that the lump is shrinking. To her dismay, nothing has changed, and for a moment, fear grips her. She can't help wondering if God is punishing her. Reason tells her she's being foolish, but the condemnation that threatened to overwhelm her in the aftermath of her botched abortion now returns with a vengeance. The fact that her fiancé coerced her into having the abortion did nothing to alleviate her guilt. The emergency hysterectomy that followed might have saved her life, but it also intensified her self-loathing. Not only had she consented to the death of her baby, but the medical complications following her tragic decision had made it impossible for her to bear children.

She might still be locked in her prison of shame were it not for a compassionate Christian counselor. After weeks of prayer and counseling, she was finally able to receive God's forgiveness, which enabled her to forgive herself. Although her sin of abortion was terrible, past imagining, God's grace was greater still.

With fear and guilt tempting her, she does what she has done through the ensuing years; she turns to the Scriptures for strength and comfort. Psalm 103 comes to mind: *"The* LORD *is merciful and gracious, slow to anger, and plenteous in mercy. He will not always chide: neither will he keep his anger forever. He hath not dealt with us after our sins; nor rewarded us according to our iniquities. For as the heaven is high above the earth, so great is his mercy toward them that fear him. As far as the east is from the west, so far hath he removed our transgressions from us."*

The lump in her breast is not God's punishment, no matter what the enemy tries to tell her. She is forgiven, and Father God desires only the best for her—no matter that her mind is playing havoc with her emotions. After a time, she is able to still her anxious thoughts and allow the soft pinging of the rain on the roof to coax her toward sleep. As she is drifting off, she remembers one of the sweetest things Bryan ever said to her: *"No matter where my life's journey may take me, the drumming of rain on a tin roof will always sound like love to me—your love."*

Chapter 39

FORT COLLINS, COLORADO

Diana has now been in the States a little more than three weeks. As I feared, the lump in her breast turned out to be malignant, stage three, according to the surgeon. She underwent a radical mastectomy and spent several days in the hospital before being discharged. At Carolyn's insistence, she moved into the second bedroom at her apartment while recovering. Her prognosis is grim, and she is facing weeks, maybe months, of radiation therapy. If the cancer has metastasized, it is likely she will also have to undergo chemotherapy.

One of the things I have always admired about Diana is her unwavering faith, and while she has tried to keep up a brave front for Eurico, I have seen the fear in her eyes. Every day since she got out of the hospital, Eurico and I have made the nearly two-hundred-mile roundtrip from the small cabin where I live west of Fort Collins to Carolyn's apartment in Aurora. Television fascinates him, and he can spend hours glued to it, giving Diana and me plenty of opportunity to get reacquainted.

The first few times we were alone were pretty uncomfortable, and we found ourselves watching every word we said. Finally, I asked her if she knew how porcupines made love.

"What kind of question is that?" she asked, trying not to laugh. When I just grinned, she said, "Okay, wise guy. Tell me how porcupines make love."

"Very carefully," I said.

Because of her surgery, she did her best not to laugh, but ended up laughing anyway while hugging a pillow to her chest. "Please don't make me laugh. It hurts too much."

"Sorry. That wasn't meant to be funny."

"What do you mean?"

"I was trying to find a non-offensive way to describe how it feels when we talk. It's like we're watching every word lest we say something wrong."

When she nods in agreement, I continue, "There's an elephant in the room and we both know it. It's called cancer, but neither one of us will talk about it. Instead we make polite conversation, pretending everything is going to be fine. With all my heart, I want to believe you are going to beat this thing, but who knows. Every night, Eurico and I pray for the Lord to heal you. I hope He does, but I don't know if He will."

A tear glistens in the corner of her eye, and without thinking, I brush it away with my finger, and she takes my hand in hers for a moment. When she doesn't say anything, I go on, "I have a lot of regrets, but I don't regret anything as much as I regret the way we parted. If I could go back and do it again, I would do things differently."

Putting her finger on my lips, she silences me. "Please, Bryan, let's not go there. It hurts too much to play the 'if only' game. It's too late. We don't get 'do overs.'"

For several minutes, we sit in silence, the only sound being the television in the other room. Finally, she asks, "Can we talk about Eurico?"

"Of course."

"I've tried to shield him from the seriousness of my situation, but I'm not sure I've done very well."

"Why do you say that?"

"When we boarded the plane in Miami, he reached over, took my hand, and said, 'It's going to be all right, Di. Jesus healed me when you prayed, and He will heal you. You'll see!' He was so sincere. If I'm not healed, I'm afraid it will destroy his faith."

I want to assure her that everything is going to work out, but I know only too well, that's not always the case. Well do I remember praying desperately for my father to return from his mission of mercy into the jungle, but to no avail. Even now, nearly thirty years later, I remember how that experience crushed me. Truth be told, I'm still trying to get over it.

When I don't say anything, she continues, "Only God knows how desperately I want to believe He will heal me, but I have my doubts. My mother was a woman of great faith, and God didn't heal her. My faith is nothing to write home about; in fact, it is sadly lacking when compared to hers, so what chance do I have of being healed?"

Once again, words fail me, and I just sit there with an ache in my heart. I would like to take her in my arms and hold her, but I don't think I dare. She made herself pretty clear when she said we don't get "do overs."

Finally, she continues, "I have great faith in God's omnipotence—nothing's impossible for Him. All He has to do is speak the word, and I will be healed. But I can't help thinking that in times like these, when we need Him most, it often seems He is silent, or worse yet, absent. The fact is, He doesn't heal everyone."

When she pauses, I ask, "So, why is one person healed and not another?"

"I wish I knew," she replies with a shrug of her shoulders, "but the truth be told, I don't have a clue. Faith is a factor, as Gordon Arnold likes to say, but not necessarily the deciding factor. If it were, my mother would surely be alive."

She reaches for her Bible and extracts a folded sheet of lined notebook paper from between the pages. Without a word, she hands it to me. It's yellow with age and in places the ink is blurred—probably by her tears—making the words difficult to read.

Dear God:

I love you, but I'm really angry right now. I don't want to feel this way, but I can't seem to help myself. The doctors did everything they could, but in the end, they were powerless. I did everything I could do, and still my mom died. Had I done any less, I would have never been able to forgive myself. You are the only one who did nothing—or so it seems to me. You have the power of life and death, and yet You did nothing. You could have healed her, but You didn't! All of us who have such limited power did everything we could, but it feels like You, who have all power, did nothing at all. I'm trying to understand why You didn't do anything, but right now I can't.

Hurt and anger are making me bitter, killing the relationship we once shared. I want to punish You, yet even in my anger, I know You are my only hope. With one hand, I push You away, while with the other hand, I cling to You with all my might. With a trembling faith, I lift my hurt to You, trusting You will take it from me. Replace my anger with acceptance, I pray, and my hurt with hope. I ask not for understanding, but for trust. I know I will never understand why things happened the way they did, so I ask You to give me unconditional trust that I may trust You no matter how grievous my loss. In Your holy name I pray. Amen.

When I finish reading, I don't know what to say, so I simply refold the page and hand it back to her. After carefully replacing it between the pages of her Bible, she clears her throat. "My mother and I were really close, and I was crushed when she died. Not only had I lost my dearest friend and closest confidant, but I also experienced a crisis of faith. As far as I was concerned, God couldn't be trusted. For the longest time, I refused to pray."

This is a side of Diana I have never seen. I have always thought of her as a paragon of faith. Now I realize she has to deal with the same stuff the rest of us struggle with. Finally, I ask, "So, how did you recover your faith?"

"When I was at my lowest point," she says, chewing her bottom lip, "I forced myself to attend a mission conference, although I had no desire to do so. One of the speakers was a veteran missionary who had buried two husbands on the mission field. Her first husband died after being stricken with malaria, leaving her with two small children. Some years later, she remarried and moved to what was then the Belgium Congo. One night communist rebels attacked and burned the mission station, killing her husband and leaving her for dead, after raping her repeatedly.

"Although her testimony sounded like a horror story, she radiated joy, and I was desperate to learn her secret. Considering what she had been through, I couldn't imagine how she could be so joyous. When I finally had a chance to speak with her privately, I told her about my mother's death and my own crisis of faith. I don't know what I expected her to tell me, but I sure wasn't prepared for what she said. Taking both of my hands in hers, she looked me in the eye and said, 'Life goes on—if you let it.'

"Initially, I was pretty disappointed, but I couldn't get her words out of my mind: 'Life goes on—if you let it.' Finally, I realized I had a choice. I could stay mad at God, or I could let it go and move on with my life. That's when I wrote that prayer letter to God."

Not knowing how to respond, I change the subject. "You said you wanted to talk about Eurico, but it seems we got sidetracked."

"So, we did, didn't we?"

I wait, somewhat impatiently, while she organizes her thoughts. "I'm worried about how he's going to adjust. Do you realize he's never seen a supermarket, or a shopping mall, or a television, nor used a telephone?"

When I nod, she continues, "Thankfully I taught him English, insisting that we speak it when communicating with each other. At least he will be able to converse with his peers."

I hasten to assure her that he will adjust just fine, given his zest for life and his irrepressible spirit, but my words don't seem to reassure her. Finally, she works up the courage to address her real concern. "Have you thought about what will happen to him if I die?"

"You're not going to die," I blurt out without thinking.

"I hope you're right, but we have no assurance of that. Cancer is an insidious disease, and it kills lots of people of all ages."

"Diana, let's not talk about dying. You haven't even started treatments yet, and you're at one of the best cancer hospitals in the country."

"Now who wants to ignore the elephant in the room?"

When I don't say anything, she continues, "I'm not being morbid—just realistic! My chances of surviving for five years or more are probably no better than fifty/fifty. I intend to do everything I can to beat those odds, but if I don't, I want to make sure Eurico is taken care of."

I should have seen this coming, but I haven't been willing to think seriously about the possibility of Diana's death or what would happen to Eurico if she should die. I know what she wants me to say—that I will take care of Eurico—but I'm not sure I can make that kind of commitment, no matter how much I love the little guy. As unlikely as it may seem, I am right back where I was four years ago—afraid to make a commitment I might not be able to keep—only this time it involves Eurico.

He was a nine-year-old orphan—a street urchin, really—when I met him. His parents had died three years earlier, and without any family he found himself living on the streets in Cruzeiro do Sul. He managed to keep body and soul together by shining shoes, picking pockets, and begging. Wise beyond his years, he soon found ways to make himself indispensable to me, introducing me to Dr. Peterson and finding a *mateiro* to guide me in my search for my missing father. In short order, we became inseparable—an unlikely pair—the *gringo* with a father wound and the street urchin.

As much as I love him, I can think of all kinds of reasons why it wouldn't work. I mean, what do I know about parenting a teenager? I'm single, a solitary person, and my cabin is too small and too remote.

As a writer, I need lots of solitude to be productive. A case in point—I've written almost nothing these past two weeks. How would I get any serious writing done if Eurico came to live with me permanently? I love the little guy, but I just don't see how it can work.

When I don't say anything, she asks me point-blank, "If I die, will you consider adopting Eurico?"

I don't want to disappoint her yet again, and I sure don't want to let Eurico down, but I can't bring myself to make a commitment I'm not sure I would be able to keep. Instead, I say, "I couldn't love Eurico more if he were my own flesh and blood. I think you know that. But right now, I'm not emotionally prepared to make that kind of commitment."

I see the hurt in her eyes, and I realize that once again I have let her down. I can't help thinking that if Diana were willing to marry me, I would leap at the chance to adopt Eurico, but I can't imagine taking on that responsibility without her.

With a sigh of resignation, she says, "At least promise me you will think about it. Better yet, promise me you will pray about it."

Chapter 40

It's been nearly three weeks since Diana's mastectomy, and she is slowly regaining her strength. Although she has not made a final decision regarding treatment, her first session of radiation therapy is scheduled for Monday. Once that is completed, they want her to undergo chemotherapy. The oncologist told her that even though the cancer had already spread to her lymph nodes, there was still a good chance she could beat it, given recent advances in chemotherapy. She wants to believe him, but she can't help thinking that chemotherapy is really just a dance with death. The doctors try to give the patient enough chemical poison to kill the cancer without killing her in the process. Best-case scenario, she will be deathly ill for weeks on end—nausea and vomiting, diarrhea, extreme fatigue, weakness, and it's likely her hair will fall out.

In her mother's case, the treatment destroyed her health but did nothing to stop the spread of the cancer. She can't help thinking it might be better to forgo radiation and chemotherapy in order to enjoy a few months of relatively good health, than to suffer the ravages of chemotherapy and still die.

Once or twice she tried to talk with Bryan about her fears, but he deftly turned the conversation to other things. Instead of talking seriously, they played table games, put jigsaw puzzles together, or just watched TV—anything to keep from discussing her uncertain future.

To her, it seemed he was determined to avoid any mention of her illness and impending ordeal. Finally, she decided to discuss his troubling behavior with Carolyn, who just smiled sadly. "That's so Bryan. He acts like he doesn't care, but the truth is, it's nearly killing him. He won't talk about it because he doesn't want you to see how scared he is."

"Do you really think so?"

"Absolutely. That's one of the things that made being married to Bryan so difficult. The deeper he felt about a situation, the more closed he became."

Not being able to discuss her fears with Bryan grieved her, but she decided not to bring it up unless he did. Instead, she began confiding in Carolyn. As an oncology nurse, Carolyn worked shift work, but on those nights when she wasn't working, she and Diana talked into the early hours of the morning. She proved to be a knowledgeable and compassionate listener, never making light of Diana's concerns or pretending everything was going to be all right. More often than not, their conversations turned to Bryan.

Although it's been more than five years since their divorce was final, Carolyn is still in love with him. Listening to Diana as she talks about the love she and Bryan once shared makes her heart hurt. Only by exercising the strictest self-control is she able to hide her feelings from Diana. It pains her deeply to realize that although Bryan a.... intimate, they once shared a clo... were never physic.... knew. Many nights, she cries into h... he and Bryan neve.... conversations have ended. ...w long after their

Late one night she dared to ask Diana w.... he and Bryan had never married. Taking a deep breath, Dian... said, "It's a long story. Are you sure you want to go there?"

"We've got all night," she replied, giving Diana's hand a squeeze. "I'm off tomorrow."

"It might take all night," Diana said, with a rueful smile. "I think I fell in love with Bryan while I was nursing him through his bout with malaria. As you know, it's a hideous disease, and without medication it is often fatal. He had all the symptoms—a violent headache, high fever, night sweats and chills. Every joint in his body ached, and fever had made his skin as sensitive as an exposed nerve.

"When he fell ill, he was in the jungle a day's journey upriver. With no medicine at hand, he might have died if Lako hadn't been knowledgeable about organic treatments. He brewed a bitter-tasting potion from the bark of the cinchona tree and forced Bryan to drink it."

When Carolyn gives her a puzzled look, she adds, "Boiling the bark produces a primitive form of quinine. It probably saved Bryan's life. Nonetheless, by the time they returned to the mission station, he was delirious and in critical condition. I spent several nights sleeping in a rocking chair at the foot of his bed. Hour after hour, I bathed his forehead with cool washcloths and forced him to swallow quinine pills. He often called your name into the darkness, mistaking me for you. Of ourse, at that time knew she was so

While Dian the ill-fated l mind wand a part of ne

...o idea who 'Carolyn' was. I just

...Bryan loved."

...inues to talk, spinning out the story of

...he and Bryan had shared, Carolyn lets her

Although she loves Diana like a sister, there's that wishes she had never come back to the State. Before Diana arrived, Bryan had seemed to be taking a renewed interest in her. They had become good friends, often spending her days off doing things together. Once they went whitewater rafting on the Arkansas River; another time, they drove over Independence Pass into Aspen, then spent the afternoon picnicking and hiking at Maroon Bells. It was late when they finally got back to her apartment, so she invited him to crash on her couch rather than drive another two hours back to his cabin, west of Fort Collins. Secretly she was hoping they might rekindle the love they once shared, but apparently it wasn't meant to be. Once Diana arrived, the interest she had seen growing in his eyes vanished. Now it seems he has eyes only for Diana.

Forcing herself to concentrate, she hears Diana say, "I was willing to marry Bryan, even if that meant giving up my missionary appointment and returning to the States to practice medicine, but he wouldn't hear of it. No matter how much we loved each other, he said he could never permit me to give up my missionary appointment. He was convinced that turning my back on my call would kill something vital inside of me. In time, he said, I would come to resent him. I would blame him for the loss of my life's purpose, and then my love for him would die. It was better, he reasoned, to suffer a clean break,

298

painful though it was, than to slowly destroy each other, as inevitably we must."

Tears are glistening on her cheeks, and she pauses while struggling to regain control of her emotions. Taking a deep breath, she says, "If I'm honest with myself, I would have to say I'm still in love with him. The last four years have done nothing to change the way I feel. I have no idea how he feels, not that it matters now. Even if he's still in love with me, it's too late for us."

"Why do you say that?"

Giving Carolyn an incredulous look, Diana says, "Look at me. I'm damaged goods. No man wants a woman with only one breast." Without giving Carolyn a chance to reply, she continues, "Even if Bryan could get past my deformity, there's no future for us. I couldn't let him marry me. Not when I'm facing an uphill battle with stage-three cancer."

"Have you discussed your feelings with Bryan?"

"Of course not. You know he refuses to talk about my illness."

"I'm not talking about your illness. I'm talking about your feelings for him."

"What's the point? There's no future for us as long as I'm dealing with cancer. No man in his right mind would marry a woman in my condition."

"Don't you think you should let Bryan decide that for himself?"

"No. I couldn't risk it. He might think he can handle whatever is coming down the pike, but he has no idea how hideous this disease can be. Or worse yet, he might marry me out of pity."

"Stop for just a minute and listen to yourself. You're doing exactly what you said Bryan did to you."

"What do you mean?"

"Didn't you tell me that Bryan didn't have the right to decide whether you should resign your missionary appointment and marry him or not?" When Diana nods, Carolyn goes on, "Now you're doing the same thing to him. First, you decide he wouldn't want to marry you because you've had a radical mastectomy. Maybe you're right, but it's not your place to make that decision. And then you say you couldn't allow him to marry you even if he wanted to, because he doesn't really know what he's getting into—"

"I could hardly bear to watch my mother die," Diana says, interrupting Carolyn. "Between the chemo and the cancer, she suffered terribly. I don't think Bryan could bear to see me suffer like that. He might abandon me when I need him most."

"He might," Carolyn concedes, "but you don't know that."

"So, what am I supposed to do?"

"I can't tell you what to do. But I can tell you this: Given another chance, I would choose love regardless of the risk. And I would refuse to make any decision based on fear. Fear does not stop death. It stops life."

Chapter 41

The sun is high in the sky and shining brightly as I help Diana into my 1962 Ford pickup. It's thirteen years old but in good condition, and clean as a whistle. Eurico and I spent all afternoon yesterday washing and waxing it. There was no way I was going to let Diana take her first foray into the Rockies in a dirty truck. Eurico called "dibs" on the window, so she slides across the seat to sit next to me. I cannot help noticing how pale she looks, but there's a sparkle in her eyes and a look of determination on her face.

We're heading west on Highway 70 toward Idaho Springs. Although I have driven this route in the past, I didn't remember how scenic it was, with towering mountains on each side of the highway, and next to it a crystal-clear stream rushing down the mountain. Eurico is nearly beside himself with excitement, and he keeps up a running monologue. Diana simply takes it all in, almost in awe, while I can hardly take my eyes off her. She has French-braided her honey-colored hair, which emphasizes her high cheekbones and sets off her eyes. I don't think she has ever been more beautiful, and my heart aches with love for her, although I am careful to keep my feelings to myself. According to Diana, we don't get "do-overs."

Rounding a curve, we come face-to-face with a rustic waterwheel situated at the base of a sheer cliff. A clear stream falls down the face of the cliff and spills over the waterwheel. "Please stop!" she exclaims excitedly. I quickly glance in my rearview mirror to make sure no traffic is bearing down on us before touching my brakes. I ease off the highway and come to a stop. In an instant, Eurico is out of the pickup and running toward the waterwheel. I help Diana get out before reaching behind the seat for my Nikon camera. The spray from the waterfall is diffusing the sunlight into shimmering rainbows. I position Diana and Eurico and frame several shots. Then I take several photos of Diana alone. I can't help thinking that if she doesn't beat cancer, these photos may be all I have to remember her by. Finally, I show Eurico how to look through the viewfinder and frame a picture before joining Diana. I slip my arm around her waist and hold her close before smiling at the camera. We clown around for several more shots, and for a moment I am almost able to forget that she is scheduled to begin radiation therapy on Monday.

Once all three of us are back in the pickup, I start the engine and put it in gear. Turning to Diana, I say, "If you think this is beautiful, wait until I bring you back next winter and that entire stream has become a silver-blue icefall."

"You have to bring me, too," Eurico exclaims, nearly beside himself with excitement.

"That's a deal," I say as I pull back on the highway.

"Promise?"

"I promise."

In a matter of minutes, I turn off the interstate and enter Idaho Springs proper. We wander through the narrow, twisting streets until we find a quaint restaurant overlooking the crystal-clear stream. It is still early, and the lunch crowd has not yet arrived, so we have our pick of tables. I nod toward a corner booth overlooking the patio, and we are seated. The sun streaming through the windows is pleasantly warm, backlighting the bouquet of wildflowers sitting in the center of our table. Diana and I order the rainbow trout, but Eurico has to have a hamburger and French fries. Lunch is good but not spectacular, and by the time we finish eating, the dining room is filling up.

Once outside, I direct Diana's attention to Mount Evans, which towers majestically over Idaho Springs before losing itself in the low-hanging clouds. I tell her that's where we're going. "It's a fantastic drive, and near the summit, just under the timberline, there's a small, but picturesque lake."

It begins to rain softly when we are about two-thirds of the way up the mountain. For several minutes, we drive in silence. Even Eurico is quiet; the only sounds are the noise of the tires on the wet pavement, the whirr of the wipers on the windshield, and the patter of rain on the roof of the pickup.

"When I was a little girl," Diana muses, "I hated the rain. Our house was big and empty, and the rain always made me sad, but just now I love it. It makes me feel like we're cut off from the world, as if there were no past, no future, just right now, just us."

I reach over and give her hand a squeeze. Like her, I wish we could make the world go away, but we can't. No matter how hard we try, we can't make Diana's diagnosis, or her scheduled treatments, just disappear. Nor can I undo the mistakes I have made. I have wounded her in ways that seem to be past forgiving. I have no idea how to rebuild her trust or restore the love we once shared.

The lake materializes out of the mist, and I ease the pickup off the pavement onto a graveled area overlooking it. Quick as a flash, Eurico leaps out, heading for the lake. "Not so fast, young man," Diana calls after him. "Come back here and put your jacket on. Try not to get your shoes wet."

"Yes, ma'am," he mumbles as he pulls on his jacket, and then he is gone.

I switch off the ignition, and a damp silence envelops the pickup, the only sound being the pinging of the engine as it cools. In the distance, the lake is visible, looking gray and pitted in the rain. We watch Eurico exploring the shoreline and skipping rocks on the lake until our breathing fogs the windows. I start the engine and reach for the defroster, but Diana stops me. "Don't turn it on. I like feeling shut in with you." Turning toward me, she adds, "I just wish you would have told me how cold it was going to be up here so I could have worn something warmer."

"Not to worry," I reply. Reaching behind the seat, I produce a wool blanket that I wrap around both of us.

As Diana nestles against my shoulder, I can't help thinking this is the first time we have truly been close since I removed her arms from around my waist and walked away from her more than four years ago. There are many things I would like to say to her, but I don't want to spoil this moment, so I don't say anything. I want to tell her that I've never stopped loving her; that rejecting her was the dumbest thing I've ever done. I want to beg for her forgiveness. Instead, I put my arm around her shoulders, and she snuggles close to me, laying her head against my chest.

I brush the top of her head with my lips, luxuriating in the delicate scent of her hair. I can't help thinking that she must use a scented shampoo, because her hair smells like crushed berries or fresh-cut flowers. She turns her face toward me, and after a moment's hesitation, I kiss her, gently at first, then with more passion as she responds in kind. When we finally disengage, she says, "I thought you were never going to kiss me."

"Why this change of heart?" I ask. "The last time we talked, you made it pretty clear it was too late to rekindle our love. If I remember correctly, you said we don't get 'do-overs.'"

"I was afraid you would break my heart again."

"And now?"

"I'm still scared, but cancer changes everything."

"What do you mean?"

"Cancer makes you realize you're not immortal. This thing could kill me. If it does, I don't want to go to my grave filled with regrets. As risky as loving you is, this may be the only chance we have, so I've decided to throw caution to the wind and go for broke. You may break my heart again. I hope not, but it's a chance I'm willing to take."

Tears are glistening in the corner of her eyes, but the look she gives me is fiercely determined. It is obvious this is not a decision she has made lightly. She has counted the cost, and she is willing to pay the price, whatever it may be. I pull her close and gently kiss her tears. Once before, she offered herself to me, and I walked away because I was afraid. I was afraid our love wasn't strong enough to endure whatever life might throw at us.

Holding her close, I realize I'm still afraid. I'm afraid radiation therapy will ravage her body, robbing her of her zest for life. I'm afraid her suffering will be more than I can endure. I'm afraid cancer will cut our time together short. I'm afraid we may only have a few months instead of years together. I'm afraid—but like Diana, I'm not going to allow fear to dictate my decisions. I did that once, and I've spent the last four years regretting it. We could have had four wonderful years together, but I let fear rob us. Not now. Not this time. Whatever the future holds, we will face it together.

"Does this mean you will marry me?" I ask, almost afraid to believe my good fortune.

"Yes. More than anything, I want to be your wife. But before we set a date, I want you to think long and hard about what you're getting yourself into."

"Are you thinking about returning to the mission field?"

"No. When we marry, I will resign my missionary appointment and practice medicine here in the States."

"Are you sure?"

"Absolutely."

"If you're concerned about Eurico, let me put your mind at ease. I would be honored to adopt him. The three of us will make a wonderful family."

"Eurico will be ecstatic," she replies, a soft smile touching her lips. "He talks about you incessantly. It's Bryan did this, or Bryan did that. No matter how hopeless things looked, he always believed we would get back together."

"Smart boy," I say.

Taking a deep breath, she says, "Stage-three cancer means I might not make it. To tell you the truth, I'm not very optimistic. Most days, I feel like I'm looking death in the eye, and I haven't even started the hard stuff yet. Radiation therapy is hell. I know. I watched my mother go through it, and then she died.

"Even if I beat cancer, the first months of our marriage will be a marathon of suffering. Most likely, I won't be able to be a wife to you. I will be deathly ill. Radiation therapy is really just a dance with death. The doctors try to bombard you with enough radiation to kill the cancer without killing you in the process. Best-case scenario, I will be terribly sick for weeks on end—nausea and vomiting, diarrhea, extreme fatigue, weakness, and it's likely my hair will fall out."

I knew it was going to be bad, but I had never allowed myself to really think about it. It doesn't change anything—not how I feel about Diana nor the fact that I want us to get married, and the sooner the better. Still, I hesitate before responding, not because I'm uncertain, but because I want her to know how seriously I am considering her concerns. Finally, I say, "Diana, I want to be there for you, whatever the future may bring. Obviously, cancer is hideous beyond imagining, but if you have to endure it, I want to endure it with you—'in sickness and in health, till death us do part.'

"I can understand if you are afraid I might abandon you when the going gets rough, given how I deserted you when I thought Eurico was dying. What I did was inexcusable, and in my mind, it was the unpardonable sin. Yet you found it in your heart to forgive me—an act so selfless that it renders me speechless even these many years later. Now I am asking you to do something even more difficult. I'm asking you to trust me, to believe that I will be there for you, no matter how difficult things become."

Putting my finger under her chin, I tilt her face up and kiss her tenderly. "Diana Rhoades, I love you more than life itself, and I want to spend my life with you...for better or for worse. I give you my most solemn promise—I will never leave you. May the Lord strike me dead if ever I go back on my solemn promise."

It is a holy moment, and we seal it with a kiss, long and tender. Never have I felt closer to anyone in my life. Diana's willingness to trust her life to me, to believe that I will be there for her no matter how horrible she may suffer, is a gift I will always cherish. Like the grace of God, it is undeserved, and all the more precious because of it. For the first time since I walked away from her more than four years ago, I feel like a whole man. Gone is my shame and ever-present guilt. Gone is my bitter regret. Gone is my hopelessness. As unbelievable as it seems, Diana has given me a 'do-over.'"

Who knows how long we might have lingered there, wrapped in our love, if a flash of lightning, followed by a crash of thunder, hadn't let loose a deluge of rain. In an instant, Eurico jerks the pickup door open and throws himself into the cab. He is drenched, but neither the cold rain nor his soaking wet clothes has done anything to dampen his enthusiasm. "Look at this!" he says, thrusting a piece of driftwood at Diana. "It's for you. I'm going to clean it up, and you can keep it as a souvenir to remind you of this day."

Chapter 42

It is nearly dark when I turn off the highway and head up the path that leads to the old cabin that I call home. Diana has never been here, and I'm a little nervous, given the spartan conditions in which I live. Although it is no more primitive than her cottage on the mission station, I can't help wondering if she will be disappointed. It's plenty good enough for me, but it will be too small for the three of us. We'll give her the bedroom for the weekend, and Eurico and I will take our sleeping bags outside, but we will have to make other arrangements once we are married.

Eurico gets Diana's suitcase from the bed of the truck while I help her out of the pickup. I hand him the keys, and he takes her suitcase into the cabin while Diana and I take a moment to enjoy the sunset over the snowcapped Rockies. Taking a deep breath of the pine-scented air, she exclaims, "It's beautiful and so peaceful."

It has been a long day, and I can tell she is tired, so I put my arm around her waist and walk her toward the cabin. Once inside, I put some kindling and a half dozen pieces of split pinion in the potbellied stove. While I get the fire going, Diana surveys the small room that serves as a combination living room and office. The dominant feature is a makeshift desk I have fashioned out of two sawhorses and a sheet of plywood. It sits before the west window facing the mountains.

On the left-hand corner, there is a framed black-and-white photo of the Whittaker family taken in 1946. We are standing in front of the mission house, and behind it, the towering trees of the Amazon rain forest block out the sky. Helen is clutching a homemade doll while looking shyly at the camera. I'm glaring up at my father, who has a firm grip on my shoulder. Of course, both Mother and Father look severe. Diana picks it up and studies it. Turning to me, she says, "You were a cute kid, but you obviously didn't want to have your picture taken."

When I just smile, she replaces it and continues to inspect my desk, noting the framed photos that sit on the opposite corner. In the first, she and Eurico are sitting side by side in the swing beneath the towering sumauma tree. She has her arm around his narrow shoulders, and he is smiling up at her. In the second, she is sitting on the porch step in front of her small house on the mission compound. Her hair is the color of new honey and streaked by the sun. She is smiling bravely, but there is sadness in her blue eyes, and I cannot look at that photo without getting a lump in my throat.

My father's Bible and his journals are sitting between two bookends at the front edge of my desk, directly below the window. Next to them, there is a coffee cup full of cheap ballpoint pens, a pair of scissors, and a letter opener. "May I?" she asks, picking up one of my father's journals. When I nod, she opens it and begins scanning my father's entries.

Once the fire has taken hold, I shut the door on the stove and adjust the damper. Diana moves her chair closer to savor the warmth and settles down to read, clearly engrossed in my father's journal.

"Would you like some coffee or a cup of tea?" I ask.

"Coffee please, if you have some milk or cream."

I know my way around the kitchen, having lived alone for several years, and in short order, the coffee is percolating. In the cupboard, I find some oatmeal cookies that aren't too stale, and I arrange them on a plate. Diana is still absorbed in my father's journal, so I go to the bedroom to check on Eurico. He has fallen asleep across the bed with that piece of driftwood clasped in his hand. I cover him with a blanket, being careful not to wake him. Back in the kitchen, I pour two cups of coffee, adding a splash of milk to Diana's, before joining her near the stove.

Closing the journal, she takes a sip of her coffee before turning to me. "Did you know your father and mother had only known each other for six weeks when they married?"

"Amazing, isn't it?"

"And on top of that, your mother's parents were opposed to the wedding."

"Yep."

"Did you know all of that?"

"Not until I read it in my father's journal."

Opening the journal, she flips through several pages until she finds the page she's looking for. "Listen to this," she says, and begins reading.

Tomorrow Velma and I will commit the rest of our lives to each other. It is a decision we have made only after much prayer. There are any number of obstacles, not the least of which are her parents. They are opposed to our marriage and have threatened to boycott the wedding. Nonetheless, Velma is determined to go through with it.

If the truth be told, we hardly know each other. Two years ago, my sister suggested I write to Velma and thus began a long-distance friendship. When I graduated from Bible college, I hitchhiked halfway across the country to meet her. I was determined to see if she was as pretty as her picture. Of course, she was even prettier than her picture, and it was love at first sight. We've seen each other every day for the last six weeks, and tomorrow we will marry.

As pretty as Velma is, I know marriage has to be built on something more than physical attraction, more than "moonlight and music." In time, age will do its work, and our passions will cool, so there must be something more. That "something more" for us is our shared faith in Jesus Christ. Like Joshua of old, we have both vowed, "As for me and my house, we will serve the Lord."

Because we are flawed human beings, we will hurt each other. Sometimes we may do it deliberately, out of anger or vindictiveness; more often, we will do it unintentionally, out of ignorance. Whatever the case, only forgiveness can heal our hurts and restore our marriage. Therefore, we pledge to forgive one another even as Christ forgave us.

With God's help, I will love Velma more than I love myself even as Christ loved the Church and gave Himself for it.

When Diana closes my father's journal, I just sit there. I can tell his words have touched her, and I consider saying nothing lest I disillusion her. Finally, I tell her, "The relationship I witnessed between my parents wasn't anything like that. It wasn't romantic. In fact, I would describe it as utilitarian. Apparently, my father had high ideals, but that's all they were—just ideals. It scares me to think I might turn out just like him, that I, too, might enter marriage with high ideals, only to fail to live up to them."

Taking my hand, she looks me in the eye. "You're not having second thoughts about marrying me, are you?"

"Absolutely not. I just pray I can be the kind of husband you deserve."

"Our marriage won't be perfect, Bryan. No marriage is. We will both make mistakes, no matter how much we love each other."

When I nod, she continues, "As best I can tell, all marriages go through hard times, some harder than others, but with God's help, we can make it."

Outside, night has fallen, and the cabin is dark, so I light two kerosene lamps before moving to the couch. When we are settled, I take her in my arms and hold her, drawing strength from her closeness. After a couple of minutes, she asks, "Can we talk about the wedding?"

"Of course."

"I would like to postpone my radiation therapy and get married right away. That way, we can have a short honeymoon and a few days together before I begin my treatments."

"Is that dangerous?" I ask. "I wouldn't want you to do anything to jeopardize your health."

"I don't think three or four weeks is going to make much difference one way or another. Even if it does, having that time together is important to me."

"Have you thought about where you would like to get married?"

"In a church," she replies. "I definitely want to be married in a church."

Her declaration brings an unbidden memory to mind. That's the one request Carolyn made—to be married in a church. I quickly vetoed it, wounding her deeply, and I'm determined not to make that mistake again. For years, I allowed anger and selfishness to control my life, but with the Lord's help, I'm changing. According to my pastor, sinful habits become spiritual strongholds. He says their roots go deep and they're hard to kill. If I want to live a victorious life, I have to "crucify the flesh"—that is, I have to deliberately deny my selfish desires. In this case, that means that although I would much prefer an outdoor wedding, I will defer to Diana's desire to be married in a church, thus dealing my selfishness a killing blow.

Smiling at her, I say, "A church wedding sounds good to me. Do you have a church in mind?"

"Not really," she replies. "I've thought about First Assembly in Aurora, where Carolyn attends, but the sanctuary is so large. Since our wedding will not be elaborate, I think something smaller would be better."

I'm hesitant to make a suggestion, since the bride usually chooses the wedding venue, but finally I say, "There's a small Pentecostal church here in Fort Collins that might work. The sanctuary is pretty plain, nothing fancy. If you're interested, I can call the pastor and set something up so we can see the church."

"Please," she says, "I would like that."

Her voice is weak, and I can tell she is exhausted. I start to stand up, but she puts her hand on my arm. "Before you wake Eurico, let me finish. I want Carolyn to be my maid of honor, and if you don't mind, I would like Eurico to be your best man."

I can't help thinking how weird that will be—my ex-wife being the maid of honor. I'm tempted to object, but I don't. If Diana and Carolyn are okay with it, I guess I can manage. Instead I ask, "May I invite my pastor to marry us? We've become good friends, and I would like him to do the honors if you have no objection."

"Of course," she says, giving me a tired smile.

Getting to my feet, I say, "Let me wake Eurico, and we'll get our sleeping bags and head for the backyard and let you get some rest."

"Aren't you forgetting something?"

"I don't think so."

"Aren't you going to kiss me good night?"

"Duh!" I say, as I slap myself on the forehead.

Taking both of her hands in mine, I help her to her feet and wrap her in my arms. Holding her close, I can't help thinking how easily we fit together, as if God's own hand cradled only us. She looks up at me, and I kiss her, tenderly at first and then with passion, trying to express all the love I feel welling up in my heart. The moment would have been perfect, except for the memory of the insidious disease threatening her life.

Chapter 43

At precisely two o'clock, my pastor and I enter the small sanctuary and make our way to the platform. When we turn and face the guests, my heart swells with gratitude for those friends and family who have come to celebrate with Diana and me. I'm especially thankful that my sister and her two boys were able to come. In a few days, they will be leaving for her first four-year term as a missionary to the indigenous tribes living in the Peruvian jungle, and I don't know when I will see her again. Her life is a madhouse right now, and I told her I would understand if she couldn't make it, but she wouldn't hear of it. She gives me a brave smile, and I can't help thinking how difficult this must be for her, bringing back memories of her own wedding and also of her late husband's untimely death.

Out of the corner of my eye, I see the pastor motion for the guests to rise, as the organist plays the first notes of the "Wedding March." For just an instant, Diana and Eurico are framed in the doorway, and I freeze that image in my memory. Everything about this day is special, and I don't want to forget a single thing. In the years to come, each memory will be important. Now I reflect on how grown-up Eurico looks in his first-ever store-bought suit. His dark hair is parted perfectly and slicked down. He does his best to appear serious, but not even his determined expression can hide his joy. At last, he is going to be part of a family with the two people he loves most in the entire world.

In my wildest dreams, I could never have imagined this moment, not after the way I abandoned Diana and left her to nurse Eurico, who was writhing in the death throes of spinal meningitis. Amazingly, God healed him, and Diana forgave me. To this day, I cannot decide which was the greater miracle—Eurico's healing or the gift of Diana's forgiveness.

Now I have eyes only for Diana, and never has she looked more beautiful. She is wearing a sleeveless wedding gown with a high beaded collar and a long train, but what I notice is not the gown but the sparkle in her blue eyes. Beneath her wedding veil, she is glowing with happiness, and she smiles at Eurico as they begin their slow journey down the center aisle. Since her father is deceased, she decided that Eurico would walk her down the aisle before joining me as the best man.

We exchange vows, promising to forsake all others and to love and cherish each other as long as we both shall live. In a voice choked with emotion I say, "Diana, I promise to love you all the days of your life. When you are lonely, I will comfort you. When you are tired, I will refresh you. When you are sick, I will care for you. I will share all your joys and sorrows your whole life long. We will celebrate growing old together, warmed against winter's chill by the memories of a lifetime cherished and shared."

Tears are glistening in her eyes when I finish and lift her veil in order to kiss her. Although we are both believing God for the best, the dark scepter of cancer is never far from our minds, and we have determined to live each day to the very fullest. We have vowed to never leave a solitary word of love unspoken or a single act of kindness undone.

Now we turn our attention to the pastor one final time. "Brian, Diana," he says, pausing to emphasize the importance of his words, "we all assume we'll have tomorrow to correct any oversight, that we'll always have another chance to make everything right. We all assume that there will always be another day to say that 'I love you.' But just in case you might be wrong and today is all you get, go ahead and say it. Tomorrow is not promised; you have no assurance that you'll see another night. Today could be your last chance to love and hold your sweetheart, so hold her tight. Instead of waiting for tomorrow, show your love now. For if tomorrow never comes, you'll wish you had done it. Hold your loved one close today and whisper in their ear. Say, 'I'm sorry, please forgive me, you're the best, it's okay.' So if tomorrow never comes, you'll not regret today."

That's good counsel for anyone, but in our case, it is especially relevant. Stage-three breast cancer was a wake-up call for both of us, and now it serves as a constant reminder to live each day as if it were our last. And if God should give us a lifetime together, we are determined to cherish each moment, living each day to the very fullest.

The pastor's booming voice draws our attention back to the moment. "I present to you for the very first time, Mr. and Mrs. Bryan Scott Whittaker." Our family and friends erupt with joy, filling the small sanctuary with applause, cheering and whistling as Diana and I make our way down the aisle. The rest of the afternoon passes in a blur of activity. There are photos to be taken, gifts to be opened, and of course, the cake-and-punch reception in the church's small fellowship hall. Finally, Diana changes into her going-away outfit, and she and I run for my 1962 pickup under a deluge of rice and good wishes.

I want to stop at the first car wash to wash off all the "just married" graffiti, and get rid of all the tin cans tied to our rear bumper, but Diana won't hear of it. As far as she's concerned, it's all part of the wedding celebration, and she wants to enjoy it as long as possible. Of course, she doesn't know that I have booked us into the historic Brown Palace Hotel in downtown Denver, or she might reconsider.

Once we are on our way, Diana slides across the seat to rest her head on my shoulder. Although she tries to hide it, I can tell she is exhausted, and an icy hand squeezes my heart when I think of what we are facing. Thinking about the trauma of radiation therapy is bad enough, but what chills my blood is the threat of the cancer returning.

Chapter 44

Diana awakens when I turn on Seventeenth Street and she stares in amazement at the historic Brown Palace Hotel. Built in 1892, it is a landmark in Denver, and it sits diagonally on the corner directly in front of us. When I turn into the portico and stop, she looks at me with disbelief and asks, "Are we staying here?"

"Just for one night," I reply as the bellman opens Diana's door and helps her out of the pickup. I slip my arm around her waist and guide her into the lobby as the bellman collects our luggage. She gasps as she surveys the atrium, which soars eight stories above the ground floor. Dramatic Florentine arches surround it, and intricate wrought-iron panels decorate six stories of balconies. Her reaction is just what I hoped it would be, and as I hand the clerk my credit card, she whispers, "Can we afford this?"

The clerk hands me our room keys and a valet ticket before directing us to the elevators. Although all of this is new to me, I nonchalantly make my way toward the elevators, as if staying in five-star hotels with all the amenities is old hat to me. Diana is obviously more accustomed to elegance than I am, her father being a surgeon, but even she is impressed.

Once we reach our room, she immediately opens the drapes and stands before the floor-to-ceiling windows, which overlook downtown Denver. Dusk shrouds the city in fading golden hues, and the city lights blink on, glowing like brightly colored Christmas tree bulbs as night falls. Before I can join her at the window, the bellman arrives with our luggage. He treats me with professional deference, but I suspect he thinks we're out of our league. I hand him a generous tip and heave a sigh of relief when he is finally gone.

I join Diana, who is still standing before the windows. "It's beautiful," she murmurs, as I slip my arm around her waist and pull her close. When I do, I can't help noticing how tense she is.

"Are you okay?" I ask, fearful that the day's events may have worn her out. She's not yet fully recovered from her radical mastectomy, and I can't help but be concerned. I hope she hasn't overdone it. The last thing she needs is a relapse.

Turning toward me, she gives me a brave smile. "I'm just really tired. I'll be fine in a few minutes."

"Can you believe this room?" I say, as she turns to survey our suite. It is spacious, with an elegant king-sized bed and ornate furniture. I take her by the hand and lead her into the bathroom, which is huge with marble countertops, sophisticated silver fixtures, an oversized tub, and a separate, walk-in shower. "What's that all about?" I ask, pointing to a small sign informing us that the bath and shower water comes from an artesian well.

When we return to our bedroom, Diana kicks off her shoes and stretches out on the bed. She tries to nap, but she's too tense to relax, so I try to interest her in the room service menu. The hotel has three first-class restaurants and twenty-four-hour room service. We've hardly eaten anything all day, and I'm starving so I order a rib-eye steak sandwich and fries. She says she's too tired to eat and falls into a troubled sleep before my food arrives.

She's still sleeping when I finish my meal, so I cover her with the throw that is on the foot of the bed, being careful not to wake her. I undress and make my way to the shower. It's nearly as big as the bedroom in my cabin, and I marvel at the soaps and shampoos at my disposal. There's plenty of hot water, too, a true luxury as far as I am concerned, hot water being in short supply at my place. I spend the next twenty minutes luxuriating under the pounding spray. In reality, I'm just killing time while I wait for Diana to wake up. My concern about her health is like a nagging toothache, never far from my mind. Although I am eager to consummate our marriage, I remind myself that it may not be possible given her recent surgery.

After toweling myself dry on the thickest towels I've ever seen, I shave and splash Old Spice lotion on my cheeks, before putting on a terry-cloth robe with the Brown Palace Hotel emblem on the breast pocket. When I return to the bedroom, Diana is awake. "How was your nap?" I ask as I lie down on the bed beside her.

Without answering, she turns toward me and lays her head on my shoulder. "You smell nice," she mummers as she runs her fingers down my freshly shaven cheek.

We make small talk for a few minutes, reminiscing about the wedding and discussing plans for the rest of our honeymoon. Being something of a free spirit, I have only put together a loose itinerary that will allow us to visit several of the most scenic spots Colorado has to offer. Tomorrow we will take Highway 36 to Estes Park and then make our way through the Rocky Mountain National Park and over Trail Ridge Pass if it is open. On Tuesday, we will drive to Steamboat Springs, a ski town with a rustic western motif. From there, we will play it by ear. We may go to Ouray and take the million-dollar highway to Telluride and down into Durango, or we could go to Aspen and see the Maroon Bells. If we go to Aspen, we can drive over Independence Pass and down into Twin Lakes. I haven't made any reservations, so nothing is set in stone. How much or how little we do depends on Diana's strength.

Giving me a quick kiss, she extracts herself from my embrace and eases off the bed. After collecting her overnight bag, she heads for the bathroom. At the door, she turns to me. "Don't go anywhere. I'll be right back."

I may have dozed off, because the next time I glance at the bedside clock, forty-five minutes have passed. I wait another five minutes and then make my way to the bathroom. Through the door, I hear what sounds like sobbing. I knock softly and ask, "Diana, are you okay?" The weeping subsides, but she doesn't respond so I knock again. "What's wrong, sweetheart? Please talk to me."

"I can't do this," she sobs. "I can't do this."

Although I plead with her, she can't bring herself to tell me what's troubling her, and I think my heart will break as she continues to sob. I beg her to talk to me, but to no avail. "Let me hold you," I plead. "There's nothing we can't get through together."

Finally, I give up and sit down on the floor, determined to wait her out. I'm not sure how long I sit there with my back against the bathroom door—at least an hour, maybe longer. From time to time, I call her name and tell her how much I love her. Her only response is to beg me to go to bed and forget about her. "Not a chance," I say. "If you plan on spending our wedding night locked in the bathroom, I will spend it on the floor just outside the bathroom door."

When she realizes I am not leaving, she finally relents. As soon as I hear the lock release, I quickly get to my feet. When the door opens, I take her in my arms and hold her against my chest. She is trembling; whether from cold or emotional exhaustion I am not sure, so I hold her close and walk her to the king-sized bed. Once she is tucked in, I lie down beside her and take her hand in mine. Her face is red and blotchy, her eyes puffy from crying. Never has she looked so sad, never, not even when she was sure Eurico was dying and there was nothing she could do to save him. That's how I feel now, helpless. I don't know what to say, so I simply kiss her tears and tell her how much I love her, over and over again.

I may have fallen asleep, but I'm instantly awake when I hear Diana's voice. She has closed the drapes and turned out the lamp, leaving our room pitch-black. "Bryan Scott Whittaker," she whispers into the darkness, "I love you more than I've ever loved anyone in my life. More than anything, I want to make love with you, but I can't. At least not tonight, maybe never."

When I open my mouth to question her, she silences me by putting her finger on my lips. "Hear me out, Bryan. I knew our wedding night was going to be difficult, but I had no idea it would be impossible. I went into the bathroom to put on my negligee and freshen up for you, but when I saw myself in the mirror, I nearly gagged. I looked grotesque. I knew it was bad, but I never realized how terrible I looked until I tried to imagine how I would look to you. Believe me when I tell you, no man in his right mind would want to make love to a woman who looks the way I do."

She has turned her back to me and is sobbing into her pillow. I'm shaken. I had no idea how traumatic this would be for her. We had discussed it once, briefly. She wanted to make sure I knew what I was getting into. She even showed me some photographs in a couple of medical journals to make sure I understood how invasive a radical mastectomy was. "Of course," she assured me, "I will have reconstructive surgery as soon as I've completed my treatments."

The photographs were hard to look at, I'll admit that, especially when I realized that Diana was trying to prepare me for the way her body now looked. Of course, I assured her that it made no difference, and it doesn't. I love her, not because she has a perfect body, but because of who she is. To my surprise, I now realize her appearance may be a bigger issue for her than it is for me.

This isn't how I imagined our wedding night. When I booked this suite in the Brown Palace Hotel, I envisioned tender moments interspersed with romantic fireworks. I thought that at long last we would put the ghosts of our past disappointments behind us. I thought they would be swallowed up in our love. I knew that in the weeks and months ahead, we would have to deal with the trauma of radiation therapy and that the dark shadow of cancer would always hang over our heads, but never in my wildest dreams did I imagine that Diana would be undone by the shame of her scarred body.

I'm tempted to take her in my arms and make wild passionate love to her, to prove to her, once and for all, that she is the most desirable woman in the world to me. But that might be the very worst thing I could do. She might feel that I am taking advantage of her, that I am simply using her to satisfy my own needs, and that's the last thing I want to do. I want her to feel loved, not used.

Yet if I don't do anything to let her know how much I desire her, she may conclude that her scarred body has turned me off. Maybe I'm overthinking this, maybe I simply need to take her in my arms and kiss her tenderly and see what happens. With that thought in mind, I turn on a small light and put on the pajamas I bought just for tonight, then I crawl into bed beside her. Her back is to me, so I spoon my body next to hers.

She doesn't say anything, but I can feel the tension in her body. For a moment I just hold her close, enjoying her nearness and the smell of her hair. In a voice that is hardly more than a whisper, I begin reminiscing about our time in the Amazon. "I will never forget how you looked the first time I saw you. You were examining a feverish Indian baby. Your hair was pulled back, but a few strands had worked loose, and you had to keep brushing them out of your eyes. You were wearing a white lab coat over blue jeans and some kind of pullover shirt. The lab coat was loose fitting; still, it did nothing to conceal the pleasing contours of your body.

"You invited Dr. Peterson and me to join you at the Arnolds' for dinner. I wanted to impress you, so I bathed in the river and trimmed my hair. I put on my best pair of jeans and a clean chambray shirt. Last of all, I applied a liberal dose of Old Spice cologne—all to no avail. I don't think you gave me a second thought. You were seated next to Dr. Peterson, and he held you spellbound all evening with his tales of the Amazon. It was crazy. I had just met you, and I had no reason to be jealous, but I was!"

She doesn't respond, but I can feel her body relaxing, so I tell her that when I first came down with malaria, I was nearly delirious with fever. "In my feverish dreams, you came to me—a yellow-haired angel whose touch was as soft as air—and you cooled my parched throat with spoonfuls of sweet tea. Your breath was warm on my face, and your words soothed me, although I couldn't understand what you were saying. I reached for you, but you drifted away, like fog carried by the wind.

"Days later, I awoke in the wee hours of the morning. I was back in Whittaker House, in my own bed, but I had no recollection of how I had gotten there. Night sweats had soaked my sheets, and the smell of my illness nearly gagged me. In the far corner, there was a small table with a kerosene lamp turned down low, making the circle of yellow light small and dim. Still, it hurt my eyes, spreading needles of pain deep inside my head.

"Later that morning, you and Eleanor helped me into a rocking chair. She stripped my bed, turned the mattress, and remade it. While she was doing that, you bathed me. The soapy water was warm, the fresh smell of soap replacing the rancid odor of my sickness. Although I was so weak I could hardly sit up, I never wanted that bath to end. You were the consummate medical professional, giving me a sponge bath with practiced skill; still, I found your touch more erotic than anything I had ever experienced."

For once I am not tongue-tied. The words and phrases simply flow out of me the way they do when I am writing. For an hour or more, I spin out the memories of our time together in the rain forests of the far western Amazon Basin. As the richness of those memories superimposes themselves on the anxiety that has overtaken Diana, I can feel the tension leaving her body. Finally, she rolls over, and now we are lying face-to-face. Slowly she traces the contours of my face with her fingers, and I can feel my heart beating. At last, she kisses me tenderly.

I want her, and it is all I can do to restrain myself, but I know I must, or I could well destroy the progress we have made. Her kisses are becoming more urgent, and I can sense her desire, but I caution myself to move slowly. Whatever happens must flow naturally; it can't be forced. I am kissing her throat when she puts her lips next to my ear. "Please put out the light. I want you to make love to me."

"Are you sure?" I ask in a husky voice.

"Don't make me beg," she says, as I reach to turn off the lamp.

The love we made was both tender and passionate, and spiritual—a kind of sacrament, healing our hurts and restoring our souls—and physical that our aloneness might be swallowed up in the body of our beloved. Long after Diana fell asleep, I lay awake trying to wrap my mind around all we had experienced. I never imagined that making love with Diana could be like that. It was not simply a physical act, not simply the merging of our flesh without the touching of our souls, but the merging of self into self until we truly became one. As I drifted toward sleep, more at peace than I had been in years, maybe ever, the words of Scripture kept playing over and over in my mind: "Therefore shall a man leave his father and his mother, and shall cleave unto his wife: and they shall be one flesh."

Chapter 45

e had a wonderful week honeymooning in the
Rockies. That is, we had a wonderful week until
the last couple of days—but more about that
in a minute. The weather was absolutely perfect, with the
temperatures climbing into the mid-seventies under brilliant
blue skies, before cooling off each evening. One night we
stayed in a rustic cabin located on the Elk River just below
Hahns Peak. At the firepit situated between the cabin and
the river, we grilled hamburgers, and later we fed each other
smores while huddled together beside the fire. We slept with
the window open so we could hear the river and smell the
pines. By early morning, at an elevation of nearly 7,500 feet,
the temperature had dropped into the high thirties. When we
whispered our love, we could see our breath, but wrapped
in each other's arms, beneath a pile of quilts, we were, as my
mother used to say, as snug as a bug in a rug.

Later that morning, we were having breakfast at a small
café in Steamboat Springs when Diana showed me an ad in
the classified section of the *Steamboat Pilot*:

*Wanted: Experienced family practice physician to
partner with older physician in an established practice. Send*

résumé to: Ronald Davis, M.D., PO Box 2721, Leadville, Colorado 80461.

"What do you know about Leadville?" she asked.

"Not much," I replied, "other than it was a boomtown in the late eighteen hundreds. Gold originally, and then silver, I think. As a kid, I loved stories about the Old West, and if my memory is correct, the famous Doc Holliday spent some time there. I think he killed a man over a gambling debt."

"No history, please?" she said with a smile. "I'm talking modern-day Leadville. Nineteen seventy-five Leadville."

"I'm not sure I can help you there, but we could forego our trip to Grand Junction and head to Leadville if you'd like? That way, you can check it out for yourself."

"Let's do it," she said, her voice alive with excitement.

When we finished breakfast, we took State Highway 131 through Oak Creek to Interstate 70, where we turned east for a short distance. Once we reached the Minturn exit, we turned off the interstate and took Highway 24 toward Leadville. In Minturn, we picked up a brochure, and Diana regaled me with interesting bits of trivia as we passed through Redcliff and crossed over a high arched bridge that provided a spectacular view. As we headed up Tennessee Pass, she pointed out the remains of Camp Hale, where the Tenth Mountain Division received specialized training for fighting in mountainous and arctic conditions during WWII.

Once we crested Tennessee Pass, we crossed a high plain as we descended toward Leadville. From time to time, we caught sight of abandoned log cabins that had once been used by early miners, reminding us that Leadville was once a mining boomtown. We spent the better part of an hour driving in and around Leadville in an attempt to get the feel of it. With a population of less than three thousand, it shouldn't have taken that long, but we didn't want to miss anything.

At the local chamber of commerce, we got the address for the Davis family practice clinic, and we drove by to look it over. It was housed in a grand two-story house that had been converted into a clinic with a reception area/waiting room combination, examining rooms, and a private office for Dr. Davis. As best we could tell, it looked like his living quarters were on the second story. All in all, it was quite an improvement over the primitive clinic at the mission station.

From there, we checked out the Tabor Opera House and the National Mining Hall of Fame and Museum. By then, it was mid-afternoon and we were starving, but before we had lunch, we drove by the high school, and then we headed to the Golden Burro, an eatery dating back to the turn of the century, for lunch.

Both Diana and I were intrigued by the possibility of relocating to Leadville. Joining Dr. Davis's family practice would give her an opportunity to assist him while building her own caseload of patients. Some physicians might have found Leadville's remote location a challenge, but for someone like Diana, who had spent several years serving in the interior of the far western Amazon Basin, it was no challenge at all. As far as I was concerned, it would be a Godsend; affording me the solitude I so desperately needed in order to write. Our last stop before leaving town was a real estate office to get some information on rental properties that were available.

We were so excited about the possibilities of moving to Leadville that for the remainder of the afternoon and early evening, that was all we could talk about. For the first time in weeks, my thoughts were not dominated by the scepter of Diana's ongoing battle with stage-three breast cancer. Of course, those thoughts returned with a vengeance in the dark of night, when sleep fled. Unconsciously, I found myself counting the days, and then the hours, until she would begin her radiation treatments.

The joy of making love to Diana was only marred by the embarrassment she felt in regard to the disfigurement she had suffered as a result of her radical mastectomy. Initially, I was understanding when she insisted on making love only under the cover of darkness, but as the week wore on, I began to resent it. Instead of realizing that her reluctance was rooted in her feelings about herself, I concluded it was about me. As far as I was concerned, she didn't trust me; I felt she was afraid I would reject her if I saw how scarred she was. That made me angry—never mind she had reason enough to doubt my commitment, especially in light of the way I had abandoned her when I thought Eurico was dying.

At first, I was able to conceal my growing irritability, but as the week wore on, I found myself picking at her in an attempt to make her angry. The old Bryan was rearing his ugly head, and I was spoiling for a fight. I hated what I was doing, but I felt powerless to do anything about it. The more she tried to appease me, the angrier I became.

Things came to a head late Friday evening, our last night before heading home to Fort Collins. We were staying in a small cabin just outside of Telluride, Colorado. The view from the front porch was spectacular, and as the day died a slow death, the sunset painted the snowcapped mountains in vivid hues. Diana marveled at its beauty, but I was too irritated to pay it any mind. Several times, she tried to make small talk, but I only grunted. Finally, she gave up and went inside to prepare for bed.

It was fully dark when she opened the front door and said, "Let's not fight. Making love is so much more fun."

Without a word, I stood up and headed for the door. I wanted to make love, but not if she insisted on doing it in the dark with her negligee on. She was already in bed, with the covers pulled up to her chin, when I came out of the bathroom after brushing my teeth. She had a come-hither look in her eye when she said playfully, "You're not going to make me beg, are you?"

When I didn't respond, she said, "Please turn out the light, and let's make love."

That did it! Instead of switching off the lamp, I stormed around the room, turning on every light until the room was nearly as bright as day. I should have known better than to give my anger an inch, experience having taught me that once I gave in to it, it became a raging monster, impossible to control.

I stood at the foot of the bed, glaring at her, nearly trembling with rage. She had never seen me like this, and she was clearly frightened. In a shaky voice, she asked, "What is it, Bryan? What has gotten into you?" When I didn't say anything, she pleaded, "What have I done?"

"You're a smart woman, a doctor," I snarled. "If you try, I'm sure you can figure it out."

The hurt in her eyes was killing me, but I was too angry to care. This was the man I used to be, and I hated myself, but I seemed powerless to stop. A saner voice inside my head told me I was going to destroy our marriage and hurt the woman I loved in ways I couldn't even imagine, but I ignored it. She was crying now, but her tears couldn't touch me. Instead, they seemed to fuel my anger.

"You know what this is about," I hurled my words at her like deadly projectiles. "Don't pretend you don't. That just makes me angrier!"

I turned on my heel and started for the door. Then I whirled around and glared at her. "You want to know what this is about? Okay, I'll tell you. I'm sick of watching you hide in the bathroom to change your clothes, lest I catch sight of your 'damaged' body—your words, not mine. I'm sick of making love to you under cover of darkness. I'm sick of feeling like you don't trust my love. I'm sick of… Oh, what's the use? You don't care how you make me feel!"

She is angry now, her eyes blazing. Throwing herself out of bed, she jerks her negligee over her head and hurls it on the floor. She spreads her arms wide and takes a step toward me, daring me to look away. "Are you happy now that you've humiliated me? Do you feel better?"

I don't say anything, but I force myself to look at her. Although the scar from her mastectomy is vivid and disfiguring, I am not repulsed. She glares at me. "Now tell me you want to make love to me." I reach for her, but she turns away, stumbling toward the bathroom, choking on her sobs.

The anger that has been building up for days is suddenly gone, leaving me disgusted and sick of myself. It's a pattern I've lived with most of my life, but I thought I had put it behind me once I made peace with my late father. Apparently, the roots go deeper than I could ever have imagined. I'm tempted to excuse myself. This isn't really me. I'm just under a tremendous amount of pressure. If Diana weren't fighting for her life, I wouldn't have reacted this way. Then I remember something my pastor told me when we were having coffee: "Pressure doesn't make us into someone we are not; it simply reveals who we are."

Now that I'm not blinded by my anger, I can think more clearly, and I realize I'm not really angry with Diana. She was just someone on whom I could take out my anger. I'm angry because Diana is battling stage-three breast cancer and I can't do anything about it. I'm angry because she has to undergo radiation therapy with all of its dreadful side effects. On top of that, it may not kill the cancer. I'm angry because cancer may kill her, and there's nothing I can do to save her. And as much as I hate to admit it, I'm angry with God. Again! How could He let a good person like Diana suffer this atrocity?

Understanding the roots of my anger does not make me feel any better. In fact, it makes me feel worse, much worse. How could I make Diana the brunt of my rage? She's has enough to deal with without having to deal with my stuff. I can still hear her sobbing softly in the bathroom, and I hate myself for what I've done. I may have wounded her in ways past forgiving. I hope not, but I'm tempted to think she would be better off without me.

I want to apologize, but not even the most sincere apology can undo the damage my words have done. In fact, apologizing feels almost insulting. I mean, how pathetic is "I'm sorry" in light of the terrible pain I have inflicted? While I'm trying to decide what to do—to apologize or to ignore what I've done in hopes that it will just fade away—I'm reminded once again of something my pastor said in a recent sermon: "If you ignore an offense, pretending nothing evil has happened, it becomes like a piece of misplaced furniture in the soul of your relationship. You may never talk about it, but anytime you try to get close to each other, you bump into it."

Going to my bag, I rummage around until I find a yellow legal pad and a cheap ballpoint pen.

Dearest Diana:

As I put pen to paper, I can hear you sobbing softly behind the locked bathroom door, and I am sick with shame. I feel like an ogre, and well I should. There is absolutely no excuse for what I did. There is no one to blame but me. I do not deserve your forgiveness, but I pray you can find it in your heart to forgive me.

I will do my best to make it up to you, even though I know there is not enough goodness in the world to undo the damage I have done. Carolyn once told me that my apologies and acts of penance only set her up for my next angry explosion. I pray that will not be the case, but honesty forces me to confess that I have an anger problem, and I often end up hurting those I love the most.

I thought I had put this anger behind me when I "forgave" God for letting my father die, for not answering this little boy's prayers. I guess I still have some work to do. Only God can help me, but with His help, I am determined to become a kinder and gentler man.

Please believe me when I tell you that you are the best thing that ever happened to me and I love you more than life itself. I am so sorry I humiliated you, and I promise you it will never happen again. You can wear a flannel nightgown and socks to bed if you want to. I promise I will never complain. Making love to you is a gift from God, a gift I will always treasure and never take for granted.

> *With all my love now and always,*
> *Your grieving husband,*
> *Bryan*

I am crying as I reread what I've written, my tears smudging the words. After folding the page in half, I bow my head and confess my sin to Jesus. I know He will forgive me. I just wish I could be sure that Diana will. I take hope because in the past she has demonstrated a remarkable capacity for forgiveness. I only pray that my repeated failures have not exhausted her mercy.

I slide the folded pages beneath the bathroom door before making my way to the porch. I don't know how much time has passed, at least an hour, maybe two. As far as I know, Diana is still locked in the bathroom. I haven't heard her stirring, and the lights are still blazing in the bedroom. Fear has become a hard knot in the pit of my stomach, and I am afraid I have gone too far this time.

After what seems an eternity, the front door opens, and Diana joins me on the porch swing. She is wearing fuzzy slippers and has wrapped herself in a bulky quilt against the mountain chill. In the dim light, I can see that her cheeks are blotchy, and her eyes are swollen from crying. We rock in silence for a few minutes, then she reaches over and takes my hand. In a voice I can hardly hear, she says, "I forgive you, but this can never happen again. No matter how much I love you, your anger will kill my love."

That's all she says, nothing more, but now I can breathe again. That piece of misplaced furniture is gone, and in the soul of our relationship, there is only love, albeit a wounded love.

Chapter 46

LEADVILLE, COLORADO
OCTOBER 1975

I watch as Diana and Eurico climb into the four-wheel-drive Jeep Wagoneer and head out. It's not new, but it is newer than my 1962 pickup, and a considerable step up. Our routine is the same each morning, Monday through Friday. I start the coffee and fix breakfast while Diana and Eurico are getting dressed. After breakfast, they head for town, where she drops him off at the high school before heading for the clinic. I usually stand on the front porch and watch them until they reach the bottom of the hill and turn out of sight. Returning to the cabin, I stoke the fire before cleaning up the kitchen. Finally, I brew a fresh pot of coffee, have my devotional time, and prepare for a day of writing.

When we moved into the cabin, Diana insisted I abandon my makeshift desk, which consisted of two sawhorses and a sheet of plywood. At a used furniture store in Minturn, we found a refurbished rolltop desk that now sits between two windows on the east wall of the living room, overlooking the meadow. It's certainly more attractive, but I have to admit I sometimes miss my makeshift desk where I wrote my first novel.

We also bought a secondhand typewriter, but as of yet, I've refused to give up my cheap ballpoint pens and yellow legal pads. There's an intimacy in putting a pen to paper that I can't imagine duplicating with a typewriter, an intimacy that is an integral part of the creative process for me. Besides, there's been more than enough change in my life in recent weeks—I don't need any more.

Writing my first novel was relatively easy, maybe because it was somewhat autobiographical. It was part adventure and part love story, loosely based on my experiences in the rain forest of the far western Amazon Basin. At times, the story seemed almost to write itself and the characters took on a life of their own. I knew where the story was going, and I made sure not to get off track, but within those boundaries, it took some twists and turns that caught me by surprise. All in all, it was a deeply satisfying experience.

It has been pretty well-received and modestly successful. Several reviewers were complimentary. One of my favorites was recently published in the *Denver Post*. Carolyn saw it and cut it out and mailed it to us. Diana framed it, and it now hangs on the wall above my desk.

> *"Jungle Doctor"* is a surprisingly good debut novel by Bryan Whittaker, a local author. The author's insights into human nature come wrapped in a story of rare beauty. His prose is lyrical but never gets in the way of the story, and the descriptions of the Amazon rain forests are so real I felt like I was there. The real strength of the book, however, is the characters. Pedro will steal your heart, Shirley is unforgettable, and Keith's struggle to overcome his

past and reach his ultimate triumph will inspire even the most cynical reader."

On the wall beneath it, she stuck a handwritten note: *"Don't get a big head!"*

I don't think there's any danger of that, not as much trouble as I am having writing my second novel. It's a totally different genre—with family secrets and political intrigue. The working title is *Shattered Trust*, and it follows three generations of the politically powerful Drake family of Tulsa, Oklahoma.

Although the genre is different, I don't think that's the problem. The last nine or ten months have been chaotic. From the moment I received Diana's letter informing me that she was coming to Denver for medical treatment, my world has turned upside down. Diana and I married in late May, then she underwent six weeks of radiation treatment for stage-three breast cancer. When she recovered, we moved to Leadville, Colorado, where she is now practicing medicine. Although being married to her is a dream come true, it hasn't been without its stresses.

After living alone for several years, sharing living space with Diana and Eurico has been joyously difficult. Unfortunately, it has made it nearly impossible for me to write. I need solitude to be creative, and that was impossible when the three of us were living in my small cabin west of Fort Collins. Hopefully, things will be better now. Not only is the cabin we have leased with an option to buy considerably larger than the one we lived in west of Fort Collins, but with Diana and Eurico gone all day, I should have several hours to myself. Although I am hopeful, it remains to be seen whether I can recapture my earlier creativity. I'm a creature of habit, and now that my routines have been turned upside down, I'm having trouble reestablishing them.

Concerns about Diana's health continue to plague me, but I should be able to put them behind me now that her radiation treatments are over. We are encouraged because the oncologist has declared her "cancer free." Of course, the possibility of a recurrence remains real, and she has to return to the hospital every three months for a checkup. Sometimes I wonder if we will ever be completely free of cancer's haunting presence. Hopefully, it will continue to fade as long as she remains cancer free.

I feared the worst going into the radiation treatments, but it was not nearly as bad as I imagined. According to Diana, the treatment itself was painless—like getting an X-ray, except the radiation was multiple times more powerful. While an X-ray takes only a few seconds, radiation treatments can last as long as an hour. For Diana, each treatment seemed endless. Not only did she have to remain virtually motionless to make sure the radiation hit the targeted area, but she also had to control her thoughts. It was a mind game, and if she relaxed her self-control for even a moment, she was overwhelmed with memories of her mother's losing battle with cancer and her agonizing death. She strengthened herself by quoting Scriptures and singing the great hymns she learned as a child.

Her side effects were mostly minimal. She had considerable skin irritation, like what you would experience with a bad sunburn. The worst, however, was the constant fatigue. Some days it was all she could do just to get dressed. Part of that may have resulted from the fact that we had to drive into Aurora five days a week for six weeks. That meant a two-hundred-mile round trip every day, Monday through Friday. That wore me out, so I can only imagine the toll it took on her.

Although it has been weeks since my angry meltdown in Telluride, I'm still grieved, and well I should be. Diana has forgiven me, but I can tell her heart has not completely healed. It's like she's walking on eggshells, trying to make sure she doesn't do anything to set me off. Seeing her like this breaks my heart, especially since it is my doing, but I don't know what I can do. I believe she has truly forgiven me, but I can tell she doesn't fully trust me.

We still make love under the cover of darkness, and I'm okay with that. The last thing I want to do is make her uncomfortable or cause her needless pain. Unfortunately, the joyous spontaneity that once characterized our lovemaking has now been replaced with tentativeness. Some of that may have to do with the lingering effects of the radiation treatments, but I fear it is more than that. I sense that while she wants to give herself fully to me, she's afraid, and who could blame her?

While my anger is deeply rooted in my troubled childhood and the insecurity it produced, it also has spiritual roots. Without realizing what I was doing, I allowed it to become a stronghold in my life. According to my pastor, my anger is like a "strongman" sitting on the throne of my life. He said the only way to overcome him is to starve him. When I asked him how to do that, he said, "Every time you give in to your anger, you are feeding the 'strongman,' but when you refuse to lash out in anger, you are starving him. Feed him, and he becomes stronger and more controlling. Starve him, and he becomes weaker."

I'm not sure I'm capable of starving my anger, but I'm doing my best. I'm sure prayer is a vital component in binding this "strongman," but it must be a discipline I practice daily, not just a cry for help when I get angry. Physical exercise seems to help defuse it, so when I feel my anger building, I go for a run or split firewood. As an added benefit, I'm getting in shape and stockpiling firewood, which the neighbors tell me I will need since the winters in Leadville are long and cold.

Eurico is fourteen now and a ninth grader. While living on the mission station, he was homeschooled by Diana, so going to high school has been a big adjustment. Knowing how cruel kids can be, I feared for him. He is small for his age and speaks English with an accent, so I thought he might be intimidated. Boy, was I wrong! I guess immigrating to a new country and starting high school is no big deal if you had to fare for yourself at the age of six while living on the streets of Cruzeiro do Sul. With his infectious personality and his enthusiasm for life, he has had no difficulty fitting in.

His biggest concern is that Lake County High School doesn't have a soccer team. He's too small to play football, a game he detests although he knows almost nothing about it, so he decided to go out for the cross-country team. To my surprise, he is a remarkably gifted runner, demonstrating both speed and stamina. His first meet is scheduled for this coming Saturday, and Diana and I plan to be there.

Diana is enjoying her new life, but I can tell the adjustment has been more difficult than she anticipated. As long as her missionary colleagues assumed she was resigning her appointment for medical reasons, they were understanding and supportive. But once they learned that we had married, their attitude changed. Although only two or three actually said anything, it was obvious nearly all of them thought she had made a terrible mistake. In their opinion, it was bad enough that she was willing to give up her missionary appointment to marry, but when they learned I was divorced, that was the last straw. I thank God for Gordon and Eleanor, who have been supportive through it all. I don't know what Diana would have done without their friendship.

Much to my surprise, Diana and Carolyn have become close friends. They exchange letters weekly and talk by telephone at least once a month. At Diana's insistence, Carolyn is planning on spending the Thanksgiving weekend with us. Eurico is excited, but I have mixed emotions.

Although Diana tries to hide it from me, I can't help noticing how pensive she is at times. On several occasions I have caught her staring off into space or lost in thought. It makes my heart hurt to see her that way, but I don't know what I can do to help her. Maybe if she would talk about it, I could comfort her, but to date she hasn't been willing to confide in me. When I press her, she says she's just tired or it's work-related, before brushing my cheek with a kiss as she heads to the bedroom to prepare for bed. I can't help fearing the cancer has metastasized and she's not telling me. Maybe it is already slowing sucking life out of her. At other times, I can't help but wonder if she is having second thoughts about giving up her missionary appointment to marry me. Whatever it is, it worries me.

After Diana and Eurico left this morning, I discovered a half-finished letter she was writing to Carolyn. It was lying on the dresser in plain sight. I guess she must have gotten distracted and forgot to put it away before heading to work. Maybe I shouldn't have read it, but curiosity got the best of me. I quickly scanned the first couple of pages, and then these words stopped me in my tracks:

> *I love Bryan with all my heart but being married is much harder than I could have ever imagined. After living single for so many years, both of us are set in our ways. I don't consider myself a neat freak, but Bryan's messiness is about to drive me crazy. What's so hard about putting the cap on the toothpaste when you've finished brushing your teeth? Why leave your dirty clothes on the bedroom floor when the clothes hamper is within arm's reach? What's worse is that he is teaching Eurico bad habits.*
>
> *I could go on, but I think you get the picture. I don't want to be a nag, so most of the time I just bite my tongue and do it for him, but I'm not his mother, and I don't want to spend my life picking up after him. When I try to talk to him about it, he just tells me to be cool. Give me time, he says, and I will do it, but in the meantime, I am growing more and more resentful. I hate the person I'm becoming, but I can't live in a messy house!*

That's really no big thing. I just needed to get it off my chest. So, what's really bothering me? The horrible fight we had on the last night of our honeymoon. I don't want to go into the details, just let it suffice to say we both said some terrible things, especially Bryan. I forgave him and we made up, but I can't seem to get over it. I keep telling myself that my heart will heal in time, but I'm beginning to wonder if it will. It's been several weeks, and my heart still hurts. Sometimes it hurts so bad I don't think I can bear it.

When I finish reading, my emotions are all over the place. Her pain is obvious, and in several places, her tears have stained the page. Knowing I'm the cause of her grief is nearly more than I can bear. Yet another part of me is angry, too, mad clear through. How dare she share the intimate details of our personal lives with Carolyn? What happens between the two of us is none of Carolyn's business. If I'm honest with myself, I have to admit that my pride is hurt. I don't want anyone to know what a jerk I can be, least of all Carolyn.

Putting the letter back where I found it, I go into the living room and sit down at my desk. I should force myself to write. I'm behind and my agent is pushing me, but I'm too angry to put pen to paper. Instead, I go outside and walk across the backyard to the woodshed. There's a pile of fresh-cut logs, so I pick up the splitting axe and go to work in hopes of working off some of my anger.

Although the temperature is only in the forties, it doesn't take me long to work up a sweat. I shed my jacket and rest for a minute before going at it again. When I have split nearly a rick of firewood, I stack it in the woodshed and sit down on the porch step.

Now that I've worked off most of my anger, I'm starting to think more clearly. Maybe Diana intended for me to find her unfinished letter. Maybe leaving it lying on the dresser wasn't an oversight. Maybe she wanted me to read it. I know I'm not the easiest person to talk to. I get defensive and clam up, or I lash out in anger. Maybe it was a cry for understanding.

My heart's hurting, too. I still haven't been able to forgive myself for the hurtful things I said. More than anything, I want to heal Diana's wounded heart, but I don't know where to start. I wish I could talk with my pastor, but he's in Fort Collins and I'm here. In desperation, I go inside and get my Bible. Before opening it, I pray, "Lord Jesus, give me a word. Show me how to heal Diana's wounds, the ones I've inflicted in my anger."

Although I know it is not a wise practice, I close my eyes and open my Bible at random, then let my finger fall on the page. "Stop being angry! Turn from your rage! Do not lose your tempter—it only leads to harm" (Ps. 37:8).

Conviction from the Holy Spirit overwhelms me, and I fall to my knees. I repent of my reckless words. I ask the Lord to forgive me, but also to change me. I ask Him to set a guard over my lips, to keep me from lashing out in my anger. Finally, I ask Him to make me wise, that I may speak words that bring healing, especially healing for Diana.

When I finish praying, I am more at peace than I have been in weeks—and more hopeful. With God's help, I can become a kinder, gentler man. I make my way into the bathroom, and sure enough, I have left the cap off the toothpaste and my toothbrush is lying on the counter. Vowing to do better, I put the cap on the toothpaste and place it in the drawer. Then I put my toothbrush in the holder before wiping down the sink and counter. In the bedroom, I pick up my discarded clothes and put them in the hamper. It's no big thing, but at least it's a start.

Chapter 47

It's Saturday morning, and Diana and I are standing with a small group of parents near the starting line for the Lake County Invitational cross-country meet. It snowed earlier in the week, and although most of it has melted, there are still patches of snow in the shaded areas. At midmorning, the temperature is hovering around freezing, never mind that it is early October. Things, as I am discovering, are different at ten thousand feet above sea level. Eurico is clad only in shorts and a sweatshirt, and I can't help thinking he must be freezing.

It's the first cross-country meet of the season, and he was so excited last night that he could hardly sleep. Unbeknownst to him, I took a break from my writing a couple of times this past week to watch him train. To my surprise, he is one of the fastest runners on the team, even though he is just a freshman. Unfortunately, he is so excited that he has a hard time pacing himself, and he usually fades near the end of the race. The course is 3.1 miles long and winds its way through some pretty rough terrain, making stamina as important as speed.

Several of the area's high schools have entered teams, and the runners are milling around the starting line. A number of them are stretching or jogging in place to loosen up. Diana slips her hand inside my elbow and leans close. "Are you sure these are all high school students? Most of them look so much bigger than Eurico."

Giving her hand a reassuring pat, I remind her that many of the runners are probably juniors and seniors, while Eurico is just a freshman. As we watch, the starter calls the runners to the starting line. Once they are lined up, he fires the starting gun, and they are off. Not surprisingly, Eurico explodes off the line, and he is in the lead by several yards as they disappear into the trees, heading for the first incline. It's a good thing, too, because as the trail narrows, several of the runners have to battle for position. Giving his diminutive size, he would have been at a distinct disadvantage.

Diana and I move with the crowd toward the finish line at the far side of the meadow. Twenty minutes later, the first runner bursts out of the trees heading for the creek, which he clears in a single bound. He is slim, and obviously an accomplished runner, and he is nearing the finish line before the next runner exits the tree line. The second-place runner is almost to the creek when two more runners enter the meadow running stride for stride. Diana is jumping up and down, screaming, "It's Eurico! It's Eurico!"

Having watched him run in practice several times, I can tell he is struggling, but with a renewed effort, he begins to pull ahead. The second-place runner has already crossed the finish line, and now all eyes are on Eurico and the tall boy a half stride behind him. Suddenly Eurico takes a nasty fall, landing on his hands and knees on the rocky trail. He is up in an instant, with blood running down his shin from a cut on his knee, but it is too late, and the tall boy crosses the finish line ahead of him.

"He tripped him," I scream, looking around for an official to disqualify the guilty runner. To my dismay, I seem to be the only one who saw what happened. It may have been an accident, but I don't think so. From where I was standing, I had a clear view, and it looked like the tall boy deliberately stepped on Eurico's heel.

We make our way toward Eurico, who is bent double trying to catch his breath. Diana wants to examine his injuries, but he brushes her off and makes his way to the tall boy who edged him out for third place. I watch in amazement as he thrusts out his injured hand and congratulates him. As he turns and heads our way, I can't help but notice the sheepish look on that boy's face.

Eurico finally allows Diana to examine his skinned hands and the cut on his knee. While she is doing that, his coach walks up. Patting him on the shoulder, he says, "Good job, son. You ran a good race."

Taking me by the elbow, he moves us a few yards away. Before he can say anything, I tell him what I saw. He just grimaces. "Sometimes things like that happen, but not too often. Most of the runners play by the rules and practice good sportsmanship, but occasionally you'll find a kid who is determined to do whatever it takes to win. It's not right, but it is what it is. The fact that Eurico is so small makes him as easy target."

"What can we do?"

"Very little," he says, "given that much of the course is cross country, making it difficult to officiate. Eurico may be small, but he's a tough kid. He'll figure out ways to take care of himself."

Although I'm hardly satisfied, I let it go. "Was there something you wanted to speak with me about?"

"As a matter of fact, there is," he replies, his voice taking on a tinge of excitement. "I just wanted to tell you I think Eurico has a lot of potential. He's obviously inexperienced, but I have seldom seen a boy with his natural ability. If he develops the way I think he can, he may well become a state champion before he graduates."

Diana is looking my way, and I can tell she is ready to go. After thanking the coach for his encouragement, I make my way to our Jeep Wagoneer. As I slide behind the steering wheel, I ask, "Anybody hungry?"

Of course, Eurico is starving. What else is new? Even after all this time, I am still amazed at the amount of food the kid can put away. As I turn onto the highway, Diana suggests we have lunch at the Golden Burro before heading back to the cabin. It has become our favorite eatery, and Eurico quickly seconds her suggestion.

The restaurant is buzzing when we walk in, and when I glance around the room, I see several familiar faces. At a large table in the far corner, I spot three of the runners and an older man who must be their coach. After we have placed our orders, he and one of the boys make their way over to our table. He introduces himself and then nods to the young man standing beside him. "Jason has something he would like to say to all of you, but especially to your son."

Jason is obviously embarrassed, and he shuffles his feet awkwardly before clearing his throat. "What happened near the end of the race was no accident. I deliberately stepped on your heel, and I want to apologize."

Eurico nods an acknowledgment, but before he can say anything, the waitress arrives with our food. Once she is gone, Jason invites Eurico to bring his food and join him and the other two guys at the table in the corner. Eurico hesitates only long enough to glace a question in Diana's direction. When she smiles her approval, he shoves his chair back and heads across the room.

Turning the now empty chair around backward, Coach Phillips straddles it and rests his arms on the chair back. I motion for the waitress to bring him a fresh cup of coffee. While waiting for it to arrive, I introduce Diana and myself. I tell him that Diana and I are fairly new to the area, having moved to Leadville in late August. In addition, I tell him that she is a family practice physician and I'm a writer. Before I can say more, the waitress returns with his coffee.

When she leaves, he picks it up and blows on it for a moment before taking a sip. "Jason's a good kid," he says, "but he has a very demanding father. His dad is a local businessman and the mayor of Twin Lakes. No big deal in the grand scheme of things, but he thinks pretty highly of himself and he puts a lot of pressure on Jason, demands that he excel at everything he does. As a result, Jason vacillates between thumbing his nose at his father and trying to measure up to his expectations. Today he was trying to measure up."

In between bites of some of the best *huevos rancheros* I've ever eaten, I tell him about Eurico. He can hardly believe it when I describe the three years Eurico spent faring for himself on the streets of Cruzeiro do Sul. From time to time, I glance at the table in the corner where Eurico seems to be holding court. I've no doubt that he is regaling them with outlandish tales of his adventures in the Amazon. Jason, I can't help noticing, appears to be particular captivated.

As we prepare to leave, Coach Phillips tells me he wishes Jason had a friend like Eurico, someone to keep him out of trouble. When I look at Diana, I can tell she's thinking the same thing I am—his apology notwithstanding, Jason looks like trouble. He's hardly the kind of friend we would choose for Eurico.

I have just started the car when Eurico leans over the front seat to tell us that Jason has invited him to a party at his house three weeks from today. "Can I go?" he asks, hardly able to contain his excitement. I am about to tell him absolutely not, when Diana intervenes.

"Doesn't he live in Twin Lakes?" she asks.

When he acknowledges as much, she continues, "So, how will you get there, and who's going to bring you home?"

"I thought maybe you and Bryan could drive me over. It's not very far. Jason said it was less than thirty miles."

"Let me discuss it with Bryan. Then we can talk about it again."

He's obviously disappointed, but he's not ready to give up. "If you guys don't want to drive me, Jason said maybe he could come and get me. He has his own car, a 1969 Ford Mustang. Isn't that cool?"

I've heard enough. There's no way I'm going to allow that kid to drive Eurico anywhere, nor is it likely either Diana or I is going to make that drive. The highway between here and Twin Lakes can be treacherous during the winter.

Diana senses my anger rising, and she lays a calming hand on my arm. Turning to Eurico, she says, "That's enough, young man. You have made your case, now let us discuss it and then we can talk about it again."

He's obviously not happy, but he knows better than to push Diana when she speaks to him in that tone of voice. I glance in the rearview mirror and see him scrunched against the back door, his arms crossed, with a scowl on his face.

"What's gotten into him?" I ask in a whisper only Diana can hear.

She mouths her answer, *"He's a teenager!"*

Chapter 48

The next few days pass in a haze of routine activities. Diana's caseload at the clinic continues to increase as word gets around regarding her medical expertise and her compassionate care. Eurico excels in cross country although he is only a freshman. He has yet to finish first, but he has placed in every meet. He loves running and is passionate about training. As a result, his stamina is much improved. If he is not the best runner on the Lake County High School team, he is close.

After considerable discussion, Diana and I decided to let him attend Jason's party, although we had some misgivings. In retrospect, it was not a wise decision, but at the time it seemed the thing to do. He was desperate for a friend, and Jason was the only boy who had gone out of his way to befriend him. To my surprise, none of his teammates reached out to him. Maybe they were jealous of his success, or it could be they all have been friends since elementary school, and he was an outsider.

In spite of our concerns, we allowed Jason to pick up Eurico and drive him to his home in Twin Lakes for the party. He arrived at our cabin a few minutes early on a

Saturday evening in early November. I expected him to sit in his Mustang gunning the engine while he waited for Eurico, but to my surprise, he came inside and spent several minutes conversing with Diana and me. He assured us that he would drive carefully, that his parents would be chaperoning the party, and that there would be no booze. Before departing, he handed me a folded sheet of paper on which he had typed his address and phone number.

Diane and I stood on the front porch until the Mustang's taillights disappeared down the hill. Turning to her, I asked, "So, what did you think of Jason?"

Before answering, she took my hand and said, "Let's go inside. It's getting cold out here."

Once inside, she headed for the kitchen to brew coffee, while I opened the damper on the stove and poked at the coals, before adding four or five pieces of split pinion. I adjusted the damper and extended my hands toward the stove as it warmed up. I've known Diana long enough to know that when she delays before answering a question, something is bothering her. I'm troubled, too, but I can't put my finger on why. Hopefully, she can. As a doctor, she works with people all the time, and she is one of the most perceptive people I know.

The stove is radiating heat when she returns with two mugs of steaming coffee. I sit down at my desk, and she takes a seat near the stove. For a minute or two, we sit in silence, the only sound being the crackling of the fire and the wind whistling around the eaves. I take a sip of my coffee and twirl a ballpoint pen between my fingers while waiting for her to speak.

Finally, she sets her coffee mug on the end table beside her and says, "I don't trust him—Jason, I mean. He's too smooth for me."

"What do you mean?"

"I'm not sure, but I can tell you this, I felt manipulated. I would have been more comfortable if he had just stayed in his car and honked his horn for Eurico to come out. That's pretty typical behavior for a teenager. In that case, I would have walked to the car with Eurico and asked the kinds of questions moms always ask: 'Will your parents be home all evening?' 'Will there be any booze or drugs at the party?' You know, things like that. But he didn't give me a chance. He answered our questions before we could even ask them."

When she winds down, I raise my eyebrows questioningly. "So...is that a bad thing?"

"All I'm saying is that's not how teenage boys act unless they're trying to con you."

"Are you sure you aren't overreacting?" I ask, playing the devil's advocate. "Maybe he just comes from a better home than most kids. His father is the mayor, so he's probably been interacting with adults most of his life. In addition, he's probably had good manners hammered into him."

"Maybe you're right," she says, before swallowing the last of her coffee. "At least I hope you are, but my female intuition tells me otherwise."

Although it is still fairly early, she takes our coffee mugs into the kitchen and rinses them out, before heading into the bathroom to prepare for bed. I know she works hard, and it's the end of a demanding week; still, I can't help feeling there's more to her exhaustion than just that. Always in the back of my mind is the fear that the cancer may have metastasized and is even now spreading throughout her body.

With an effort, I push that thought aside and reach for my yellow legal pad. I am working on a scene in my novel that requires a measure of subtlety that I fear exceeds my capabilities. I've written and rewritten it at least a half dozen times, and the wastebasket beside my desk is filled with crumpled pages torn from my legal pad. Something my creative writing professor said returns to haunt me: *"And there was that poor sucker Flaubert, rolling around on his floor for three days looking for the right word."* I haven't resorted to rolling around on the floor yet, but I'm getting close.

With renewed determination, I put my pen to paper and try again. Suddenly the scene opens up, and I can't write fast enough to keep up with the torrent of words pouring out of me. This is a rare experience for me. Normally I am a painfully slow writer, doggedly plowing ahead, more out of sheer determination than any flight of inspiration. Not tonight. In what feels almost like no time, I have filled several pages with my cramped scrawl. Of course, I will have to rewrite them to get them into publishable form, but that's just grunt work, like cleaning up the baby when the birthing is done.

"Bryan," Diana calls from the bedroom, "do you know what time it is?"

Glancing at my watch, I realize I am running late. I was so absorbed in my writing that I lost track of the time. I pull on my jacket as I'm heading for the door. Over my shoulder,

I call, "'Bye, sweetheart. Don't wait up for us. It will be late when we get home."

It is snowing lightly as I turn onto Highway 24, heading south toward Twin Lakes. The farther I go, the heavier the snow becomes. The highway is covered with a thin coat of ice, making me thankful I brought the four-wheel-drive Jeep Wagoneer rather than my pickup. Having lived in Colorado all of my adult life, I'm used to driving in snow, but there's something a bit unnerving about tonight. It's nearly midnight, and I haven't met a single car, and to my dismay there is not a snowplow in sight.

As I start up a steep incline, the Jeep fishtails on the slick road in spite of the four-wheel drive. I turn into the skid and the car straightens out; still, I can't help but imagine what would happen if I slid off the road. I could be out here all night before anyone found me. Under my breath, I berate myself for not getting the studded snow tires put on the Jeep. Winter comes early at this elevation, and I knew it was time to get it done, but I kept putting it off.

After nearly an hour, I finally see the lights of Twin Lakes. It has taken me that long to traverse the thirty miles from Leadville, and I am tense from the strain. Just thinking about the return trip makes me tired. Following the directions Jason had typed for me, I find his house without any trouble. To my surprise, it is dark, and for a minute I think the party is over, but when I turn into the circle driveway and near the house, I hear the heavy throb of rock music.

I leave the Jeep running as I make my way up the snow-covered sidewalk toward the front door. The music is louder now, and although I ring the doorbell repeatedly, no one comes to the door. Finally, I let myself into the house. The music emanating from the basement is so loud it feels like a physical force as I make my way down the stairs in the dark. In the basement, several candles are burning, providing the only light. The sickly-sweet smell of pot hits me in the face, and as my eyes adjust, I see several couples making out.

No one is paying any attention to me, and I work my way around the room looking for Eurico. By now, I am mad clear through! If I could get my hands on Jason, I fear what I might do. Just as Diana suspected, he conned us. He assured us his parents would be chaperoning the party, but as far as I can tell, they are nowhere to be found, and empty beer cans are everywhere.

I finally find Eurico passed out behind the couch in the far corner of the room. Taking him by the arm, I drag him to his feet and march him across the room and up the stairs. When the cold slaps him in the face, he revives a little, but as soon as he settles into the warm car, he passes out again.

I am nearly shaking with anger as I ease the Jeep down the driveway. Of course, I'm mad at Eurico—how could he do this to Diana? But I'm probably angrier with myself. I knew allowing him to come to this party was a bad idea, so why did I permit it? Because I succumbed to what my pastor calls "misguided compassion." Eurico was lonely, and I wanted him to have friends, so against my better judgment I gave in. Diana was opposed to the idea, but I convinced her it would be okay. Now I dread facing her. She's going to be devastated when she discovers Eurico is stoned.

The lights come on in the house next door as I turn the corner at the end of the block, and I meet a police cruiser heading toward Jason's home. Apparently, the neighbors have gotten tired of the loud music and called the police. Thankfully, I got Eurico out of there before the police arrived. The last thing we need is for him to be charged with underage drinking and possession of illegal drugs.

As I turn onto Highway 24 for the return trip to Leadville, it is snowing so hard I can hardly see the road, and the wind has picked up, making matters worse. Although I am running the defroster full blast, I have to stop every few miles and clear the buildup of ice off of the wipers if I hope to have any chance of keeping the windshield clear. Once again, the highway is deserted, although I do see a single snowplow fighting a losing battle against the storm. I can't help thinking no sane person would be out on a night like this.

Ninety minutes later, I finally reach the turnoff to the road leading to our cabin, and I am tense with exhaustion. When it started snowing earlier this evening, the ground was warm enough to cause it to melt, and then it froze, coating the road. By now, the snow is nearly a foot deep, and underneath is a thin layer of ice. The road to our cabin is hardly more than a track. In several places, it is steep with hairpin curves, and I am having trouble maintaining traction even with the four-wheel drive. We are still nearly a mile from the cabin when we lose traction on a particularly steep section of the road. Once our forward progress is stopped, I apply the brakes, but even with the wheels locked, we slide to the bottom of the hill. Once again, I berate myself for failing to have the studded snow tires mounted on the Jeep. Still, I'm not sure they would have made much difference. To be safe, I probably should buy a set of tire chains. I would hate for Diana to get stranded like this.

For a few minutes, I sit with the Jeep running while trying to decide what to do. There are only a couple of options. We can spend the night in the Jeep, or we can try to hike the rest of the way to the cabin. Neither option is ideal. Although I am wearing hiking boots, Euriko is wearing sneakers, not suitable footwear for a hike through nearly knee-deep snow in freezing temperatures. Besides, hiking in the dark with limited visibility due to the heavy snow and high winds is a risky venture at best. We could become disoriented and lose our way. In that case, we might freeze to death.

Thankfully, we always travel with an emergency bag in our vehicles during the winter. It contains wool blankets, extra coats and gloves, a gallon of water, and a small amount of nonperishable food. I ease out of the Jeep and make my way to tailgate. After sweeping away the heavy accumulation of snow, I lift the lid and retrieve the emergency supplies. Once I deposit them in the Jeep, I use my hands to clear the snow away from the exhaust pipe. We will have to run the engine periodically to stay warm, and if the tailpipe gets clogged, we could risk carbon monoxide poisoning.

I have no idea how much pot Eurico has smoked or if he also had a few beers, but he is clearly stoned, and I am having trouble helping him into a heavy coat and gloves. Finally, we succeed after a fashion, and almost immediately he passes out again. I cover him with a couple of wool blankets and berate myself once more for my poor judgment. I should never have allowed him to go to Jason's party.

The Jeep is reasonably warm, so I kill the engine and wrap myself in the remaining wool blanket to await daylight. When I do, my thoughts turn to Diana. We should have been home hours ago, and she must be frantic with worry. I wish there was some way to let her know that we are all right, but that's impossible. All I can do is pray, asking the Lord to give her peace.

We spend a miserable night in the Jeep, and I awake from my semi-sleep every hour or so to run the Jeep for ten or fifteen minutes. Finally, the first hint of daylight outlines the towering peaks, and I realize the storm has passed. As the sun pushes its way higher in the sky, the world around us blazes with a dazzling light, forcing me to reach for my sunglasses. After starting the Jeep, I turn the heater on full blast and take a long drink of water before eating some cheese and crackers from our emergency rations.

Eurico is still reeling from the effects of last night's party, and he refuses the cheese and crackers I offer to share with him. Suddenly he flings the car door open and lunges out into the snow. He bends over double, and I take a perverse pleasure in watching him heave his guts out. When he turns toward the Jeep, I hand him the water bottle and watch as he rinses his mouth out. He is clearly dehydrated, but when he tries to take a drink, he gags and has the dry heaves.

From the first day I encountered him as a nine-year-old on the streets of Cruzeiro do Sul, we have had a special connection, but now I can't reach him. He is sullen and only grunts in response to my attempts at conversation. I want to press him about the events of last night, but I don't trust myself. His attitude has ignited my anger, and I fear I might do something I will regret. Instead of questioning him further, I get out of the Jeep and prepare to hike to our cabin. Reluctantly he joins me, and we push uphill through the deep snow.

Although there is little wind, the temperatures have plunged, and I suspect it can't be more than just a few degrees above zero, maybe even colder than that. If we are not careful, frostbite could become a real problem. Thankfully, we both have parkas and gloves, but I'm concerned about Eurico's feet. His sneakers are not waterproof, and they offer little protection against the cold, nor do they provide much traction.

In my eagerness to reach the cabin and let Diana know that we are safe, I plow through the snow, oblivious to the fact that Eurico is no longer with me. When I pause to catch my breath, I realize he is nowhere to be seen. I fight down a rush of fear and begin retracing my steps. Hopefully, he hasn't fallen and injured himself or wandered off the road and gotten lost in the woods. Whatever the case, I should be able to find him. Given the snow, his tracks will be clearly visible.

After almost a quarter of a mile, I find him curled up in the snow. When I shake him awake, he simply groans. "I can't go any further," he whines as I pull him to his feet. "I'm sick, and my feet are frozen."

I'm angry clear through, and I want to shake him until his teeth rattle, but I'm scared, too. "Listen to me," I say through gritted teeth. "These temperatures are deadly. No matter how sick you are, you have to keep moving. If you lie down in the snow and fall asleep, you may never wake up. Do you under-stand me?"

He nods his head, but I am not sure he grasps what I'm saying. His jeans and sneakers are soaked and crusted with snow, making frostbite a serious danger, especially for his feet and toes. There's nothing I can do about it except get him to shelter as quickly as possible. With that thought in mind, I lock arms with him and redouble my efforts, determined to drag him to the cabin if I have to.

We are still more than a hundred yards from the cabin when Diana catches sight of us through the frost-fringed living room window. In an instant, she flings the door open and rushes to the edge of the porch, waving at us. I wave back, but Eurico simply slogs on through the heavy snow, refusing to even acknowledge her presence. Several times he slips as we push our way up the steep hill toward the front steps, and I have to drag him to his feet. When we reach the porch, Diana tries to hug him, but he pushes her aside and stumbles into the house. Turning to me, she asks anxiously, "Is he okay?"

Inside the mudroom, we shed our parkas and hang them on wooden pegs before removing our snow-covered footwear. Diana is hovering over us like a mother hen, and as soon as Eurico removes his sneakers, she bends to examine his feet. From where I am standing, I can see that the skin around his toes is a grayish-yellow color, and when she touches them, he flinches. Under her breath, I hear her say, "This doesn't look good."

Although he tries to resist, she takes him by the arm and marches him into the bathroom. Working quickly, she fills the bathtub about half full of warm water and tells him to soak his feet. Immersing his feet in the warm water sends shooting pains through his frostbitten toes, and he instantly jerks them out of the water. Diana gives him a stern look and orders him to soak his feet. Reluctantly he eases them back into the warm water, grimacing in pain as he does. Every few minutes, she adds more hot water to keep it the right temperature.

While he's soaking his feet, she tries to engage him in conversation, but he just grunts in reply. After two or three unsuccessful attempts, she glances a question in my direction, her concern obvious. I'm tempted to tell him to be respectful to his mother, and in no uncertain terms, but I don't. Something about his painful silence reminds me of my own troubled youth, and my heart goes out to him. When I was hurting, the last thing I needed was a harsh word, and I suspect that in this moment, he's not all that different from the wounded boy I was. Stepping behind him, I massage his narrow shoulders, hoping my touch lets him know how much I love him. Nothing he did last night will change that. I can feel him trembling, and after a couple of minutes, he turns and throws his arms around my waist, burying his face against my chest.

"I'm sorry, Bryan," he sobs. "I'm so sorry."

Diana's concern is obvious, and I tell her that I will explain later. As she continues to stare at us, I hug him fiercely, willing his shame away. As his sobs subside, I hand him my handkerchief, and he dries his tears and blows his nose. When he looks at Diana, she nods her head toward the bathtub, and he returns his feet to the warm water.

After about thirty minutes, she tells him he can take his feet out of the water. When he complies, she dries his feet and carefully examines them, paying particular attention to his toes. While she's doing that, I go to his bedroom closet and return with sweats and a pair of fur-lined moccasins. Eurico limps to the couch and lies down. Diana covers him with a wool blanket before heading to the kitchen to prepare a late breakfast. While she's doing that, I stir up the fire in the potbellied stove and add more wood, noting that Eurico is already asleep.

Now that the crisis has passed, I am suddenly overwhelmed with a bone-crushing exhaustion, and I collapse in the nearest chair. Diana brings me a mug of fresh brewed coffee, and I gulp it down, nearly scalding myself in the process. A few minutes later, she calls me to the kitchen, and I make my way to the table. "Is Eurico going to eat with us?" she asks as she sets a plate of ham and eggs before me.

"He's asleep on the couch," I reply, as I dig into my ham and eggs. "He had a pretty rough night. I don't think he feels like eating right now. Maybe you can make something for him a little later."

When she sits down at the kitchen table across from me, I fill her in in regard to Jason's party. After I finish, she sits without speaking for two or three minutes, maybe longer. Finally, she says, "I'm terribly disappointed in Eurico, but I'm not surprised about the party. As you may recall, I've had a bad feeling about Jason from the beginning."

I can tell she holds me responsible, at least in part, and with good cause. If I hadn't insisted it was time we allowed

Eurico to grow up, there's no way she would have allowed him go to Jason's party. In retrospect, I can see how misguided my decision was, but at the time I was convinced I was doing the right thing. Rather than trying to justify my poor decision, I simply nod in agreement, and she continues, "Thankfully Jason lives in Twin Lakes, so we shouldn't have any trouble keeping Eurico away from him in the future."

She stands up and begins to clear the table. Belatedly, I carry my cup and plate to the kitchen sink. Normally we do the dishes together, but when she sees how tired I am, she takes my hand and says, "Let's get you to bed."

In the bedroom, she helps me undress, and when I crawl into bed, she tucks me in. When she bends down to brush my lips with a kiss, I see a tear escape the corner of her eye. Before I can say anything, she puts her finger on my lips and says, "Thank God you both are safe. You have no idea how scared I was when you didn't come home last night. I don't know what I would do if something happened to either of you."

At the doorway, she pauses and turns toward me. "Don't be too hard on yourself or Eurico. We'll get through this. You'll see."

Once again, I am amazed at her kindness. Had our roles been reversed, I might well have railed at her again and again for her poor judgment. As I'm nearing sleep, I hear her puttering in the kitchen, and I thank God for her. As my pastor says, "Houses and lands are inherited from parents, but a godly wife is a gift of the Lord." That may not be an exact quote, but that's the essence of it.

Chapter 49

As often happens following an early snowstorm in the Colorado Rockies, the following day a warm front pushed the midday temperatures to nearly fifty degrees, ushering in several days of Indian summer. By the weekend, nearly all of the snow was gone, except for a few stubborn patches the sun couldn't get at, making for a nearly perfect day for the final cross-country event of the season.

Diana and I were in the crowd on Saturday morning when the starter fired his gun. As per usual, Eurico got off to a fast start and was ahead of the pack as they rounded the first turn and headed up a steep incline to disappear into the trees. I was excited, but not necessarily hopeful, as I had seen him take an early lead several times before, only to be run down at the finish by runners who had paced themselves.

Today he heeded his coach's advice, and following his fast start, he allowed several runners to pass him, although it was all he could do to restrain himself. With a half mile remaining, he lengthened his stride and began to overtake one runner after another. With just three hundred yards remaining, he burst out of the trees hard on the heels of the lead runner. I watched in amazement as he drew on reserves of stamina and determination I never knew he possessed. Just before the finish line, the lead runner faltered, and with a burst of speed, Eurico lunged across the line just ahead of him. Diana and I were nearly beside ourselves as we jumped up and down, screaming ourselves hoarse.

To celebrate, we had lunch at the Golden Burro before heading back to the cabin. Once we got home, I quickly changed into a pair of worn jeans, a plaid flannel shirt, and hiking boots, before heading to the woodpile. In a few minutes, Eurico came out to join me. Ever since Jason's party, he has been a model son, doing everything he can to make up for his irresponsible behavior. Today we work as a team. I split the logs using a heavy splitting axe, and he stacks the split firewood in the woodshed. We work all afternoon and add nearly a cord of firewood to our winter supply.

The sun has slid far down the western sky when Diana brings each of us a tall glass of sweet tea. When I see her approaching, I bury the axe deep in the nearest stump and wipe my sweaty face on my shirtsleeve before taking the glass she hands me. I drain nearly half of it in one gulp. Her nearness and the rich taste of the sweet tea carry me back to the Amazon. We are sitting in the swing beneath the towering samuma tree in front of Whittaker House. We are still recovering from our ordeal on the mountainside, following our accident, while returning from the Kachinawa village. Her broken leg is still in a cast, and it will be for a few more weeks, but her scrapes and bruises are mostly healed. My knee continues to give me fits, but its nothing I can't live with. Out of the corner of my eye, I study her, taking pleasure in her radiate complexion with its sprinkling of freckles across her nose and cheekbones. She thinks they make her look like a tomboy, and she hates them, but I think they are cute. I remember thinking she was a truly special woman—compassionate, caring, capable, and very attractive. I think that's when I fell in love with her, although I didn't acknowledge it, not even to myself, until weeks later. Never, not in my wildest dreams, did I imagine that one day she would be my wife—but she is.

After handing Eurico his glass of tea, she comes to stand beside me, and I slip my arm around her waist and pull her close. We stand there without speaking as the sun slides beneath the towering peaks. Almost instantly we feel the temperature drop, even as the soft light lingers in the sky a few minutes longer. I take a deep breath, savoring the fragrant, pine-scented air. Somewhere across the meadow, a bird calls, and in the background, I hear the sound of the creek rushing down the mountain.

Turning to Eurico, I say, "Let's have a wiener roast, what do you say? Winter is just around the corner, and this may be the last chance we have until next summer."

His excitement matches my own, and when Diana heads to the cabin to get the hot dogs and condiments, he carries chairs from the porch and places them around the firepit. I get an armload of wood for the fire. By the time she returns with a picnic basket containing the food and paper plates, we have a fire blazing. We move our chairs closer to the fire to enjoy the warmth while waiting for it to burn down to a bed of hot coals. Eurico is talking a mile a minute as he recounts his winning strategy in this morning's race. Diana makes an effort to interact with him, but I have tuned him out as my thoughts return to her upcoming PET scan. It's never far from my mind and a constant cause for concern.

She is scheduled to see her oncologist for a checkup in about a week. We haven't talked about it, but I can sense that it is weighing heavy on her mind, as well, although she tries to hide her concerns from me. Of course, I'm doing the same thing. I don't want her to know how anxious I am. As far as I know, there is no reason for us to be worried, but the possibility of the cancer returning is always lurking on the edge of our minds.

Ever since I found Diana's letter to Carolyn, I have made a conscious effort to clean up after myself. Occasionally I slip up, but for the most part, I am turning into something of a neat freak, much to Diana's delight. Of greater concern is the hurt that lingers in her eyes, a hurt I put there our last night in Telluride. I would give anything if I could unsay the hurtful things I said, but I now realize that once words are spoken, they can never be unsaid; they take on a life of their own. I've apologized, but the hurt in her eyes remains. I truly believe she's forgiven me, but I sense she can't bring herself to fully trust me.

In my mind, I'm still searching for a way to restore her trust when she hands me a long-handled fork with two hot dogs skewered on the prongs. Now the three of us lean forward to extend our hot dogs over the white-hot coals, toasting our faces as we do. It only takes a couple of minutes to roast our hot dogs, and then Eurico and I chow down while Diana is loading hers with condiments. I'm still working on my second one when he gulps down his last bite. Diana is only half finished with her first hot dog, so she hands her second one to him. He devours it in three or four big bites before reaching for his long-handled fork and skewering two more hot dogs on the prongs. As always, I am amazed at the amount of food that little guy can put away.

When we finish eating, we toss our paper plates and napkins into the fire and wrap ourselves in blankets to watch the stars decorate the dark sky. The night is still, without a breath of a breeze, the only sound being the crackling of the fire. Diana reaches over and takes my hand, and belatedly I realize I've never been more content than I am right now, with the two people I love most in the entire world close to me. When I was younger, I hungered for adventure and excitement, but now I wouldn't trade all the excitement in the world for the contentment Diana and Eurico have brought me.

We huddle by the fire until it burns down and the cold coaxes us into the cabin. Eurico and I clean up the kitchen while Diana gets ready for bed. He has developed a love for reading, and when we finish in the kitchen, he browses through the books on my shelves until he finds one that catches his interest: *The Adventures of Huckleberry Finn* by Mark Twain. He shows it to me, and I give him a thumbs-up as he heads for his bedroom.

Diana is already in bed when I enter our bedroom with a basin of warm water and a towel draped across my arm. Looking up from her book, she asks, "What do you have there?"

Before answering, I carefully arrange my paraphernalia on the floor at the foot of the bed. In addition to the basin of warm water, I have a washcloth, a towel, and a bottle of lotion. I position the bedroom chair directly in front of where I am kneeling and invite Diana to take a seat. Puzzled, she hesitates before laying her book aside and getting out of bed.

Once she is seated, I pick up one of her feet and place it in the basin of warm water, and then I begin to gently wash it. As I do, I tell her how grieved I am for the pain I have caused her. "What I said to you that night at the cabin in Telluride was evil, pure evil. I was so full of myself, so consumed with my own needs, that I was blind to how embarrassed you were by your surgically scarred body. I couldn't wrap my head around how it made you feel—like less of a woman somehow."

I am weeping now. No sobs, just silent tears slipping down my cheeks. It seems as if God has allowed me to experience Diana's pain in ways I can't even put into words. Taking a deep breath, I force myself to continue. "I would like to put all of this behind us, but I can't, because I see the hurt in your eyes each time I look at you. When we make love, I sense your tentativeness, and it breaks my heart because I know that I am the cause of it. In my anger, I shamed you. I humiliated you. I wounded you in ways that left freezer burns on your soul."

While I have been baring my soul to her, I have been gently washing her foot. Now I wrap it in the soft towel and dry it.

After a moment, I place her other foot in the basin of water and repeat the process. As I gently wash her second foot, I tell her that I truly want to serve her in ways both great and small. "With God as my witness, I promise to take care of you all the days of your life. Each morning, I will get up before you do so I can brew a cup of coffee for you and build a fire in the stove to warm the cabin. On cold winter mornings, I will scrape the snow off the windshield of your car and start it for you, so it will be warm when you get in. When you are exhausted after a difficult day at the clinic, I will massage your aching feet and anoint them with lotion. And because I know you hate going to bed between cold sheets, I will use my body heat to warm your side of the bed, so when you crawl in, you will feel warm and cozy."

I want to look at her, but I can't make myself meet her eyes. I long for her to say something, anything, but she remains silent, and I fear I may have acted presumptuously. Maybe she feels manipulated, as if I am pushing her to act before she is ready to do so. Maybe she feels I'm being disingenuous, that the whole foot-washing thing is nothing more than an act. Maybe this was a bad idea. I thought the Lord impressed me to do it, but it may have just been my imagination. I can only pray I have not made a hurtful situation worse. It's the last thing I want to do, but who knows what she is feeling.

After drying her foot, I pick up the bottle of lotion. I pour a generous amount in the palm of my hand and warm it for a moment before gently rubbing it into her feet. She groans with pleasure. "Oh, that feels good."

Her eyes are closed, and the expression on her face is serene. For the first time since that ill-fated night in Telluride, she seems to truly be at peace. As I continue to stare at her, she opens her eyes, and the look she gives me is filled with such tenderness I feel the terrible burden of my guilt lift. She doesn't say anything, but when she lays her hand against my cheek, I know all is forgiven.

Without a word, she stands to her feet and slips her nightgown off. She wraps her arms around my neck and gently pulls my face against the scarred tissue where the surgeon has removed her breast. I hesitate for just an instant, and then I cover her scar with kisses. After a moment, she takes my hand and leads me to our bed. I reach to shut off the lamp, but she stays my hand, and for the first time ever, we make love without embarrassment or shame, wrapped in the soft glow of the light from the bedside lamp.

Chapter 50

Although I've lived in Colorado much of my life, winters in Leadville are unlike anything I've experienced before. With an annual snowfall of 140 inches, winter seems to last forever. The locals like to say Leadville has four seasons just like other places, only in Leadville it is winter, June, July, and August. On bitter cold days, they attempt to encourage me. "Wait till July," they say. "It's the perfect time to live in Leadville. The days are sunny with mild temperatures, the average high being only seventy-one degrees."

Rather than complain about the long winter, Eurico and I have taken advantage of the snowy conditions to learn to ski. He took to it like a duck to water, and after a half day of lessons, he was zooming down the green slopes at breakneck speeds. By the end of his third day of skiing, he was tackling the black diamond slopes with fearless enthusiasm. His reckless abandonment resulted in several spectacular spills, but that didn't deter him. He just bounced up and pointed his skis down the mountain, and away he went.

Watching him made me wish I had learned to ski when I was his age. Unfortunately, in those days our family's perilous financial condition prohibited skiing, not to mention the fact that Sterling was nearly two hundred miles from the nearest ski slope. Still, I caught on fairly quickly, and I was soon racing him down the blue slopes, but I have yet to risk the blacks. Our styles are different. We both ski aggressively, but I stay under control while he gets bored if he is not pushing the envelope.

Maybe the best part of our ski outings was the time we spent together on the trips to and from the ski slopes. It gave us time to talk, and we had some in-depth conversations. Although he tried not to show it, concerns about Diana's health weighed heavy upon him, and we talked at length about the possibility of her cancer recurring. He wanted to know what the risks were and whether she might die. I was tempted to dismiss his fears out of hand, but I decided he deserved the truth. So, I told him there was always a chance the cancer would return, and if it did, her chances of a long life were minimal. As I explained to him, once breast cancer metastasizes, it usually spreads throughout the body, making chemotherapy, with its debilitating side effects, the last line of defense.

A tear slipped down his cheek, and he quickly wiped it away. Giving me a brave smile, he said, "With God, all things are possible. That's what Diana told me. God will heal her. You'll see."

We drove for several miles in silence, and I focused my thoughts on him. He is still small for his age, but he is in the midst of a growth spurt, and he now stands nearly five-foot-seven. With training for the fall cross-country season beginning in just a few weeks, his excitement is building. Although he was only a freshman, he had qualified for the state meet by finishing second in the district meet last fall. Earlier this spring, he had received a letter from the coach at Adams State College in Alamosa, Colorado. He's something of a legend when it comes to coaching long-distance runners, having coached several Olympic and national cross-country champions. In his letter, he wrote, *"I'm impressed with your achievements and at such a young age. It appears you have a natural gift for distance running, but that's not enough to make you a champion. If you hope to fulfill your potential, you will have to train diligently. I will be watching your progress as you hone your skills. If you continue to develop the way I think you can, I may be able to offer you an athletic scholarship to Adams State College when the time comes."*

Helen writes infrequently, but I check the mailbox every day in hopes of receiving one of those light-blue, tissue-thin aerogram envelopes with a Peruvian postmark. According to her letters, she is living on a remote mission station located in the Iquitos Amazon jungle region with another missionary couple. Like the mission station where we grew up, it is accessible only by riverboat. She is truly her father's daughter, and like him, she is consumed with a desire to take the gospel to those indigenous groups who have never been reached. Although the living conditions are primitive, she has adjusted quickly, thanks in part to her childhood in the far western Amazon Basin in Brazil. The hardest part for her has been being separated from her boys. They are attending boarding school in Lima, the capital city. It was a painfully difficult decision for her, but in the end, she decided it was for the best.

Her letters are filled with exciting accounts of her life and ministry, but I sense an underlying loneliness. That's understandable, given all she has gone through the last four or five years—her marital difficulties, the untimely death of her pastor husband, and now, separation from her boys. Still, she continues to assure me that she has no regrets. I can't help but wonder whom she is trying to convince—herself or Diana and me.

Our life has fallen into a fairly predictable routine. Each weekday morning, Diana takes Eurico to Lake County High School before going to the clinic, where she spends her day seeing patients. Once they are on their way, I do the breakfast dishes, brew a fresh pot of *cafezinbo*, and sit down at my writing desk. I begin each day by rewriting what I wrote the day before. This allows me to polish yesterday's work while "warming up" for what I plan to write today. Occasionally I get bogged down, and try as I might, I can't seem to write my way out of it. When that happens, I go to the mudroom, where I pull on my snow boots and don my parka. Outside, I make my way to the woodpile and start splitting firewood. There seems to be something about physical labor that unlocks my creativity, and usually by the time I have worked up a good sweat, my creative juices are flowing again.

Night comes early during the winter, and it is usually dark by the time Diana and Eurico get home in the evening. As expected, he is usually starving, and he goes directly to the kitchen in search of something to tide him over until dinner, while Diana heads for the bedroom to change into something more comfortable. Since my cooking leaves much to be desired, we have worked out a routine. She cooks, and Eurico and I clean up the kitchen and do the dishes. While we're doing that, she reads or corresponds with friends, usually Carolyn or Helen. Occasionally she writes to Gordon and Eleanor.

Once we are finished with the dishes, Eurico usually grabs a book and heads for his room while I brew *cafezinbo* for Diana and me. I got addicted to it while searching for my late father in the far western Amazon Basin. Once it is ready, I fill two mugs and head to the living room, where I join Diana near the potbellied stove. Sometimes we talk about her day or what's going on with Eurico, but more often than not, we drink our coffee in comfortable silence or reminisce about the time we spent together in the Amazon. Although we seldom discuss it, her health issues are never far from either of our minds. I know she is concerned, because I have seen her doing a self-examination when she didn't realize I was watching. Returning to the University of Colorado Hospital in Aurora every three months for a scan serves as a constant reminder of the risks she is facing, as if we needed one.

We usually drive to Aurora the afternoon preceding her scheduled scan and spend the night with Carolyn before going to the hospital the next morning. Once we arrive at the hospital, Diana's care team checks her blood sugar, then starts an IV line before injecting a radiotracer that allows the PET scan to show where the sugar metabolizes in her body. That will enable the oncologists to determine whether the cancer has metastasized. It normally takes sixty to ninety minutes for the radiotracer to start working. During that time, I drink too much coffee while pacing the floor nervously. Diana, on the other hand, sits as still as a statue. Only her lips move as she strengthens herself by silently quoting Scriptures.

Although the procedure is painless, it is decidedly uncomfortable. Diana must lie flat on her back on a hard platform inside a long tube the entire time. It usually takes between twenty and forty minutes to complete the scan, and she must remain perfectly still. Any movement could adversely affect the results. Needless to say, the whole experience is extremely stressful, as are the two or three days we spend waiting for the results.

While Diana is undergoing the PET scan, I browse through the rack of pamphlets on the wall in the family waiting room. They provide detailed information about cancer, its treatment, and the prognosis. Although the information is presented in the most sterile medical terms, reading it makes my blood run cold. Diana was diagnosed with stage-three breast cancer, which means that the cancer in her breast had spread to several nearby lymph nodes, but not to her bones or organs. She was treated with radiation therapy, and according to the literature I'm reading, she has about a fifty/fifty chance of surviving for five years. It doesn't say what her chances of survival are after that. If the cancer metastasizes, it will likely spread to her lungs, her bones, or her vital organs, making further surgery out of the question. If that happens, aggressive chemotherapy will be the only treatment option, and she would have less than a 20 percent chance of surviving five years. Not encouraging information no matter how you look at it.

When I look up, I see a nurse bidding Diana good-bye as she steps into the family waiting room. Hastily I stuff the pamphlets I've been reading into the back pocket of my jeans and make my way across the room to her. I take her in my arms and hold her close. She is trembling, but as I continue to hold her, I can feel her begin to relax.

Glancing at my watch, I realize it's nearly noon. She hasn't had anything to eat yet today, so I suggest lunch at the Northwoods Inn. We've never eaten there, but Carolyn says it's great. It offers a traditional steakhouse experience with peanut shells on the floor and a rustic décor. Diana hesitates, so I encourage her. "We've got time. We can still make it home before dark, and besides, I'm starving."

She gives me a tentative smile before acquiescing. I realize she would rather get on the highway right away, but I'm convinced this will cheer her up. Besides, we both need something to eat, and the last thing she needs is a sandwich from a fast-food place.

It is not yet noon, and the traffic is fairly light, making the drive to the Northwoods Inn in Littleton uneventful. Once we are seated, I shell several peanuts and pop them in my mouth before throwing the shells on the floor. I've never been in a restaurant where you are allowed to make such a mess. It's quirky, but I like it. The waitress brings our drinks, and Diana orders a salad and clam chowder.

"Are you sure that's all you want?" I ask.

When she assures me it is, I order a rib-eye steak sandwich on sourdough bread with homestyle fries. I continue to eat peanuts and throw the shells on the floor while watching the midday news on the television above the bar. "Can you believe that?" I ask, directing her attention to the television.

She glances at the TV screen for just a moment before losing interest. I try to engage her in conversation, but it is no use, so I turn my attention back to the news.

Our food is served, and after saying the blessing, I dig in. My steak is cooked perfectly—medium rare on the rare side—and it is as good as advertised. Carolyn was right. This is my kind of place, right down to the peanut shells on the floor. I just wish Diana was enjoying it as much as I am. As I watch, she makes a show of eating, but in reality, all she is doing is toying with her food. Normally she loves clam chowder, but she's hardly taken a taste of it. Thinking it might not be to her liking, I offer her a portion of my steak sandwich and some fries, but she declines.

Finally, I ask, "What is it, sweetheart? What's bothering you?"

A tear slips down her cheek, and she quickly wipes it away. Taking a breath, she speaks in a voice I have to strain to hear. "I'm scared, Bryan, really scared. I think the cancer has metastasized."

Before she can say more, I bombard her with questions. "What makes you think the cancer has returned? Did the doctor say something? Have you discovered a lump in your other breast or in your lymph nodes?"

She holds up her hands to slow my torrent of words. "No. Nothing like that. It's just a feeling I have. My body doesn't feel right. Maybe it's just my imagination, but I can't shake this feeling."

The fear I've been holding at bay ever since I learned she had stage-three breast cancer months ago returns with a vengeance and now settles like a heaviness in the pit of my stomach. With an effort, I ignore my fear and move to comfort Diana. Sliding into the booth beside her, I slip my arm around her and hold her close. I must not let her see how frightened I am, or it will only make things worse. I always struggle for words in times like this, but somehow I manage to say, "Of course you're scared. Anyone in your situation would be. The feeling you have, and your fears, are real, but they are not necessarily accurate. A feeling is just a feeling if it's not rooted in objective fact. There is absolutely no medical evidence to suggest your cancer has returned—all of your PET scans have been clear, and you haven't discovered a lump anywhere in your body." I pause before continuing, "Without any evidence to the contrary, I would say the only thing you have to fear is fear itself."

My words seem to have the desired effect, and I can feel her relaxing just a little. Once more, she begins to quote the Scriptures she first learned as a child and that have been her comfort through this whole ordeal. Under her breath she whispers, *"Yea, though I walk through the valley of the shadow of death, I will fear no evil: for thou art with me; thy rod and thy staff they comfort me..."*

The waitress returns with our check, but sensing the intensity of the moment, she simply places it on the table and slips away. After she is gone, Diana reaches for a napkin and dries her tears before handing me the check. "Why don't you take care of this while I freshen up in the ladies' room, and then we'd better be on our way. I would like to get home before dark if possible."

As we head west out of Denver on Interstate 70, she leans her seat back and falls into an exhausted sleep. I'm a heavy sleeper, and I can only conclude that while I have been slumbering like a hibernating bear, she has been lying awake night after night, tormented by her fears. Although I tried to minimize her fears in order to comfort her, I have to admit I am more troubled than I let on. She's one of the strongest people I know, and certainly not someone given to flights of emotion. If she senses something is not right with her body, I suspect something may be going on.

Chapter 51

In spite of Diana's premonition her scan was clear, as was the following one, three months later. Unfortunately, following her July scan, Dr. Church's nurse called to inform us that some abnormalities had shown up on Diana's PET scan. I thought I had prepared myself for that kind of news, but I was wrong. Her words caused my head to spin, and I had to ask her to repeat herself. I understood the words she was using, but I couldn't get them to make any sense. It felt like I was wrapped in layers and layers of gauze, making her words sound garbled. I kept asking her to repeat herself, and finally she was able to make me understand that Diana needed to make an appointment to see Dr. Church as soon as possible. Before ending the call, I managed to ask her if that meant the cancer had returned.

"I'm sorry," she said, "but you will have to discuss that with Dr. Church."

After hanging up the telephone, I make my way to the front porch, where I collapse in a wooden rocker. My heart is beating slow and heavy in my chest as the full impact of her message sinks in. I try to tell myself not to jump to conclusions, that it may not be all that serious, but in my heart I know better. Her call simply confirms what some secret vein in Diana's body already knew—the cancer has metastasized.

I take a deep breath and force myself to look around. At first glance, everything appears to be the same—the sun is still shining, the sound of the wind still whispers in the aspens, the creek still rushes down the mountain—yet I can't help thinking everything has changed. The life Diana and I are living has been rudely interrupted. I don't know that for a fact, but I can't help but fear the worst. In the past, Dr. Church's office has simply informed us that Diana's scan was clear and she needs to return in three months. Given the change in protocol, I fear the cancer has spread throughout her body. If that's the case, her PET scan must have lit up like a Christmas tree.

I consider calling Diana at the clinic but decide against it. It's not likely she can reach Dr. Church, and his nurse isn't going to give her any more information than she gave me. Besides, the shock of an abnormal PET scan will weigh heavy on her mind, making treating her own patients more difficult. It's better, I conclude, to wait and tell her about the call when she gets home this evening.

Having settled that, I force myself to look southwest across the meadow toward Mount Elbert, Colorado's tallest peak, standing 14,433 feet above sea level. The three of us—Eurico, Diana, and myself—had planned to hike to the summit this weekend, but I guess we will have to postpone our climb until later. I can't help thinking that's probably just the first of many things we will have to cancel or reschedule.

Against my will, my thoughts return to the call from Dr. Church's office. If the cancer has metastasized, surgery is probably out of the question. We are most likely looking at chemotherapy. I dread the thought. As Diana told me, chemotherapy is just a dance with death. The oncologist tries to give the patient enough chemo to kill the cancer without killing her. The side effects are horrendous—vomiting and diarrhea, mouth ulcers, baldness, anemia, extreme fatigue, even heart damage.

I want to pray. I want to fling myself facedown on the rough plank flooring of the porch and cry out to the Lord, but I don't. I don't, because right now I'm not sure I can trust Him. We asked Him to remove the lump in her breast, and He didn't. Then we asked Him to make it benign, and it turned out to be malignant. For the past several weeks, we have been praying that the cancer wouldn't metastasize but apparently it has. No matter how desperately we have prayed, it seems He has turned a deaf ear to our cries. Right now, I am angry with the Lord, and praying is out of the question.

Although I'm a grown man with a wife and an adopted son, I feel like a helpless child, just the way I felt when my father disappeared in the jungle of the far western Amazon Basin. Once again, I am tempted to rail at God, to demand to know what kind of a God turns a deaf ear to a seven-year-old boy's desperate prayer, or for that matter, to the frantic prayer of a newlywed husband who is undone by the possibility of losing his wife to the ravages of cancer. It seems to me God is either incompetent or uncaring. Either He cares but is incapable of doing anything about our situation, or He is all-powerful but He just doesn't care. Like I said, He is either cruel or incapable. Either way He's not the kind of God I feel I can trust with my life. Yet what alternative is there? The thought of returning to the dark place in which I lived for so many years following my father's disappearance is unthinkable.

In desperation, I bury my face in my hands and pray. *"Lord Jesus, I don't want to feel this way. I don't want to question Your love or Your wisdom, but I can't seem to help myself. Fear and disappointment have turned me into a conflicted person. With one hand I shove You away, and with the other, I cling to You for dear life. Help me to trust You even if I cannot understand Your ways, for You are my only hope, my only help. In Your holy name I pray. Amen."*

I wish I could tell you that when I finished praying, my faith was restored, but it wasn't. I am still afraid and angry, but I'm determined to lean into the Lord rather than away from Him. The thought of facing the uncertain future alone is simply unbearable. Besides, I will need to be strong for Diana, and I am determined not to let her down.

After a time, I go inside and sit down at my desk. The first thing I see is a letter from my agent, encouraging me to finish my manuscript as quickly as possible. He reminds me that I have already missed one deadline, and the extension the publisher granted me is looming ever nearer. Usually that would motivate me, especially since I have already exhausted the small advance I received when I signed the contract. If Diana can't work while taking chemotherapy, things could get dicey around here in a hurry, making my meager contribution to our livelihood critical. My next advance payment is not due until the publisher receives the completed manuscript. With that thought in mind, I pick up my cheap ballpoint pen and reach for my yellow legal pad, determined to be productive.

Unfortunately, I spend the better part of the next two hours doodling, without producing a single coherent paragraph. The disciplines that have worked in the past fail me. No matter what I try, I can't concentrate. All I can think about is the phone call from Dr. Church's nurse and what it portends for our lives. Finally, I fling my pen down in exasperation and head for the door.

Once I'm outside, I head for the woodpile. The long months of bitter cold have taken a heavy toll on our supply of firewood, and I have a lot of wood to split to get ready for next winter. Grabbing the heavy splitting axe, I go to work, and in short order, I work up a good sweat. Unfortunately, my physical exercise does almost nothing to relieve my anxiety or get my creative juices flowing. No matter how furiously I work, all I can think about is losing Diana, and the thought of life without her is devastating. Looking around, I can't help thinking that none of this will mean anything without her— not this rustic cabin, or the ten acres it sits on, or the books I write.

Exhausted, I bury the axe head in a stump of wood and walk across the meadow to the creek, where I scoop up handfuls of cold water to wet my hair and beard in an attempt to cool off. I'm finger-combing my hair when I see an unfamiliar car coming up the trail. "I wonder who that can be," I mutter to myself as I start back toward the cabin.

Before I reach the cabin, the car pulls to a stop, and Eurico jumps out, followed by a man who looks to be slightly older than I am. He has the lean build of a long-distance runner, and the hair showing beneath his ball cap is flecked with gray. He's clad in shorts and a T-shirt, with a whistle hanging from a cord around his neck, so I assume he's the new cross-country coach Eurico has been raving about.

As I approach, he sticks out his hand and says, "You must be Bryan. Eurico has told me about you. I'm Coach Robinson."

"A pleasure to meet you."

"Do you have a few minutes? I would like to talk with you about Eurico."

I am not in any mood for company, but I can't think of any way to graciously refuse, so I say, "Sure. Let's sit on the porch out of the sun."

Once we are settled, I ask Eurico to bring us each a glass of iced tea. He returns in no time and hands each of us a tall glass, before making himself comfortable on the porch step. I take a gulp of my tea, savoring its flavor and sweetness. Turning to Coach Robinson, I say, "I hope you like sweet tea. It's a Southern delicacy. My wife introduced me to it, and it's become a summer staple in our house."

"I take it your wife is from the South?"

"No. She grew up in Minnesota, but she did her residency in Florida. That's where she fell in love with sweet tea. According to her, it's the official state drink."

Taking a sip of his sweet tea, he grimaces and hands his glass to Eurico. "If you don't mind, I would prefer water. I haven't used processed sugar in years."

Eurico quickly gets to his feet and heads into the cabin. I can't help thinking Coach Robinson must be some kind of health nut. I mean, what damage could one glass of sweet tea do? If he had any manners, he would have simply pretended to like it. Oh well, I guess it takes all kinds.

"Eurico tells me you guys are fairly new to Leadville."

"We've been here nearly a year now. My wife is a family practice physician. She works in the clinic with Dr. Davis. I'm a writer."

"That's impressive," he says, although he seems to take no particular interest in what I'm saying. "So, how do you like it here?"

"The winters are long with lots of snow, but once you get used to that, it's not a bad place to live." I take another swallow of my sweet tea before asking, "So, what brings you to Leadville?"

"What brings me to Leadville?" he muses, before replying. "Burnout and a messy divorce. I was coaching in Lincoln, Nebraska, at the largest high school in the state. The pressure to win was unrelenting. It was all-consuming, leaving little time for anything else. As a result, I neglected my family. I didn't realize what was happening until it was too late. After the divorce, my wife took our boys and moved back to the West Coast to be near her family."

As per usual in situations like this, I don't know what to say, so I say nothing. Thankfully, Eurico returns and hands him a tall glass of ice water. After taking a long drink, he continues, "I love coaching, but I hate the pressure to win that is a huge part of most large high schools, so I looked for

398

a different kind of situation. After considering several opportunities, I settled on Lake County High, and here I am."

Turning to Eurico, who is sitting on the porch step, he puts a hand on his shoulder. "What I didn't expect to find in Leadville was one of the most naturally gifted distance runners I have encountered in nearly twenty-five years of coaching."

With that, he launches into a monologue about a specialized diet for distance runners, special running shoes, and a twelve-month training program. I try to concentrate, but my mind keeps returning to Diana and what she's facing. When he finally runs down and excuses himself, I am only too happy to see him go. I'm proud of Eurico and excited about what the future holds for him, but right now I have a one-track mind.

Chapter 52

It is Saturday morning, and the sun is just edging above the rim of the earth as I ease the Jeep down the trail toward US Highway 24. Against my better judgment, I have allowed Diana to convince me we should hike to the summit of Mount Elbert as we had planned. To her way of thinking, it may be the last chance we will have until next year. She has an appointment to see Dr. Church, her oncologist, on Monday afternoon. She's convinced the cancer has returned, which means he will probably want her to begin chemotherapy sooner rather than later, hence the urgency. As she told me, once she begins chemotherapy, she won't be able to do anything strenuous, and she certainly won't be in any condition to make a nine-mile hike to the summit and back. Given her exhaustion, and the trouble she's had breathing of late, I'm not sure she's up to it today, but that's another story. I have tried to talk her into letting Eurico and me make the climb without her, but to no avail. Once she makes up her mind, there's no changing it.

Like most teenagers, Eurico likes to sleep late, and he tried to talk me out of getting up at the crack of dawn, but he grudgingly acquiesced after I explained that it's critical to be off the peak shortly after noon, as Mount Elbert and the surrounding peaks are notorious for afternoon thunderstorms this time of the year, making lightning a real hazard for climbers. Consequently, he's asleep in the backseat as we turn west onto Colorado 300 and cross the railroad tracks heading for the turnoff to the Halfmoon Creek Campground. Roughly a half mile later, I make a left turn onto Lake County Road 11 and drive just over a mile before turning right. The next five miles are rough. The road is filled with washboard and potholes, making it impossible for Eurico to sleep, and he's wide awake when we reach the North Mount Elbert trailhead.

From here, we will hike nearly five miles up a relatively easy trail, "relatively" being the key word. We will ascend a little over one thousand feet in elevation for each mile we hike. I am told the route becomes much steeper at roughly 13,400 feet above sea level. The next section of trail climbs the rugged talus-scree ridge and gains almost five hundred feet in elevation in under three-tenths of a mile. Once we get past that point, the path to the summit levels out some and shouldn't be much of a challenge.

Although it is fairly early, I'm still surprised there are no other vehicles in the parking lot as we exit the Jeep and unload our gear. Eurico and I are each carrying a backpack with our lunch, a water bottle, and a rope. Mine also has a first aid kit. Diana has only her walking stick and a water bottle. The trail to the summit is supposed to be clearly marked, so I let him lead off, and I bring up the rear in order to keep an eye on Diana.

The two greatest dangers, other than lightning, of course, are dehydration and not being sufficiently acclimated. Neither should be a problem for us. We have plenty of water, and we have been living at an altitude of over ten thousand feet for several months now.

We haven't gone much over a mile when I holler at Eurico to take a break. Although the temperature is barely above 50 degrees, I have worked up a sweat, soaking the back of my shirt. Being a competitive cross-country runner, this climb has been a piece of cake for him, but Diana is gasping for breath, and I'm a little winded myself.

I ease up the trail until I am standing beside her. She is bent over with her hands on her knees, struggling for breath. "Are you okay?" I ask, trying not to sound overly concerned.

"I will be in a minute," she gasps. "Just let me catch my breath."

I'm no doctor, but even I can tell something has changed in Diana's body over the last few weeks. After mentioning her concerns when we were having lunch at the Northwoods Inn, she has refused to discuss it, but it is obvious that her stamina isn't what it was. A day at the clinic exhausts her, and the least bit of strenuous activity leaves her short of breath. Although she goes to great lengths to pretend otherwise, I can tell she's scared. Since Diana won't talk about it, I've shared my concerns with Carolyn. She tried to minimize my fears, but when I pressed her, she finally conceded the cancer might have spread to Diana's lungs, and that could be what is making it difficult for her to breathe.

Pushing those thoughts from my mind, I try to force myself to notice the scenery. It is stunning from this vantage point, but I hardly notice. I have eyes only for Diana, and she looks unusually pale as she sits down on an outcropping of rocks and reaches for her water bottle. Her hands are shaking, and she is having difficulty opening it, so I take it from her and unscrew the cap. Her breathing has almost returned to normal, and after taking a long pull on her water bottle, her color is better.

Having grown impatient, Eurico has moved up the trail nearly a hundred yards. Now he motions for us to join him. I glance at Diana, and it is obvious she needs a few more minutes to recover, so I holler at him and he reluctantly starts back down the trail toward us. By the time he reaches us, Diana is on her feet and ready to go—at least, she pretends she is.

The farther we hike, the more often she has to rest, and soon Eurico's impatience gives way to concern. I suggest that we call it a day and head back to the Jeep, but she won't hear of it. Stubbornly she says, "You can quit if you want to, but I'm going to the summit with or without you." With that, she gets to her feet and heads up the trail. I look at Eurico and shrug my shoulders before starting up the trail after her.

After several more stops to rest, we finally reach the most challenging the part of the trail, and as we start up the rugged talus-scree ridge, I take Diana's arm and help her. Even with my help, she is exhausted and gasping for breath before we reach a stretch of trail that seems to level off, or nearly so. The summit is clearly visible now, and after one final break, we reach it, and Diana collapses on a nearby boulder.

The view is stunning in all directions. Slipping my arm around her waist, I direct her attention to the north, where the skyline is dominated by Mount Massive, the second highest peak in Colorado. Turning her 180 degrees so that she is now facing south, I point out La Plata Peak, with a summit towering 14,336 feet above sea level.

Eurico is hungry, so we look around for a shaded place to eat our lunches, but at this elevation, we are far above the tree line, and there is no shade to be found. That's unfortunate, because the sun is unbearably intense at this altitude, even though the temperature is barely above 60 degrees. While we are eating, I try to help them get their minds off the relentless sun by telling them we are having lunch at the highest point between Mount Whitney in California, Fairweather Mountain in Canada, La Malinche Mountain in Mexico, and Mont Blanc in France.

Giving me a wan smile, Diana says, "You're just an encyclopedia of information, aren't you?"

Eurico laughs, but I just grin at her.

Once we've finished eating, he explores the summit while Diana tries to nap, using her floppy hat to shade her face. I remove my trusty Nikon from my backpack and begin shooting pictures. The scenery is spectacular, but what interests me more are the candid shots I take of Diana and Eurico without their knowledge. Although it's not a conscious thought, some part of me knows these photos will be important in the years ahead.

I've been so focused on my photography that I haven't paid any attention to the thunderstorm building in the west. Belatedly I realize the wind is picking up, pushing the towering thunderheads across the face of the sun, and in an instant the summit is in shadow. The first jagged flash of lightning rends the sky, and an instant later, thunder rocks the mountain. I see Eurico running toward me as Diana reaches for her hat, but she is too late. The wind has snatched it away. The first raindrops, huge and icy cold, pelt us as we hastily gather our things and scramble for the trail heading down the mountain.

Now it seems the sky is on fire as lightning flashes hysterically and thunder rumbles relentlessly. The first huge raindrops have become a deluge, making it impossible for us to see more than two or three feet in any direction. Desperately I reach for Diana while grabbing Eurico's arm with my other hand. I pull them close and try to shelter them with my body as we are now being pelted with marble-sized hail.

Suddenly a bolt of lightning strikes the ground a short distance from us, creating a potentially deadly ground current. As a former lineman, I know how dangerous that can be, and exposed as we are, we are at great risk. Our only hope is to get off this mountain as quickly as possible. Unfortunately, the heavy rain is making it nearly impossible to see where we are going, and the trail across the rugged talus-scree ridge is dangerously steep. One false step could send us plunging to our death. Still, it's a chance we have to take. We have no other choice. It's get off this mountain or die.

Thankfully, these summer thunderstorms are usually as short as they are violent. They often last fifteen minutes or less; still, that can seem like an eternity when you are caught in one like we are. The blinding rain and marble-sized hail continue to pound us as we stumble down the steep trail, but the real danger is the lightning. It doesn't have to strike us directly to be fatal. When lightning strikes the ground, it creates a dangerous and potentially deadly ground current capable of killing anyone or anything in the immediate vicinity.

Suddenly Diana slips on the rain-slick trail, and for an instant I think we are all going over the precipice. Desperately I fling myself backward and dig my heels into the rocky ground, seeking a foothold. Thankfully, Eurico has done the same thing, and the two of us manage to stop our downward skid. Diana has slipped off the trail, and I am holding on to her with one hand, as she hangs in thin air. It feels like my shoulder is being pulled out of joint, but I grit my teeth and ignore the pain. If I lose my grip on her wrist, she will plunge to her death. The muscles in my shoulder and arm are cramping as I strain to pull her up inch by inch, and I can't even imagine the pain she must be experiencing. Finally, she is able to fling her leg over mine, and with Eurico's help, she is able to pull herself back onto the trail.

We are both gasping for breath, and Diana is sobbing uncontrollably as she collapses on top of me. Eurico is lying next to us with his arm tightly wrapped around her waist. Overhead, lightning flashes and thunder crashes, reminding me that we still have to get off this mountain before lightning kills us. Between the roar of the rain and the crash of the thunder, it is nearly impossible to make ourselves heard. Putting my mouth close to Eurico's ear, I tell him to get the rope out of my backpack and tie us together.

Although the pounding rain makes it nearly impossible to see, he somehow manages to get the buckles undone and extracts the length of rope. Next, he loops it around his waist and makes it fast with a figure-eight knot, just the way I have taught him. Now he plays out about ten feet of rope before looping it around Diana's waist and making it fast with a second figure-eight knot. Finally, he tosses the rest of the rope to me, and I repeat the process. Now that we are linked together, I feel better. Such precautions should not be necessary on a trail like this, but given the weather conditions and Diana's situation, it makes sense.

It is still raining hard, but the hail has let up and the lightning seems to have moved off to the east for the most part. We are not out of danger yet, but our chances of surviving have improved considerably and will continue to do so as we descend. Now that we are able to see a little better, I realize we have wandered off the trail. No wonder Diana almost fell to her death. I carefully study the terrain, looking for the best route back to the trail. Finally, I decide on what appears to be the safest, if not the most direct route. We pick our way up the mountainside, being careful to avoid areas that are too steep or covered by rocks that appear to be unstable. It is a slow process, given the rain-slick surface and the treacherous footing, and by the time we finally reach the trail, Diana is nearly out on her feet.

Now that the storm has passed, I am able to examine her more closely, and when I do, I discover she has suffered a badly dislocated shoulder. She tries to tell me what to do to get her shoulder back in place, but when I try to follow her instructions, she screams in pain. After the third try, I give up and help her sit down with her back against a boulder. The first aid kits we brought are sorely inadequate, so I end up taking my shirt off and use it to make a crude sling.

I'm afraid she is going into shock. Her skin is cold and sweaty and slightly gray. Eurico and I lay her down and elevate her feet by placing them on his backpack. As best I can tell, her pulse is weak but rapid. I wish we had some way to keep her warm, but all we have is our jackets. I quickly untie mine from around my waist and wrap it around her torso. Eurico does the same and wraps his jacket around her legs. I rummage in our first aid kit in search of a packet of aspirin, and I put four of them in her mouth. Gently I lift her head and give her a drink of water so she can swallow them.

While Diana is resting, Eurico and I take stock of ourselves. Neither of us is any worse for the wear, except for some scrapes and bruises. We let Diana rest for nearly an hour before we help her to her feet. I wish it could have been longer, but if we want to get off this mountain before dark, we have to get started. Her color is better, and her pulse is steady, but the inactivity has caused her muscles to stiffen, and moving her is painful. I wrap my arm around her waist to steady her, and we start down the trail. Although she's in a great deal of pain, she doesn't complain. She simply bites her lip and puts one foot in front of the other.

Descending is easier than climbing, but it is difficult in its own way, and by the time we finally reach the parking lot at the North Mount Elbert trailhead, Eurico and I are both worn out, and Diana is beyond exhausted. While he is loading our gear in the back of the Jeep, I help Diana into the Wagoneer. I try to be as gentle as possible, but she still groans in pain.

Once she's situated, I take a moment to examine her. As far as I can tell, her only major injury is her dislocated shoulder, but we will know more once we get to the emergency room, where they can examine her and take X-rays. When I think of the rough road between here and the highway, I cringe. It's going to be an excruciatingly painful trip for her.

When we reach the emergency room, they place her in a wheelchair and wheel her into a cubicle. The emergency room doctor examines her and immediately orders X-rays, which reveal no broken bones, although it does show a small mass in her lungs. An orthopedic specialist is called in from Vail to put her severely dislocated shoulder back into place. Thankfully, they give her some strong pain meds, as the process is excruciatingly painful, and it is nearly midnight when they finally finish immobilizing her arm. The doctor wants her to stay in the hospital overnight for observation, but she refuses. After helping her into the Jeep, I ease out of the parking lot, and turn onto US Highway 24 toward home with a heavy heart.

Chapter 53

Although she was in no condition to travel, Diana insisted on keeping her Monday appointment with Dr. Church, her oncologist. As we feared, the cancer has metastasized, having spread to her lungs and to her bones. The only treatment is aggressive chemotherapy. The treatment protocol outlined by her oncologist calls for her to be hospitalized for five to seven days every two or three weeks, depending on how fast she recovers from the chemo. For the first three days, she will receive intravenous chemotherapy around the clock. Then she will remain in the hospital until her white blood cell count returns to a safe range. This usually takes two or three more days.

Her first treatment is not scheduled to begin until the next Monday, so following our consultation with the oncologist, we head home. Although the news was not unexpected, it still has thrown us for a loop. Of course, my first concern is Diana. The thought of the ordeal ahead of us and the possibility of her death is overwhelming. Then there's Eurico. I fear this grim news will rock his faith. I can't help recalling how my father's disappearance sent me into a tailspin that lasted more than twenty years. It wasn't just due to his disappearance, but also because I felt God hadn't answered my desperate prayers. The possibility that Eurico might experience something similar is simply unthinkable.

On a more pedestrian level, training has begun in earnest for the upcoming cross-country season, and Eurico is fully invested in it. Coach Robinson has developed a training plan designed especially for him, and he is adhering to it faithfully. If we can't find anyone for him to stay with during the week Diana is undergoing chemo, he will be hard-pressed to continue his training. We've made several friends during our time in Leadville, but no one I would feel comfortable asking to keep him. Diana suggests I return home and stay with him while she undergoes her treatments, but there's no way I'm going to do that except as an absolute last resort.

I think about asking our pastor and his wife if Eurico can stay with them, but Diana immediately vetoes that idea. "Bryan, they have three children of their own and live in a tiny eight-hundred-square-foot parsonage. They simply do not have room for him."

Reluctantly, I concede her point, but that puts us back to square one. He may simply have to come to Aurora with us, at least until school starts. I realize that will cut into his cross-country training, but we may have no other option. There are other things weighing heavy upon us, as well. Who will cover for Diana at the clinic when she can't work? How am I going to get my novel finished on time? Where will I stay while Diana's in the hospital? If she has a private room, perhaps I can stay at the hospital with her. If not, I may have to impose on Carolyn. There's no way we can afford a hotel, not with Diana unable to work.

When we finally arrive at the cabin nearly three hours later, she is exhausted and in pain. I help her out of the Jeep and into the house before unloading the Wagoneer. By the time I finish, she has taken a pain pill and collapsed on the bed. It's chilly in the bedroom, so I cover her with a throw and brush her forehead with a kiss before tiptoeing out. In the kitchen, I brew *cafezinbo, and* when it is finished, I fill a mug and carry it out to the porch.

To the west, the sun is painting the sky in vivid hues as it slides below the towering peaks, but the beauty of the sunset is mostly lost on me. I'm emotionally exhausted and tempted to despair. Stage-four breast cancer is about as bad as it gets. In reality, our only hope is a miracle, and in my experience, those are in short supply. The thought of watching Diana die an agonizing death is nearly more than I can bear, and the thought of life without her is simply unthinkable. I tell myself to get a grip, as Eurico will be getting home any time now. I have to be strong for him.

I'm just finishing my *cafezinbo* when Coach Robinson's car tops the hill and comes to a stop in our driveway. Eurico hops out and thanks the coach for the ride home before joining me on the porch. Eschewing the empty rocker beside mine, he makes himself comfortable on the porch steps. For a couple of minutes, we sit in silence, and then he asks, "So, how bad is it?"

"It's bad," I say, "but not hopeless. She has a malignant mass in her lungs—that's why she is having so much trouble breathing. The cancer has also spread to her bones."

His deeply tanned face turns a sickly white, and he uses the heel of his hand to wipe the tears that have escaped the corner of his eyes. "Is she going to die?" he asks in a strangled whisper.

"Not anytime soon," I reply, trying to put a positive spin on it. "Maybe not for years." The truth is, she has about a 20 percent chance of surviving the next five years, and who knows what her quality of life will be, given the aggressive chemotherapy required to stop, or at least delay, the spread of the cancer. Of course, I spare Eurico those grim details.

Instead, I ask him how practice went. He simply shrugs his shoulders without answering. When I tell him that we will have to find a place for him to stay for the weeks Diana is in the hospital, he protests that he's old enough to stay by himself. He has a good argument, considering he survived on the streets of Cruzeiro do Sul for three years when he was just a child. I counter by pointing out he has no way to get to and from school. Finally, he suggests that maybe he could stay with Coach Robinson. I hadn't thought of that, and at first blush it seems like a workable plan if he is willing, "Let me discuss it with Diana," I say. "If she's agreeable, we will approach Coach Robinson and see what he thinks of the idea."

Diana is still sleeping, so we close the bedroom door softly and make our way into the kitchen. I'm not really hungry, but Eurico must be starving, so I decide to make something to eat. Yesterday we had baked ham and mashed potatoes for dinner, so I take the leftovers out of the refrigerator and place them on the counter. I cut two thick slices of ham and place them in a cast-iron skillet. In a second skillet, I put a dollop of butter and brown the leftover mashed potatoes. When they are ready, I scoop them onto two plates, being careful to give Eurico the biggest serving. Next, I put six eggs in the skillet while he butters the toast.

He gorges himself, but I can hardly force myself to eat. I leave most of the ham and fried potatoes untouched, plus a slice of toast. I place them on a clean plate and cover it with tinfoil. If Diana is hungry when she wakes up, I will warm it up for her. Once we finish cleaning the kitchen, Eurico goes to his bedroom while I get my jacket and head to the porch. I sit in the rocker for a few minutes, but I am too restless to be still, so I make my way across the meadow toward the creek. The night is cloudless, and overhead the sky glitters with a million or more stars. I don't know whether to be in awe of God's creative power or to simply feel like an insignificant speck in this vast universe. An insignificant speck, I decide, given how God seems unmoved by the things that trouble us.

The porch light comes on, and I see Diana step outside. After a moment, she calls my name. It's dark where I am standing, under the aspens at the edge of the creek, making it impossible for her to see me, so I quickly move into the meadow. It takes her a moment to spot me, but when she does, she descends the porch steps and starts across the yard toward me.

I take her in my arms and hold her close, being careful of her injured shoulder. I see a tear glistening on her cheek, and I gently wipe it away. "Are you okay?" I ask.

"I am now, but when I woke up and couldn't find you, I thought you had left me."

It breaks my heart to hear her say that, but I understand why she would feel that way, given my history. When it seemed Eurico would die writhing in pain, his body twisted and misshapen by meningitis, I abandoned her, leaving her to face the ghastly end alone. When she offered to give up her missionary appointment and return to the States with me, I turned her down cold and walked away without a backward glance. Shame and guilt nearly overwhelm me, and I search for some way to make up for what I've done. I search for a way to assure her that I will never leave her, no matter what the future holds, but I come up empty.

Finally, I simply whisper, "For better or worse, for richer or poorer, in sickness and in health, till death do us part."

She is shivering as we walk toward the porch, whether from fear or the cold I do not know. When we reach the cabin, I offer to heat up the ham and potatoes for her, but she tells me she's not hungry. I make her a cup of hot chocolate, and we sit at the kitchen table while she drinks it. In the glare of the overhead light, her skin is pale, and there are dark smudges under her eyes. It breaks my heart to see her like this, and I know it is only going to get worse.

"Eurico suggested that I speak with Coach Robinson and see if he could stay with him when we have to be in Aurora for your chemotherapy."

Diane frowns before replying, "I don't know if I'm comfortable with that. He's new in town, and we hardly know him."

"Granted, but we are running out of options. Besides, he seems to have taken a special interest in Eurico, and Eurico really likes him."

When Diana still seems hesitant, I suggest we speak to him together. "If you still have reservations after we talk with him, we'll drop it."

She thinks about it for a moment before replying, "I don't think I'm up to that. You will have to handle this one without me."

Although it is still fairly early, we decide to go to bed. Actually, she decides to go to bed and I tag along because I don't think she should be alone. While she is brushing her teeth and preparing for bed, I crawl between the sheets on her side of the bed and warm them, since I know she hates going to bed between cold sheets. Once she told me that when she snuggled between sheets I had warmed for her, it was like wrapping herself in the warmth of my love.

Usually I fall asleep almost as soon as my head hits the pillow, but tonight sleep eludes me. I can't tell if Diana is asleep or just pretending, but I force myself to lie perfectly still nonetheless, lest I awaken her or irritate her injured shoulder by thrashing about. I wish there was something I could do to ease her fears and the toll they are taking on her. She cares more about Eurico than just about anything in the world, and the fact that she doesn't have the strength to speak with Coach Robinson tells me more than I want to know. I can take care of the physical chores—the cooking, the cleaning, the laundry—but I don't know what I can do to help her bear the emotional trauma. Just be with her, I guess. I think my pastor called it the "ministry of presence."

Chapter 54

A Sunday afternoon in late October arrives, and it is time once again to make our pilgrimage to the University of Colorado Hospital in Aurora. This will be Diana's fourth chemotherapy treatment in a series of six. Initially, her arm remained in a sling, as a result of a dislocated shoulder she suffered in a fall while climbing Mount Elbert, and that made her treatments more difficult. Thankfully, her shoulder has healed, but she continues to suffer debilitating side effects from the chemo. During the three days she receives the chemo intravenously, she experiences extreme nausea and uncontrollable diarrhea. On a number of occasions, she has soiled herself and her bedding. It is terribly humiliating for her, and I have heard her crying in the shower as the nurses tried to clean her up. In addition, she has huge sores in her mouth and throat and a painful rash over much of her body.

Thankfully, she has a private room on the oncology wing, so I am able to stay with her. It is a good thing, too, because the medication is causing her to have terrible nightmares, or maybe even hallucinations. She thrashes about and cries out in her drug-induced sleep. When I take her hand to comfort her, I discover she is burning up with fever. Gently I place cold washcloths on her forehead and feed her bits of crushed ice. After a while, she seems to settle down and I think she is asleep, but I am mistaken.

"I had a terrible dream," she says, slurring her words slightly, "only it wasn't a dream. It was a memory, but more real. It was like I was living it again."

Her voice trails off, and I wonder if she has fallen asleep, but then she speaks again, in a slightly disjointed fashion, and I have to struggle to make sense of what she is saying. "They could only find one arm… I saw her in my dream, and she was tragically beautiful, but she only had one arm… I tried to get away from her, but everywhere I looked, she was there, staring at me with her enormously sad eyes… Finally, I cried, 'Who are you? Why are you following me?' In response, she uttered a single word: 'Mommy.'"

Suddenly she is seized with a coughing spell, and when she is finally able to stop coughing, she lies back against her pillow, exhausted. A nurse slips into the room silently and checks her IV to make sure she didn't jerk it out when she was coughing so hard. Satisfied, she gives me a tired smile and exits the room. When she has gone, I sit there trying to make some sense of Diana's incoherent ramblings. As best I can figure, it must be the drugs.

I am about to doze off when she speaks again. "In my dream, it seemed I was drowning. Desperately I fought to swim to the surface, but that beautiful, blond-headed child had wrapped her one arm around my legs and was clinging to me with a deathlike grip."

Exhausted, she falls silent once more, and I have the feeling she is waiting for me to say something, but what? I scoot my chair closer to her bed and take her hand in mine. "It's just a dream," I say, trying to ease her mind.

Instantly, she jerks her hand free and hisses at me, "It's not just a dream. Why can't you understand that?"

Her chest is heaving as she struggles to breathe. "They killed my baby," she says through gritted teeth. "They killed my baby, and I let them."

"Who killed your baby?" I ask, trying to make some sense of what she is saying.

She doesn't answer, and as she drifts toward a drug-induced sleep, she begins to hum softly, filling the semi-dark room with a haunting melody from her childhood. In a voice I have to lean close to hear, she sings:

"Hush, little baby, don't you cry.

"Momma's so sorry she let you die..."

Her voice is so sad and the words are so poignant that I feel myself tear up. If she is not simply talking out of her head, it appears she had an abortion sometime in the past. I find the thought nearly inconceivable. She is not that kind of person. She loves children, and I remember how she grieved she was when she lost both the Kachinawan mother and her baby during an unsuccessful breech birth.

I am about to decide there is absolutely no way Diana could have ever had an abortion when another memory forces its way to the front of my mind. After her tragic accident in the Amazon, when she didn't know whether she would live or die, she begged me to hear her confession. "Bryan," she said, "I don't want to die with this on my conscience." And then she proceeded to tell me she had allowed her boyfriend to convince her to have an abortion. She was suffering from a concussion, and I simply attributed her "confession" to her confusion. In retrospect, it seems I shouldn't have been so quick to dismiss it.

Now she is weeping softly, and I think my heart will break. I would give almost anything if I could heal her memories. Whatever happened is years in the past, and yet it continues to torment her to this day. I can't help thinking that God may tread our sins underfoot and hurl all our iniquities into the depths of the sea, but they will likely haunt us as long as we live. God may forgive us, but life doesn't, and seldom do we forgive ourselves.

After a time, she grows quiet, so I make my way to the recliner that makes into a sort-of bed. Unfortunately, it wasn't made for men who stand three inches over six feet tall. Nonetheless, I arrange my pillow and stretch out on it, in hopes of getting some sleep. Of course, it is a waste of time, and when I'm sure Diana is sleeping soundly, I tiptoe out of the room and make my way to the family room at the end of the hall. At this late hour, the room is empty, but some kind soul has made a fresh pot of coffee. I pour myself a cup and find a reasonably comfortable chair in a dark corner where I hunker down.

I may have dozed off, but I awaken quickly when I sense I am no longer alone. Carolyn has poured herself a cup of coffee and taken the chair across from me. Giving me a wan smile, she says, "When you weren't in Diana's room, I thought I might find you here." When I don't say anything, she continues, "Things are pretty quiet on the floor, and I thought you might need some company."

Now that I'm fully awake, I can't help noticing how pretty she is with her heart-shaped lips, beautiful eyes, and flawless, porcelain skin. In spite of my determination not to, I can't help comparing her healthy good looks to Diana's emaciated appearance. Hardly has that thought entered my mind before I push it aside. A wave of guilt washes over me, and I castigate myself for being disloyal to Diana.

Picking up the Styrofoam cup from the end table beside me, I swallow the dregs of my coffee before addressing Carolyn. "I'm glad you're here. I have some concerns about Eurico, and I don't want to trouble Diana."

I pause to gather my thoughts, and Carolyn asks, "What is it? Nothing too serious, I hope."

"He hasn't been himself lately—not for several weeks, really."

When I hesitate before continuing, she interjects, "In what way hasn't he been himself?"

"He has become really moody, withdrawn. He hardly talks to us. You know that's not like him. He's usually the life of the party." When she nods, I continue, "At first, I assumed he was just scared and worried about Diana. I'm sure that's part of it, but something else is going on, as well. I'm sure of it."

"This may be a dumb question, but have you tried to talk with him?"

"Several times, but he just clams up. Last Friday, I got a telephone call from the school counselor. She said Eurico is failing several classes and in danger of being disqualified from the state cross-country championships. I told her I would talk with him, but he just blew me off."

"Have you discussed this with his coach? What does he say?"

Before I can reply, her beeper goes off, and she dashes out the door. Alone in the room, I consider the situation. I can't help thinking that Eurico may simply be overwhelmed given Diana's condition. Most of her hair has fallen out, and she looks like a holocaust survivor. It's enough to depress anybody. I know it depresses me.

Then there's the situation with Coach Robinson. Initially, Eurico was so excited about staying with him, and he talked incessantly about the things he was learning about training techniques and racing strategies. Now I can't get him to discuss it at all, and when it is time for him to stay with Coach Robinson, he withdraws inside himself and no one can reach him, not even Diana.

I drink one more cup of coffee before returning to Diana's room. In the small bathroom, I relieve myself and quickly brush my teeth before stretching out on the too-short recliner in hopes of getting a few hours' sleep. I am physically exhausted, but my mind is hyperalert, and I can't turn it off. There's something about Eurico's situation that I'm missing, I'm sure of it. For the better part of the next hour, I examine it from all sides without finding a clue. But as I am finally drifting off to sleep, it hits me, and I sit up in bed fully awake. I don't want to believe it, but now that I've thought of it, it makes perfect sense.

I'm so angry I'm ready to kill somebody. I keep telling myself to calm down and not do anything crazy. Although I have no doubt I've discovered the cause of Eurico's depression, I have no proof. And before I act, I will have to have irrefutable proof lest I make a fool of myself. Once more, I consider all the pieces, and the more I think about it, the more convinced I am. In the morning, I will begin the tedious process of collecting the proof I need.

Chapter 55

Diana completed her fifth series of chemotherapy treatments this morning, and her only remaining IV is administering fluids and antinausea meds. She is sleeping, so I scrawl a quick note telling her I will return shortly and slip out of the room. Exiting the hospital, I make my way to a nearby branch bank where I change a twenty-dollar bill into two rolls of quarters. Back at the hospital, I situate myself in a phone booth in the lobby and start feeding quarters into the pay phone.

My first telephone call is to Lincoln High School in Lincoln, Nebraska. The receptionist answers, and I ask to speak with the athletic director. When he comes on the line, I introduce myself as a freelance journalist. I tell him I'm writing an article about outstanding high school coaches for an upcoming issue of *Sports Illustrated*. After mentioning three or four well-known coaches, I tell him I'm considering including Coach Robinson in my article.

"I'm sorry," he tells me, "but I don't think I can help you. Lincoln High no longer employs Coach Robinson. He resigned last spring."

"I'm surprised to hear that. My sources tell me he was one of the most innovative track coaches in the entire country." I pause to allow him to comment, but he remains silent. "If my research is correct, he coached the Rockets' track team to two state championships in the last five years. Several of his long-distance runners have gone on to have success on the collegiate level."

Although this is an opportunity for him to brag about some of the best athletes the school has produced, he refuses to take the bait. "I don't mean to be rude," he says, "but I'm extremely busy this morning. If you will excuse me, I really do need to go."

After he hangs up, I rearrange the stack of quarters on the shelf beneath the phone in front of me and consider our conversation—or lack thereof. Normally a high school athletic director would jump at the chance to have one of his coaches included in a *Sports Illustrated* article, but he couldn't get off the phone fast enough. His response makes me think I'm on the right track.

Next, I call the *Lincoln Star Journal* and ask to speak to the sports' editor. Once again, I identify myself as a freelance journalist working on an article about high school coaches for *Sports Illustrated*. When I ask about Coach Robinson, he is much more forthcoming.

"Robinson was far and away the best high school track coach in the state of Nebraska. His specialty was long-distance runners, especially cross-country runners."

"I've heard that from several sources," I interject. "That's one of the reasons I would like to include him in my article."

He's in a talkative mood, and he needs no prompting to continue. "Several of Robinson's runners went on to have outstanding college careers. Terry Baker even made the 1972 Olympic team, but he wasn't the best long-distance runner to compete for Lincoln High. That would be Bobby Stecker."

I wait for him to continue, but he falls silent. Finally, I say, "So, tell me about Bobby."

"He was a natural, a rare combination of speed and endurance, plus he had an uncanny ability to strategize and adapt on the run. He thrived under Coach Robinson's innovative coaching techniques. He won the Nebraska State cross-country championship last spring as a junior and set a new state record in the process."

There's a note of wistfulness in his voice, and I immediately pick up on it. Something tells me there's more to this story, and I intend to get to the bottom of it. "Can you tell me how I can get in contact with Bobby?" I ask. "I may want to include him in my article."

"Bobby is no longer with us."

"What do you mean? Did he transfer to another school?"

"I wish. Unfortunately, he committed suicide—took his own life."

The telephone operator tells me I'm nearly out of time. Frantically, I feed several more quarters into the pay phone.

Above the clink of the quarters, I can hear the editor's voice in the background. "He parked his car on a lonely stretch of road out in the sandhills and killed himself. As far as anyone knows, he didn't leave a suicide note. According to the police report, he used a 410-gauge shotgun." Almost as an after-thought he adds, "It was a birthday gift from his father."

"Do you have any idea why he took his own life?"

"Nothing concrete. There were some rumors floating around for a while, but nothing ever came of them. Some people think Coach Robison was involved somehow, but that makes no sense to me. A few weeks later, Robinson's wife divorced him, and he resigned. Rumor has it, he took a coaching position at a small high school somewhere in Colorado."

My mind is racing. Given what's going on with Eurico, I need to talk to Bobby's parents. "Do you have a telephone number for the Stecker family?"

"Let me check my Rolodex." I hear him moving things about on his desk, and then he says, "Here it is," and reels off a string of numbers, which I quickly jot down on a scrap of paper I have torn from the telephone book.

I feed my last four quarters into the phone and dial the number I've jotted down. An electronic voice answers: "The number you have dialed has been disconnected or is no longer in service." Disappointed, I hang up the telephone and glance at my watch. I see I have been gone over an hour, so I decide to go back upstairs and check on Diana.

Chapter 56

Two days later, on a bitterly cold December day just before Christmas, Diana is dismissed from the hospital, and we prepare to head for Leadville. Carolyn invited us to spend Christmas with her, but Diana insisted on going home. As she told Carolyn, "This may be my last Christmas, and if it is, I want to spend it with Bryan and Eurico in our cabin high in the Colorado Rockies."

I also realize this may well be her last Christmas with us, but it is too painful for me to consider, so I push that thought out of my mind and concentrate on the task at hand. A hospital orderly pushes her wheelchair to the car, but I insist on helping her into the Jeep. Although the heater is running full-blast, making the Jeep toasty warm, she is freezing. I quickly recline her seat, place a pillow beneath her head, and cover her with two wool blankets.

Last night a storm system out of Canada dumped eight inches of snow on the mile-high city, and more on the higher elevations, but the snowplows have been busy, and Interstate 70 is mostly clear. An arctic cold front followed, plunging temperatures into the single digits, and it is expected to be even colder tonight. It makes me thankful for a well-stocked woodshed and a weather-tight cabin.

Diana sleeps most of the way to Leadville, or at least she pretends to, giving me time to consider how to best deal with Eurico. Once the cross-country season was over, he refused to stay with Coach Robison. Thankfully, our pastor and his wife stepped in to save the day. They insisted that we allow Eurico to stay with them. We tried to talk them out of it, pointing out what a burden he would be, given their three boys and the small parsonage. They simply waved our objections aside.

In no way is Eurico his normal exuberant self, but he seems less depressed now that he's away from Coach Robinson, which leads me to believe that something untoward was going on. I wish he would confide in us, but he simply clams up when we try to talk to him. Unless he's willing to talk to us, there's not much we can do. I have no idea what kind of threats Robinson may have made to keep him quiet, but they seem to be working. He's probably convinced Eurico that whatever happened was his fault.

I've made several attempts to contact Bobby Stecker's parents, but to no avail. They seemed to have dropped off the face of the earth. As best I can tell, they moved shortly after Bobby's suicide and left no forwarding address. Even if I had the time and the money, which I don't, I wouldn't know how to find them.

Without realizing it, I am gripping the steering wheel so tightly my knuckles are turning white and my jaw aches from gritting my teeth. I know I'm supposed to love my enemies, but surely the Lord doesn't mean for me to love a scum like

Robinson, a scum who preys on vulnerable boys. A small voice inside my head attempts to reason with me, reminding me that all I have to condemn him are suspicions and circumstantial evidence, but I brush it aside. As far as I'm concerned, he's guilty of unspeakable crimes against a boy whom I love more than life itself, and I want to make him pay.

I'm so absorbed in trying to think of a way to hold Coach Robinson accountable for what I'm convinced he's done to Eurico, that I nearly miss the turnoff for the trail heading up to our cabin. After slamming on the brakes, I make a sharp turn onto the trail we call a driveway. It runs uphill for nearly a mile before ending in front of our cabin. Given last night's storm, I was afraid I might have to chain up to make it to the cabin, but someone has plowed the trail for us, probably our pastor. He has a heart as big as the out of doors, and it's just the kind of the thing he would do. He has a four-wheel-drive pickup with a snowplow blade, and he plows parking lots and driveways during the winter to help make ends meet.

When I top the last rise and start the descent toward the cabin, I see there is a light on in the living room and smoke is rising from the chimney. Eurico must be home, and I can't help thinking how nice it is to come home to a warm cabin. Coming to a stop, I shut off the ignition, and Diana asks, "Are we home?"

Before I can answer, Eurico steps onto the porch and waves at us. I climb out of the Jeep and call to him, "Can you help me get Diana into the house?"

She is so weak she can hardly walk, even with Eurico and me supporting her. In the mudroom, I help her out of her coat and gloves, as well as her snow boots. Knowing how exhausted she must be, I start for the bedroom, but Eurico directs me toward the living room. "I've made a bed on the couch for her so she can be with us."

Slowly she shuffles into the living room, clinging to my arm. To her delight, he has cut a Christmas tree and placed it in the corner of the living room. It is strung with lights, but there are no decorations. Tears are glistening on her cheeks as she wraps her arms around him, holding him tightly. "Thank you," she says, her voice choked with emotion. "It's beautiful."

His face is full of joy, and he is smiling in a way I haven't seen him smile in weeks. "I didn't decorate it," he explains, "because I was hoping we could do it together, like we always do."

He stumbles to a stop when he realizes how weak Diana is and hurries to turn the quilts back. I help her lie down on the couch and cover her before putting a couple of pillows beneath her head. Once she's settled, he asks, "How about a cup of hot chocolate? I made some to celebrate your homecoming."

When Diana smiles her approval, he heads for the kitchen, calling over his shoulder, "I'll put lots of marshmallows in it, just the way you like."

In short order, he returns, bearing a tray with three mugs of steaming hot chocolate. After serving Diana and me, he sets the tray on my writing desk, pulls a chair close to the couch, and sits down beside Diana, who is struggling to sip her hot chocolate. She is too weak to hold the heavy mug, so he helps her. The love in her eyes when she looks at him makes my heart ache.

I can't help noting the toll chemotherapy has taken, leaving her weak and emaciated. Eating or drinking anything is extremely painful, as she continues to battle huge ulcers in her mouth. Her beautiful honey-colored hair has fallen out, and she has a painful rash over much of her body. Seeing her like this is ripping my heart out.

Although she tries to stay awake, she soon dozes off. I motion to Eurico, and we slip out of the living room. In the kitchen, we each get a second mug of hot chocolate and take a seat at the table across from each other. I was hoping he might open up and talk to me about what happened with Coach Robinson, but he doesn't, so after a couple of minutes, I decide to take the plunge.

"I learned something really sad this week while talking to the sports editor of the *Lincoln Star Journal*. As you probably remember, Lincoln High is where Coach Robinson coached before coming here. According to the sports editor, a boy named Bobby Stecker was the best long-distance runner to ever run for the Lincoln High track team. As a junior he won the state championship in cross country, setting a new state high school record in the process."

"Wow! That's awesome," Eurico exclaims, his eyes lighting up with excitement. "What was his time?"

I pause before continuing. "A few days later, Bobby drove out into the sandhills and killed himself."

In an instant, Eurico turns as pale as a sheet, and he can't meet my eyes. Finally, I ask, "Why would he do something like that? He had the world by the tail. He was a state champion with a bright future. If he continued to develop he had a chance to make the Olympic team."

When Eurico doesn't say anything, I continue, "A young man like Bobby Stecker doesn't kill himself for no reason. He came from a good family, he was strong academically, and a stellar athlete. So, why would he commit suicide?"

When he still doesn't respond, I go on, "The whole community was stunned. They simply couldn't believe it. Shortly thereafter, the Stecker family moved out of state. Then Mrs. Robinson filed for divorce, and Coach Robinson resigned and left town.

"Are those three events connected—Bobby's suicide, Mrs. Robinson filing for divorce, and Coach Robinson's resignation? Maybe. Maybe not, but if they're not connected, it's a pretty interesting coincidence."

I move to the stove and pour the remainder of the hot chocolate into my mug before returning to the table. After taking a sip, I say, "Do you know what I think? I think Coach Robinson sexually assaulted Bobby and then threatened him should he tell anyone. Somehow, he convinced Bobby the whole thing was his fault and that if his parents or his friends found out, they would be disgusted, maybe even despise him. Bobby couldn't live with that, so he killed himself."

Silent tears are running down Eurico's cheeks, and he is trembling. I want to take him in my arms and tell him everything is going to be all right, but I don't. As emotionally fragile as he is at this moment, I am afraid he would shove me away. Instead, I move my chair next to his and put my arm around his shoulders. "One of the things that makes this so sad is that it wasn't Bobby's fault. He was the victim. Coach Robinson was the abuser. Neither his parents nor his friends would ever have blamed him."

Now he forces himself to look at me. "What are you going to do?"

"What do you want me to do?"

"Nothing! I don't want you to do anything. I don't want anyone to know what he did to me."

"What he did to Bobby and what he did to you is called sexual assault, and it is a crime. If you tell the police what he did to you, they will arrest him."

"No. I won't talk to the police, not ever."

He's trembling with emotion, and I can tell he is afraid I will try to make him press charges against Coach Robinson. "I wish you would go to the police," I say after a moment, "but that will have to be your decision. I won't force you to do anything you don't want to do."

He takes a deep breath, and his trembling seems to ease a little. "I can't, Bryan," he mumbles. "I just can't."

"I understand. There's just one thing I want you to think about. If Bobby Stecker had gone to the police instead of killing himself, Coach Robinson would probably be in prison. But because Bobby didn't report him, he came to Leadville and did the same thing to you."

I leave it at that, and he stands up and turns to go. "There's one more thing I need to say."

He stops, but he cannot turn and face me, so I step in front of him and put both of my hands on his shoulders. "Whatever happened, it wasn't your fault."

He's weeping again, and this time I take him in my arms, and he buries his face against my chest. "I'm so sorry," he sobs. "I'm so sorry."

Again, I tell him it was not his fault, but I can tell my words have little or no effect. In that moment, I hate Coach Robinson. He has wounded my son and robbed him of his innocence. I can't help thinking that hell is too good for a man like that!

Chapter 57

With the deadline for my manuscript looming ever nearer, I arise early each morning—well before daylight—and tiptoe out of the bedroom, lest I awaken Diana. Before sitting down to write, I stir up the fire in the stove, then add some kindling and an armload of split pinion. In the kitchen, I pour brown sugar and coffee grounds into a battered old coffeepot and brew *cafezinbo*. I developed a taste for it in the far western Amazon Basin while searching for my father. It is so sweet and strong it makes my teeth ache.

Back at my desk, I light a vintage kerosene lamp, which we salvaged from an antique store in Minturn. The pungent odor and the circle of yellow light it casts on my desk reminds me of my childhood growing up on the mission station deep in the Amazon. It takes a while for the woodstove to warm up the cabin, and my breath is clearly visible in the cold room. The window above my desk is fringed with an intricate pattern of frost, and I suspect the outside temperature is well below zero. It makes me thankful for my heavy corduroy pants, my thick wool sweater, and my fleece-lined moccasins. I warm my hands, cupping them around my mug of steaming *cafezinbo* while contemplating our uncertain future.

Diana has one more scheduled treatment in her first series of chemotherapy treatments, but that may have to be postponed. Yesterday we received a telephone call from her oncologist, informing us that some of her bloodwork looked suspicious. He wants to do a PET scan to see if he can determine what is going on before continuing with the chemotherapy. Of course, anytime something like that comes up, it sets off alarm bells for us, and we spent a good part of the night discussing the future.

If I have learned anything at all about life in my thirty-six years, it is that life is a mixed bag—joy and sorrow, laughter and tears, hope and despair. When Diana is having a good day, hope returns as joyous as the first barefoot day of spring, and I feel like all things are possible. When she's having a bad day, despair descends like a nuclear winter, and I feel as helpless as I did as a seven-year-old boy when my father disappeared. Sometimes, like now, our emotions are all over the place.

Diana is convinced she is going to die, and she wants to discontinue all treatment—chemotherapy, radiation, everything. Of course, I argued against it. I'm desperately believing for an eleventh-hour breakthrough, some kind of miracle cure for cancer. When my pleas fell on deaf ears, I changed tactics. I told her that if chemo could increase her life expectancy by even a few weeks or months, she owed it to herself and to Eurico to go for it. She responded by saying, "Look at me. This isn't living. I'm so weak I can hardly walk across the room. I would rather have one good week with you and Eurico than a year like this."

We debated the pros and cons until late into the night without resolving anything. In retrospect, I know I'm being selfish, but I can't imagine life without her. Watching her suffer is nearly more than I can bear, but the thought of life without her is even worse. If she dies, I will only be half a person.

Normally, I can keep my grief at bay, but last night's conversation has left me drained. A lump the size of a man's fist has lodged in my throat, and I find myself tearing up. I close my eyes tightly and use the heel of my hand to wipe the tears away.

With a determined effort, I push my grief into a place deep inside myself and reach for my mug of *cafezinbo*. I take a sip, relishing the bitterness of the coffee combined with the sweetness of the brown sugar, as I watch the first fingers of light push the darkness from the eastern sky. As the sun slowly eases its way above the towering peaks, I deliberately turn my thoughts to the good times Diana and I have shared. On an impulse, I set my mug aside and reach for my pen.

Dearest Diana:

I realize we've had some bad times, we've hurt each other, but I choose not to remember those times. Sitting here at my desk, in the predawn darkness, I choose to recall the good times, the sunshine, and the laughter. Like the time we were sitting in the swing beneath the towering samauma tree in front of Whittaker House and I said, "Hey, in the sun you have freckles."

And you asked, with a mischievous grin, "Don't you like me in freckles?"

I thought about it for a moment before replying, then I said, "I love you in freckles."

Then there's the time you declared, "What you've done to me is criminal."

Feigning surprise, I asked, "What do you mean? What have I done to you?"

"Oh, nothing," you replied. "Nothing at all, except make me fall madly, crazily, head over heels in love with you."

Protesting my innocence, I inquired, "Is that so bad?"

"It's worse," you replied with mock seriousness.

"Are you sorry you fell in love with me?"

"Absolutely not! I just want you to feel responsible. Before I met you, I was a dedicated missionary doctor, living my life in service to God and others. Now look at me—I'm making out with a handsome guy in a pickup truck. You've ruined me!"

"Well," I said in my defense, "at least I've always been a perfect gentleman."

"I know," you replied with a sigh, "but there are times I wish you weren't quite such a gentleman."

That's one of the things I love most about you— your quick wit and wacky sense of humor.

And there's more, much more—little things I never even realized I was noticing. Subconsciously, I must have been memorizing them, because when I think of you now, they come back to me as clear as light itself.

Like the way your mouth turns down at the corners when you're afraid or about to cry. Or the way you always take a long breath just before saying good-bye. "Good-bye breath," you called it when I drew it to your attention. And the way you always touched my face as I was leaving, like a blind person reading a love story in Braille.

Then there's the poetry. "I'll Think of You" by Naomi Sheldon and "Your Body" by James Kavanaugh, plus a lot of others I can't think of just now, but which have a haunting way of suddenly possessing my mind when I least expect it.

There are so many things. Not big things really, but important to me nonetheless, because we shared them. They are us. If you die, whom will I share them with? Even if there was someone I could talk to, it wouldn't be the same. Besides, they probably wouldn't understand. I mean, what would the fragments, the snatches of conversation I remember, mean to them?

If you die, what do I do with the dream we shared of having a big old country house with a bright sunlit kitchen and a huge stone fireplace? And what do I do with the fruit cellar we planned, or the home-baked bread you were going to make, or the garden we were going to plant out behind the house? What do I do with me?

Whom will I share my day's writing with? Who will suggest subtle changes in the plot and character development? Who will bring me coffee when I need a break? Who will massage my neck after hours of writing have knotted it? Who, I ask you, who?

I'm crying. I'm trying not to, but I can't seem to help myself. There's no sound, just silent tears dripping off my chin to smudge this page...

I hear the bedroom door open, and I quickly slip the handwritten pages beneath my yellow legal pad before turning to greet Diana. A night cap covers her bald head, there are dark splotches beneath her eyes, and they are bright with fever. She stops in front of the potbellied stove and stretches her hands toward the warmth. I slip up behind her and wrap her in my arms, noticing as I do that she is hardly more than skin and bones.

Chapter 58

Diana's appointment with the oncologist isn't until late Tuesday afternoon, so we make plans to spend the night with Carolyn. It is a good thing we do, because the news we receive is not good, and emotionally we are in no condition to drive home. The PET scan reveals the tumor in her lung is continuing to grow and the cancer has spread to her liver. The oncologist informs us there really isn't anything more they can do. He wants to refer her to M.D. Anderson Cancer Hospital in Houston, as she fits the patient profile for an experimental chemo protocol they are testing. There are only a limited number of openings, and he presses us to make an immediate decision.

The news is not unexpected, but it still rocks us to our core, and we are reeling when we leave his office. Of course, I try to talk Diana into going to M.D. Anderson, but she remains adamantly opposed. Although she is just a general practice physician, she is knowledgeable enough to know that her situation is terminal, and she is determined not to spend what little time she has left playing guinea pig in Houston.

Reluctantly, I concede, and I take her in my arms and hold her while she sobs into my chest. When she finally dries her tears, she tells me there are several things she wants to do before she dies. "I want to leave a journal for Eurico. I know how much your father's journals have meant to you, and I want to leave something like that for him."

I squeeze her hand and give her the best smile I can manage. "He will love that, especially when he gets older."

"Maybe I can use some of your legal pads," she muses.

"You may if you want to, but I have a better idea. Before we go home, we will go by a bookstore and buy two or three nice journals for you."

Her eyes shine with joy for just a moment, and then she grows pensive. "If we can locate him, I would like to speak with the boy who got me pregnant and coerced me into having an abortion."

I didn't see that one coming, and before I can stop myself, I blurt out, "Why in the world do you want to contact him?"

"I have never forgiven him, and I don't want to die with unforgiveness in my heart."

After a moment, she softly quotes Matthew 6:14 and 15: *"For if ye forgive men their trespasses, your heavenly Father will also forgive you: But if ye forgive not men their trespasses, neither will your Father forgive your trespasses."*

It's a passage that has troubled me through the years and still does from time to time. I've harbored bitterness toward any number of people—my father, my mother, my sister, my ex-brother-in-law, even Carolyn. Thankfully, with God's help, I've been able to forgive them. I thought I had put all of that behind me, only to discover that I'm struggling with unforgiveness again. When I think of what Coach Robinson did to Eurico, I don't know if I will ever be able to forgive him. And that's not the worst of it. I don't know if I even want to. Like I said, "Hell's too good for a man like that."

With an effort, I push those troubling thoughts out of my mind and ask, "Do you have any idea how to contact him?"

"Not really," she says. "I've stayed in touch with a couple of girlfriends from college. Hopefully, they will know how I can reach him."

It's fully dark now, and I can tell that she's hanging on by her fingernails, so I turn on the headlights and drive out of the clinic parking lot. When we reach the apartment complex where Carolyn lives, she puts her hand on my arm and says, "There's one more thing."

When I turn toward her she says, "You're probably going to think I'm crazy, but hear me out. When we get home, I want you to finish the natural hot tub you started last summer. I would love for us to use it at least once before I die."

I help her out of the Jeep and up the stairs to Carolyn's second-story apartment. As exhausted as she is, I suggest she might want to go directly to bed, but she refuses. She doesn't want to be alone, so Carolyn and I make her comfortable in the recliner situated in a corner of the living room. In almost no time, she is asleep.

Carolyn has prepared dinner, so I join her at the dinette table. I don't feel like eating, but I force myself to swallow a few bites since she has gone to all this trouble. She doesn't seem to have much of an appetite, either, and we end up just moving the food around on our plates. Finally, we give up and she fixes a small plate for Diana should she feel like eating when she wakes up.

While I clear the table and load the dishwasher, Carolyn prepares coffee. Rather than taking our coffee in the living room, we remain at the table, lest we disturb Diana. She thrashes about in her sleep and groans in pain from time to time, but she doesn't wake up. I'm grieving, and Carolyn's presence is a comfort. She's a good listener, so I tell her what's going on with Eurico. She's outraged and wants to know what I'm going to do.

"Kill the coach, maybe," I tell her, "or just beat him within an inch of his life." When she looks at me aghast, I hasten to add, "Of course, I won't really do that, but I would like to."

Noticing that my coffee has grown cold, she dumps the dregs in the sink and pours a fresh cup. Without consciously intending to, I find myself studying her while she's moving about in the kitchen. Although she's in her mid-thirties, she hardly looks a day older than she did the first time I saw her more than ten years ago. We were married a few weeks later in a small ceremony at the base of Hahn's Peak high in the Rockies. We were madly in love, but our marriage was doomed from the start. She was an insecure person and desperately needy, while I was a wounded man, distrustful of everyone. When we divorced, I never expected to see her again, but here we are.

"Would you like something sweet to go with your coffee?" she asks, interrupting my reminiscing. "I picked up some pastries from the bakery on my way home from the hospital. Cream cheese Danishes, your favorite."

In an instant, I have a flashback. It's a Sunday morning in our tiny apartment, and I'm still in my pajama bottoms and a T-shirt, with the Sunday *Denver Post* spread out on the floor around me. Carolyn has gotten up early and walked several blocks to the neighborhood bakery, where she bought apple fritters and cream cheese Danish pastries. Now she's grinding coffee beans in the kitchen, and in a couple of minutes, the rich aroma of freshly brewed coffee has me salivating like one of Pavlov's dogs.

A wave of guilt washes over me, and I quickly push that memory out of my mind. I have no business entertaining memories like that when the woman I love is in the next room suffering from terminal cancer.

"Just coffee for me," I say when I realize Carolyn is still waiting for a response. "Let's save the Danish for in the morning."

"Are you sure? I think there's plenty. We could have one now and one in the morning."

"Thank you, but no," I reply, still trying to get my feelings under control.

She returns and places two cups of steaming hot coffee on the table between us before laying her hand on my arm. "I'm sorry, Bryan," she says. "I truly am. You and Diana are made for each other. You deserve a lifetime together."

She's done nothing inappropriate, nor have I, yet I feel disloyal to Diana. I hurriedly gulp my coffee and push back from the table. Out of habit, I take my cup to the sink and rinse it out before placing in the dishwasher. Carolyn offers to help me get Diana into bed, but I tell her I can manage.

In the bedroom, I help Diana undress and take her pain meds. She is feeling nauseous, so I offer to get her something to eat, but all she wants is her antinausea pill. Once we are in bed, I hold her hand while we pray together. By the time we finish, she has fallen into a fitful sleep. Although I'm exhausted, I can't sleep. Every nerve in my body is vibrating, yet I force myself to remain perfectly still, lest I disturb her. Her breathing is labored, and from time to time she groans in pain. Each time she does, I think my heart is going to break.

After Bryan and Diana go to bed, Carolyn straightens up the kitchen. Although it is nearly ten o'clock, she's not sleepy. She's been working the three-to-eleven shift, and according to her body clock, it's still early. In the living room, she folds the blankets Diana was using and places them on the floor beside the recliner. She considers turning on the TV, but neither the late news nor the *Tonight Show* holds any appeal for her.

Picking up a magazine, she begins leafing through it, but nothing catches her eye, and soon her thoughts return to Bryan and Diana. She can't help thinking how unfair life can be. Bryan and Diana should have had a lifetime together, and now it doesn't look like Diana will make it to their second anniversary. Being a nurse working on the oncology wing at the hospital, Carolyn is not unfamiliar with cancer's insidious evil, but nothing has prepared her for this. Watching cancer destroy her friend from the inside out is far worse than anything she's ever experienced.

She can't help remembering how vibrant and alive Diana was the first time she met her on the mission station deep in the Amazon. Not just vibrantly alive either, but stunningly beautiful in a wholesome, girl-next-door sort of way. No wonder Bryan fell in love with her.

Now cancer is destroying her from the inside out, and she looks like a holocaust survivor. Her beautiful honey-colored hair has fallen out, and her eyes are dull and sunken. It's heartbreaking to remember how beautiful she was on her wedding day, barely eighteen months ago. She wore a sleeveless wedding gown with a high beaded collar and a long train. Beneath her veil, she had been glowing with happiness and her blue eyes had sparkled. Never had she looked more beautiful. Carolyn can't help thinking that Bryan's heart must be breaking, seeing Diana the way she is now.

Thinking of Bryan makes her heart hurt. He looks so tired, and he's losing weight. His shirt just hangs on him. How she wishes there was something she could do to help him through this terrible time.

If she's honest with herself, she has to admit that she's never stopped loving him—not during the horrible, nightmare days of their marriage, when it seemed they were determined to destroy each other. Not even after their divorce was final, and she thought she would never see him again. Not even after he and Diana were married, and she was forced to come to grips with the fact that he would never be hers.

For a time, before Diana returned to the States, it seemed that she and Bryan might rekindle the love they once shared. They became best friends, something that had never happened while they were married. They had fun together, going to the movies, picnicking in the park, and hiking in the mountains. Nursing school was hard, and without his encouragement she might never have graduated. Several times she was ready to quit, but he was always there for her, telling her she could do it. But once Diana returned, he had eyes only for her. He and Carolyn remained good friends, but any hope of rekindling their love faded, and in a few weeks Diana and Bryan were married.

Standing up as Diana's maid of honor was one of the hardest things she ever had to do. She had pasted a brave smile on her face and made it through the wedding and the reception, although her heart was breaking. She kept telling herself how happy she was for them, and she meant it, but on the inside, she was dying. Back in her apartment later that night, she sobbed into her pillow. She genuinely wished them every happiness, but a part of her grieved because she would never have the only man she had ever loved.

Sitting alone in her living room, in the dark of night, a forbidden thought takes shape in her mind. If Diana dies, maybe she and Bryan can get back together. In an instant, she is ashamed of herself. What kind of a friend would think such a thing? She doesn't want Diana to die—of that she is absolutely sure. In fact, she prays for her healing daily, but the truth is, there seems to be no hope of recovery.

For just a moment, she allows herself to imagine what it would be like to marry Bryan. She knows it's wrong, but she does it anyway. This time they will be married in a church with family and friends in attendance. She will be gorgeous in a shimmering white wedding gown, and Bryan will be handsome in his tux. Grief will have touched his dark hair with a sprinkling of gray, but it will simply add a touch of maturity to his good looks.

Her whimsical thoughts are interrupted when she hears Diana coughing and struggling to breathe. A moment later, the bedroom door opens, and Bryan urgently calls to her, "Can you help me? Diana is choking."

Chapter 59

In an instant, Carolyn realizes that Diana is in serious trouble. Grabbing the bedside extension, she punches in 9-1-1. In less than ten minutes, the paramedics arrive and immediately get Diana started on oxygen, before loading her onto the gurney and wheeling her out the door. Carolyn and I rush after them and follow the ambulance to the University of Colorado Hospital emergency room entrance.

While Carolyn parks her car, I try to keep up with Diana as the paramedics wheel her into an examining cubicle in the emergency room. When she sees me, she reaches for my hand. The oxygen seems to be helping, but she's still struggling to breathe, and her hand is unnaturally cold when I take hold of it. I may be overreacting, but I'm afraid she's not going to make it.

A nurse walks in and thrusts a clipboard, containing several pages of forms at me, then turns to leave without even glancing at Diana. I'm furious and demand to see a doctor. "My wife has stage-four cancer, and she can't breathe. If she doesn't get help soon, she could die!"

Without so much as a backward glance, the nurse says, "The doctor is on his way. He'll be here shortly."

Carolyn overhears our exchange as she walks in, and she just shakes her head, her disgust obvious. Moving to Diana's side, she quickly examines her before turning toward me. "Her oxygen level is still low, but it appears to be steady. I suspect she has a fluid buildup around her lungs, which is making it difficult for her to breathe. It's extremely uncomfortable, but I don't think she's in any immediate danger."

In spite of her reassuring words, I'm too upset to deal with the forms, so she takes the clipboard from me and proceeds to fill them out. Before she finishes, the doctor walks in. He asks me a few questions about Diana's medical history as he is examining her. He listens to her lungs and confirms what Carolyn suspected—there's a buildup of fluid around her lungs, a condition called pleural effusion. He goes on to tell me that in extreme cases, a person can have up to four liters of excess fluid in their chest.

"How do you treat it?" I ask, anxiously.

"The first thing we have to do is remove the fluid that is collecting between the sheets of tissue that cover the outside of the lung and the lining of the chest cavity. We do this by inserting a wide needle called a cannula into the pleural space, then we connect it to a drainage tube."

"Is it painful?"

"It's definitely uncomfortable, but I will give her a small injection of a local anesthetic before I insert the needle."

"Do you have any idea how long it will take to drain the fluid?"

"If she has a lot of fluid, and I suspect she does, considering how difficult it is for her to breathe, it could take several hours."

"Once you've drained the fluid, what's the next step?

"Step two is called pleurodesis. After we have drained all the excess fluid, we will insert sterile talc into the space between the tissues covering the lung. This will enflame them and make them stick together, eliminating any space where the fluid can collect."

"Is this an outpatient procedure, or will Diana have to be admitted?"

"I'll start the procedure here, and then we will move her to outpatient surgery to complete it. Of course, given her condition, we will want to observe her overnight."

When I have no more questions, the doctor steps out while Carolyn and I help Diana undress and put on a hospital gown. I am shocked when I see how much weight she has lost in just the past few days. Her ribs are clearly visible beneath her translucent skin, and there is not a trace of fat or muscle tissue. She is cold, and I am covering her with a blanket when a nurse returns with a package of sterile instruments needed to drain the fluid. When I see the size of the needle, it is all I can do not to gasp.

I hate any medical procedure involving needles, and I would prefer to step out while the doctor works on Diana, but I don't. I know she is looking to me for support, so I stand beside her and hold her hand. She gasps with pain, and squeezes my hand, when the doctor inserts the needle between her ribs before attaching the drainage tube.

Shortly thereafter, she is transported to outpatient surgery and placed in a private room. It takes several hours to drain the fluid off her lungs, and we pass the time in mostly exhausted silence. When the morning shift arrives, Carolyn offers to stay with Diana while I go downstairs to get something to eat. When I return, she bids us good-bye and departs for home to get some sleep. She has to work the evening shift, so she needs to get some rest.

A new nurse comes in to check on Diana, and I ask her how she's doing. Giving me a quick smile, she says, "Better. Her oxygen levels are rising, and she seems to be breathing much easier."

"Can you tell me how much fluid you have removed?"

She studies Diana's chart before replying. "Almost three liters. That's a lot. No wonder she was in such distress."

After listening to Diana's lungs, she checks the drainage tube before turning to me. "It looks like the drainage has stopped. The doctor should be in shortly to complete the procedure, and then she will be moved upstairs for observation overnight."

For the first time since we arrived, I can feel myself relaxing just a little. It looks like this crisis is over, but something tells me it is only the beginning. In the days and weeks ahead, I'm sure there will be other crises. Turning from the window, I see Diana is awake. When she sees me, she asks for a drink of water. I quickly pour some ice water into a glass and hold it to her cracked lips, while she takes a sip. When she pushes the glass away, I ask her how she's feeling.

"With my fingers," she says, rubbing her thumb and forefinger together. Shaking my head, I can't help marveling that even at a time like this, she hasn't lost her quick wit.

She's just dozing off again when the doctor comes in to do the pleurodesis procedure. After disconnecting the drainage bag, he injects the sterile talc into the pleural space using the drainage tube. Although the doctor is careful, it is still a painful procedure, and Diana grips my hand tightly while trying not to cry out. When he has inserted the last of the sterile talc, he removes the tube from between her ribs. Every ten minutes, for the next hour, a nurse checks on Diana and helps her change her position to make sure the talc gets spread around. Finally, they move her upstairs.

Diana sleeps most of the day, and shortly after noon, I slip out and drive to a nearby bookstore. When I walk in, I am pleased to see my first novel, *Jungle Doctor,* prominently displayed in the center aisle. My agent tells me it is doing far better than the publisher expected, and it is now in its third printing. He also informed me that he is in negotiations with the Book of the Month Club. I hope all of that means that I will get a hefty royalty check. We're going to need it. It doesn't look like Diana will be returning to her practice any time soon, maybe never.

A matronly clerk approaches and asks if she can help me.

"Can you direct me to the journals? I'm looking for something special. Leather-bound, if you have it."

"Right this way," she replies with a smile.

When we reach the shelves where the journals are displayed, she asks, "Is the journal for you, or is it for someone else?"

"It's for my wife," I say, and suddenly find myself choking up.

Without intending to, I tell her the whole story—about Diana and Eurico, about living in Leadville, where Diana is a family practice physician, and about her stage-four breast cancer. "She probably only has a few weeks to live, and she wants to leave something for Eurico, hence the journals."

She smiles her sympathy and dabs at the corner of her eye with a tissue before getting down to business. "Are you sure you want a leather-bound journal? They're not very feminine."

"I'm sure. Although Diana will record her thoughts and feelings in them, they're really for Eurico."

After looking at several leather-bound journals, I settle on a soft calfskin journal with a clasp. She only has two of them, and I purchase them both. While I am paying for them, she shows me a beautiful Sheaffer Imperial fountain pen. On an impulse, I decide to buy it for Diana, even though it's sinfully expensive. When she finishes ringing up my purchases, she asks, "Would you like me to gift-wrap them for you?"

"That would be nice," I reply.

When I get back to the hospital, I discover that Carolyn has dropped in to check on Diana before starting her shift on the oncology floor. She and Diana are involved in an animated conversation, so I stand just outside the door rather than interrupt them. It does my heart good to see Diana enjoying herself.

When Carolyn leaves, I step into the room and give Diana a gentle kiss. She appears to be feeling much better, so I move her tray table into position and take a gift-wrapped package from my sack and hand it to her.

"What's this?" she asks.

"Open it," I say. "It's a late Christmas present."

When she sees the stunningly beautiful gray and black fountain pen, with a solid 14K gold semi-flex nib, she's speechless. While she's still in a state of shock, I place a second package on her tray.

"Another late Christmas present?" she asks with a soft smile.

When I nod, she removes the wrapping paper and discovers two soft brown calfskin-bound journals. "They're beautiful," she murmurs, hugging them to her chest.

"No cheap ballpoint pens or yellow legal pads for you," I say with a grin.

I make myself comfortable in the recliner located at the foot of her bed, while she examines her new fountain pen. I got almost no sleep last night, and when I try to read, I keep dozing off. Finally, I give up and lay my book aside. From time to time, I partially awaken, and each time I do, I see Diana is writing in her new journals.

Chapter 60

Last summer, before Diana became so sick, we were planning on building a natural hot tub at the hot springs, located about a quarter mile behind our cabin. It was her idea, and she was eager to get it done. Unfortunately, once her cancer metastasized, those plans were quickly forgotten. All my energy was devoted to caring for her as she underwent chemotherapy treatments, with their insidious side effects. Lately, that project has been much on my mind, especially since she asked me to finish it. Although it is bitterly cold, with at least two feet of snow on the ground, I'm considering tackling it. If I wait until summer, I'm afraid it will be too late.

Since discontinuing her chemo treatments, Diana seems to be regaining a little strength. Her hair is growing back, and she has a thick layer of fuzz all over her head. Much to our surprise, it is no longer blond, but dark brown. She hardly eats enough to keep a sparrow alive, but still, she's putting on a little weight. As thankful as I am for the reprieve, I'm not fooled. This is just the calm before the final storm.

She spends most of her days ensconced in the recliner, situated near the potbellied stove, with a view of the snowcapped peaks in the distance. I made her a simple writing table out of red cedar. It fits across her lap and rests on the arms of her recliner. It has an inkwell in one corner, and in the opposite corner, I made her a cupholder.

If we can keep her pain under control, she seems to sleep a great deal; nonetheless, she has still managed to fill page after page in her journals. Already, she has nearly filled one. As much as I admire her efforts, I can't help thinking that no matter what she writes, her journals will never be able to fill the empty place her passing will leave in Eurico's life. Yet, in another sense, they may enable him to know her in a way he might never have experienced otherwise. At least, that's how it was for me when I discovered my father's journals.

I don't know what I was expecting when I opened his journals for the first time, but nothing in my experience could have prepared me for what I experienced. When I was a boy, my father loomed larger than life, and he could do no wrong in my eyes. He was an imposing figure, stern and exacting, intimidating really. The man revealed in his journals was far more human, no less committed to the Lord, but certainly more approachable. Without question, he loved the Lord, but he struggled, too. He made mistakes, he failed to live up to his own high ideals, yet he pressed on with a single-minded devotion that I both envied and feared.

The man I encountered on the pages of his journals was not at all like the man I remembered as a child, or perhaps I should say, he was far more complex than the one-dimensional man I knew. In my childhood home, he was a man of few words, at least with my sister and me, but on the pages of his journals, he was profound in his insights and on occasion even eloquent. His strict adherence to discipline caused me to think he was stern, even rigid, but his writings revealed another side of him.

Thinking about it now, my throat is thick with feelings, and my eyes blur when I realize how little I would have known him without his journals and how badly I would have misjudged him. His journals provided a portrait of him far more valuable than any ever captured on film or painted on canvas. Not a portrait of his physical likeness, but a glimpse of his heart and soul, a picture of the man himself, and what a great man he was, albeit he had feet of clay, as we all do.

As close as Eurico and Diana are, as much as he loves her, there are depths to her he simply can't know. Hopefully she will be able to reveal those hidden depths on the pages of her journals, and as the years go by, I pray he will come to appreciate her in ways he simply cannot imagine now, at his young age.

She's sleeping now, and I get up from my desk and tiptoe out of the living room. In the kitchen, I fill my thermos with black coffee before pouring a fresh cup of coffee for her. I carefully add cream and sugar, making it just the way she likes. She's awake when I return, and I pause in the doorway for just a moment. I watch as she toys with her beautiful Sheaffer Imperial fountain pen before beginning to write. Stepping into the living room, I place her mug on the corner of her writing table. She looks up and smiles a thank-you as I open the door on the stove and stir the coals before adding more firewood.

I bend down to kiss her good-bye, and she asks, "Are you leaving me?"

"Just for a couple of hours. I've got some chores to do, but I will be close by if you need me."

In the mudroom, I pull on my snow boots and don my parka before stepping outside. The cold slaps me in the face, and my eyes smart. An arctic cold front has plunged the temperature to 20 degrees below zero, and the snow beneath my boots is nearly as hard as gravel. I stop by the toolshed and get a shovel, a pick, and a pry bar before continuing up the hill toward the hot springs.

I thought I might have to shovel the snow away, but the heat from the hot springs has melted it off the rocks that Eurico and I moved into place last summer. There's a pool nearly three feet deep, and with just a little work, I can convert it into a natural hot tub. For the next two hours, I rearrange several small boulders, using my pry bar to roll them into place, creating a natural windbreak around the hot springs. Next, I clear a path and arrange some smaller rocks to form steps, making it easier to enter the steaming hot pools.

Glancing at my watch, I decide I have just enough time to try it out before heading back to the cabin. Quickly, I discard my parka and snow boots before shedding my clothes. It is so cold my teeth are chattering, and I almost change my mind, but instead, I ease down the stone steps and lower my shivering body into the nearly scalding hot water. I groan with pleasure and lean back against a rock ledge, and close my eyes as the heat works the knots out of my tired muscles.

Now that it's finished, I hope Diana has the strength to enjoy it at least one time. This was her idea, and I kept putting it off. Now I feel like kicking myself. If she can't experience this at least once, I don't know if I'll ever use it again. I kept telling her that I would get to it someday, never realizing how little time we had. Had I known, I would have made it a priority, and we could have enjoyed it last spring and in the early summer before the cancer metastasized. Now it may be too late. Like my pastor says, "Today may be the only someday you ever get!"

I should be getting back. Diana is probably wondering what's happened to me, but the thought of getting out of this hot water and stepping into the frigid air is nearly paralyzing. Gritting my teeth, I lunge to my feet and stumble up the stone steps to my clothes. Instantly, my wet hair and beard freeze. I'm shivering so hard I can hardly pull on my jeans and snow boots. I throw on my parka, without putting on my shirt, and zip it up. Collecting my tools, I stumble down the hill toward the toolshed.

In the mudroom, I kick off my snow boots and head for the bathroom without shedding my parka. I quickly undress and step into the shower, luxuriating in the hot water pounding my frigid body. Slowly I begin to warm up, and I step out of the shower only after the hot water begins to cool off.

I planned to surprise Diana and take her to the hot springs, but I'm having second thoughts. What I did today was stupid. Soaking in the hot tub was safe enough, but getting out, dripping wet, in 20-below-zero temperatures was insane. I don't know what I was thinking—and I didn't even have a towel. What I did today would kill her!

"Welcome back," she says when I step into the living room. "I've missed you."

Bending down, I give her a tender kiss. "Your beard's wet," she complains playfully.

A chill causes me to shiver, and I ask, "Is it chilly in here, or is it just me?"

"It's chilly. You probably need to check the fire."

Moving to the stove, I open the door and poke at the coals. Opening the damper creates a draft, coaxing a small flame from the glowing embers, and I add some kindling before placing an armload of split pinion in the stove.

When I finish, she surprises me by asking, "Would you like to read what I wrote today?"

Chapter 61

Diana hands me her journal, and for a moment I marvel at her nearly flawless penmanship. Her writing moves across the page with a rare beauty, and I shake my head in amazement. She's a doctor, for heaven's sake. Her writing is supposed to be illegible, or at least nearly so. Belatedly, I turn my attention to what she's written.

Eurico, no one goes through life untouched, not even the daughter of a prominent surgeon, and at an early age I learned life could be cruel. You surely know this better than I do, having lost both of your parents to malaria when you were only six years old. I mention this only to say it is not life's cruelty, or the wounds it inflicts, that cripple us, but how we respond to them. We can hug our hurts, make a shrine out of our sorrows, and grow bitter, or we can forgive those who have hurt us. The choice is ours.

When I was in my second year of college, someone I loved and trusted caused me to do something that scarred me for life—physically, emotionally, and spiritually. For years, I hated myself, and I hated him.

Although I knew God had forgiven me, I couldn't forgive myself, and I wasn't about to forgive him.

Sometimes the hardest person to forgive is yourself. I know; I struggled with that for years. When success came my way, or when people affirmed me, I repeatedly found ways to sabotage my success because I didn't think I deserved it. If God wouldn't punish me, I was determined to punish myself. Yet, no matter how much I suffered at my own hands, it was never enough.

I see you doing the same thing to yourself. The only difference between you and me is that you didn't have a choice in what happened to you, and I did. I allowed someone I loved to coerce me into doing something I would regret for the rest of my life. You, on the other hand, were forced. Against your will, a person in authority forced himself on you. What happened to you was not your fault; nonetheless, you will never get over it until you forgive yourself for being weak and allowing yourself to be manipulated.

When I learned I had only a short time left to live, I decided to do what I should have done years ago—I decide to forgive the man who got me pregnant and then coerced me into having an abortion. When I contacted him, he refused to take any responsibility for what happened. When I told him I forgave him, he cut me off saying, "I don't need your forgiveness." Then he hung up on me.

Of course, that hurt me, but then I realized that the weight of unforgiveness, which I had carried for years, was gone. When I forgave him, I freed myself!

I tell you this because the only way you will ever be able to get past the terrible thing Coach Robinson did to you is to forgive him. When you forgive him, you will free yourself.

There's more, but I put my finger between the pages and mull over what she's written. It rings true for me. For years, I carried a grudge against my father. I couldn't forgive him for disappearing into the jungle on a mission of mercy when I was just seven years old. My grief soon morphed into bitterness, not only against my father, but against the Lord, as well. Unforgiveness poisoned my soul, turning me into an angry man, and destroying all my relationships.

In desperation, I returned to the Amazon twenty years later in search of my father. I had finally come to realize that I would never be able to get on with my life until I made peace with my past. Weeks later, I found myself kneeling beside his grave deep in the Amazon rain forest, and I was finally able to forgive him. I forgave him for not giving me the affection and affirmation I so desperately needed as a child. I forgave him for not taking the time to be a daddy to a little guy who needed his daddy more than anything in the world. I forgave him for turning my mother into a clone of himself, and for making her repress her natural affections to please him. Most of all, I forgave him for dying and leaving me to grow up alone.

When I finished, it felt like a great weight had lifted off me. I had carried that grudge for so long I had no idea how heavy it was. Forgiving him gave me hope and a new lease on life. It also gave me the grace to forgive myself for all the damage I had caused to those who tried to love me.

When at last I look up, I realize that Diana is staring at me, trying to judge my reaction. Finally, she asks, "So, what do you think?"

I take a deep breath, while trying to collect my thoughts, which are all over the place. Of course I'm reliving my own experience, as well as wondering how Eurico is going to handle the information Diana has revealed about herself. That's a lot for a fourteen-year-old boy to take in. Another part of me is ready to tear Coach Robinson's head off. Anytime I think about what he did to Eurico, I seethe with anger. Revenge, not forgiveness, is what I have in mind. And then I can't help wondering why Diana didn't tell me she had talked with her ex-boyfriend. If I'm honest, I'll have to admit that hurt my feelings.

Finally, I say, "At first, I thought the part about getting pregnant and having an abortion might be too much for Eurico."

"I considered that," she replies, "but given what's happened to him, I decided he could handle it. Besides, he probably won't be reading my journals until he's older."

"True enough. Besides, it's your call. I don't want to second-guess what you've written."

"How do you feel about the part about forgiving those who've sinned against us?"

"You're right, of course, but it may be years before Eurico gets to the place where he's ready to forgive Coach Robinson. Look how long it's taken you to forgive your ex-boyfriend."

"Ex-fiancé. We were engaged."

"Whatever."

"You and I both know that Eurico will never get past this if he doesn't forgive Coach Robinson."

"You're right," I say, as I close her journal and return it to her.

I can't help thinking that at some point, Eurico may be able to forgive him, but I don't know if I will ever get there. In fact, I spend a considerable amount of time thinking of ways to make him pay. Of course, given Eurico's reticence to speak to the authorities, there's very little I can do, but that doesn't mean I'm not exploring my options. In fact, I'm considering a couple of possibilities. I may not be able to get Robinson fired, but I believe I can make his life miserable.

Chapter 62

As often happens in early spring, a Chinook wind ushered in surprisingly warm temperatures. Although the elevation at our cabin is over ten thousand feet above sea level, daytime temperatures have climbed into the mid-thirties for several days in a row. And at night, it hasn't gotten colder than 25 degrees.

I have been waiting for a break in the frigid temperatures to bring Diana to the hot springs behind our cabin. She knows I've been working on something out here, but she doesn't know exactly what I've been doing. In addition to enhancing the natural pool created by the hot springs, I have made a firepit, and a few minutes ago, I built a large bonfire. Utilizing some tin roofing, which I was able to salvage off an old barn, I made a heat reflector to create a reasonably warm area. Given Diana's sensitivity to cold, it was absolutely necessary.

When everything is ready at the hot springs, I return to the toolshed and collect the utility sled I have borrowed from my pastor. I connect it to an ancient snow machine I picked up in a yard sale. The utility sled is flexible with raised sides. I have made a pallet using several quilts for bedding, and it should provide an ideal way to transport Diana to the hot springs.

It has been so cold that she hasn't ventured outside the cabin since we returned from Denver nearly two months ago, and she is suffering from "cabin fever." As you might imagine, she is excited about the excursion I have planned for tonight. All I told her was that we were going to the hot springs. Enhancing the pool to create a natural hot tub was originally her idea, so she probably suspects what I have in mind. She gave me a knowing look when I asked her to dress only in her bra and panties, and the luxurious robe I bought her for Christmas. It has an ultra-absorbent terry-cloth interior, a hood, and patch pockets. Of course, I will bundle her up in my parka, as well, and cover her with wool blankets once I get her on the sled.

When I step into the bedroom, she is frowning as she studies herself in the full-length mirror. She is wearing a frilly set of bikini panties and a ruffled bra that almost hides the scar from her mastectomy. It's the first time I've seen her in anything sexy in weeks, and I give her a wolf whistle. Embarrassed, she quickly wraps herself in her robe.

"I hate for you to see me without clothes," she says with a catch in her voice. "I'm so thin. I look terrible."

I take her in my arms and hold her close, resting my chin on the top of her head, which is now covered with thick brown fuzz. Stepping back, I place my finger under her chin and lift her head and gently kiss her lips. "You always look beautiful to me."

"Liar," she says, giving me a sad smile. "But say it again."

We both laugh, and after kissing her once more, I go to the dresser and take out a small, gift-wrapped box, which I hand to her.

"What's this?" she asks.

"It's your birthday present."

"It's not my birthday"

"Just open it," I say, and in her eyes, I see that she realizes that I fear she may not make it to her next birthday. It's not a new thought. We've talked about it before, but something about receiving an early birthday present makes it painfully real for both of us.

Her hands are trembling as she unwraps the small box, being careful not to tear the wrapping paper, although why that should matter is beyond me. She opens the box and gasps when she sees a 14K gold chain with two intersecting 14K gold hearts. The words "My Heart Will Always Be Yours" are inscribed on the back.

Her eyes are shining with unshed tears, as I take the necklace from her and place it around her neck. "Thank you," she says. "It's beautiful."

"Let's get your snow boots on," I say, blinking back tears of my own.

Outside, I help her get comfortable on the sled, before tucking the heavy wool blankets around her. Even in the dark, I can tell her eyes are bright with excitement, but when I bend down to kiss her, it seems I taste death on her breath. Maybe I'm imagining things, but it breaks my heart just the same. How can it be that our time together is almost gone?

Once we reach the hot springs, I build up the fire before helping Diana to her feet. She stands close to the fire while I strip off my clothes, before helping her out of my huge parka and her terry-cloth robe. When I take her in my arms to carry her to the hot pool, I am shocked to realize how little she weighs. Although it has only been a few moments since she shed her robe, she is shivering violently by the time I ease her into the natural pool fed by the hot springs.

I immerse myself in the geothermally heated water and wrap my arm around her. She leans against me and groans with pleasure as the hot water drives the chill from her thin body. The night is clear, and overhead a million or more stars are spread across the dark sky. I have brought a thermos of hot chocolate, and now I fill the silver thermos cup and both of us drink from it.

Looking me in the eye, she smiles a sad smile and whispers, "Thank you, Bryan. Tonight is so special."

Never have I loved her more, and my heart is breaking, thinking of how little time we have left. There are so many things we planned to do, and now we will never get to do them. She wanted to show me Niagara Falls and Lake Louise in the Alberta Rockies. I wanted to take her on an Alaskan cruise departing from Seattle, traversing the inland passage to Sitka, and then on to Anchorage. She wanted to camp in Yellowstone National Park and see Old Faithful erupt. I wanted us to take a road trip to Mount Rushmore in South Dakota. She wanted us to see the giant redwood trees in California, and I wanted us to take a float trip down the Colorado River through the Grand Canyon.

How many nights did we spend pouring over the maps, planning our adventures? Now that's all they will ever be— just plans, imaginary trips taken only in our dreams. There won't be a trip to the Grand Tetons in Wyoming or a holiday in Glacier National Park in Montana. I feel tears of regret stinging my eyes, but I blink them away and hold Diana tight.

For several minutes, we sit in comfortable silence, enjoying the heat of the hot springs and the stillness of the night. Laying her head against my shoulder, she says, "We need to talk."

Something about the way she says it makes my heart hurt. I think I know what she wants to talk about, and I don't know if I can handle it. Finally, I manage to say, "Can't it wait?"

She takes my hand in both of hers and holds it tight. "I want to talk about my funeral."

"Please," I say, "not tonight. Let's enjoy this special time. We may never get another chance."

"It can't wait, Bryan. Something's going on in my body. I can feel it."

Her words scare me.

"What are you talking about? Your hair is growing back, and you've gained a little weight."

"Granted, but don't be fooled. Have you noticed my color? I've got jaundice. That means the cancer in my liver is blocking the bile ducts. It's only a matter of time before it will kill me. It may also cause fatal blood clots in either my lungs or my heart. In that case, death could be sudden."

I can see she won't be dissuaded, so I steel myself for what will likely prove to be a painfully difficult conversation. With my free hand, I reach up and grasp the alabaster cross that hangs on a leather thong around my neck. It was a symbol of my father's faith, and I never saw him without it. When he died, he bequeathed it to me. I know it doesn't possess any special power, but it reminds me of his faith, and that gives me strength.

Although her head is leaning against my shoulder, her voice seems to come to me from far away. "I would like to be buried in the cemetery here, near a blue spruce tree, if possible. Please buy two burial plots, side by side. It gives me great comfort to think that one day you will be buried beside me."

I simply nod my head, grief making speech impossible.

"I want three songs sung at my funeral, two before the sermon and one at the conclusion of the service. I want the service to open with 'God Took Away My Yesterdays,' followed by Andrae Crouch's 'The Broken Vessel.'"

Her voice cracks, and she pauses to regain her composure before continuing. "If Gordon and Eleanor are still in the States, I would like for him to give the sermon, and if she's willing, I would like Eleanor to give the eulogy. Then I want the service to conclude with 'It Is Well with My Soul.'"

My chest is tight, and it feels like I've been holding my breath forever. When I try to speak, my words come out in a croak, and then I am sobbing. After I finally manage to get my emotions under control, I say, "Wow... This isn't how I expected our evening to go. I thought we would drink hot chocolate while soaking in the hot springs, maybe smooch a little, and reminisce about the good times we've had."

She squeezes my hand, and for a time, neither of us speaks. Then she says, "There's just one more thing."

"Okay," I say, as I brace myself.

"Bryan, you're still a young man, and I don't want you to spend the rest of your life alone."

I start to protest, but she places her finger on my lips to silence me. She is trembling, and I can only imagine the toll this conversation has taken on her.

"I know how much you love me, and I'm sure you can't conceive of ever getting married again, but in time that will change. Your heart will heal, and when it does, I want you to know you have my blessing to fall in love again. Just promise that you'll never forget me."

She's weeping now, and I hold her close, my tears mingling with hers. When I am finally able to speak, I say, "I could never forget you. Never."

It's been an exhausting evening, and my emotions are raw. If I'm exhausted, I can only imagine how Diana is feeling. I know I should get her home and put her to bed, but I'm not willing for this night to end, knowing there will never be another one like this for Diana and me. Once we return to the cabin it will be all downhill—what someone described as a long night of dying. I take her in my arms one last time and kiss her deeply, trying to express all the love that is in my heart.

When at last I release her, I immediately climb out of the hot pool, lest I lose my resolve. I collect Diana's robe and warm it at the fire before returning to help her out of the hot springs. I immediately wrap her in her robe and put on her snow boots before helping her to the fire. Her teeth are chattering as I wrap her in my parka, before getting dressed myself. The fire is blazing, and when she is warm, I help her to the sled and cover her with the wool blankets. Soon, as my mother used to say, she's as snug as a bug in a rug, and I move to douse the fire before heading for the cabin to face whatever the future holds.

Chapter 63

For the next two weeks, Diana seems to hold her own, and I push all thoughts of her impending death from my mind. Maybe she was wrong about what she thought she was feeling in her body. Maybe she has months to live and not just a few weeks. Who knows—maybe the Lord is healing her. Eurico and I pray for her healing every morning and night, as does Carolyn. I don't have much faith, but Eurico is convinced the Lord is going to intervene.

Diana spends most of her days writing in her journal or sleeping in her recliner near the stove. My desk is in the living room, not far from her, and that's where I spend a good part of each day. My editor has returned my manuscript with his editorial suggestions, and I am working on the final rewrite. For the most part, he is enthused about my writing, but occasionally his tone can be a little sharp, or so it seems to me. For instance, at a critical point in the story, he wrote, "A grand opportunity missed!" That hurts my feelings, but when I show it to Diana, hoping she will soothe my bruised ego, she just looks at me and says, "You can do better than that."

I return to my desk in a huff, although I try not to let her see how upset I am. The truth be told, I had never been satisfied with that scene either, but no matter how many times I rewrote it, I could never get it right. Now both my editor and Diana are holding my feet to the fire. With renewed determination, I pick up my pen and attempt to rewrite the scene yet again. It isn't easy—good writing never is—but by sharpening the dialogue, the characters go from flat, two-dimensional caricatures to real flesh-and-blood people. When I read it to Diana, she gives me a thumbs-up.

Dr. Davis—her partner at the clinic—comes by weekly to check on her. He is monitoring her situation, and from time to time he increases her pain medication. On his last visit, he suggests that at some point Diana will probably need to be moved to the hospital where they can better manage her pain, but she is adamant about spending her last days at the cabin with Eurico and me.

After Dr. Davis leaves, she asks me what I think about asking Carolyn to come and live with us when the end is near. That way Dr. Davis can prescribe a morphine pump for pain, and being a licensed oncology nurse, Carolyn can oversee her treatment. At first, I am hesitant and play the devil's advocate. "That would be imposing on Carolyn," I say, "and besides, she probably can't get that much time off work. Even if she can, the cabin's too small." When Diana continues to insist, I finally agree to think about it.

When she asks me if I have made the funeral arrangements, I hang my head and admit that I haven't. I know it's crazy, but I'm still in denial. Once I purchase the burial plots and contact Gordon and Eleanor to give them a heads-up about Diana's impending funeral, I can't pretend anymore. I will have to come to grips with the painful truth: Diana is dying.

"Please take care of it," she says.

I know I can't put it off any longer, so I call Morrison's Funeral Home and make an appointment. Then I call Gordon Arnold. I'm relieved when he tells me they're going to be in the States for several more weeks, before returning to the mission station in the far western Amazon Basin. Diana would have been terribly disappointed if he wasn't available for her funeral.

Two days later, I have a meeting with the funeral director. He drives me to the Evergreen Cemetery, where I pick out two burial plots surrounded by several beautiful Colorado blue spruce trees. He encourages me to select a casket, but I decline. Buying the cemetery plots is hard enough. I'm not up to looking at caskets yet.

Before going back to the cabin, I decide to pick up a few things at the supermarket. When I come out, I look across the street and see Coach Robinson's car parked in front of the Golden Burro. This is the opportunity I have been waiting for. After putting my groceries in my pickup, I head across the street.

When I step inside the door, I hesitate for a minute, letting my eyes adjust. It is still too early for the dinner crowd, and the dining room is mostly empty. I spot Coach Robinson seated at a table in the far corner of the room.

"Do you mind if I join you?" I ask. Without waiting for him to reply, I pull out a chair and sit down across from him. I nod to the waitress, and she brings me a mug of coffee.

This is the first time I've seen Robinson since I learned what he did to Eurico, and I am struggling to keep my anger in check. It's all I can do not to reach across the table and slap him silly.

He seems totally oblivious to how angry I am, and after taking a sip of his coffee, he asks, "How's your wife?"

Instead of replying, I pick up my mug and blow on my coffee to cool it.

He continues to make idle conversation, not really caring about Diana's condition, not really realizing I haven't responded to his question. "Her illness," he said, "really took a toll on Eurico, especially academically. I'm sure you're aware he was almost disqualified from the state cross-country championships."

When I nod, he continues, "I had to pull some strings with the administrators to get him reinstated. When I explained what was going on with your wife, they talked with his teachers, and they allowed him to make up some of the work he had failed to turn in."

When I still don't say anything, he finally asks, "Is something bothering you?"

"Tell me about Bobby Stecker."

For just an instant, there's a hint of something in his eyes— fear maybe, or shame—then it is gone. "What's there to tell?" he says, with a shrug of his shoulders. "Bobby was probably the best distance runner I've ever coached. He won the state championship in cross-country as a junior. Set a national high school record in the process."

"And?"

"What do you mean, 'And'?" he demands.

"Tell me the rest of it," I say. "Tell me how Bobby took his 410-gauge shotgun, drove out in the sandhills, and killed himself. Why do you suppose he did that?"

When he doesn't say anything, I go on. "I'll tell you what I think. I think you destroyed that boy. I think you sexually molested him, just the way you molested Eurico. And I bet, if I dig back through your résumé, I'll find other boys whom you ruined."

If I thought I was going to shame him, I couldn't have been more wrong. He just sits there smirking at me, and I realize he is a sexual psychopath. He has absolutely no feelings for Bobby or Eurico. No empathy—none whatsoever.

The waitress is headed our way to refill our coffee cups, but she quickly retraces her steps when she senses the heated emotions emanating from our table. Standing to my feet, I deliberately knock my coffee cup over, spilling hot coffee in Robinson's lap. I lean across the table and get in his face. "You had better start looking for another job," I say, my voice as cold as ice, "because your days are numbered in this town. And don't think about getting another coaching position, because if you do, I will be coming after you."

As I turn to go, he says, "He liked it. Eurico liked it, and he'll be back for more."

Before I realize what I am doing, I backhand him across his face, breaking his nose. Blood is dripping off his chin, but he's still smirking at me. Too late, I realize that nothing I do to him will ever undo what he has done to Eurico. The manager is calling the police as I exit the café and head to my truck.

I consider heading home, but I decide it will be better to deal with the police here rather than at the cabin. The last thing I want to do is upset Diana. When the police have not come after twenty minutes, I decide Robinson probably isn't going to risk pressing charges. As I am starting my pickup, I see him leave the Golden Burro, holding an ice pack of some sort to his swollen nose. I watch him get in his car and drive slowly down the street toward the high school.

I know what I did was stupid, but I have no regrets. I can't help feeling he had it coming. Even more satisfying is the knowledge that he knows I'm on to him. Even if he is shameless, even if he doesn't regret anything he's done, he has to be concerned about his reputation. If this gets out, it will be difficult for him to find a coaching position anywhere in the county. He can't be sure Eurico and I won't go to the school board or the police. Given the way he left Lincoln High School in Nebraska, things must have been heating up after Bobby Stecker killed himself. I take a perverse pleasure in the knowledge that I've rattled his cage.

As a Christian, I know I should feel bad about punching him, but given the chance, I would do it again. I know we're supposed to turn the other cheek and love our enemies, but in this case, that was beyond me. I can identify with Peter, when he took out his sword and cut off the ear of one of those who came to arrest Jesus. Even though Jesus rebuked him, I suspect he got no little satisfaction from his defense of the Lord. Although the Lord says that vengeance is His and that He will repay the evildoer, in this case I'm glad I was able to give Him a helping hand.

Chapter 64

It soon becomes obvious that Diana needs more care than I can provide. Her pain is increasing exponentially, and the pain meds the doctor prescribes hardly touch it. In desperation, I telephone Carolyn and explain the situation. Before I can even ask, she volunteers to come and care for Diana. She is granted a leave of absence from the hospital, and two days later, she moves into Eurico's bedroom. He moves into our bedroom, and we rent a hospital bed for Diana and set it up in the living room near the woodstove. I spend my nights in a recliner next to her bed.

The morphine pump eases her pain, but it doesn't totally eliminate it. Although she seldom complains, it's obvious she's suffering. As weak as she is, she tosses and turns a great deal, seeking a more comfortable position, but to little avail. She is terribly jaundiced; her skin and the whites of her eyes have grown increasingly yellow. Even the smell of food makes her nauseous, and she eats almost nothing.

What little sleep she gets usually occurs during the day. At night, especially during the wee hours after midnight, she is restless and unable to sleep. Sometimes she asks me to help her move to the recliner. Once she's settled, I light the kerosene lamp on my desk and move my chair close to her. Sometimes we talk, but mostly I just hold her hand or read to her from her well-worn Bible.

Once she falls asleep, I use my finger to trace the veins on the back of her hand, clearly visible now through her nearly translucent skin. Sitting there, alone in the darkness, I realize I have a choice. I can spend the night grieving over what might have been, or I can remember the good times we've had. I choose the latter, and as I turn my thoughts toward the past, the painful realities of Diana's illness seem to fade, and an earlier, healthy version of the woman I love comes into focus.

My memories come to me in no particular order, rather like random slides projected on a screen. In the first one, Diana and I are swimming in the uncomfortably chilly creek located behind my cabin, in the foothills west of Fort Collins. We've only been married a couple of weeks, and we're madly in love. We splash and play for two hours or more, oblivious to the sun's deadly rays, and Diana suffers a painful sunburn. That evening I rub aloe vera gel on her sunburned shoulders, and later we make love, awash in the moonlight streaming in through our bedroom window. Aloe vera gel and moonlight will always remind me of the love we shared.

As that memory fades, it is replaced by another. Now I'm standing in the arrival gate at the Stapleton International Airport, awaiting the arrival of the American Airline flight from Miami. It is fifteen minutes late, and I pace the corridor impatiently. It has been four years since I've seen either Diana or Eurico, and my heart hungers fiercely for the sight of them.

When the passengers finally begin deplaning, I stand on my tiptoes, looking over the heads of those in front of me, searching for a woman whose smile lights up every room she enters. When I catch sight of her, my heart leaps, and I ask myself for the hundredth time how I could have ever left her in the far western Amazon Basin and come home alone.

Diana hacks a cough, drawing me back to her bedside, and I lean close to make sure she doesn't choke. After a moment the hacking stops, and she resumes her labored breathing. I hate what is happening to her, and I hate the thought of living in a world without her. And I hate that I threw away four years we could have spent together.

Involuntarily, I find myself reliving our final days in the Amazon. We discussed every possible scenario, left no option unexplored. Late into the night, we planned and schemed and argued, but when all was said and done, we could not find a course of action suitable to both of us.

For two or three days, Diana seemed to withdraw inside herself, and I set about making preparations for my trip downriver. She found me late one afternoon as Lako and I were putting the last of my things into his boat in preparation for leaving early the next morning. As she approached, Lako slipped away. I could tell she had been crying, but there was a stubborn determination in her eyes when she looked at me. She told me that since I had no intention of living on the mission field, she would give up her missionary work, marry me, and practice medicine in the United States.

I'm not sure how she expected me to react, but I surely disappointed her. Instead of taking her in my arms and crushing her to my chest, I turned and walked to the river's edge. Slipping up behind me, she wrapped her arms around my waist and laid her cheek against my back between my shoulders. In that moment I loved her so much, and more than anything I wanted to take her in my arms and cover her face with kisses, but I knew I didn't dare. If I allowed my resolve to waver even the least bit, I would be lost.

Her willingness to sacrifice herself on the altar of our love was heartrending in its selflessness, but I knew it would never work. It was a price neither of us could afford to pay. God had first claim on her life, and whether she realized it or not, turning her back on her call would kill something vital inside of her. In time she would come to resent me, to blame me for the loss of her life's purpose, and then her love for me would die. It was better, I reasoned, to suffer a clean break, painful though it might be, than to slowly destroy each other, as inevitably we must.

I remember removing her arms from around my waist and turning toward the trail that led to the mission compound and the small house that had been my home for the past few weeks. I could hear Diana sobbing, but I did not look back. She may have called my name, or it might have been a voice inside my head. I will never know, for I did not turn around to see.

My bittersweet reminiscing goes on for most of the night, although I am sure I dozed from time to time. The ache in my heart never goes away, and to make it through these difficult days, I have put my grief in a box and clamped the lid down tight. Unfortunately, the lid keeps coming off, and this is one of those times. There are no wrenching sobs—maybe those will come later, maybe not—but for now there are just silent tears slipping down my cheeks to lose themselves in my beard.

It's Good Friday, and later today our pastor and his wife are coming to the cabin so Diana can receive communion one last time. She wants to look her best, and she has asked Carolyn to help her do her hair and makeup. When they finish, Carolyn helps Diana into the beautiful bed jacket she bought for her, then she hands her a mirror. When she sees herself, she exclaims, "I look almost pretty again."

I holler at Eurico to bring my camera and flash attachment. When he does, I take several candid shots of Diana, realizing as I do that these will probably be the last photos I will ever take of her. I show Carolyn how to use my Nikon, and then Eurico and I get on either side of Diana and smile at the camera. She takes several pictures of all three of us and then several of just Diana and me. When we finish, Diana is absolutely exhausted, but she refuses to get into bed, opting instead to stay in the recliner.

My heart is breaking, and I can't bear to be still, so I put on my jacket and snow boots and go outside. Although it is April, there is still snow on the ground as I make my way down the hill toward the creek. I find a spot in the sun and make myself comfortable on a fallen log. I don't know how long I've been gone, but the sun is working its way down the western sky when I hear someone approaching.

"There you are," Carolyn says. "I've been looking all over for you."

"Is everything all right?" I ask, suddenly concerned.

"Yes. Diana is still sleeping, and Eurico is sitting with her."

She sits down on the log a short distance from me, and I study her out of the corner of my eye. I can't help thinking how completely I misjudged her. Of course, a lot of water has passed under the bridge since then, and we are both different people. Still, I never could have imagined the woman she has become—independent, competent, and compassionate. I don't think I've ever known a more compassionate person, unless it's Diana.

We sit without talking for several minutes, and I find myself drawing strength from her presence. I don't know how we would have made it without her. She's the consummate caregiver, making Diana's last days as comfortable as possible. Any time Diana has a crisis, she knows just what to do. If she hadn't been here, I would have had to put Diana in the hospital, and that's the last thing she wanted. And she's been a godsend for Eurico. Watching Diana die is killing him, and several times she's comforted him when I had nothing left to give.

She's also been there for me, listening when I needed to talk or just being there when grief rendered me mute.

Now she clears her throat to speak, and when I look at her, I see tears glistening in her eyes. "If you have any final words you want to say to Diana, now would probably be a good time to share them. She could go at any time, but more likely she will slip into a coma for three or four days before she passes."

I knew the end was near. Still, hearing her say it shakes me to my core. This is worse than losing my father. It's worse than the pain I experienced when I learned that Carolyn had been unfaithful to me. It's worse than the hopelessness that consumed me when I was sure Eurico was dying. It's worse than anything I could have ever imagined, and I don't know how I'm going to bear it.

Without a word, I get to my feet and start toward the cabin. Carolyn hurries after me and touches my arm. I pull it away and say, "Please. I just need to be alone."

She freezes where she's at, and I can tell that my rejection has wounded her. I didn't mean to hurt her, but right now I need to be alone to prepare myself for what's coming. I turn toward the woodshed, and Carolyn continues on toward the cabin.

It is nearly dark when I see headlights coming up the trail toward our cabin. It's our pastor and his wife and Carolyn steps out onto the porch to greet them. Leaving the woodshed, I quickly make my way to the mudroom, where I shed my jacket and snow boots before joining the others around Diana's recliner for worship. For the most part, she seems oblivious to what we are doing, but when it comes time to receive Communion, she opens her eyes and reaches for the cup and the bread. Pastor kneels beside her recliner and takes her hand. As he begins to quote John 14:2–3, "In my Father's house are many mansions…" she moves her lips, soundlessly mouthing the words along with him. As we sing her favorite hymns, she seems to draw strength from them—not strength to live, but the strength to pass from this life to the next without fear.

After everyone has gone, Carolyn and I help Diana prepare for bed. She removes Diana's stylish bed jacket and replaces it with a flannel nightgown, before Diana allows us to help her into bed. Carolyn checks her morphine pump and administers the appropriate dose. It's been an unusually busy day, and Diana is exhausted. Although she's in considerable pain, sleep soon overtakes her.

I follow Carolyn into the kitchen, and she asks if I would like something to eat. "No, thank you," I reply. "But if you're not too tired, I would like to talk to you for a minute."

"Sure. Just let me pour myself a cup of coffee."

After pouring her coffee, she sits down at the table and rests her head in her hands for a moment. I take a chair across from her and wait until she looks up and makes eye contact, before I speak. "First I would like to apologize for my rudeness this afternoon. It wasn't directed at you, and I'm truly sorry."

She reaches across the table and squeezes my hand. "Apology accepted. These are difficult times for all of us."

"As you are well aware, I'm not very good at expressing my feelings, but I hope you know how much I appreciate all you've done." When she nods an acknowledgment, I continue, "I'll never be able to repay you. Not just for your nursing care, but also for all the little things, like the bed jacket. That was such a nice touch, and it meant the world to Diana. I never would have thought to do anything like that."

We sit in silence, each of us immersed in our own thoughts, while she finishes her coffee. I watch her go to the sink and rinse her cup before putting it in the rack to dry. When she turns to go, I say, "There's just one more thing."

She pauses and gives me a tired smile. I take a breath and force myself to go on. "Are you sure the end is so near?"

"There's no way of knowing exactly when a person is going to die," she replies, her voice full of sorrow, "but all the signs are there. Her blood pressure is slowly decreasing, as is her body temperature. Her breathing is becoming more labored, she has stopped eating, and she is taking almost no fluids."

Stepping behind my chair, she gives me a hug and says, "I'm sorry, Bryan." In the living room, she checks on Diana one more time before going to bed.

After she has gone, I sit at the kitchen table and mull over her words. Do I have any last words for Diana? If I had a lifetime, I couldn't tell her everything that is in my heart. Yet, when I try to put my feelings into words, I find I'm tongue-tied. Grief has rendered me mute.

I hear Diana coughing and thrashing about, and I hurry into the living room to make sure she is not choking. I push the recliner close to her bed and take her frail hand in mine. When I do, she settles down, and after a couple of minutes, I think she's fallen asleep, but she hasn't. "I'm scared, Bryan," she says in voice so tiny I think my heart will break.

I don't know what to say, so I simply kiss her hand and hold it next to my heart. She's so still that for an instant I fear she's passed, but then she gasps for breath and my heart begins to beat again. "How will I ever find you in heaven," she asks, "with all those millions of people?"

Quick as a flash, I say, "In heaven, we won't be separated by time or distance. As soon as you think a thought, it becomes reality. As soon as you think, 'I want to be with Bryan,' I'll be right there."

"Really," she whispers in a breathy voice. "What a comforting thought."

I'm no Bible scholar, certainly no theologian, so I have no idea if my explanation has merit or not. But the more I think about it, the more convinced I am that it or something like it is a real possibility.

She grows still, and I fall asleep holding her hand next to my heart. When I awaken several hours later, morning is just a smear of light outside the window. Being careful not to wake her, I tiptoe to the bathroom and step into the shower. I shampoo my hair and shave in the shower, using a tiny handheld mirror. When I'm finished showering, I pull on a pair of heavy corduroy pants and fleece-lined moccasins, before donning a flannel shirt. In the kitchen, I spoon coffee and brown sugar into a battered coffeepot, fill it with water, and put it on the stove to boil, before returning to the living room to stir up the stove.

Almost instantly, I sense something is amiss. Diana is lying with her head thrown back. Her mouth is hanging open, and her eyes are rolled back in her head, leaving only the white of her eyeballs visible. At first, I fear she has passed, but then I hear her take a shallow breath.

I holler for Carolyn, and quick as a flash, she is beside me. She immediately takes Diana's blood pressure and listens to her heart. When she finishes, she turns to me. "She's slipped into a coma. All we can do now is keep her as comfortable as possible till the end comes."

Somehow, I manage to find my voice, and I ask, "How long will she be like this?"

"Probably not long. Three or four days. Maybe less."

For the next three days, I maintain my bedside vigil, only leaving to go to the bathroom. Carolyn is in and out, sometimes sitting with me for hours at a time. Eurico makes a pallet on the floor at the foot of her bed, and that's where he sleeps. On the third day, her breathing slows noticeably. We sense the end is near, and the three of us gather around her bed. As she draws her last breath, she closes her mouth and opens her eyes. She focuses on something only she can see, smiles, and tries to sit up—and then she is gone.

When she took her last breath, I lost an irretrievable part of myself. The woman I loved more than life was gone, leaving me with a huge hole in my heart, a hole I knew could never be filled. Yet, on another level, I was rejoicing because I knew she was now more alive than she had ever been. Never again would she struggle to breathe, or writhe in pain, and even as I choked on my grief, another part of me was celebrating with her. There was no death angel in the room when she died— just the Lord of life, coming to call her to her eternal reward as He promised He would.

Kneeling beside her bed, I hold her now-lifeless hand to my lips and whisper, "Go with God, Diana Lorraine Whittaker. Go with God."

Epilogue

More than two years have passed since I lost the love of my life, and not a week has gone by that I haven't visited her grave. I know she's not here; still, it gives me comfort to come. Sometimes I simply clean her tombstone while reflecting on our time together. At other times, I have imaginary conversations with her. I took great pleasure in informing her that Coach Robinson had resigned unexpectedly, a few weeks after our encounter in the Golden Burro. I also informed her that Eurico was doing better now that Robinson was out of the picture. He and I come together sometimes, but not often, which is fine by me, as I don't really like to share this time with anyone. The last time he came with me was a couple of days after he won the state cross-country championship. He kissed his championship medal and hung it on her tombstone. When he turned to go, I saw tears glistening in his eyes. His medal still hangs there, although the elements have tarnished it.

As I read the epitaph I had inscribed on her tombstone—*Selfless in Love, Magnanimous in Forgiveness, Faithful Always*—I reflect on the fact that this will probably be my final visit, at least for a while. It's time, as Diana often said, quoting the words of Jesus, to "let the dead bury their dead."

Another time she told me, "Life goes on if you let it." She was encouraging me to focus on the future and not the past, something that is easier said than done. I know now that I will never stop loving her, but that doesn't mean I cannot love another. That's what she was trying to tell me the night we soaked in the hot springs, just before she took her final turn for the worse.

On the first anniversary of her death, I received a letter. The envelope was postmarked in Aurora, Colorado, but the address was in Diana's handwriting and easily recognizable. I sat in the Jeep, in the post office parking lot, for several minutes before I found the courage to open it. Inside was a letter dated a few days before her death.

My Dearest Bryan:

If you are reading this letter the first anniversary of my death has passed. I cannot even imagine how difficult the last year has been for you. I trust that the God of all comfort has been very near to you and Eurico. And I pray that your grief has been richly seasoned with hope—the hope of eternal life!

I want to thank you for caring for me with such love and devotion these past months. I know it hasn't been easy, and that makes your patience and kindness even more special. Forgive me for ever doubting your commitment. No husband could ever love a wife more than you have loved me. You have made these difficult days not only bearable, but also blessed. Truly my heart will always be yours.

Now comes the most difficult part of this letter for me. I want to encourage you to remarry, sooner rather than later. The Bible says it's not good for a man to be alone. That's why God created Eve for Adam, and that's why God created us for each other, but when I am gone, God will have someone else for you. When you find her, you will likely be tempted to feel you cannot love her without betraying your love for me. Nothing could be farther from the truth. You do not have to stop loving me in order to love her, nor do you have to divide your love between us. A mother does not divide her love between her children; rather, she multiplies it. In the same way, you do not have to love me less in order to love the woman God has now prepared for you. When I am gone, there will be love enough in your heart for both of us.

My only concern is that you find a woman who will love you as I do and who will also love Eurico. At the risk of speaking when it might be wiser to hold my peace, I must say I only know of one woman who meets that criteria. Of course, I am referring to Carolyn. From the first time I met her at the mission station years ago, I knew she was in love with you. Please don't misunderstand me. She has never done anything inappropriate. In fact, she has gone out of her way to behave toward you in the most circumspect manner. Still, I know she's in love with you, and I truly believe she is capable of loving you as I have loved you.

Of course, marriage cannot be built on a one-sided love. For it to work, you will have to love her as deeply and as passionately as you have loved me. Is it possible for you to love Carolyn like that? I think so, but you are the only one who can answer that question. I think you loved her that way once, but you both had too much emotional baggage for your marriage to work. Things are different now. I'm not telling you to marry Carolyn, but I am asking you to open your heart to whomever God has for you.

I'm terribly tired now, and my handwriting has become nearly impossible to read, so I will close. Soon I will join that great cloud of witnesses mentioned in Hebrews 12, and I will be watching over Eurico and you. Always know that wherever you go and whatever you do, I will be there with you.

> *With all my love now and forever,*
> *Diana*

> *PS. Go with God, Bryan Scott Whittaker!*

I have carried her letter in my pocket every day since I received it. It is bent and wrinkled from being read so many times. After today, I will put it away in a safe place. Maybe I will read it again at some point in the future, maybe not. It has served its purpose, having guided me through the dark days of my grief, when I nearly lost my way.

I kneel one last time at her grave and trace the name on her tombstone with my finger: *Diana Lorraine Rhodes Whittaker.* I press my first two fingers to my lips, touch them to her name, and whisper, "Diana, I will always love you." Getting to my feet, I walk to the Jeep without looking back.

The sunlight is shimmering off Carolyn's auburn hair as I watch her walk toward me across a high mountain meadow just below Hahn's Peak, located a few miles north of Steamboat Springs. She has colorful ribbons and flowers in her hair, and she is carrying a bouquet of wildflowers native to the Rocky Mountains. A close friend of hers from the hospital is playing the flute, and the ethereal tones float in the alpine air, brilliantly clear, soft, and penetrating. My pastor, who is standing beside me, leans over and whispers, "She's stunningly beautiful." I can only nod, my throat thick with feeling.

My mind is racing as I replay the events that have culminated in this moment. Following Diana's death, Carolyn became a ray of light in a world gone dark for Eurico and me. Of course, she couldn't remain in Leadville. She had to return to her job at the hospital in Aurora, but she came to visit us as often as her schedule permitted. Thankfully, she was there for Eurico, as I was not fit company for anyone in the weeks and months immediately following Diana's passing. I had fallen into a dark place from which I feared I might never return.

This was different from anything I had experienced before. Instead of being angry, as I was following my father's death, I just felt dead. In fact, I often prayed to die. As far as I was concerned, I had no reason to go on living now that Diana was gone.

Nonetheless, I forced myself to go through the motions for Eurico's sake, but there was no joy in it, absolutely none. My second novel was doing even better than the first one, but I took no pleasure in it. Both my agent and my editor implored me to write, but I couldn't. Grief had sucked my creative juices dry.

Slowly, little by little, over many months, Carolyn coaxed me out of the dark cave of grief into which I had hibernated. To say I was happy, even a tiny bit happy, as I emerged, would have been exaggerating, but for the first time in months, I wasn't unhappy. I was just numb. I forced myself to go to Eurico's cross-country meets, and I was present when he took first place at the state championships. Carolyn had taken the weekend off, so she was present also, and afterward we celebrated with dinner at the Hideaway Steak House in Alamosa.

We returned to the cabin late Saturday night, and on Sunday, Eurico spent the day with friends, so Carolyn and I had the afternoon to ourselves. After church, she packed a picnic lunch, and we hiked to the hot springs behind the cabin. Although the wind blowing through the aspens was chilly, it was pleasantly warm sitting in the sun, out of the wind. We enjoyed a leisurely lunch, and I was content in a way that I hadn't been since Diana's long ordeal began. Of course, I was still grieving, but I was able to keep my grief at arm's distance. I could feel Diana's letter in my shirt pocket, and strengthened by her encouragement, I determined to give life and love another chance.

Turning to Carolyn, I asked her if she was ready to try the geothermally heated hot pool, and she readily accepted.

We had our swimsuits on under our clothes, so we stripped down and eased ourselves into the steaming hot water. It had seemed like a good idea when I suggested it, but as soon as I lowered myself into the hot pool, I knew I had made a mistake. I had modified this natural hot pool especially for Diana, and I had never shared it with another person. My emotions were all over the place, and after a couple of minutes, I lunged to my feet and climbed out. I hurriedly stuffed my feet into my boots, grabbed my clothes, and plunged down the hill toward the cabin.

Over my shoulder, I called to Carolyn, "I'm sorry. I can't do this."

That's how our courtship went, if you want to call it a courtship. In my grief and loneliness, I was attracted to Carolyn, but if I allowed myself to make the slightest overture toward her, I was assailed with guilt. I tried to explain my feelings to her, and she said she understood, but I don't know if she really did. How could she? I didn't even understand them myself.

Things might have continued that way until Carolyn tired of the emotional roller coaster I had put her on, if it wasn't for Diana's letter. It was written a few days before she died, and she gave it to Carolyn, in a sealed envelope addressed to me, with instructions to mail it just before the first anniversary of her passing.

It took me several readings, over many weeks, and with lots of tears, before I slowly began to emerge from the fog of my grief. I not only had Diana's permission to pursue a relationship with Carolyn, but also her encouragement, even her blessing. Of course, that didn't alleviate my conflicted emotions, but it gave me the strength to work through them.

I liked Carolyn a lot, but I was unsure about pursuing anything other than a friendship. We had been married once, and it was disastrous. Why should I think it would be any different now? Of course, as Diana said, a lot of water has passed under the bridge since then, and Carolyn is not the same person she was, nor am I.

With Diana's blessing, I allowed myself to see what I had heretofore been willfully blind to. Although Carolyn was careful never to do anything inappropriate, it was readily apparent that she had feelings for me. And as I allowed myself to feel again, I soon realized I had feelings for her, as well.

When I finally got up the courage to propose to her, I told her I would be happy to get married in a church and she could invite as many people as she wanted. To my surprise, she told me she wanted to be married in the meadow at the base of Hahn's Peak. Instead of a traditional wedding gown, she wanted an off-white, old-fashioned, floor-length gown, with a high neck and puffy sleeves. She wanted it to be made out of soft cotton and covered in lace, with three big ruffles on the bottom of the skirt.

Although I loved the thought of an outdoor wedding, I was skeptical at first, finding it hard to believe she didn't want a church wedding, considering how important that had been to her the first time we married. At that time, I was angry with God and refused to step inside of a church building, so over her tearful protests, we were married in this same meadow at the base of Hahn's Peak.

As Carolyn draws near, I put those thoughts out of my mind and focus on the moment. Now I have eyes only for her. The joy I see in her face and the way her dark eyes shine with happiness makes my heart swell with thankfulness. When I take her hand and turn to face our pastor, I can't help thinking how wise Diana was when she wrote, *"When I am gone, there will be love enough in your heart for both of us."*

I can't help thinking how different the circumstances are this time. Following our first wedding, I awoke on our wedding night to find Carolyn weeping softly. She tried to tell me her tears were tears of happiness, but in my heart I knew better. She was crying because I had refused to allow her to invite any of her family to the wedding. It grieves me to realize that was not the only time I reduced her to tears. If the truth be told, I had a special talent for hurting her.

If there are any tears tonight, I am determined they will only be tears of joy, for on this day we are surrounded by a host of family and friends. Helen and her two boys have flown in from Peru, and Carolyn's mother and her brother are both present. A number of friends from our church in Leadville also drove over for the wedding, as did several of Carolyn's co-workers from the University of Colorado Hospital in Aurora.

I am determined not to make the same mistakes I made when we married the first time. This time I will love her with all my heart, and she will never have to beg me to love her more. When she is hurting or lonely, I will never again respond with indifference. Instead, I will hold her in my arms until her loneliness is swallowed up in my love.

And if she should ever ask me, as she did in our first marriage, if I will love her forever, I won't hesitate before answering. And I won't tell her that forever is a long time, either. Instead, I will declare my undying love: "Carolyn, I will love you forever, as long as time shall be. And when time is no more, I will still be loving you."

When the last of the guests have departed, Carolyn and I drive a half mile down the road to the Glen Eden Guest Ranch, where we spend our wedding night in a refurbished cabin. Since the evening is surprisingly chilly, I build a small fire in the fireplace. Later we consummate our marriage on the bearskin rug in front of the fireplace with the firelight dancing over our intertwined bodies. We didn't plan it that way, but when we started kissing, we couldn't stop. The love we made was tender and passionate, a healing gift from God. And for the first time since Diana's funeral, I am not haunted by grief.

Carolyn has her head on my shoulder and my arm has gone to sleep, but I refuse to move lest I break the spell of this magic moment. "A penny for your thoughts," she says in a voice husky with sleep.

"They're worth more than that," I reply.

"Okay, I'll give you a dollar," she says, as she repositions herself next to me, laying her shapely leg across mine.

"I was just thinking how grateful I am for Diana's letter."

"What letter?"

"You know. The one she gave you to mail to me on the first anniversary of her death."

My voice trails off, and after a moment, she says, "And?"

"In her letter, she gave me her blessing and told me to remarry sooner rather than later."

"Wow!" Carolyn says. "I don't know if I could write a letter like that." And after a moment, she adds, "What a remarkable woman."

"I know," I whisper into the darkness, as I kiss the top of her head, "and it gives me great joy to know she is looking down on us and smiling."

ABOUT THE AUTHOR

Richard Exley is a man with a rich diversity of experiences. He has been a pastor, conference and retreat speaker, as well as a radio broadcaster. In addition he has written more than 30 books including *Authentic Living, The Rhythm of Life, The Making of a Man, Man of Valor, When You Lose Someone You Love, Dancing in the Dark* and *The Alabaster Cross. The Making of a Man* was one of five finalists for the Gold Medallion Devotional Book of the Year. In 2003 the Methodist Episcopal Church USA and the National Clergy Council Board of Scholars awarded him the Doctorate of Divinity honoris causa for his life's work in ministry and writing.

He loves spending time with his wife, Brenda Starr, in their secluded cabin overlooking picturesque Beaver Lake. He enjoys quiet talks with old friends, kerosene lamps, good books, a warm fire when it's cold, and a good cup of coffee anytime. And he hopes to become one of your favorite authors.

You may contact Richard at –
pastorrichardexley@gmail.com

BOOKS BY RICHARD EXLEY

Dancing in the Dark

Deliver Me

Encounters at the Cross

Encounters with Christ

From Grief to Gratefulness

Intimate Moments for Couples

Man of Valor

One-Minute Devotion

Perils of Power

Strength for the Storm

The Alabaster Cross

The Making of a Man

The Gift of Gratitude

When You Lose Someone You Love

When Your World's Falling Apart

www.RichardExleyBooks.com

PRAISE FOR *THE ALABASTER CROSS*

I am on the plane flying from Chicago to Tulsa and I just finished reading *The Alabaster Cross*. Wow! This is no ordinary novel! Yes, the story is told in a wonderful way and it certainly keeps you turning the pages, but it is so much more. It is also a collection of deep spiritual truths and nuggets of wisdom discovered as the story unfolds. I am certain it will have a profound and meaning impact on those who read it, as it did on me.

–Kurt D. Green
Founder and President, Sequoyah Technologies

When I was given, *The Alabaster Cross* I was very lukewarm about reading it. I suspected it would be either a sermon or a lecture on living a righteous life disguised as a novel. Boy was I surprised. *The Alabaster Cross* is riveting! I almost never read a book in one setting, but I couldn't put it down. Excellent writing style and character portrayal! The characters are so real I often felt like I was looking in the mirror. I want more! Is there a sequel on the horizon?

–Candace Dombrosky
Athens, Georgia

The Alabaster Cross was a great read! It was difficult to put down and even when forced to, I found myself thinking about the characters and anticipating what might happen next. Bryan's struggle with anger and forgiveness is so palpable that when he finally accepts God's love and forgiveness, I found myself engulfed in relief and peace! I can't wait for the sequel. I want to know what happens to Rob, Helen, and Carolyn.

–Kenda Blackwood
Pastor's wife – Greensboro, North Carolina

Richard Exley has an extraordinary gift of painting pictures with words. Black letters on white pages became brilliant in color with emotion while unraveling the tale of the Whittaker family. When I closed my eyes after reading certain passages, it was as if I could smell the atmosphere that had been created on the pages before me. *The Alabaster Cross* led me on a journey of emotions that I would gladly take again, through the Amazon Rain Forest. Richard is truly a gift to the body of Christ.

–Mari-Lee Ruddy
Pastor's Wife – Littlestown, Pennsylvania

PRAISE FOR DANCING IN THE DARK

Dancing in the Dark, is Richard Exley at his best. He packs more soul stirring truth in a single story than many writers do in an entire book.

> –KAREN HARDIN
> President, PriorityPR Group & Literary Agency

Richard Exley's writing is moving, practical, vivid, filled with the Word, often raw, and in a style he might refer to as "Blue Collar." His stories evoked memories of my past and I found myself tearing up on more than one occasion. Although he often speaks of the frailties and troubles of man, he always gives us hope through the Word and the grace of Jesus. I intended to read only a few selections from *Dancing in the Dark,* but once I got started, I couldn't put it down.

> –FRANK DAVIS
> "Life's A Marathon!"
> Pastor, Author, and Attorney

Dancing In the Dark is a great gift to us all. Richard Exley's sage musings and crisp writing style bring coherence to life's confusions and Rock solid encouragement for a brighter future. Do your soul a favor and read this insightful book – slowly.

> –DAVID SHIBLEY
> Founder / World Representative Global Advance

Richard Exley has done it again! *Dancing in the Dark* is a must read. His heartfelt stories and penetrating insights will encourage you no matter how dark the night.

> –SHARON STEINMAN
> Author, *Shattered: Coping With the Pain of Divorce; A Devotional Journal of Hope and Healing*